Coming of Age

COMING OF AGE

Volume 1: Eternal Life

by Thomas T. Thomas

COMING OF AGE
Volume 1: Eternal Life

All rights reserved. This is a work of fiction. Any resemblance
to actual persons or events is coincidental. For more information,
contact TomThomas@thomastthomas.com.

Copyright 2014 Thomas T. Thomas

Cover photo © 2008 Roberto A. Sanchez, iStockphoto.com

ISBN: 978-0-9849658-5-4

Contents

Prologue – 2115: Orphan on the Wind
1. Traveling Light — 3
2. Carbon Copy — 7

Part 1 – 2018: First You Die …
1. Morning in Court — 17
2. The Heart Stops Beating … — 30
3. The Brain Explodes … — 40
4. … And Then You Live — 46
5. Afternoons on a Rooftop — 64

Part 2 – 2019: Run for Your Life
1. Coming Home — 81
2. Slow-Motion Train Wreck — 99
3. The Twenty-Nine Points — 115
4. Breaking Up Is Hard to Do — 136
5. Total Loss of Control — 158
6. The End of an Era — 182

Part 3 – 2028: Plumbing Work
1. In the Ninth Year of War — 207
2. Sixth or Seventh Armistice — 229
3. Getting Into Bed — 247
4. Family Ties — 263
5. Mad Scramble — 281
6. The Next Generation — 302

Appendix 1: Praxis Family Tree, c. 2030 — 318
About the Author — 321

*Have you heard of the wonderful one-hoss shay,
That was built in such a logical way
It ran a hundred years to a day ...*

—Oliver Wendell Holmes

Prologue – 2115:
Orphan on the Wind

1. Traveling Light

THREE DAYS AFTER her aunt's death—at the advanced age of 153 years—and with the swift execution of her living testament through the intelligences in the San Francisco Municipal Records Office, Angela Wells was evicted from their five-bedroom luxury condo on the forty-second floor of 333 Market Street. According to terms of the testament, recorded in Antigone Wells's own voice with the dry accents of a Calvinist preacher, Angela was to be allowed one suitcase, to be packed under supervision of a Hall of Records mech, "in order that my niece may learn the virtues of traveling light."

The mech came programmed with a list of authorized items: three casual tops, three pairs of slacks, two pairs of shorts, one semi-formal dress—"but not the backless burgundy taffeta"—two pairs of ballet pumps, one pair of sandals, four days' supply of fresh underwear, a week's supply of basic toiletries. Specifically proscribed was Angela's collection of tiny crystal animals, bought with her own money—well, money from her allowance, and with her aunt's approval required before buying each piece. Also on the forbidden list was her musicbot with all the songs, scenarios, and player roles she had collected over the years, as well as her old tennis racket, her hockey skates and stick, and her carbon-fiber street luge with vibrafoam impact suit and helmet.

As directed in the testament, her aunt's estate—which included proceeds from the condo's sale and holofax auction of all its furnishings and contents, combined with her liquid assets—had been donated to St. Brigid's Home for Orphaned Girls in the Sunset District. So other, nameless orphans were going to benefit from a long lifetime of professional work, saving, and investment—but not the orphan who bore her aunt's own last name. For some reason, Angela found that typical. Capricious, quixotic, callous, and cruel—but also typical of her aunt's sometimes mysterious reasoning.

When Angela picked up the jewelry box from the dresser in her own room, the mech took it from her with two plastic-and-steel hands and a strength of arm she could not resist. The mech then opened the box and rummaged about in its contents, picking up various brooches and necklaces—clearly in pattern-matching mode—and finally selected one: a heart-shaped silver pendant on a chain, both blackened with a hard glaze of tarnish. It was a piece Angela hadn't worn since she was, oh, seven years old—half a lifetime ago. She remembered her aunt had called it a locket, but it had no catch or hinge. She assumed it was just solid silver without any insides.

"Can't I have the diamond circle?" she asked. "It wasn't expensive."

"That is not permitted. All you may take is the heart."

Angela accepted it from the mechanical hand and put it in her pocket—which presumed she would be allowed to leave in the clothes she was wearing.

"You will put the charm around your neck."

"But it's so dirty. The tarnish will—"

"You must put it on, please."

Angela knew of ways to override the mechs, even the ones that proctored for the law—her aunt had taught her all about that. But since this one was doing her aunt's final bidding, she guessed those tricks wouldn't work. She put the chain around her neck and tucked the heart inside her blouse.

"Anything else?" she asked.

The mech paused. With these intelligences, a two-second pause was enough time for anything. The house butler, which had been deactivated and wiped by legal order that morning, could plan a party, order assorted hors d'oeuvres from three different South of Market shops, restock the wine cellar, and send out the invitations in that much time and still have spare capacity to balance the household checkbook and sort the laundry.

"I have ordered your transportation," the city's machine said.

"Thank you. And where do you think I'm going?"

A pause. "I am not permitted to say."

The mech laid the jewelry box on the dresser and picked up her suitcase. It gestured for Angela to go out into the hall. At the side table by the front door, she picked up her purse. The mech took it—not rudely but firmly—extracted her identity card, left the cash cards, and put the purse back on the table. It triggered the front door and waited for her to leave.

Angela walked over to the elevator. Before she could press the down arrow, the other one lit up—the mech taking control again.

"I guess I'm supposed to go to the roof and jump off?" she suggested.

No pause this time. "There is a barrier, and I will stop you."

"That wouldn't be a kindness," Angela replied.

When they arrived at the rooftop pad, the morning fog was just beginning to burn off. An ariflect was already landing. Not one of the low-altitude town cabs, but a model equipped for supersonic, with appropriate pressure-fittings around the door, military-style belts across each seat, and explosive bolts lining the canopy. The mech stowed her suitcase in the luggage bin, turned, and walked away. Unlike the house butler, Angela knew civil-service mechs were not programmed for the courtesies, like saying good-bye.

She belted herself in and waited.

"I'm ready," she told the pilot.

The door latched itself, the cockpit pressurized, and her ears popped. The rim vanes on the wing nacelles engaged and spun up. The 'flect lifted straight into the air, then rose past the city's skyline, through the last wisps of marine layer overcast, into hard sunlight and a view of the Bay that reminded her of a traffic satellite's omnipresent eye. She shifted her attention to the nacelle on her right as the vanes stopped spinning, the wing slats closed and reshaped the machine into a gunmetal-gray dart, and the revs increased by several thousand rippems as the turbine became a jet engine. Where before the seat frame and cushions had been gently pressing against her thighs and bottom, the direction suddenly changed and they pushed against her spine. Pushed hard.

In three seconds San Francisco Bay had disappeared behind her, followed by the East Bay Hills, the Livermore Valley, and Altamont Pass. She was out over the curved plate of the San Joaquin Valley, which held steady in her view for all of half a minute before the eastern edge began wrinkling up with the foothills of the Sierra Nevada.

"Can you tell me where I'm going?" she asked the pilot. Given that the Hall of Records mech had refused to tell her, Angela expected no better from the city's chartered taxi service.

"Tuolumne County, ma'am," the pilot said. "To the Praxis Estate."

Their privatization of the former Stanislaus National Forest.

"Why there, I wonder? I don't know any Praxises."

"That's not in my memory hole, ma'am."

Angela hoped the ariflect was armored and programmed for evasive tactics. From everything she had ever heard about the Praxis family, they were touchy about their privacy—and not shy about defending their airspace.

2. Carbon Copy

CALLISTA PRAXIS WATCHED the dark-gray flyer circle once at high altitude, cued as a bright spark in the second sight of her neural eyepatch. It was shedding speed while it negotiated landing rights with the estate's air defense system. She followed that exchange through her patch, too, and gave the final approval. Then the dart dipped toward the earth and changed shape as its wings unfolded and sprouted daisies. It descended smoothly on vertical thrust.

Last night her mail folder had included a bonded message from the San Francisco Attorney General's intelligence concerning a transfer of wardship. A minor female named Angela Wells—age fifteen, no priors except three traffic citations for recklessness with a "suicide sled," and no current wants—was being written off the municipal rolls and expelled at the request of her only living relative, an aunt, Antigone Wells, who was deceased as of sixty-seven hours prior to transmission.

Antigone again. Disposing of another "niece." Well, this one would be her last.

Callie had instructed the family lawbot to accept the transfer of allegiance and assign Angela Wells provisional status as a ward—stipended but without shares—until the girl's situation could be evaluated and her place in the family established.

The ariflect settled with just a whisper from its fans and a tiny bounce as the hydraulic gear took its weight on the estate's landing pad. The door popped out of its seals and swung open. A young girl in a white blouse and corduroy jumper stepped out.

"The air's thinner here," she said with a little gasp.

"We're at forty-seven hundred feet," Callie said, then offered her hand. "I'm Callie, by the way."

The girl took it, holding on for a second longer than customary, perhaps to catch her balance. "I'm Angela."

"Yes, I know." Callie busied herself with retrieving a single suitcase from the ariflect's cargo hatch. She turned quickly then, before her own face could give the game away, and led their guest through the radiating pathways of the sunken formal garden and up a flight of granite stairs to the Gate Tower of Resurrection House.

Angela Wells was a slender girl, with as-yet unformed features and a still childish body. She had long, ash-blonde hair that was clearly used to regular shampooing and a bedtime routine of one hundred brush strokes. She was an unexceptional girl, except for her eyes, which were a pale, almost iridescent green, the color of old apothecary bottles, and seemed to glow with their own light. They were the same eyes that looked out of Callie's vanity mirror every morning.

―――

Angela followed the Praxis woman along the gravel path through a low-lying plot that was full of coniferous shrubs in geometric arrangements and long, orderly rows of roses and other flowering perennials in every imaginable color. She wondered how the garden fared when winter came to the mountains and the snow level fell to 4,700 feet of elevation. But then, her internal newsfeeds suggested, the family was rich enough that they probably could tent over this whole area, heat it all winter long, and provide a couple of mechs to maintain the flowerbeds.

Then the name she had heard almost in passing came into focus, confirmed by her eyepatch: Callie—Callista—Praxis. There had only ever been one. Daughter of John. The most senior woman of this fabled family. And she had come out to the landing pad personally to meet Angela. What was going on?

She couldn't help noticing that Callie was not only beautiful, as reported, but also young looking. She moved with grace, poise, and a perfect centering, the way Angela's yoga instructor had tried to teach her. Callie might have been only thirty or forty years old, judging by her face. Her hair was dark and luxurious, her skin still smooth and lovely, even around her eyes and mouth—the places where women, even those in regeneration, were quickest to age. By contrast, her aunt's face had been a wreck, with wrinkles, indented creases, and the powdery look of old silk left hanging too long at the back of the closet.

The other thing she had noticed was Callie's eyes. They were bright, green eyes like Angela's own. Except that where Angela's eyes were merely strange, like insets of cold green glass stuck in a mask, Callie's were warm and alive, full of expectation and caring and … well, wisdom. Angela hoped one day she would have eyes like that.

From the rose garden the women climbed a short flight of steps, turned a corner, and came to a round tower. It was four stories tall, made of hard white stone, trimmed in gray granite, with a conical roof of black slate. The tower was remarkably bare of windows. All Angela could see was a single arched casement on the front of the first two upper levels, aligned directly above the door on the ground floor. But at the very top, right under the overhang of the roof, the wall was set with a series of small, black-framed windows, one every thirty degrees, like the numerals on a clock face. Angela thought they might be for lookouts—or for shooting arrows.

Directly in front of the two women, at ground level, was an arched door of ancient-appearing oak, supposedly darkened with age, although Angela knew the whole estate could not have been built much more than thirty years ago.

"That door's big enough to drive a truck through," she said in admiration.

"If we allowed any truck to get that close," Callie said over her shoulder.

They walked into the Gate Tower's central chamber, thirty feet across and empty except for a single reception desk. The receptionist—or rather, a guard with holstered side arm—recognized Callie with a nod and passed her and Angela through into the Gallery.

During the circling descent of her ariflect, Angela had studied the layout of the Praxis Estate and compared it with feeds from her patch. The Gate Tower stood on the northern shore of Cherry Lake, a man-made body of water at the southeastern edge of the former national forest lands. From the lake side of this tower the Gallery crossed the water on five stone piers supporting six high, rounded arches. These in turn supported two tiers of white stone arcades pierced with square windows in granite frames, while the top tier was roofed in steeply-pitched black slate with round windows set in white dormers.

At the far end of the Gallery was the Chateau proper, built right out to the edges of a rocky island that was set deep into the lake. The building rose three stories above its foundation, a wedding cake in white and gray masonry, with rounded towers built into each corner. The top floor presented more pitched slate and white dormers with tall, peaked windows as well as chimneys topped with granite lintels. On the east side of the Chateau she had noted an anomalous structure, like a hexagonal half-dome clinging to the outer wall, which spanned the first and second floors with tall, gothic-arched windows in stained glass. Her patch had confirmed this extrusion had been designed as a chapel, although the database showed it as having no denomination or actual sanctification.

She and Callie entered the Gallery, which was more than two hundred feet long and thirty feet wide, floored in an alternating pattern of black and white marble and brightly lit by the morning sun coming in through the line of east-facing windows. Angela did a rapid internal scan of available architectural studies. One leapt out at her.

"You modeled this house on the castle at Chenonceau, in the Loire Valley."

"That's very perceptive," Callie said, "since you've never been there."

"But I have seen pictures. My aunt said she adored the place."

"You should definitely travel one day. France is lovely."
"But with your choice of almost any architect—"
"Why copy a design over six hundred years old?"
"Well, yes. You studied architecture, didn't you?"
"It's a form of homage. Good design is timeless."

As they made the long walk through the Gallery, Angela looked up, expecting a low ceiling. From outside, the arcades and tiers of windows had suggested three separate levels. But inside it was one massive hall whose wooden hammer beams soared fifty feet overhead between the white-stone dormers.

"I would call that a waste of space," she observed.

Callie Praxis gave her a brief smile. "This might look big and empty to you now. But wait until the whole family gathers here for a wedding—or a proxy fight. Then you'll see how small it really is. The high ceiling helps with the acoustics, not to mention claustrophobia."

"Oh!" Angela said. "And how many …?"

The woman gave another smile. "Why don't we let John explain these things? He's expecting you."

She led Angela through a smaller, arched passage and into a narrow hallway of polished limestone with a vaulted ceiling at the center of the Chateau. It was dark, lit only by a window at the far end, but glowed with the whiteness of the stone. They crossed to a granite stairway, went up two flights, and entered another stone-flagged hallway. At a far door—more antiqued wood—Callie Praxis waved her signet ring, which obviously had an embedded radio-frequency chip. A very modern-sounding *click!* freed the door in its stone frame.

"This is the Residence," she explained, and Angela could hear the capital "R" in her use of the word. "Very few people come up here, and none without being asked."

Callie conducted her past what was obviously a lounge area with chairs, a sofa, and ottomans in butterscotch-colored leather, arranged for conversation, as well as a wet bar. The side where they crossed contained what looked like a workout area—half filled with machines for weight and cardio training, half left as open space with mirrors for floor exercise. Hurrying through, Angela caught sight of a piste, laid out on the floor in black stripes, for fencing, with a rack of swords against the paneled wall.

Finally, Callie knocked softly at an interior door and opened it to reveal a man's study with a wide desk and wall cases on three sides for books—not disks or memory blocks but real paper books bound in cloth and leather. Hundreds of them. The room's fourth side was bare stone with one of those granite-cased and mullioned windows that pierced the outer wall of the Chateau.

Standing by the desk was the oldest man, the oldest person, Angela had ever seen. She knew this not by his face or posture, which might have been those of a vigorous man in his early sixties. Instead, she had the authority of the newsfeeds into her patch. This was John Praxis, patriarch of the family, who at the age of 161 was certified to be the world's oldest living human—so far.

He waited for her to approach. His expression was quizzical, not quite smiling. He looked as if he was expecting something strange or wonderful or terrible to come from their meeting.

Callie hung back, allowing her to walk up to the edge of his personal space. Angela didn't know whether to offer her hand, or curtsey, or just stand there. She wanted to drop her eyes under the pressure of his gaze, but something told her that would be a mistake.

Finally he said, simply, "I see."

"The city releases her to us," Callie said. "Antigone is dead."

He glanced across at his daughter. "When?"

"Three days ago. Natural causes."

"I was afraid of that," he said. Then he turned his attention back to Angela. "What do you know about your mother?"

"My mother died, sir," Angela said, expecting such questioning. "Both my parents died when I was a baby, so I never knew them. My aunt took me in and raised me. She was always very good to me—well, until today, when they read to me the terms of her trust document."

John Praxis absorbed this quietly but without showing any sympathy. "And what was your aunt like?" he asked.

"She was—" Angela hesitated. She knew she must not speak ill of the dead.

"—the warmest, most caring, fun-loving, sweetest little old lady you've ever known?" he suggested with a grin. "All lace doilies, gingerbread, and chocolate milk?"

Angela had to smile at that. "Well, no. She liked to have her own way, sir. Have everything just so. She could be pretty strict, too. But she also encouraged me to go out and try new things, learn things. She said she wanted me to grow up strong." Angela paused to reflect, because this man's face and stance demanded a level of personal honesty. "I think, in some ways—some important ways—she was really disappointed with her own life."

"Yes, exactly!" he exclaimed. "That was Antigone to the core."

This made Angela brave. "So why am I here?" she asked.

Rather than answer her question, he asked, "Did your aunt *give* you anything? Oh, isn't that a foolish question! Of course she gave you lots of things. But did she, in particular, give you a token to wear? A locket?"

"You mean this?" She fished the blackened heart out of her blouse.

He stepped closer, reached out his hand, and held the pendant gently, without pulling on the chain. After a moment, he said: "You are here because we need to establish your true identity. The contents of this locket will do that."

"But it doesn't open, sir. So it's not really a locket."

"It opens with the right tools," he said. "And inside is a chip with a message written in the world's oldest code. We'll need to take a sample of your blood to see if it matches."

"But I know who my parents were! My father was Antigone Wells's young nephew. So Miss Wells was my great aunt."

"You look like an intelligent child," the senior Praxis said. "But do you know how to count? Antigone Wells's true age was a matter of public record, as is mine. So how old would her sister have been? How old would any hypothetical son of her sister's be—and still able to father a child your age? That story fails by at least two generations, more likely three."

Now Angela was really confused. She took the locket out of his hand and stepped back. "But then it can't be *my* DNA in there. This heart is an antique. It's more than eighty years old, or so my—aunt—said."

"Of course it's old. You don't you think you're the first girl to wear that heart, do you?"

"What are you telling me, that I'm a *clone?*"

"No, you're real, but a genetic remix."

"How is it that you know all this?"

He smiled. "Because I gave Antigone that locket." He turned to his daughter, who straightened attentively. "Angela is to have provisional acceptance, with the usual benefits. Oh, and you might tell Alexander he has a new baby sister."

Callie Praxis nodded and held out a hand. "This way, my dear."

Part 1 – 2018:
First You Die …

1. Morning in Court

DEPARTMENT 606, SUPERIOR Court of California, County of San Francisco, The Honorable Oscar W. Bemis presiding, was a thoroughly, almost reassuringly human place for Antigone Wells.

Morning sunlight coming in through the deep-set casements had, over the years, bleached and cracked the varnish on the lower portions of the room's oak paneling. At the same time, caustic ultraviolet rays from the fluorescent ballasts had darkened that same paneling up near the ceiling until it looked almost like old walnut. Although the janitors waxed the floor's linoleum to a high gloss each month—or, with recent cutbacks, more likely once each quarter—the passage of many feet had scuffed dull pathways through the room's center. Contact with the moist palms, ring binders, and briefcases belonging to generations of attorneys had dulled the polished wooden surfaces of the two tables for opposing counsel. Only the angular dentils in the wooden fretwork across the front of the judge's bench seemed sharply defined and unworn. Only the vivid colors sewn into the flags of both the United States and the State of California hanging behind his high-backed leather chair stood out bright and fresh.

Antigone Wells thought she could smell the age of the room, although that might have been her imagination, based on hundreds of other courts she had appeared in over close to three decades. The lingering ghosts of old sweat and stale perfume would follow those tracks in the linoleum from the endless parade of plaintiffs, defendants, their attorneys, and witnesses. The bindings of the blue-and-beige law books on the shelf behind the clerk's desk would exude odors of fine, acid-free paper and crackling buckram. The very air would hold dust from the mill of the law, which ground slow but exceedingly fine.

Someone had once told Wells that partners were not supposed to appear in court themselves. Or if they did, they never stood up, addressed a jury, and fired questions at witnesses. Partners were the elder statesmen, the grand strategists, the generals who led from the rear. Instead, the associates, younger attorneys like Carolyn Boggs and Suleiman "Sully" Mkubwa, who were seated at the table next to her, were the ones who stood forth and gave battle. But Antigone Wells loved the law. She loved the battle. The courtroom was her playing field, her boxing ring … sometimes her bull ring. Bryant Bridger & Wells, LLC had enough other cases in the backlog to keep their associates in good voice.

Wells drew in a little breath, after her precisely timed pause, and began to drive into the heart of her case against Praxis Engineering & Construction Company *et al.* She had already seen her first expert witness sworn in and had worked to establish his professional credentials for the jurors. Ralph M. Townsend had flown out from the American Institute for Structural Analysis, or AISA, in Fair Oaks, Virginia. Now it was time for him to enlighten the jurors on the facts of the case—none of which, as Wells had made clear during her opening statement, were in dispute between the two parties.

"Mr. Townsend," she began, "would you please describe what you discovered when the Board of Directors of St. Brigid's Hospital Foundation retained you to examine specimens of the reinforced concrete from their new medical center at Alemany Boulevard and Ocean Avenue in San Francisco?"

"Yes, of course." The blade-thin man licked his lips—but more from nerves than from hungry anticipation. "We received fifty-four fragments, ranging in size from nine ounces to more than five pounds, taken from various parts of the complex. Each piece was accompanied by a photograph showing exactly where it had been cut, or in some cases where it had spalled—that is, had already expelled itself from the surrounding material …"

Praxis Engineering & Construction had contracted to build St. Brigid's new hospital complex in the Outer Mission District. While the main building and its two conjoined wings, each three and four stories tall, were constructed of steel frame with glass curtain walls, the basements and the floor pads in all three parts of the building, as well as the entire five-story, open-air parking garage, had been poured—supposedly to specification—with reinforced concrete. Even before the structures were completed, they had betrayed evidence of cracks and spalling. The workmen on the site had dutifully patched over these spots and proceeded on schedule.

After the complex was finished and accepted by the hospital foundation, after all of the facility's expensive, delicate, and complicated equipment had been installed, and after it was opened for business and occupied by staff and patients, only then had divots the size of dinner plates begun dropping out of the floor pads. Two load-bearing walls in the basement— one at the far end of the east wing, the other at the junction of the west wing and main building—had partially collapsed, jeopardizing the entire structure. Concrete chunks the size of a cocoanuts began raining down in the parking garage. Within a month, the entire hospital had to be shut down and condemned. It was a write-off to the tune—at the time—of $90 million, plus compensation for injuries to staff and patients, as well as damage to equipment and automobiles. And none of *that* was in dispute in this case, either.

Townsend began to describe the composition of those concrete fragments: various percentages of moisture content; a small but pervasive amount of calcium silicates mixed with clinker or slag containing aluminum and iron oxides, collectively known as "portland cement"; and then a much larger amount of aggregate. And there Wells interrupted him. "Excuse me, sir. 'Aggregate'? What is that?"

"Oh, that's a vital component of any concrete mix—in fact, as much as sixty to seventy-five percent, on a volume basis."

"But what *is* aggregate?"

"It could be many things: graded amounts of sand, gravel, small stones—even bits of used construction materials, like concrete rubble and crushed brick. Aggregate is what gives the concrete its strength. Without those solid bits, the liquid portland cement surrounding them dries to a hard but brittle mass, like porcelain, and is likely to crack under strain. The cement really only serves to bind the sand and stones together."

"You mentioned 'crushed brick.' Do builders use a lot of that?"

"Very sparingly, ma'am. Never more than five percent."

"What about the kind of brick called 'refractory'?"

Until this case came to her, Antigone Wells wouldn't have known a refractory brick from a refried bean. Refractory was made from the kind of clay formulated for high-temperature environments like ovens, kilns, boilers, and open-hearth furnaces. She had been introduced to this special kind of brick when AISA returned their initial report on the concrete fragments. It was one of the chief discoveries of the plaintiff's case.

"Oh, no, ma'am! Refractory brick is specifically excluded from use as construction aggregate. It contains large amounts of magnesium oxide, also called 'periclase,' and so it tends to absorb water. Then it expands. When mixed with wet portland cement, particles of refractory brick gradually become slaked. That is, they kind of explode in slow motion. They crumble, lose their strength, and weaken the concrete."

All of this—and much else—had been stipulated between the parties before the case even went to trial. But Townsend and his technicians had uncovered a long and winding trail of errors of both omission and oversight. Unknown to anyone at the time of construction—although since confirmed with sample borings throughout the condemned hospital complex by Townsend's field team—was the fact that the aggregate added to the cement at the batch plant had contained between eight and ten percent of not just crushed red brick but of refractory brick.

What was in dispute between the parties was how to account for its presence. Saint Brigid's Hospital Foundation sought to recover damages from Praxis Engineering & Construction—which was at once the overall building contractor, construction manager, and deepest pocket—for failure to adequately monitor and test the concrete pours. Praxis blamed the batch company, Chisholm Cement of Stockton, California, for providing bad concrete. Chisholm in turn blamed its aggregate supplier, Yucca Sand & Stone of Indio, Riverside County, for improper fulfillment of their order. Yucca blamed the software integrator, Datamatron of Los Angeles, for faulty material coding when they installed the system that coordinated between its automated order-intake software and the mapping of the stockpile yard and the printing of instructions for the drivers of their front-end loaders that filled the trucks. And Datamatron blamed the original software supplier, Jian Zhu Anye Company of Taiwan, for various untrapped bugs in their underlying code.

Wells had already written out her closing arguments, to be polished and supported by testimony over the coming days. "What we have here, ladies and gentlemen of the jury," she planned to say, "is a simple matter of human negligence, a failure of human oversight of the machines they use. We all tend to think computer systems are infallible, because they supposedly cannot make mistakes. And in matters like adding two plus two, I suppose this assumption is usually correct. But they are only machines, after all. And we are all aware, too, of the programmer's watchword: 'Garbage in, garbage out.' " She would pause here for the obligatory chuckle, then again for the jurors to apply the maxim to loading refractory brick on a truck. "It's only when a person begins to think that computers and their calculations can incorporate any kind of awareness or common sense, well then, you put yourself on greased rails toward the disaster that occurred at Saint Brigid's Hospital."

The foundation's Board of Directors didn't care who paid, ultimately, so long as someone did. But until the hospital had actually brought suit, no one had bothered to follow the trail backward from the concrete samples and test borings to the batch plant, to the stone yard, to the software assumptions and the faulty system. Antigone Wells and her associates at Bryant Bridger & Wells had brought in Townsend's analytical firm, and they had traced the whole unlucky chain and proved that the concrete's failure was not any kind of unforeseeable circumstance or *force majeure*. None of it was hard to unravel—it had just taken persistence and digging.

Normally, Wells hated going after a family-owned business like Praxis. Such companies tended to be small, honest, mom-and-pop affairs. They were usually under-funded in terms of subsidiary functions and supporting staff, and so vulnerable to predation by the better-funded giants of the corporate world. Family-owned businesses were traditionally the underdogs that juries loved to favor. But in the case of Praxis Engineering & Construction, the better descriptive would be "privately held."

Praxis was either the third or fourth largest—depending on how you counted certain state-owned Chinese enterprises—of the world's civil engineering, architectural design, and construction firms. Praxis had grown rich from the building boom in the Middle East during the past forty years. In the previous decade, they had moved strongly into joint ventures in China and Indonesia. The company's strength was in projects generally known as "infrastructure"—roads, bridges, transit systems, water and sewage projects, power stations, industrial plants, and medical facilities like Saint Brigid's.

Once Praxis might have been a small family business—way back in the early 1900s. Then Alexander Praxiteles, a Greek immigrant to the United States and sometime fisherman, had started taking on paving jobs in the new beach communities of Pacifica, Montara, Moss Beach, and El Granada that began springing up as the now-defunct Ocean Shore Railroad made its way from San Francisco down the western side of the Peninsula. But now, more than a century later, the eagle-browed, silver-haired man sitting in court behind the defense table was the surviving grandson of Alexander Praxiteles—whose surname had long since been shortened to "Praxis." The two gray-haired men sitting at his side were the great-grandsons of that earnest entrepreneur. All of them were prosperous and well-fed. None of them had ever lifted a shovelful of dirt in their lives, other than at some formal groundbreaking using brand-new shovels spray-painted in gold. Antigone Wells would have bet money on that.

She finished questioning her expert witness and turned him over to the Praxis Engineering counsel for what was sure to be a perfunctory cross examination. As she did so, the thought again crossed her mind—although she would never mention it to the jury, even obliquely—that the Praxis people should have settled when St. Brigid's made their offer. After all, the initial claim had only been for $140 million, and that was chicken feed in the current economic environment. Then Praxis Engineering & Construction could have gone after the subcontractors themselves for recovery. But instead they had held out from the beginning and then propounded that weak-kneed *force majeure* defense. It only made them appear brazen and callous—not to mention just a little bit stupid. … And juries loved *that*, too.

The San Francisco courtroom where the civil trial against his company was being argued was not, John Praxis decided, a place that seemed completely comfortable with technology.

The tables where the lawyers sat were festooned with power cords and data cables leading down from their laptop computers to exposed junction boxes on the floor, rather than more modern, molded-in-place connections. The last-generation WIFI repeater with its upright horns sat on a makeshift shelf above the door to the judge's chambers, with more wires hanging down. A flat-panel television screen—a full five inches thick, so not the latest generation—was bolted under the clock on the wall that faced the jury box and had its own dangling wires. The computer monitors on the desks of the clerk and bailiff were positioned at odd, oblique angles, so that those officials could perform their duties while still facing the court itself. Only the judge, high above the proceedings, operated in a virtual technology-free zone.

Praxis knew his mind was wandering now. He had been sitting for the past two hours in the folding, theater-style seats for spectators behind the courtroom's central railing. They were surprisingly small seats, more like transplants from a junior high school auditorium. They were too narrow for his hips and too close to the row ahead for his knees. With his six-foot-four-inch frame, Praxis could only perch stiffly upright, unable to cross his legs and afraid to move his arms for poking his sons on either side—and, Heaven knew, Leonard and Richard had resented such familiar contact even as boys.

He looked at his watch. If the testimony of the plaintiff's first witness took more than another hour, then the judge would call a noontime recess and send them all off to lunch. Praxis could wait that long. He was only putting in the obligatory, opening-day appearance. Then he and his sons would leave the whole matter with the attorneys they had on retainer and go back to the corporate headquarters on Steuart Street overlooking the Embarcadero.

The woman speaking now, this Antigone Wells, was a pretty sharp lawyer. While she and her witness patiently worked through the massive snafu that had added refractory brick to concrete aggregate, Praxis recalled the color photographs she had sent scrolling across that big-screen television during her opening statement: cratered floors, collapsed bearing walls, and crumbling parking ramps, alternating with shots of damaged and tilting medical equipment, dented car roofs and hoods, entry doors X'ed across with yellow CAUTION tape, and a sign at the gate reading "CONDEMNED" in big, red letters. Even John Praxis, hardened as he was to lawyers' rhetorical tricks, had to admit it was damned effective.

Antigone Wells was a trim woman. She still had her figure at—what? Fifty-something? Late fifties, probably. She wore her ash-blonde hair meticulously combed back in a wave and tied in a bun, like Tippi Hedren in that old San Francisco movie, *The Birds*. She dressed the part, too, in pastel-colored suits that might have come from Chanel. She even had gray eyes—but not smoky and smoldering, like some of the gray-eyed women Praxis had known. These eyes, when you saw them close up—as he had, during their various meetings for depositions, negotiations and, finally, the settlement offer—were sharp and hard, like agates. And that, too, was a bit of the old Tippi.

He looked at the backs of the heads at the defense table. The team of attorneys representing Praxis Engineering & Construction were hunched over, already defeated even before their turn to cross examine. They had stacks of manila folders in front of them, full of construction orders, waybills, and inspection results. They even had rolled printouts of structural drawings on the old E-size vellum—although, of course, nobody drafted with ruler and T-square on paper anymore; all the design work was done in CAD these days. But still, none of that technical documentation could stand up to those pictures on the big television screen.

Praxis looked slowly from side to side at his two sons. Leonard was the firm's president and chief of operations. Richard was chief financial officer. Both of them sat stone-faced and slit-eyed. To the casual observer at a distance—someone in the jury box, say—they might not even seem to be awake. But Praxis could see beads of sweat at Richard's hairline. The boy was terrified. Good!

A hundred and forty million buck-a-ding-dongs was a terrifying number. And the actual cash amount was only going to go up from there. Since the start of the Continuing Currency Crisis—which the news media promptly shortened to "C3"— a couple of years ago, the value of money had been eroding faster than a sugar cube in hot tea. In previous inflations, that might have been a good thing: take on a big debt today, watch it become pocket change in a decade or so. But these were modern times, and everyone had access to fast computers. All future payments—and that included jury awards, which would not become final until the verdict was in, as well as any scheme for amortization or delayed distribution—were now made in constant dollars, calculated with the "C$" button on the latest banking apps, and indexed to the value of money at the point of sale or, in this case, the date of actual loss. By the time this lawsuit played out, PE&C might be in the hole for a billion dollars of current value. While that might not be such a horrific number in the sweet by-and-by, the prospect of it bearing down on future balance sheets gave everyone the heebie-jeebies.

Technically, ultimately, the buck stopped with John Praxis himself as chief executive officer and chairman of the board—for even a private company had bylaws and needed the appearance of being run by a council of elders. However, for the past two years he had been transitioning into an emeritus position, heading for semi-retirement, and was trotted out mainly for diplomatic functions like ribbon cuttings with governors and heads of state. And for buck-forty-million foul-ups—all right, *fuck*-ups—like the St. Brigid's contract.

At sixty-four years of age, he was now the firm's strategic thinker and hadn't involved himself in its daily operations for six or seven years, and not at the technical level, the ground level, for a dozen years more. That level of involvement was where you walked the site, smelled the dirt, and used your eyes and brain and accumulated knowledge from a hundred other sites to know the land and its geology, know which way the water table flowed, and which part of a hill was likely to collapse in a slide. Where you occasionally put a bare hand into the outflow from the cement mixer and rubbed it between your fingers, to know the consistency and quality of the sand and gravel you were pouring. Where you could just look in the eyes of your subcontractors and tell that a braying jackass like Stephen Macedo, their site superintendent on St. Brigid's, wouldn't question when his men started patching over cracks in the foundation. Where you could just shake hands with an operator like Howard Chisholm and tell from his distant, distracted manner that he didn't know where he was getting his aggregate from and, furthermore, didn't really care, so long as the price was right.

Once John Praxis had those skills, because he'd worked his way up. Despite his standing as the sole male in the family's third generation, and his holding an advanced engineering degree from Stanford University, his father Sebastian had still made John walk the ground, know the men, and run the numbers on each of his projects. At first, he was only allowed to assist a more experienced project manager. Only later, with experience of his own, did he get to manage the work himself. It was training he should have demanded of his own sons. But Leonard had never been any good at math, had flunked out of engineering while taking calculus and gone into art history, and finally earned a master's degree in fine arts. He had come into the company on the administrative side, marketing and sales, and worked his way up from there. Richard, on the other hand, had the math skills but preferred the tidy columns of figures in an accounting ledger to the slippery numbers of strain coefficients and cohesion factors. He was a financial genius, John supposed, but he wouldn't know anything about refractory brick or why it was so dangerous. Neither would Leonard, for that matter.

At least there was some hope with his third child, Callista. She had started as an architect, doodling pretty houses full of Frank Lloyd Wright angles, had quickly grown bored with that, and transferred into architectural engineering. Callie might have smelled a rat at St. Brigid's, but she happened to be in Dubai at the time.

All of which still didn't explain this hundred-forty-megabuck mistake. When Antigone Wells and her team had uncovered the whole sorry story of the crumbling brick, they had offered Praxis Engineering & Construction a settlement. Leonard had turned it down flat. He'd argued, behind closed doors, among the family, that computer glitches like that were simply acts of God. No one's fault and in no way negligence. Hey, the paperwork had all checked out. The Chisholm order said "clean quartz gravel with 4% recycled construction materials." The Yucca waybills all said "clean quartz gravel with 4% recycled construction materials." The two samples they'd taken at the batch plant—by some law of unholy averages—showed "clean quartz gravel with fractional red brick and crushed concrete." So how was anyone to know there was contaminated firebrick all over the site? Leonard hadn't just argued against settling; he'd made it a test of his leadership, his place in the company. And John Praxis had let his first-born son have his way.

In Leonard's defense, and before twenty-twenty hindsight kicked in, it hadn't been much of a settlement. When you added up all the clauses and stipulations, St. Brigid's was asking for $1.55 on the dollar—which amounted to excess of damages plus court costs. It was an offer that gloated, that screamed, "We've got you nailed, sucker!" And, as the PE&C attorneys had argued, to pay it would amount to an admission of professional negligence—which might make it harder for them to go after the subcontractors.

Now they were all going take a big dump. Praxis had seen it in the jury's eyes as they looked at those slowly repeating pictures. There was just no acceptable explanation for what had happened. And when this case with St. Brigid's was finished, and PE&C had lost, there would be more trials. The insurance bond wouldn't cover the costs and damages, so PE&C in turn would have to sue the suppliers and their computer contractors. Praxis figured the whole thing would end up costing the company somewhere north of three hundred megabucks—or more like $3.33 on the dollar. And that was before the inflation clock kicked in.

Oh well, it was only money. … Richard was going to have to give up buying Ferraris for a while. Leonard would have to sell one of his vacation homes and make do without the pretty, twenty-something, live-in housekeeper who came with it. And John himself? He was going home to his lovely wife and have a good, stiff drink.

2. The Heart Stops Beating ...

"THE THUNDERBOLT"—AS JOHN Praxis would later describe it—struck on the sixth green of the Cliffs course. It was only nine holes, the shortest of the Olympic Club's three golf courses, but the fairways offered sudden, surprising views of the Pacific Ocean. The selection of the Cliffs that morning was part of a strategy, because it allowed someone to comment that the magnificent view must stretch all the way to China.

Ever since he got out of bed, Praxis had been feeling tired and cranky. If it had been merely his choice, he would have stayed home with Adele and read a book or something. But he and his son Richard were scheduled to entertain the visiting Chinese Minister of Transportation, whose entourage included the president of Shanghai's second largest bank. China was planning to extend its high-speed rail system westward from Chengdu into the Tibet Autonomous Region and Lhasa. With the Continuing Currency Crisis, American labor—especially of the advanced technical kind—was potentially the cheapest in the world, and Praxis Engineering & Construction needed to exploit every opportunity. Essential to their bid strategy was allowing these high-level functionaries to meet with the nominal head of the firm, practically one of its "ancestors," in a social setting. An ancestor's work, it seemed, was never done.

And besides, Praxis had wanted the opportunity to take Richard aside and ask how they were going to handle the financial fallout of the St. Brigid's mess. The verdict, and the wallop that would come with it, loomed larger each day as the trial drew to a close. But Richard was avoiding him this morning, wasn't even making eye contact, and Praxis had felt himself getting angrier and angrier.

Then he noticed, as he swung his Two Wood for the last time, that his shoulders were feeling achy. Also, he briefly thought he might have pulled a muscle in his left biceps—but he put that down to being out of practice. In truth, he had not touched a club in two weeks, maybe three. By the time he was on the green, however, he was panting—short, sharp, hard breaths—and the fairway wasn't that steep. He thought the two Chinese officials were giving him anxious looks, but Richard was totally involved in his own golf game. Richard played seriously, to win, and not to make nice.

Praxis was staring at his son, wondering why he couldn't at least flub his putts once in a while, so their guests, who were good but not great players, might feel better about themselves, when someone hit him in the chest with a baseball bat. *Wham!* Pain shot across his whole front, as if his ribs and arms were being broken at the same time.

Without remembering exactly how, Praxis was suddenly lying on his side. His vision was cocked. One eye seemed to stare across acres and acres of brilliant green grass, clipped as smooth as a billiard table, while the flag that was held by his caddy, Sam—whom everyone called "Peaches," either because he had come from Georgia or because he brought peaches from home for a few favored members—was receding into the distance at a million miles an hour. The other eye was looking up at the edge of the tree line, with the soft, misty blue of a San Francisco morning sky looming beyond it, and a sea gull cartwheeling up there, drawing closer and closer.

A face appeared above him, hidden by its own shadow. John Praxis thought he should know that face, but now he just couldn't remember. All he could hear was the screaming of the gull, a single word repeated: "Papa! Papa!" Praxis knew he should be scared, but he was more concerned for that gull and its own sense of panic.

Then somehow he was lying on his back, and a Caterpillar 120 road grader was driving across his chest. The pressure of those massive, cleated tires was making rubble of his bones while the shiny, angled blade cut deeper and deeper.

His vision closed to a tiny white circle, a closeup view of smoothed feathers from the gull's immaculate white breast, which glowed like white neon. And suddenly Johnny Cash was singing, in his ears or in his mind, "Down, down, down … to a burning ring of fire …" as the earth sank beneath him and the darkness enfolded him.

Not until his father fell over on the golf course did Richard Praxis have any idea that something was wrong. The Old Man had always been the strong one, the healthy specimen, the sturdy oak among the bending, compliant willows and bamboo trees that were other men—including his own children. That morning his father had been playing slowly, sure, but then his golf game was usually careful and methodical, practicing his swings and assessing the ground before each shot. He had been rubbing his left shoulder a bit, but that could just be a touch of neuralgia or bursitis or whatever. There was nothing wrong with his father.

When John Praxis toppled sideways, like a statue knocked off its pedestal, Richard suddenly understood the situation was serious. He dropped his putter—barely conscious of how its head nicked his ball and disturbed the lie—and rushed to his father's side. "Papa!" he called. And again, "Papa!"

His father's eyes were open, their gaze fixed but at slightly different angles, almost cross-eyed. And he was not breathing—not straining or gasping, just not breathing. Richard realized his father was dying.

"Papa!"

He dug out his cell phone and tossed it to the caddy. "Don't call nine-one-one," he instructed. "That just gets you the Highway Patrol and a layer of bureaucracy. Call the clubhouse and tell them to call the nearest hospital with a helipad and arrange a medevac chopper. Get it out here *now!* Put any charges on the Praxis membership."

Without waiting for the caddy to acknowledge, Richard rolled his father over on his back. It was the first time he had physically touched the Old Man, other than a handshake, in more than twenty years. Richard had taken the company's mandatory training in office safety and high-rise disaster preparedness, which included basic first aid and cardio-pulmonary resuscitation. He couldn't remember the rhythm—was it twenty or thirty chest compressions? two or five breath-of-life ventilations?—but he suddenly realized the exact number didn't matter. He just had to do it.

He crossed his palms over his father's breastbone and started pumping. He dimly recalled the fire department instructor describing the beat of that old Bee Gee's song "Stayin' Alive" as the perfect pace. Push, push, push, push, staying alive! Push, push, push …

After what he guessed were twenty or so compressions, he pulled opened his father's jaw, used his index finger to probe the airway and depress the tongue—which was rough and dry as sandpaper—took a deep breath, and bent to close his lips around his father's mouth. He blew as hard as he could, forcing air into his father's lungs, and out of the corner of his eye saw the chest rise an inch or so. He took another breath and blew. Then he went back to pumping along with the Bee Gees.

As Richard worked, the two Chinese government officials knelt quietly on the grass beside him. When he could spare them a glance, he saw their faces held reverence, even awe. He remembered that Chinese culture valued respect for one's parents and elders. That was what they were feeling now. Then he put that thought out of his mind and kept on pumping.

A long time later—push, push, push, push, breathe—he could hear the familiar *thwock-thwock-thwock-thwock* and the jingling mechanical whine of a helicopter descending. It took effort not to change his rhythm to match the beat of those blades. A frenzied downwind battered his hair and shirt collar. He glanced over to see skids dig into the perfectly manicured green. After a minute, a pair of hands in purple nitrile gloves at the end of dark-blue uniform sleeves gripped Richard's arms to stop him and then take over the compressions.

He sat back on his heels. The med tech moved into position above his father while others brought a stretcher from the helicopter.

As they loaded John Praxis through the fuselage doors, Richard confirmed the hospital where he would be taken. He retrieved his cell phone from the caddy and called his office, told his administrative assistant to find his brother Leonard and sister Callie, tell them what had happened, and get them over to the UCSF Medical Center at Mission Bay. Richard himself was allowed to ride in with his father.

Two hours later, with John Praxis still in surgery, the three children sat on the cold, slate-blue vinyl furniture of the waiting area. Callie was next to Richard and held his hand. After he had described giving the Old Man mouth-to-mouth and CPR, she had smiled and murmured, "You saved his life."

Leonard, on the other hand, was unusually quiet. As the time dragged on and still no word came from the doctors, he became restless, crossing and uncrossing his legs, then tapping his fingers. Finally, he signaled to Richard with a toss of his head. He got up, went a short way down a connecting corridor, and paused to let Richard catch up.

"What were you thinking of?" Leonard asked in a fierce whisper.

"What do you mean?" Richard asked, surprised.

"Giving him CPR like that."

"Dad was dying."

"So?"

Richard shook his head, not understanding. What was he supposed to do? They gave everyone the training so that, when the time came, they could all save lives. It was what they expected of you. "I still don't know what you mean," he said.

"People die. It's natural. It was his time."

"You *wanted* him to die?" Richard asked.

"No … no, of course not. But, after all, he's not that young. How much longer could he expect to live? And it was the perfect opportunity for him—doing something he loved, on a beautiful spring day, no pain, no lingering. He probably didn't even know what hit him."

"But I could save him. The doctors can—"

"Come on! You heard what they said. Massive heart attack. Irreversible tissue damage. Possible *brain* damage. Yes, he could live, but what kind of life? He'll be an invalid, maybe a vegetable, still dying, just more slowly."

"But these days, with transplants—"

"Get real, will you? There are waiting lists, criteria, priorities. Who would assign a fresh, young heart to a man his age?"

"I guess I didn't think about that," Richard said.

"I know, and it's just too bad you didn't."

"Well, would *you* have let him die?"

Leonard's eyes went opaque.

"In hindsight … yes."

———

Whirrr-Click! … Whirrr-Click! … Whirr-Click! …

John Praxis came awake slowly to the sound. With each *whirr*, he felt growing pressure in his chest. With each *click*, a little thud and release of the pressure. Over and over again. He still felt pain in there, but it was an ache, a throbbing, like the remembered pain after the dentist had drilled a tooth. Not the deep, cutting pain that went along with the Thunderbolt. This was pain he could handle.

He opened his eyes to the muted wash of fluorescents shielded inside tiny egg crates against blue-white ceiling tiles. He breathed in through his nose and caught the scents of a hospital—fresh vinyl rubbed down with mouthwash. So this wasn't the morgue. So he was awake and not dreaming. Or not *mostly* dreaming.

"How are we doing?" asked a female voice from somewhere above his head.

Praxis thought about this for a long time. "Not dead yet, I gather."

"That's the spirit! But you should go back to sleep now."

"What happened to me? Why do I feel this—?"

"Sleep now. You'll get answers later."

The next time he awoke, the ceiling was different and someone had raised the head of his bed slightly, so he could also see a fair amount of the opposite wall, with a television set mounted high in the corner—its screen dark now. The *whirr* and *click* were still taking place inside his chest. He moved his head to one side and saw a familiar face.

"Hello, Dad." Callista Praxis, who was sitting close to the edge of his bed, put down her magazine and reached for his hand.

He tried to reach for hers and felt a restraining cuff. "What the—?"

"It's to keep you from moving around. Please don't struggle."

"What happened …?"

"You had a heart attack."

"How …?" Wait, he already knew the answer to that one—walking uphill on the damned golf course. He changed direction to ask, "How bad?"

"Pretty massive." Callie never could tell a lie. "But they say you'll be all right."

"Adele …?" He turned his head to look around.

"Mom sat here for twenty-three hours straight. She's gone home to rest."

"Tell her …" He struggled with the thought. What could he say? *I'm sorry? I love you? I didn't mean to almost die on you?*

"You can tell her yourself in a little bit. Why don't you go back to sleep now?"

He decided to go back to sleep. The *whirr* and *click* were becoming just a white noise that no longer meant anything. The pressure buildup and release inside his chest were like the impacts of his feet on a carpeted floor. No longer the focus of his awareness. There wasn't even any pain.

The third time he awoke, it was to a bright light shining into his right eyeball. Flicking to one side. Flicking back. A large pink thumb was holding his eyelid open.

"Don't do that," he muttered. He tried to push the nuisance away but his hands were still cuffed to the bed.

"Pupil response is good," said a voice.

"Are you a doctor?" Praxis asked.

"I'm Doctor Jamison, from your OR team. I'm just checking vital signs."

"That means I'm still alive, does it?"

"Yes, very much so," the man said.

Praxis looked around. The head of the bed was even higher now. On one side was a window, drapes drawn, dark outside. On the other side a wall with a credenza-thing and a couple of straight-back chairs, now empty. No sign of an enclosing curtain, so he was in a private room, not recovery, not intensive care. That would be good news, wouldn't it? No sign of Callie or the boys, either, so there was no death watch—another good sign?

He looked down at his chest to see what all the *whirr*ing and *click*ing were about—and saw that the thin front of his hospital gown, lower down below his stomach, was pushed out by strange shapes that pulsed in time with the muted sounds and distant thuds. It took him a minute to interpret those shapes as loops of hose that came up over the edge of the bed, went under his gown, and stopped somewhere … inside his chest.

"What is that?" he asked, nodding at the hoses.

"Ah … we need to explain that," Jamison said.

"So explain," Praxis said, using his CEO voice.

"You suffered a major infarction with irreversible end-stage biventricular failure."

"In English, that's a heart attack," Praxis said.

"No, in English, your heart had already died."

So that was to be his epitaph: *Your heart had already died.* Well, truth to tell, John Praxis had secretly been expecting it for a long time. Ever since a bout of rheumatic fever as a child, the doctors had been urging him at the annual checkups to take care of his heart. Then he had experienced a couple of "episodes," ten and eight years ago, that seemed to be the consequence of all that concern. But those events had been nothing like the Thunderbolt. He'd felt tired, weak, short of breath—and had some discomfort in his chest, like heartburn or a spell of indigestion. The doctors had called them "silent" heart attacks and said they were a warning. So he quit smoking entirely, cut way back on his drinking, and started taking exercise—ironically, most of it on the golf course. The doctors had prescribed nitroglycerin pills for him, but when Praxis started feeling so much better, he stopped carrying them. Instead, he paced himself, and whenever he felt weak or tired, he just sat down. The "heart condition" just hadn't been that big a deal. It wasn't as if he was going to *die*.

"That explains my falling over at the Olympic Club," Praxis said. "It doesn't explain those tubes and the whirligig going on inside me."

"When we couldn't get your heart back to a stable rhythm through either stimulation or percutaneous intervention," Jamison said, "we had to open your chest. We found multiple and extensive blockages and areas of previous necrosis. In laymen's terms, your heart was beating on will power alone. We had no alternative but to remove most of the ventricular muscle tissue."

Praxis tried to relate what the doctor was saying to what he felt inside his chest now. "Yet I'm still alive. How so?"

"We replaced your heart with a mechanical device. It's air driven and simulates natural systole and diastole. The hoses you can see are powering it. They're linked to a pump under the bed, which is regulated by an automated blood pressure cuff on your left arm and a fingertip oxygen monitor on your left hand."

Praxis digested all of that. He hadn't even noticed the subtle, alternating pressures on his upper arm as the cuff inflated, took its readings, and then deflated. "How long do I have to wear all this?"

"Until we can find you a replacement heart. We've already entered you on the UNOS waiting list."

"Eunos? Who are they?"

"United Network for Organ Sharing."

"A waiting list. There's a wait. ... How long?"

"Well, you understand it's all speculative at this point."

"How long?" Praxis insisted, using his command voice again.

"Seventy to ninety days. But, given your age group, that's really—"

"You're kidding me. I'm tied to this contraption for *three months?*"

"At least you're alive. And really, your prognosis is excellent—"

"Yah, but only if I don't go crazy and try to kill myself first."

"We'll make you as comfortable as humanly possible."

"You can start by getting me a glass of scotch."

Dr. Jamison hesitated. "Was that a joke?"

"Just wait until I ask for a cigar."

3. The Brain Explodes …

IT WAS A day for celebration. After six months of discovery, deposition, and dealing, six days of actual trial, and less than six hours of jury deliberation, the St. Brigid's case was finally over and won. Antigone Wells had brought everyone—the hospital foundation's entire Board of Directors, their chief witness Townsend and his field analysts, and her legal team of Carolyn and Sully—back to the Bryant Bridger & Wells offices on Trinity Place for champagne and canapés. Inside of ten minutes, of course, the whole firm was crowding into the conference room to share the joy.

With an award of construction costs plus actual damages plus punitive damages to the tune of two hundred and fifty million, the firm could afford to pour Veuve Clicquot brut like seltzer water and offer whole trays of Chef Bonnaire's special Dungeness crab puffs and those little calamari dumplings. Hell, with the firm taking a third of that award in fees, they could afford to pay their rent plus utilities for the next hundred years.

It was a shame, of course, about John Praxis and his much publicized heart attack. Wells didn't want to kick a man when he was down. But all of that had no bearing on the case. The judge had instructed counsel that the elder Praxis's medical condition could not be mentioned in front of the jurors. The suit was against the company, not the executives or the Praxis family itself.

Now Ted Bridger, the old man of the BB&W law firm—who, come to think of it, was the same age as the elder Praxis and also served in semi-retirement, while Sullivan Bryant, the most senior partner, had passed away a year ago—was proposing the afternoon's toasts. First to the AISA people, "for their hard work and diligence, which effectively made the case for us."

And a voice from the back: "And for which they will be adequately rewarded." Which brought a polite chuckle.

Then to the St. Brigid's board, "for all the good work they do in the community, and for selecting BB&W to represent them."

That voice again: "And to their newer, bigger, and better hospital."

Finally, to Antigone Wells and her team, "who played their big fish with great skill in the time-honored fashion and successfully landed him."

To which many voices responded: "Hear, hear! … Antigone! … Auntie! … Speech! Speech!"

Wells put down her glass, folded her hands in front of her stomach, and raised her chin to respond. "This has certainly been a great day," she began. "Thank you for your kind words, Ted. And I want to say thank you, as well, to my own team, who-oo-ooo—"

—and she fell right into the ceiling.

The world turned upside down. No, literally, the floor became the ceiling, and the ceiling became the floor, and she was falling up toward the ceiling. Whatever she was saying to these bright, smiling faces flew right out of her head. Her own voice became a buzzing in her ears and faded away. Her stomach turned sour and flopped over, and she was sure she was going to vomit right there in front of everyone. But before her head could hit the ceiling it filled with an amazing white light. And the world was buried in deep, soft snow.

―――――

After a long time and from a great distance she was suddenly confronted by a boy and a girl with identical short haircuts. They were not people she had seen before, none of the firm's associate attorneys or administrative assistants, no one from building security—which she could figure out because, in addition to their dark-blue uniforms, they were also wearing bright-green plastic gloves. She tried to think of the boy's and girl's names and realized she could not think at all.

They were staring intently, directly into her face—which was a rude way to treat one of the firm's partners. Then she realized she was sitting on a padded bed or stretcher inside a tiny metal room that lurched from side to side while angels wailed and hooted above her head. She felt a chill dampness around her loins, soaking her underwear, pantyhose, and skirt, and knew with sudden horror that she had peed herself. And all the time she was trying to deal with this, these uniformed people were asking her the most absurd questions.

"Can you smile for us, Miz Wells?"
"I can but I don't feel like it," she mumbled.
"What was that?" asked Boy Uniform.
"Couldn't make it out," said Girl Uniform.
"Can you raise your arms above your head?"
That was the boy again.
"Ungh … no … I can't."
"All right. Don't let it bother you."
That was the girl this time.
"Can you tell me the date?"
"May something … thirty …"
"Good, good. And the year?"
"Year of … the elephant …?"
Why were they asking her about elephants?
"Phone Admitting, we're going straight to Neurology."

Flick-*blaze!* Flick-*blaze!* Antigone Wells woke up with a bright light shining intermittently into her left eyeball. Each time the light blazed, its whiteness, brilliance, and clarity startled her. And then the world would go briefly dark as the light flicked away to the side. After a few more flashes, the annoyance itself went away.

But soon it started up again in her right eyeball. This time the effect was just the opposite, like watching a lighthouse try to send its beam out through a dense fog. Glimmer-*gone!* Glimmer-*gone!* This light was much more soothing. But all this nonsense with the lights really had to stop.

"Would you please stop doing that?" she asked as politely as possible.

"Excuse me, Miss Wells," said a male voice. "What were you saying?"

She tried again, enunciating each word clearly and slowly.

"We're having some trouble with speech here."

Wells gave up and glared at him.

"You've had a cerebral accident—a stroke," the voice said.

Now that her vision was recovering from the glare of the light, she could make out a young, dark face. It was much younger than Antigone herself, and not so dark as Sully Mkubwa, but still with dark skin, dark eyes framed by gold-rimmed spectacles, curly dark hair, and very white teeth. Indian or Pakistani, or from somewhere up country from there. Half of him was in sharp, clear focus. The other half was a soft blur.

"Whoo?" she hooted carefully at him, "Youu?"

"I'm sorry, I'm sure some of this may be confusing for you." The man tilted his head to one side. "I'm your doctor, Prabhjot Bajwa. I'm on the neurosurgery staff here. You're in the San Francisco Medical Center. Do you remember when they brought you in?"

Suddenly, Wells did remember. Two children wearing green plastic gloves had taken her in the back of a tiny fire truck, or perhaps it was an ambulance, to a place that was too cold, filled with glass and metal that moved too fast. She remembered bare hallways rushing past, bars of light strobing overhead, wide doors swinging open and then closing, and lots of cold air flowing around her. People did things to her body, then lifted her into a white machine with a narrow tunnel that made annoying, beeping, buzzing, ringing noises. That was like listening to a telephone somebody had left off the hook—except she could not reach it to put the receiver back, because the noises came from behind a curve of smooth, white plastic that pressed down right above her face. The noises went on until she wanted to scream. Her eyes went wide with the memory of it.

"Noy ... ses ..." was the best she could manage.

"Yes, we had you in the MRI for a brain scan," the dark-skinned man said. "That must have been unpleasant. You had experienced an intracerebral hemorrhage—which means you had some bleeding into your brain. Then we took you into surgery to stop the bleeding. But that's all fixed now. You're going to get better."

Antigone Wells, who had spent a lifetime of studying people, watching their eyes, reading their reactions—so that she could know the truth of their words—now worked her mouth and tongue to say as carefully as she could: "Lie ... *yarrh!*"

———

Over the days that followed, Wells suffered the attentions of others from among the hospital staff. Another doctor examined her without as much conversation—or confidence—as Dr. Bajwa. A rotating team of nurses and orderlies pushed needles into her intravenous drip tube, rearranged the electrodes attached to her chest and side for heartbeat and to the shaven patches on her skull for brainwaves, fed her oatmeal and tapioca from a bowl because her right arm wasn't working and neither was most of her tongue, changed the bottle attached to her catheter, and put a bedpan under her infrequent bowel movements. And two therapists came by to poke at her.

One, the man, alternately stroked and jabbed her limbs and the soles of her feet with blunt and pointed objects and asked, "Feel that?" Then he asked Wells to move various parts of her body and made noncommittal sounds as she flopped around on the bed. But he seemed satisfied as he went away.

The other therapist, a woman, didn't touch her but asked her questions and showed her pictures. Some of the questions Wells was supposed to listen to and answer with just a nod or shake of her head. Others required spoken answers, and the woman listened intently to interpret the warbling sounds Wells made. Then she showed cards with simple line drawings of common things—a cat, a football, a bird, a house—and asked Wells to name them if she could. Finally, she showed cards with lines that met in odd ways: twists and angles, curves and branchings. Wells studied them hard. She knew what these things were, of course, but she could not ... actually ... remember ... what they ... meant.

She looked to the side, to the table next to the bed, and reached with her good left hand for the wide plastic tube that was standing on its cap. The nurses had used this tube to squirt out and rub yellow, smelly liquid into Wells's wrists and hands, ankles and feet. Across the widest part of the tube were some of these same twisting, branching lines. She knew these shapes were terribly important, but she could not name them. She used her thumb to tap the images on the widest part of the tube.

"Hhhhgg?" Wells husked, forcing the words out. "Hh ... what? Sss-same?"

"Yes! Exactly!" the woman therapist said. "That's *writing*. Those are *words*."

"*Urrds!*" Wells agreed. But she still did not know what they meant.

4. ... And Then You Live

AFTER TWO WEEKS, John Praxis was able to contemplate the tubes entering his abdomen without feeling squeamish and wanting to gag with thinking about what was going on inside his chest. And when he didn't actually look down at the gently pulsing curves where they slid under the incisions in his skin, he could forget the whole degrading experience. Except that he was still trapped in bed, flat on his back. The only good thing was that the doctors now trusted him enough to remove the restraints on his wrists and ankles. They even let him get out of bed, under supervision, and stretch the mechanical heart's air hoses to their maximum length to use the bathroom. That was the highlight of his day.

He looked across to the visitor's chair where Adele sat. She was leafing through a magazine without really reading it. The pages flipped by faster and faster. With her legs crossed at the knee, Adele's free foot was bobbing up and down, and it, too, was moving faster and faster. Some minutes ago, maybe half an hour, it had kept pace with the *click* and *whirr* of the machine under the bed. But now her fidgeting was accelerating.

Dear Adele. ... She had stuck by him for forty-three years of the hardest life a woman could face: following him from one jobsite to the next, usually in those out-of-the-way places in undeveloped countries where a major dam or aluminum smelter complex was under construction. She had coped admirably with strange languages, strange foods bought in rural markets, sullen and inadequate domestic help, and sometimes primitive sanitation and medical conditions. Through it all, she had borne and raised three children, watched over them in sickness, taken a hand in their education, and then sent them off to boarding schools in Europe or the States when the time was right. And she never said a word against that life.

But the strains were there and the scars remained. Praxis could smell one of them now, whenever she came to visit.

By ten in the morning Adele would have taken her first and maybe even her second drink of the day. And after an hour by his bedside, when she had exhausted the possibilities of small talk and magazines, as her fidgeting became more and more pronounced, he knew she was itching for a chance to get up, go outside, light up a cigarette, and take a nip from the flask of bourbon she kept in her purse.

He couldn't blame her for these vices. They had once been his, although he had curbed them some years ago on doctor's orders. Adele had never seen the point of such abstinence for herself, nor had she made a personal commitment to it, and he certainly didn't want to nag. After all, she'd done her job with an uncomplaining will and a straight back. She could indulge herself now, when it didn't matter.

However, the irony wasn't lost on him. He was the one who had made the healthy decisions and changed his life. And he was the one whose heart had died, while Adele continued to soldier on, resolutely drinking and smoking, tough as an old pair of work gloves, virtually immortal. But this was not the time for him to mention the unfairness of life.

Praxis looked down at the tubes again. The best he could manage was the lament from a dimly remembered situation comedy in the golden age of broadcast television. He uttered it softly now: "What a revoltin' development this is!"

"Dear?" Adele asked, looking up. "Do you need something?"

"Nothing. I'm just commenting on human mortality."

"I know … and when you've done everything right," she said, echoing his thoughts. "You watch your weight. You take your vitamins. You play golf. And you're still the man I married—a strong and vital man."

Who has to wait for another man to die so he can get a new heart, Praxis thought, although he refrained from saying it. Almost three more months of this waiting, on average, they had said. He could already feel his muscles growing slack from inactivity, his weight starting to creep up—even on the prescribed diet they fed him—and his joints tightening up. Three days ago he had developed his first bedsore. And if the waiting didn't kill him, the boredom certainly would.

"You look tired, dear," he said. "Do you want to step outside? Stretch your legs?"

"You don't mind? I mean, I want to keep you company. …"

"You go now. I'm really doing all right."

She dropped the magazine, gathered up her purse, and was gone before he could change his mind.

———

During Praxis's third week in the hospital, the doctors on his team—this one with a nametag that read "Peterson"—were still coming in every morning to listen to his chest with a stethoscope.

"Why do you do that, I wonder?" Praxis said. "If you want to know how my heart's doing, lean over and read the dials on that machine."

Dr. Peterson stared at him for a long moment, clearly weighing some decision. "It's not your heart I'm concerned about," he said finally, "but your lungs."

"Is something wrong with them, too?"

"No—that is, not that we can tell. But elderly people who have been only moderately active for most of their lives, and who suddenly become bedridden, are at greater risk for pneumonia and other respiratory diseases. So we're keeping an eye on things. How do you feel otherwise?"

"Lousy … but if you'll unhook me, I'll happily get up and dance."

The doctor stared at him again. "That's one of your jokes."

"I've got nothing to do around here but make jokes."

"I see we've given you bathroom privileges."

"And I'm damned glad to have them."

"We should have started you on an exercise program by now," Peterson said. "I'll order a portable pump, one that rides along on a cart, and assign an orderly to accompany you."

"Where am I going—out to the golf course?" Praxis asked facetiously.

"No, down to the basketball court, so you can practice your jump shot."

"What!"

"That's a joke," Peterson said with the smallest of grins. "You can start by walking up and down the corridor. If you survive that and manage to build up your stamina, we'll see about more intense activity and some physical therapy."

Praxis sighed. "How much longer until they find a heart?"

"It might be any day now," Peterson said.

"Or it might still be months."

"Yes, that, too."

———

In his fourth week of purgatory, with only two months remaining on his sentence, John Praxis had worked himself up to walking the corridors for twenty minutes at a time, three times a day, and believed himself stronger for it. But he still felt shaky each time the orderly, Marcelo, helped him back into bed. Whether all of this was helping to fight off pneumonia—if two rounds of golf every week for the past ten years hadn't worked—was still open to debate.

It was a surprise then, when his medical team of Jamison and Peterson, plus two men he didn't recognize, came into his room, brought extra chairs, and sat down facing him with sober, worried looks. They reminded him of clients who had signed a fixed cost contract, changed their minds about some major specification, and didn't know how much the change order was going to cost them. In such cases, the news was generally bad.

"First, let me say," Dr. Jamison began, "that we are continuing the search for a suitable transplant candidate for you."

"But you must understand," Dr. Peterson went on, "that the waiting list is long—"

"—and the situation is made more difficult, in your case, because the donor heart must match you in both histocompatibility and blood type—"

"—blood type being more important, because we can compensate for most antigen incompatibilities—"

"—and you have fairly rare blood, type B-negative—"

"—meaning you receive from only O and B groups—"

"—and negative Rh factor, which is even more limiting—"

"—for O, it occurs in about seven percent of the population—"

"—and for B ... well, occurrence is less than two percent."

"In other words," Praxis summed up, "I'm screwed."

"Let's say the match will be difficult and take longer."

Praxis pointed to the machinery under the bed. "And what's the warranty on this thing?"

"People waiting for transplants have lived for hundreds of days with totally artificial hearts," Peterson said.

"But today we want to present you with an alternative," Jamison concluded.

He introduced the two strangers in the room as doctors Anderson and Adamson, colleagues from the Stanford Medical Center who specialized in the new field of cellular regeneration.

"It's all about taking stem cells from your own body," Anderson explained. "We isolate them from skin and nerve tissues, muscle and connective tissues. We culture the stem cells *in vitro* and induce them to grow new organs to specification."

"With such an organ," Adamson put it, "there's no need for the waiting, searching, and tissue typing, because the implanted material originated in your own body and has all the right antigen signatures."

"And also no need for a regimen of immune-suppressing medications," Anderson concluded. "We don't interfere with the body's defense system. That's one of the major benefits of autonomous regeneration."

"You're going to grow me a heart?" Praxis said. "I didn't know that was possible."

"Well, it's still in the experimental stage," Jamison said. "Technically, you would be participating in a clinical trial."

"The procedure would not be covered by your insurance," Peterson said. "And while there's a modest stipend connected with the trials, we figured in your case—"

"Screw the money?" Praxis suggested cheerfully.

"Well, something like that," Peterson said.

"So, tell me what's going to happen."

"In the early stages," Anderson said, "we started with a heart donated from a cadaver. We washed it with various enzymes and detergents to remove the previous owner's cells, leaving just the connective tissues—a set of intracellular proteins called collagens. This is simply the shape and structure of a human heart but totally inert."

"I'll bet," Praxis said.

"We would then bathe this 'empty' heart in a solution of stem cells, hormones, chemicals to control cell development, and nutritive media. We place it inside a chamber that provides the appropriate conditions for growth—temperature, pressure, oxygen supply, carbon dioxide removal, *et cetera*. And the cells arrange themselves and grow into new, living tissue of the appropriate type."

"We used to think," Adamson put in, "that it would be difficult to organize the different kinds of stem cells—muscle, artery, nerve—on such a scaffold and train them to grow into productive tissues. But the amazing thing is that the stem cells seem to be self-organizing, sending chemical signals into their immediate environment and calling forth the right kinds of tissue. It's the same process that occurs in the womb during—"

Praxis cut him short. "But you're still going to put a dead man's heart inside me?"

"Not exactly," Anderson said. "We were able to use the cadaverous hearts in experiments with baboons. But there were still issues of contamination—lingering traces of antigens, virus particles, and such. We actually found it easier to map out the heart's internal structure, model it on a computer, and then 'print' it in three dimensions using layers of fresh, uncontaminated collagen that has been grown synthetically. We can also scale the organ's size for the intended recipient. You will be getting a new heart made from your own cells that are grown on such an armature."

"How long?" Praxis asked.

"About six weeks," Adamson said. "That's the organ's incubation period in a bioreactor."

"Come again?"

"How long it takes to grow a heart in a jar," Peterson said.

Praxis didn't have to think about it. "When do we start?"

"Don't you want to hear the downsides?" Jamison asked.

"All right. What are they?"

"This is all still experimental—"

"But will I remain on the UNOS list?"

"Well, yes. This procedure won't invalidate—"

Praxis plowed ahead of him. "So if the new Frankenstein heart flops or something, you can always rush me into surgery, cut it out, and put back this little two-stroke pump while we wait for a suitable human donor. I don't lose my place in line, and I only waste about a month and a half—time that I would spend lying here anyway."

"Well, you must understand," Peterson said, "there's a limit to the amount of 'cutting out' and 'putting back' your body can tolerate."

"Yeah, sure," Praxis replied. "But you wouldn't have brought these gentlemen here if you didn't think I was a good candidate. So I presume they brought along the appropriate forms for me to sign."

Dr. Anderson reached for his briefcase.

All the rest was details.

―――

Antigone Wells had lost track of the days—more than four, less than fourteen. But she was almost certainly aware of several visits at odd intervals by the physical and speech therapists, renewed passages through that white tunnel filled with beeping noises, and repeated, one-sided consultations among her doctors just beyond the door of her hospital room. It had become clear, even to Wells herself, that she was getting better—stronger, clearer, more precise, more focused—in some ways but not in others. So Dr. Bajwa's original assessment was proving to be only halfway a lie.

She was regaining feeling and controlled movement on her right side: tongue, arm, hand, leg, foot. She still had difficulty smiling on command—but then, hadn't she always? She was able to form words more clearly, now that her tongue was working properly, or at least it did not curl around inside her mouth like a wounded snake when she tried to use it. But these were still only the words that popped into her head from that gray place behind her eyes. The words that she really needed, the words that lived out there among people and inhabited those twisting and branching graphic images, they still eluded her.

So after those many days of waiting to get better—more than four, less than fourteen—Dr. Bajwa came to consult with two new doctors. And this time they included Wells in the conversation as a person rather than an object.

"Ms. Wells, I'd like to introduce William Anderson and Peter Adamson," said Dr. Bajwa. "They've come up from the Stanford Medical Center."

Antigone Wells nodded at the new men, immediately forgetting which one was which. She did not offer to shake hands, because her right hand was still not fully under control. Anyway, neither of them seemed to expect the social contact. They just smiled at her. She told them slowly, meaning it as a way of greeting, "Don't … words …"

"That's because you've had a stroke, ma'am," Bajwa explained quickly. He seemed to be speaking for Wells's benefit, although he half-turned to the two other doctors. "We've mapped out the areas of—well, nonresponsiveness—in your left hemisphere. There's some damage to the motor functions, accounting for the obvious loss of physical control. Overall, the darkest region of the scans touches on Broca's area, which governs the brain's ability to recognize and recall words and put them into speech. You've also acquired some spottiness in areas which might account for your alexia, or receptive aphasia with regard to text. We think you might have some damage in pathways connecting the visual cortex to Wernicke's area, which interprets what you hear into language and what you see into the written word. Fortunately, Wernicke's area itself seems to be unaffected."

Otherwise, you'd be talking to a brick, wouldn't you? Wells thought to herself. *But then again, maybe I* am *a brick, and these men are not really here.*

"Of course, Miz Wells," said one of the others, perhaps Anderson, "references to 'Broca's area' or 'Wernicke's area' are merely generalizations from nineteenth-century anatomists and psychiatrists. Nowadays, with better neural imaging, we tend to think the actual processing of any function is more distributed—that is, it takes place over a much broader surface of the temporal lobes."

"Total blackout in either area?" asked the other one, perhaps Adamson.

"Oh, nothing *total*," Bajwa said. "The entire lobe shows remarkable activity."

"Good, good. We'll need that to build on," said the man named Anderson.

Bajwa turned back to Wells. "These gentlemen have a new therapy we'd like to try with you. Because you're in excellent health—I mean, other than problems resulting from the stroke—and you're of suitable age, we all feel you would be a perfect candidate. You see, they propose to take some of the cells from your body and teach them to be new brain cells. Then those cells can help rebuild the parts that you lost in the stroke."

"You see, Ms. Wells," Anderson began, "the brain is both ductile and resilient—"

"Simple words, Doctor?" Bajwa prompted.

"Ah, yes, by which I mean, the brain is … like plastic, it can mold itself, adapt, even repair itself and build new connections—given the right materials and a nudge in the right direction."

Antigone Wells tried to dredge up words from that gray place, from something she had read or heard sometime before the stroke. Her brain offered: "Stem …?"

"Exactly!" Adamson said. "Oh, very good! Yes, stem cells."

"It's a cellular regenerative therapy," Anderson went on, "that has been in trials for some years and is now coming into general use."

"Oh … kay," Wells said. "Give … words."

"Good. Now that we have your verbal consent …" Adamson laid a case on the tray table attached to her hospital bed and snapped it open. He took out papers covered with those twisting, branching images. His partner uncapped a fountain pen and handed it to him. "Next we must acquire what's called 'informed consent,' which means that we ask you to read and sign these documents …"

Antigone Wells smiled at the man expectantly, waiting for him to catch on.

"Oh, dear," he said. "But how can you …?"

"Verbal … contract …" She groped for a word, the name of an identity she knew she had once held close to her heart. It was only four days ago—certainly less than fourteen days. She tapped her breastbone. "… lawyer."

When he still hesitated, Wells reached for the papers with her good left hand and for the pen with her right. Her fingers flopped a bit as she tried to take the barrel from his unresisting grasp. She set the papers on her lap and flipped them over one by one, looking for something. She didn't know what exactly, but she would recognize … a long straight line! With uneven pressure, and not sure which way the pen's nib was pointing, she made a mark against that line. One way, then the other, leaving a long dent in the paper and a darkened hole, if not exactly a mark.

"Consent," she said clearly. She nodded at the other man and then at Bajwa. "Witness—ses ..."

Then she lay back, too tired from the effort to try anymore.

Inside the Induced Pluripotency Laboratory at Stanford Medical Center in Palo Alto, clinical technologist Tina Gonzales reviewed the list of the day's setups. Among the twenty-one treatments to be prepared were three tissue samples from a patient identified as "Praxis_J" and one from patient "Wells_A." All four had come in overnight on blue ice from the University of California - San Francisco's Medical Center up at Mission Bay.

In the old days, with dozens and sometimes hundreds of blood and tissue samples arriving at a lab like hers from around the country, mixing up patient identities would have been all too possible. Relying on just surname and first initial, or even the patient's Social Security number, would have been a recipe for life-threatening disasters, because those tags existed outside of the tissue itself. You had to find some way to tell the anonymous tissues apart after they had passed through various containers in the various stages of processing.

Each of these samples was now tagged with the thirteen genetic markers and sex differentiator of the Combined DNA Index System, or CODIS, which the FBI had originally created for forensic profiling. Before any culture was sent to Gonzales's lab, it was profiled with a DNA test kit and the results were attached. Before she sent pluripotent tissue back to the implant center, she profiled and matched it to the donor's CODIS identity. And the center that had shipped the sample in the first place performed another DNA test upon receipt, just to be sure.

But after Gonzales had logged the samples into her computer and while they remained in her lab, they traveled in two-milliliter tubes, microtiter plates, and culture dishes marked with a Sharpie and using just the last name and initial. If anyone screwed up the plates along the way, they would simply toss that batch and start another. Tissue was cheap. The lab never consumed more than a fraction of the original cells extracted from the patient. And the chemicals and nutrients used in processing them were all bio-synthesized and stocked in liter-sized bottles. Nothing was ever lost, except time. Any mistakes that she and her co-workers might make never saw the light of day—although the Food and Drug Administration required them to log botched and restarted batches as a quality metric.

The three samples from the Praxis patient were identified as muscle, vascular, and skin cells, with the notation that the latter were wanted to be made potent for a neural replacement. "I guess the heart project is finally taking off," Gonzales murmured as she keyed the protocol requests into the appropriate boxes on her computer screen.

The sample from patient Wells was from skin and also noted as a neural implant. "Somebody fell and hit their head," she said, keying in the nerve-cell protocol for a second time.

The other samples she processed without comment.

In the early days, researchers working on cellular regeneration had thought to use stem cells from human embryos to build new organs in adults, because developing embryos were rich in cells that could potentially become many different cell types. Some were even "totipotent" and could become anything at all, provided you caught the embryo early enough, at the blastocyst or hollow-ball stage. But it turned out that taking stem cells from a baby was no better than drawing stem cells or a freshly harvested organ from another adult. The risk of incompatibility between the immune system antigens was just as great, and the patient still faced a lifelong regimen of immune-suppressing drugs. And then even research into embryonic stem cells had become clouded, because raising human embryos on a routine, assembly line basis made some people queasy—for, of course, the embryo did not survive the harvesting process. The only way to use a baby's stem cells successfully was by freezing the patient's own umbilicus at birth, saving the stem cells stored there against the day when they could be used to grow new organs.

All that was ancient history now. That early research with embryos had revealed the little bits of ribonucleic acid, called "microRNAs," that were used to differentiate and make new tissues from stem cells. Unlike the messenger RNA that got translated into proteins out in the cell body, these tiny strands of genetic material never left the cell nucleus. MicroRNAs promoted complementary sites along the chromosomal DNA to express other bits of microRNA, and those bits promoted still other bits in a precisely timed cascade of cellular development and differentiation inside the embryo. Eventually, one of those branching cascades would lead to expressing the combination of proteins that determined what kind of bodily tissue the cell was to become.

By studying embryo development, researchers working in laboratories and teams around the world quickly identified the microRNAs sequences needed to tell a developing epithelial or skin cell to become part of a lung, liver, or kidney. Or a developing cell in the connective tissue to become blood, arteries, and veins. And they learned that the process could be worked in reverse. By tagging these little bits of RNA, synthesizing them in quantity, and then introducing them into an adult cell of the right type, along with other compounds that would induce or inhibit cell growth, they could reprogram an adult cell and return it to a semi-developed state which would keep its options open. That state was called "pluripotency," and the cells reprogrammed from adult cells were called "induced pluripotent stem cells," or iPSCs for short.

And that was all they did in Gonzales's laboratory at Stanford: take tissue samples from adult patients, treat them with specific sequences of microRNAs plus those other compounds according to various established protocols, and multiply the resulting iPSCs by the millions and billions. Then they would pack the reprogrammed cells on ice, perform a final DNA test to make sure that tissue-in matched tissue-out, and send them back to the originating center.

In the case of the Wells_A cells, a mass of pluripotent nerve cells was all the patient really needed. The surgeons would then open up his or her—Gonzales checked the CODIS tag for sex determination and discovered Wells was a *her*—braincase or spine or wherever the damage had occurred, inject a dose of the cultured cells, and let them begin knitting the neural network back together. Those new cells would then begin the longer process of learning from their neighbors and copying or adapting to new brain functions.

In the case of the Praxis_J cells, the frozen and type-matched package would be walked down the hall to Stanford Medical Center's newly dedicated Multiple Tissue Structures Laboratory. Pluripotent muscle tissue, connective tissue reprogrammed as potential arteries and veins, and epithelial tissue reprogrammed as nerve cells would be combined in proportion on a collagen armature to become somebody's new heart. Then the organ would be DNA-tested once again, packed on blue ice, and sent up to San Francisco, where the surgeons would cut open Praxis_J's chest, remove his old, damaged heart, and insert a new one.

Gonzales looked forward to the day when her lab could do more than just extract and expand stem cells, when the medical center could do more than simply build new hearts and other organs on the pattern of the old ones. For those tissues retained the genetic flaws, the inherent susceptibilities, which had caused problems in the first place. One day researchers would have complete access to the complex relationship between genes and proteins, and between proteins and tissue function. Then they could correct the genes while making new stem cells. They could give patients fixed hearts, free of defects and more resistant to disease.

Tina Gonzales knew that she and the rest of the medical profession were standing on the brink of revolutionary change. Evolution would soon take place *outside* the human body, under the direction of research scientists would could predict and control the entire chemical makeup of life's processes. They would draw on genes and proteins not just from the human cell line, but from the heritage of the world's animals, plants, and bacteria as well. With all of that knowledge, why not create a *better* heart? Why not program it to beat stronger, faster, longer, and all the while demand less of the body's oxygen and nutrients? Why not give it properties that even Tina Gonzales and the doctors of today could not yet imagine?

Do you fancy having purple eyes the exact, enticing shade of Elizabeth Taylor's? How about silver eyes? Or golden eyes? Bah! We can grow those irises for you in a test tube today. Think bigger!

Do you want strength equivalent to a chimp or gorilla—reckoned conservatively as twice that of a human—so you can punch through walls? Speed like a cheetah's, to run the one-minute mile? Or legs like a grasshopper's, to leap ten feet straight up in the air? We can program your metabolism, brain, muscles, lungs, and heart for that. Think bigger!

Do you want to endure exposure to microbes and viruses, eat raw poisons, take bruising, bone-breaking impacts and never get sick? Do you want to grow back lost limbs like a chameleon or salamander? Breathe under water like a fish? Grow a working set of wings like an angel? Do you want to … live forever? Ah! That would be the trick, wouldn't it?

Thinking about all the good things that might one day grow in her two-milliliter tubes and incubators, Tina Gonzales started the tissues from Praxis_J and Wells_A on their way through her lab.

———

Antigone Wells opened her eyes in the recovery room. She thought her vision was clearer now, in both eyes. She tested it by staring up at the ceiling panels, with their pattern of little holes, and slowly closing first one eye, then the other. No change. Or not much. But then, her vision had been getting steadily better all the time *before* the operation. So that was not proof.

She lowered her eyes and lifted her head slightly to look at the doorway into the hall. It had the mandatory lighted sign above it. She stared hard at the bright-orange symbols. She knew they made up a word, because the nurses had explained to her that the sign told people where to go if there was trouble and they had to leave the building. It was a short word. But still the symbols were just a branching and a crossing, a single stripe and a thing whose lines met in a T-shape.

So the operation had not given back her words.

But then, she wondered where she had gotten that notion of a "T-shape." Had somebody told her once? Was it from memory, like the way she could identify a cat, a football, a bird on the therapist's flip cards? Or was her brain, even now, making new connections?

The doctors had said the process would take a long time. She would get her words back slowly. She might even have to learn how to read all over again. Start with Dick and Jane … *See Spot run! … Run, Spot, run! Feh! It might have been easier to die back there in the ambulance.*

And as the new brain cells took over, what about the old ones? What parts of her life—her *former* life—were now gone forever, beyond the retrieval of memory? Oh, what the hell! As an attorney, Antigone Wells had always been one to make it up as she went along. Whatever she didn't have now, she would simply be forced to invent all over again.

From nowhere, from somewhere, from that gray place, a story floated into her brain, about a scarecrow who knew he was stupid because his head was stuffed with straw. So he went to see a wizard, who removed the straw and stuffed his head with pins and needles, to make him sharp. And afterwards, the scarecrow really did think he was smarter.

Better or just different? she wondered. *And does it matter?*

She laid her head back, and tears started behind her eyes.

As they prepped John Praxis for his second—and hopefully last—surgery, he wondered what it would feel like. As they shaved ten weeks of stubble from his chest and abdomen, where the thing inside him *whirr*ed and *click*ed, he wondered what it would be like to have a human heart again. To not be aware of his body unless he bothered to take his pulse or something. To be able to walk, run, dance without dragging around a cart carrying his battery, air pump, and monitors.

He had asked the doctors if it would still hurt, the way the incision over his mechanical heart still pained him sometimes. They said the sternum, which was the bone they had to crack open to reach inside the chest cavity, as well as the ribs that they spread apart in the process, would all heal in time. As for the heart itself, it wouldn't feel like anything. It was *his* heart. He wouldn't feel the sutures that held the organ inside its web of arteries, veins, nerves, and connective tissues. Those sutures would slowly dissolve and the tissues would grow together. The new heart wasn't going to fall out or flop around. It was part of him and, on a cellular level, always had been.

From out of nowhere, probably from his actively groping subconscious, Praxis recalled the scene in *The Wonderful Wizard of Oz*, where the wizard—who had proven to be a humbug from Nebraska, another visitor from the outer world, and no more magical than Dorothy herself—gave the Tin Woodman the heart he so fervently desired. It was nothing but a big, red pocket watch in the shape of a heart, which Jack Haley hung on the outside of his barrel chest. No, wait. That was the Judy Garland movie. In the original book, the wizard cut the Woodman's chest open with a pair of tin snips and hung inside it a heart made of red velvet stuffed with sawdust.

Well, Praxis decided, as they gave him the injections that would make him sleep, he already had a damned tick-tock mechanism going on inside him. ... Maybe the stem cell wizards and their heart made of velvet and sawdust would be an improvement. ... Quieter, at least, with no more *whirr-click, whirr-click ... whirr-click ...*

5. Afternoons on a Rooftop

WHY ANYONE WOULD build a garden on a rooftop in San Francisco was beyond the understanding of John Praxis. The city had only two seasons: cold and drizzly winter, cold and foggy summer. The only time you would hunger to sit outdoors under a warm and smiling sun came in May and October, although random days might come during that nominal summer when the fog would burn off by noon and the onshore breeze would not start blowing it back again until three or four o'clock. And then the nurses at the Mission Bay medical center herded their convalescent patients, like a little boy chasing pigeons across a plaza, up onto the roof "to get some fresh air."

Come to think of it, he wondered as he settled into a chaise longue, why didn't the city's pigeons ever flock up here? The glass walls surrounding the garden were no barrier, being open at the top. Visitors, if not the patients themselves, usually brought food, were not stingy about sharing it, and sometimes carelessly dropped wrappers full of crumbs and bits. It must have been the hawks, Praxis decided. Hawks lived high up, so they could dive on their prey. Every major city had its population of red-tailed hawks that stooped on the pigeons from ledges and cornices. As a new architectural feature, his daughter had shown him a dozen websites with dedicated cameras following the real-time lives of these predators and their nestlings, including the rending of smaller, gray-feathered carcasses. Probably the pigeons had learned not to fly so high anymore.

While Praxis sat and mulled this problem in urban ecology, a woman came over and took the chaise next to him. She moved stiffly and reached forward with both hands to lift her right calf up onto the long seat. Something wrong with the joints in her leg or back, he supposed. She wore a bright-blue sweat shirt and matching pants, as well as low-cut sneakers, so he guessed she had just come from physical therapy. But her head and hair were covered with a long silk scarf worn as a turban. The cloth's background was peacock blue, which color-coordinated with her sweats, but was streaked through with various greens, from forest green to aquamarine to iridescent emerald. Anywhere else, that scarf would have suggested "good taste" or "fashion sense," but here it whispered "chemotherapy."

Then he glanced at her profile, not meaning to intrude, and must have made some small, sudden movement in surprise.

"Hello?" the woman said, questioning him with agate-gray eyes.

So now Praxis felt free to look her full in the face. He saw the same strong jaw and cheekbones, the same straight nose and generous mouth. He had seen that face mostly in profile or from slightly behind, while she spoke in court addressing witnesses and the jury. But it was a memorable face. Where the turban now coiled tightly, he knew she once had worn a broad sweep of ash-blonde hair.

"Ms. Wells!" he said, inanely. "Hello!"

She smiled faintly. "Have we met before?"

Praxis supposed that the rigors of a massive heart attack, the near-death experience, and two surgeries might have changed his own face. But not that much. Adele and the children kept assuring him he looked the same as ever. So this failure of recognition—in the woman who had single-handedly taken a chunk out of his company to the tune of a third of a gigabuck—must have meant something else.

"Only briefly," he replied. "Well, on a half-dozen occasions," he corrected. "With plenty of other people in the room."

He watched her eyes as she tried—and obviously failed—to place him. "Are you an attorney?" she asked.

"No. Ah, what's the word in a civil case? 'Respondent'?"

"Defendant," she said. "I'm guessing I didn't represent you."

"No, ma'am. If you had, I think we would have won."

She smiled at that. "But I still don't know you."

"John Praxis," he said. "We were the engineers who built Saint Brigid's."

"Oh, yes!" she said, although it was clear from her eyes she still didn't know him. "I get confused about faces and names these days," she apologized.

"Chemotherapy?" he suggested, touching his own head to indicate the turban.

"What?" Her hand went up to the cloth in response. "Oh! No. Brain surgery."

"That'll do it, too." His mind turned over the remaining possibilities. "Stroke?"

"Aneurysm," she agreed. "Tiny little artery, but it blew out all sorts of things."

"You seem to be doing really well," he said. "I mean, considering that it must have happened sometime after my Thunderbolt. And that was just a couple of months ago."

"Thunderbolt?"

"You didn't hear? It was while the case was still at trial. I had a heart attack. Big one, on the golf course. My heart just … died."

"I'm sorry. If I knew that, I don't remember. But—'died,' you said? And they arranged a transplant so soon? You look like you just came in from a jog."

Praxis glanced down at his own clothing: gray sweatpants, tee shirt from the company picnic, microfiber fleece jacket with PE&C logo on the left breast, lace-up cross trainers with waffle-stomper soles. "Well, the treadmill," he said. "Downstairs."

"They must have you on a very aggressive program."

"You have no idea," he replied.

———

Antigone Wells had a new appreciation for how "ductile" and "resilient"—in the words of one of those Stanford doctors—the brain could be. Especially with a refreshment of what she had come to think of, in the words of Hercule Poirot, as "the little gray cells."

A month—no, five weeks now—after the operation to sow activated stem cells into the darkened areas of her brain, her body had recovered nearly all of its old control and most of its strength. Daily bouts with Gary, her physical therapist, were building muscle tone and dexterity. Her mind and tongue had recovered enough of her words—at least the easy ones—so that she could speak almost normally and survive without embarrassment in light social conversation. Jocelyn, her speech and language pathologist, had her working on fluency in her verbal processing and on phonetics in her visual processing. Soon she would graduate from flip-card exercises, "A-*ah*-apple … B-*buh*-ball … C-*kah*-cat," to actual sentences and then on to *Dick and Jane*. But written words were coming along more slowly than spoken words.

Jocelyn seemed pleased that Wells was meeting a mysterious gentleman on the roof every day it was sunny. "Tell me about him."

"He says he knows me."

"But you don't remember him?"

"No. Not really. Not the voice. Not his face."

"So how does he know you?" Jocelyn asked.

"It was a case I worked on—right before my stroke."

"Was he your client? Did you have a personal relationship?"

"No, not personal. He was the other side, defending. … I don't know."

"I'm not surprised," Jocelyn said. "Our brains process memories in many different ways.

"In your career, as a lawyer," she went on, "you worked with words as much or more than with sounds or visual images—and written words as much or more than spoken words. You're in the class of people I would call 'hyper-literate.' Anything you remember about his court case would be linked strongly to the text of briefs or dockets or whatever. And you've handled a lot of cases, haven't you, over the years? So I would guess you might only recall this man's face and name in relation to those documents, rather than in any emotional context."

"He's a stranger to me." Wells paused. "So … should I stop visiting with him?"

"Oh, no. It's good for you. He might even help you bring back some of those words. Did he give you his name?"

"John Praxis …" she said, still trying to place the name in some context other than the rooftop.

"Well, then!" Jocelyn said delightedly. "You two have something in common, something to talk about. He's a bit famous around here, you know. Praxis is one of the first recipients of an artificial human heart. Wait—I've got that wrong—not 'artificial' so much as grown in a test tube. They call it an 'implant' rather than a 'transplant,' because it was grown from his own stem cells instead of being donated from another person. It's the same way that your brain is rebuilding itself from stem cells."

"Uh-huh," Wells said. "So he's a what you call … celebrity?"

"In medical terms, at least."

That afternoon the sun was shining, and Antigone Wells looked forward to going up on the rooftop. She sought out the man with the close-cropped silver hair, the white eyebrows that shadowed his enigmatic brown eyes like an eagle's, and the nose whose bridge came straight down with nostrils curving back around, like a beak. The deck chair next to his was empty and she settled into it as gracefully as she could.

"I understand we share a secret, you and I," she began.

"Hello, Ms. Wells! And what secret is that?"

"They're rebuilding both of us from spare parts."

"You mean, like Frankenstein's monster?"

"No, our stem cells. My brain. Your heart."

"Someone told you about that, did they?"

"Everyone here is really quite proud of you," she said.

"Nothing I did personally. I just signed their damned papers."

"But you're advancing so fast! I wouldn't even know you were sick."

"My doctors say organ regeneration's the wave of the future. All I know is that without it, I'd still be on a waiting list. Or dead."

"And I'd be ..." She paused.

"What? What would you be?"

"Different. ... Dull witted. Crippled. Pathetic."

"You could never be dull or pathetic, Ms. Wells."

That made her smile. "Please, call me Antigone."

"Antigone!" John Praxis said with a smile that was warm and bright. He seemed so delighted to be allowed to use her Christian name that he reached across, took hold of her crippled right hand, and squeezed it.

And Wells was so shocked by the personal contact—something no man had offered her in a long, too long, a time—that, rather than withdraw her hand in ladylike fashion, she returned the squeeze and held it, twined her fingers through his, and locked them.

After a moment, they let go together and withdrew slowly.

"I'm so glad," she began. "You're not ... Did I hurt you badly? In the case?"

"You were brilliant." He sighed. "You, you really *ruined* us—"

"I'm so sorry!" she said. "I want to be your friend."

"—but, but it's only *money*, Antigone."

———

John Praxis was flattered that this woman—who was beautiful, elegant, talented, and younger than him by at least a decade—would seek him out on the rooftop every afternoon. He put aside, for the moment, what that might mean in terms of his marriage to Adele or the fact that, so far, he hadn't mentioned to anyone the growing emotional attachment between himself and Antigone Wells. For now, they were two shipwrecks cast up on the beach, existing in an isolated world of aftermath and recovery.

Their talk consisted of comparing notes about their differing stem-cell procedures, the differences in their physical therapy regimens, and the sameness of the hospital food. They talked about the medical center's unfamiliar routines, the antiseptic but still strangely biological smells, and the distant, anonymous courtesy of the professional staff. Their relationship—his and Antigone's—lived in the contrived world of the hospital. In fact, it did not actually live inside the hospital itself, because she came up from the Neurology Department and he from Cardiology. He did not even know what floor she lived on. And he had never told her about Adele and his family, nor asked her about a possible husband or companion. Those were topics for outside, in the real world.

At their fourth or fifth meeting, Antigone had hesitated after sitting down, then reached up and untied the blue-and-green scarf. She dipped her head shyly behind it as the cloth unraveled. Praxis expected either a cleanly shaved scalp or a buzz cut. But when she dropped the scarf, her head was covered in short, overlapping layers of her pale yellow hair, like rose petals clinging to her scalp.

"That's really pretty," he said.

"You probably remember it being longer."

"I do remember. But this is nice, too."

"The surgeons didn't have to take all of it off, you know. Just in patches where they planned to drill their burr holes. Then the hospital stylists did the best they could with the rest."

"You look lovely," he assured her.

Still, she sat with an uncertain expression on her face.

"What is it?" he asked.

"Some time ago, you said I had 'ruined' you," she began slowly. "I need to know … well, if you need money, I make a really good salary and have something put away. I could help you—"

"Antigone!" He laughed. "It was all corporate stuff. We carry liability insurance. And we have a really strong backlog right now. It all evens out."

"But I looked you up. Yours is a private company. At some point, that money comes out of your pocket."

"No," he said, "just a little less money goes in—and that's over a span of years. Don't worry about it. When I said 'ruined,' I really didn't mean financially. You just wiped the floor with us, is all. You did the technical homework that my supply chain team failed to do in the first place."

"I'll try to believe that …"

"No need to worry. In fact, I think I'll put Bryant Bridger & Wells on retainer for future liability cases."

"Who?" she asked blankly.

"That's your firm, isn't it?"

"Oh, right! Yes … it is."

———

Six weeks after her operation, Dr. Bajwa came to Wells's room after the routine morning brain scan. In his hands he carried a set of film images, which he spread out on her tray table.

"We're are very happy with these," the doctor said. He took out a pen and pointed to various color-matched focuses: splotches of active reds and yellows, surrounded by quiescent greens and blues, which were distributed over both hemispheres. Together, she and her doctors had watched the left hemisphere light up over the past couple of weeks. "Although we have no previous baseline of your brain to compare them with," he said, "the activity is almost normal for a woman your age."

"I'm glad …" Wells said. She waited for the "but." Announcements like this usually led up to a complication.

"Any stroke patient doing as well as you, we would have been discharged weeks ago—to a skilled nursing facility, or home if you have someone to care for you. We've only kept you in the hospital this long because your procedure is relatively new. We wanted to track your progress and, frankly, to guard against any adverse reactions."

"What would be an adverse reaction? Headaches? Hot flashes?"

"Another stroke," he said. "Failure of the new cells to thrive."

"And you're saying you don't see any of that here?"

"No, as far as we're concerned, you are good to go."

"Then why don't I have all my words?" she asked.

He paused. "You have new brain cells. They have survived and responded to the process that induced their new growth potential—a process that is still a matter of some controversy. Those cells are now growing well, adapting, and perhaps even integrating with the old neurons. So you have all the mechanical equipment. But it takes time for them to learn new functions, for the brain itself to adapt and grow, to heal itself. That's why we'll keep you on a schedule of speech and reading therapy, and physical therapy as necessary."

"When were you planning to send me home?"

"We can process the discharge in an hour or so."

"That soon?" Wells wasn't prepared for the rush.

"Do you have adequate care and support at home?"

"I have a housekeeper, Maritsa. She comes in to clean Tuesdays and Thursdays." In the last ten weeks, Wells had also asked her to collect the snail mail, scan her personal email, and refer anything important to Carolyn Boggs, who had her power of attorney.

"We'd like to have someone with you full time, at least while you're awake."

"I don't have …" Suddenly, her life choices were catching up with her.

It had been twenty-eight years since Antigone Wells made her final resolution: to stay at Boalt Hall, dedicate herself to the law, and become the Best Damn Attorney in San Francisco. Another Melvin Belli. Another Gloria Allred or Leslie Abramson. She knew that would be at the expense of becoming lover, wife, mother—and she accepted the sacrifice. So she had said good-bye to her insistent young man of the moment, Steve ... what was his name?

"We can arrange a practical nurse to come stay with you," Dr. Bajwa said. "Do you have a guest bedroom or study where—"

"It's a big enough apartment. There's room."

"Very good. I'll start the paperwork on that, too."

"Can you delay all this processing until after lunch?"

"This isn't a hotel, Ms. Wells. We do have other patients."

"Of course, I understand."

She had closed the door on a social life in favor of a professional life. But the stroke—what had Praxis called it? "Thunderbolt"?—had stolen her words and possibly even her career. The doctors could tell her what the mechanical part of her brain was doing, whether the new cells were alive and firing, but none of them could promise how much she would get back in terms of memory and ability. Oh, she would learn to read again. She might even be able to write her name and fill out the Social Security and Medicare forms, when the time came. But to regain her claim to the title of Best Damn Attorney? To be able to attract the high-profile clients, plan their cases, and deliver them to judge and jury? All of that was in the clouds, a future more filled with hope than based on evidence.

Now that other door was cracking open again. Sure, it was stupid to build a future based on half a dozen meetings with a practical and charming man. The only thing they shared was a secret, a new procedure, a new kind of medicine, no more. And besides, he was married, with a wife of long standing—she had checked on that, too. Carolyn Boggs was a fountain of information when it came to the city's social set, foundations, and fund raising. He had a family and obligations.

Antigone Wells regretted that she would not be able to see him one more time, up on the rooftop. She would be discharged into the lingering morning fog, before the afternoon sunshine. No chance to say good-bye.

But then, John Praxis wasn't exactly going anywhere. He lived in town. His roots were in San Francisco. And if he made good on that promise to put her old firm on retainer, she might even be able to wrangle him onto her client list. The senior partner, Ted … what was his name? Well, anyway, that man certainly owed her a favor. And the chance to meet Praxis again, to work alongside him, to share in his goals and dreams, at least a little bit, at second hand as it were, was incentive for her to work hard at becoming the Best Damned Attorney once more.

John Praxis waited on the roof for Antigone to come up from her physical therapy. At half an hour, then three-quarters past her usual time, he began to think she was not coming. But before he could decide what to do, stay or leave, Dr. Jamison appeared, leading a young woman who wore neither lab coat nor surgical scrubs and didn't have a staff badge.

"Mr. Praxis? I'd like to introduce Elpidia Hartzog, from the *Chronicle*. She's doing a story on regenerative medicine in the Bay Area, and she wants to interview you as one of the first recipients of a whole-heart implant."

The woman nodded and smiled, and sat down on Antigone's chaise longue. From her shoulder bag she took out a tape recorder, a pale-green steno pad, and a pencil.

"Do I mind if we have someone from the Praxis Communications Department present?" he asked. "Just for clarification."

"I can come back, if you want," Hartzog said. "But I'm not really interested in your company or its current situation. I understand you're privately held—so no implications with the Securities and Exchange Commission. I'm just interested in your experience as a transplant recipient."

"Implant," Jamison corrected. "As I've explained, there is no donor in this case."

"Right," she agreed. "So … Mr. John Praxis, shall we start?" And she very obviously turned on the recorder.

Praxis knew enough about the reportorial process that he could not expect to review or challenge her draft article. Everything he said was on record from this moment forward. He weighed possible damage to the company's reputation—calculated as nil—compared with the reassurance that PE&C's customers and employees might draw from hearing him say he felt fit and fine. "Go ahead," he said.

"So, how do you feel with a brand-new heart?"

"I feel fit and fine," he said. "Some discomfort early on, from a nine-inch-long incision and the cracking of my chest bone, but that happens with any heart surgery. Otherwise, no pain."

"I understand you were living with a 'total artificial heart,' made by CardioWest, for several weeks. What was that like?"

"No offense to anyone at that company you mentioned—Cardio-something?—but that was not my favorite vacation."

"Why did you stay with it so long?"

"My old heart was dead." Praxis shrugged. "I was on the waiting list for a donor transplant. And then the doctors—including Dr. Jamison here—suggested this new treatment."

"How did you feel about trying a new and untested procedure?"

"It wasn't exactly untested," Praxis said. "They'd been trying it out in animal models before I got my heart. And 'clinical trials' implies more than one patient. Considering my other prospects—extensive tissue matching, immune suppression, and then waiting for a suitable donor to … appear—I was thrilled to be chosen for this."

"Do you have any concerns about the ethics of the procedure?"

"Ethics? In what respect? This heart was grown with my own stem cells, on an armature of synthetic materials. Seems to me, the ethics are between me and the doctors."

"Well, yes, but there are issues of equity here. The procedure is not covered by medical insurance. You got a new heart by participating in a selective clinical trial. But you're also a wealthy man, so we can assume others will benefit only if they can buy their heart implant out of pocket. I'm left with the impression this is rich man's medicine. The rest of us need not apply."

Praxis could feel Jamison stir beside him, but he put out a hand to stop the doctor from interrupting.

"Of course, this is still a new procedure," he said. "The 'rest of us' may have to wait until the trials are over, the results studied, and the procedure deemed safe and effective. All this was explained to me by Dr. Jamison here and his colleagues, both the people at this medical center and those who came up from Stanford. In that sense, I'm glad my experience could help prove the process.

"But as I understand it, this procedure is more science than art. With all respect to my medical team, once all the steps are worked out and tested, then drawing the stem cells, inducing their potency, culturing them, and growing them on a collagen armature is a matter of protocol. Cookbook stuff that any medical technician can do. And if they happen to flub it up, they start over. The only real skill involved is the surgical team who cuts open my chest and attaches the new heart, same as in a traditional transplant.

"This is medicine on the assembly line," he concluded. "It's how Henry Ford put America on wheels. In the long run, it will be the cheapest, most available kind of medicine."

"But don't you worry," Hartzog pressed on, "about the crisis this procedure will create in Social Security and Medicare? If we go around extending the lives of old people—"

"Ye-ess?" he asked with the faint hiss of a rattlesnake.

"—doesn't that throw the actuarial tables into a tailspin?"

"It depends on what you want. Old people who are healthy and productive? Or people who are sick and dying?"

"What about those who *won't* benefit—patients with dementia, Alzheimer's, or brain damage? Do you want to extend their lives as well?"

Praxis paused. "That is a question for the doctors and the families. I'm not qualified to answer."

"Did you know there's a stroke patient in this hospital who received an implant procedure similar to yours? Antigone Wells, an attorney with the firm of Bryant Bridger and Wells? Didn't she challenge your company over malfeasance in the St. Brigid's hospital case?"

He paused again. *Gotcha!* Every reporter had a *gotcha!* question lurking somewhere in the woods. But then, Natalie Petrovska, PE&C's head of public relations, had drilled him well over the years. *Watch my lips and count the actual lies!*

"Oh?" he said. "Well, if Ms. Wells had a stroke, it must have come sometime after my heart attack. Since then, I've been too busy to read the newspapers. The last time I saw the woman, she looked very well. But in any case I wish her a speedy recovery."

Elpidia Hartzog tapped her pencil against her teeth, studying the fragmentary notes on her pad. "Thank you for your time, Mr. Praxis."

"You're welcome." He turned to Dr. Jamison. "I think I'd like to go in now."

Part 2 – 2019:
Run for Your Life

1. Coming Home

WHEN THE STAFF wheeled her out to the front entrance, Antigone Wells saw a woman standing there holding a placard with her name—just like a driver making a pickup at the airport. The woman was mid-forties, with brown hair going gray and tired, faded blue eyes, but she looked *strong*. Wells thought she might need such strength in the days ahead.

"That's me," she said, raising her hand and then gripping the chair's armrests to lift herself. The woman darted forward to assist, but Wells waved her away. "I just need to get my feet under me. Who are you?"

"Jeanne Hale, ma'am, from the MaxStaff Agency."

"Do you have some identification?"

Hale produced a wallet with cards, laminated certification as a licensed vocational nurse, and a work order from the agency.

"Very good," Wells said after examining them.

The hospital staff had already arranged for a cab, and it drove the two women out to Wells's apartment on Divisadero Street. She had the two upper floors and an attic loft in one of San Francisco's "painted ladies"—those Victorian houses that had been elegantly restored to their original, gaudy color schemes.

After paying off the driver, she turned to face the stairs: twenty-eight terrazzo-tiled steps up from the sidewalk to the outside door. Beyond that door, she knew, as many more steps went up the inside stairway to her apartment's first floor. She once used to run up and down those two flights of stairs every day—as well as the third, between levels inside her apartment—and claimed the exercise kept her in shape. Now she took them slowly, holding the railing and favoring her right leg when it balked.

"Maybe it's time to move to a newer building," Hale said as she followed behind, strategically positioned to catch Wells if she collapsed. "One with an elevator?"

"If you think I'll change my life around just because of a few scrambled wires in my head, you don't know me."

"Yes, ma'am. … They all say that at first."

"Humph!" Wells climbed with renewed vigor.

Inside her own space and looking around, she was pleased to see Maritsa had kept the place spotless. The living room spanned the width of the building in front, and Wells looked into the alcove created by the second bay window. She kept it shuttered to protect her orchids, arranged in banks of shelves against the wall, from too much direct sunlight. She cultivated the frilly *Cymbidia,* the delicate *Phalaenopses,* and the tiny, tubular *Ludisiae.* In a way, they were like her never-conceived children. Wells was glad to see Maritsa had maintained their feeding and lighting schedules, and only two had gone dormant.

"How lovely!" Hale said, and Wells began to like her better.

"Do you keep any kind of plants yourself?" she asked.

"Oh, no. I'm out on assignment too often. No home life."

"That reminds me. Bedrooms are one flight up. You get the front, with the street noise, sorry"—she made a face—"because I'm already set up in the back, over the garden. Do you have luggage and such?"

"I'll pick it up as soon as we get you settled."

"I'm home now. What more do I need?"

"Maybe a cup of tea?" Hale suggested.

"No tea, just coffee. Kitchen's through to the back. I'll show you."

Maritsa had left the kitchen just as neat and with the cupboards fully stocked, including a bag of fresh-ground Major Dickason's blend from Peet's and a new carton of two-percent milk. In her secret stash Wells found an unopened bag of Milano cookies. In the process, Wells discovered that she didn't need to read labels when she could recognize the packaging. In ten minutes the two women were seated at the dinette with a plate of cookies between them.

"I'm really not here to socialize," Hale began.

"My home, my rules. You'll do as I say so long as I'm paying."

The woman paused. "You understand, I'm not here to cook and clean, either."

"I have someone come in for that," Wells replied. "I know, your job is to follow me around and pick me up when I fall down. Right?"

"And administer meds and track your vitals."

"You can take my temperature later if you like."

The woman smiled and sipped her coffee.

When the doorbell rang, Hale started to get up.

"My job," Wells said, and went to the intercom.

"Auntie? Are you home? It's Carolyn and Sully!"

"Just got here," she said into the speaker and pressed the lock release. "Come on up!" She turned to Hale with a grin. "Oh, damn! Now we don't get to eat all the cookies."

In two minutes everyone was sitting around the kitchen table with full cups in front of them, and Wells was introducing her legal staff to her nursing aide. "Ms. Hale will be staying here with me for a while."

"Ma'am? You can call me Jeanne—if I can call you 'Auntie,' too."

"Sure," Wells agreed. "No formality—or not much when it's just us." Then she turned to business with her associates. "So, what's happened while I've been away?"

"Caseload is really backing up," Carolyn said. "Ted Bridger wants you back soonest so you can take up your share of the work."

"Bridger," Wells repeated softly. So that was the senior partner's name. A face floated up from memory: round and kindly, wrinkled, benevolent smile, silvery white hair, brown eyes as soft as stones from a riverbed. She wouldn't forget him again. "What kind of cases are we getting?" she asked.

"A lot of breach-of-contract," Sully said. "Mostly customers going slow-pay, no-pay, or dragging their accounts payable out to a hundred-twenty or two-hundred-forty days. With the inflation, their supply and logistics contractors deliver in dollars and get paid off in virtual pennies."

"But aren't there ..." Wells groped for the word. "Clauses ... with constant—?"

"Oh yeah, the C-Dollar button," Carolyn supplied. "Except these are all the old contracts, based on long-standing relationships—which are falling apart now that dollar devaluation has kicked up about a hundred percent. It's busting a lot of businesses—which is good for us, of course."

Wells grimaced. "How are we getting paid?"

"Percentage of the settlement," Sully said. "Which even in constant terms is starting to erode before we can get out of the judge's chambers."

"Bridger's talking about changing our fee structure," Carolyn said.

"To what?" Wells asked. "Do we take something up front?"

The associate nodded. "Payable in euros or yuan."

"Gold or diamonds," Sully said.

"Jesus!" Wells swore.

"We need you badly, Auntie," Carolyn said. "And, as a little incentive, we brought you a welcome-home gift." She reached into her bag and brought out a package with no special wrapping. It was a late-model touch tablet.

"I've already got one of those," Wells said. "It's nice to play with the icons and look at the pictures, but until my head clears up ..." Ah, what the hell! She had to come clean sooner or later. "I've forgotten how to read," she admitted quietly. "For a while, the Roman alphabet might as well have been the hash marks of ancient Sumerian. Now I can pick out some of the letters, guess at a few of the words. But ..."

"We know," Carolyn Boggs said. "You'll get it all back soon. In the meantime, this little fellah has an artificial intelligence that understands spoken language. You tell it what you want, and it will find the document or email, open it, and read it to you. Then it will transcribe your replies and send them off. Pretty neat, huh?"

Wells tried to think through, in her head, how it was that she really worked. This AI gadget *might* be useful—if she already knew which emails she wanted to open, or which documents she needed next, and could call for them by name. But Wells was in the situation of a blind person working with a sighted assistant who knew no law and couldn't anticipate her next move. Working at second hand might do, if someone like Carolyn or Sully were sitting at her elbow, fielding requests, making choices, and reading aloud. But would this glorified Speak 'n' Spell be able to search and skim the texts of laws and precedents in a database like LexisNexis? And what about when she herself had only a hunch and didn't know exactly what questions to ask? And the further trouble—the deep, dark secret Antigone Wells hardly dared think about—was that she still wasn't sure how much law she knew anymore versus how much had disappeared into those dark areas of her brain scan.

"That's a really nice gift," she said. "I'm sure it will be a big help."

She left the device on the table between herself and Carolyn.

Instead, she lifted the plate and passed it around.

"Does anyone want the last cookie?"

———

John Praxis went home to his wedding-cake Georgian mansion in the enclave of billionaires that lay west of the Golden Gate, in the Sea Cliff district. After weeks of overlooking the city's high-rises from his hospital window or the rooftop garden in Mission Bay, he was surprised by how small and toylike everything appeared in his own neighborhood. His mansion—actually just five bedrooms and 6,000 square feet—nestled between a tiny Tudor-style brick-and-stone manor house and a Japanese lacquer-and-tile gift box, all set among billiard-table lawns and topiary trees. It was the Disneyland version of wealth and power.

His immediate family had come home to receive him. Leonard and Richard took time off from their busy schedules, and Callie had flown in from the jobsite in Denver. Adele had asked the cook to prepare something special for lunch—a paella, which was Praxis's favorite—and then wondered aloud whether all those fats and starches fit in with his new hospital-approved diet.

"I think I'm allowed to eat anything I want," he grumbled. "I've got a whole new set of arteries in there."

"But your weight, John? Dr. Jamison wants you to lose twenty pounds."

"I'm down ten since the surgery," he replied. "And I spent half an hour on the treadmill this morning before they discharged me. This is the first real food I've had in three months, so please let me enjoy it in peace."

Adele retreated with trembling lips to her wine glass.

Callie shot him a dark glance, then looked away.

The two boys remained oblivious, of course.

"So … how's business?" he asked the table in general.

Richard glanced at Leonard. Leonard shrugged and continued eating. Only Callie put down her fork.

"How much have you been following the news, Dad?"

"Nurses turned the television off whenever it came on. Said they didn't want to upset me." But he was healthy now, and he was home. It was time to face the real world again. "What did I miss?"

"The money situation has gotten much worse since your … episode," his daughter said. "Nobody knows how bad, really, because the government isn't publishing the figures anymore. Even if they did, nobody would believe them. Stores don't put price stickers on anything, just barcodes with the product identification. You find out how much it costs at the cash register—unless you've got an app that reads the code and looks up the price online. Even then, it might change while you're walking to the front of the store."

"We've got the whole company on quarterly personnel reviews and salary adjustments," Richard said quietly. "Our labor costs are up about three hundred percent in six weeks."

"Ye gods! Are we still in business?" Praxis asked.

"Sure, because our contracts are all on a sliding scale," said Leonard, PE&C's president and chief operating officer. "Revenues are up three hundred *and twelve* percent in that time, just from inflation alone."

"Then the Fed or somebody rings a little bell," Callie said, deadpan, "and we all move the decimal point three places to the left on our calculators, to round out the zeroes. That makes it easier to keep track."

"Actually," said Richard, the chief financial officer, "revenues aren't that good."

"Not now, please," Leonard told his brother and sister with a warning frown.

Callie ignored him. "Everybody has gone slow-pay," she said. "And most of our projects are proceeding in slow motion."

"Slow motion?" Praxis said. "What does that mean, exactly?"

"Nobody gathers a pile of cash to build straight up anymore," his daughter explained. "And no bank or consortium will give them a construction loan, even on a balloon payment, knowing it will only get paid off in peanuts. That's because we overran the constant-dollar calculations months ago.

"So now, if a client gets a few bucks together," she continued, "they buy the building site, maybe do architectural design and some of the structural engineering to satisfy the building permits, take receipt of the drawings, and walk away. A few months or a year later, when they've collected more cash, they come back for demolition and excavation, and then say *sayonara* again over a hole in the ground. Later still, they come back to pour the foundation. After that, it's a year before they put up the steel—and get it all cocooned in foam and plastic against the weather. It might be two more years before they'll commit to floor pads and curtain walls. And God knows when the elevators and HVAC will be commissioned. It's like some banana republic, paying off in pesos or bolivars that melt before you can get them to the bank."

"It's not quite that bad," Richard protested.

"Then it soon will be," Callie assured him.

"How long can this go on?" Praxis wondered.

"Well …" she paused. "Until it *can't*, is my guess."

Praxis was frowning heavily. Parceling out construction funds in little dribs and drabs of effort might be the smart move financially, but it made for bad projects and worse buildings. It broke up engineering and construction teams and destroyed any kind of corporate memory as to who had done what and who promised to do how much by when. It blew the schedule of deliverables all to hell and smashed any accounting for the time value of money—which he now guessed wasn't so important when the money was melting like ice cream in the July sun. You couldn't plan anything, but instead you rushed blindly forward, expending your effort before it became worthless. Praxis just knew there had to be a better way to cope with the problem.

"I think I'd better start coming into the office," he said.

His daughter and middle son looked at their older brother. "Leonard's moved up to the thirty-eighth floor," Callie said, head down, talking to her plate.

"Only because it's more convenient to handle the chairman's business out of the chairman's suite," Leonard said. "Honestly, we didn't know when you would be coming back."

"Or even *if*," Richard put in.

"Shush!" Callie hissed at him.

"Really," Leonard said. "There's no need for you to rush back, Dad. We've got everything under control. The currency situation is just like riding a tiger—"

"—you hang on tight to its ears," Callie finished the old proverb.

"We just want you to get well, Dad."

"Think of it as early retirement—a well-earned rest."

"You'll get to do all the fun things you and Mom never had time for."

―――

"Congratulations!" said Jocelyn, her speech therapist, after administering one of her many tests. "It looks like you're now reading at the sixth-grade comprehension level."

"So I'll be on my way to high school soon?" Wells joked.

"The rest is just practice—and learning new words, of course."

"I know and understand the words while I'm reading them," Wells said, "but when I stop reading, and close my eyes, they just seem to go away. I'm afraid I won't remember—won't get them back."

"Does your house go away after you lock the door and stop thinking about it? Does your job as a lawyer go away when you leave the office and stop worrying about your cases?"

"I don't know if I'm still an attorney or not," Wells said quietly.

"Do *you* go away when you lie down to sleep and shut your eyes?"

"Well, I *hope* not, but after the stroke, I'm just not sure anymore."

"You have to believe that you are a real person, that you exist." The therapist paused. "You are actually doing very well, Antigone. Much better than the average stroke patient."

"I know. I'm learning much faster than I remember from my schooldays."

"Oh, that's because you already *know* how to read. You've got the principles stored away in other parts of your brain. You know how to deduce the meaning of unfamiliar words from context in a sentence, or by triangulation from the Latin, Greek, French, and Anglo-Saxon roots of the words you already know.

The brain stores information in many different places and in many different ways. You're simply rewiring it and reconnecting with what you already know in other circumstances."

Wells drew some comfort from that—the notion that her brain had places untouched by the stroke's annihilating darkness. That as much as she was learning new words, she was also re-creating, compiling, refreshing, and filing them away.

"Some psychologists," Jocelyn said, "think the brain's cognitive functions work compositely, like a hologram, rather by than the linear recording of data, like a compact disk. That is, the brain breaks our experiences up into related pieces—visual fragments of what we saw, aural fragments from what we heard, as well as smells, feelings, and the words we used to describe them. Each of these pieces goes off into a different part of the cerebral cortex but remains linked to the others by the unifying experience."

"Wait ..." Wells tried to remember back to an earlier conversation. "When I first met John Praxis on the rooftop, and didn't recognize him, you said that was because I associated his face and name with my legal work. When I lost the words for that work, I lost my memory of him. Now you're saying that associations can actually bring back the words?"

"We don't fully understand how the brain works," Jocelyn said, "and these are just theories. When you met that man on the roof, your brain was still in shock and repairing itself. I imagine the effects of your aphasia were dominating the encounter. But now your brain is healing, compensating, settling down. Links through association should strengthen over time."

Wells thought about that. Could the hologram thing be true as well for the principles of the law? Perhaps the exact language and interpretation of specific precedents, cases, and statutes lay just beyond the reach of her mind and tongue, still waiting to be learned or re-assimilated. But might the underlying *structure* live somewhere else deep inside her, as fragments of experience and understanding: the operations of parity, reciprocity, reparation, and retribution; the rules of evidence, examination, and cross-examination; the workings of trial and appellate courts, legislative bodies, and regulatory agencies; and all the other mental processes, upon which the mere words and intentions of statute and case law were hung like ornaments upon a tree—all still alive in there? Wells could hope these relationships were still part of her mind's organization, just as the appreciation of spatial relationships, strengths in tension and compression, and flow of forces lived in and shaped the mind of an engineer, or as appreciation of color, form, line, depth, and incidental and reflected lighting shaped the vision of an artist.

She tried to describe all this to Jocelyn, and that sparked an idea.

"Would you like to try some art therapy?" the woman asked.

"I never was any good at drawing," Wells said quietly.

"That's not the point," Jocelyn replied. "The attempt will exercise the right side of your brain, and that might stimulate some activity and associations on the left side. As you try to manipulate lines and colors for effect, the effort might stimulate the way you previously manipulated words and symbols."

"I'll try anything once. But the results won't be pretty."

Jocelyn took her hand. What seemed to start as a personal gesture became a clinical examination of her wrist, forearm, upper arm, and shoulder.

"What?" Wells said defensively.

"You're all stiff. Have you been keeping up with your physical therapy?"

"Treadmills." Wells made a face. "Dumbbells."

"You should be doing some kind of organized movement activity. Next time, I'll bring you some brochures for local yoga and modern dance classes."

"That won't be pretty, either."

———

After a week of sitting around at home, keeping up with his exercise program and pretending to catch up on his reading, John Praxis decided one morning it was time to get back to work. He woke at his usual time—which these days was closer to seven-thirty than his old workday schedule of five o'clock—and went down to breakfast with Adele.

"Think I'll go into the office today," he said as he buttered his toast.

His wife put down her coffee cup. "So soon? Do you think that's wise?"

"I feel fine," he said, then checked himself. "Better than fine, actually."

When he went up to shower and dress, Praxis was still thinking about his physical condition. He felt stronger and more alert than he had in a couple of years. The enforced hospital regimen of sleep and diet, plus his new level of physical activity, combining treadmill, elliptical, and weight machine instead of one morning a week walking the fairways behind a little white ball—and often as not riding an electric cart up to each lie—had done wonders for his body.

As he stepped out of the shower, it was a younger man who nodded back from the mirror, whose steamy surface blurred his wrinkles and filled out his thinning hair. He still had that ugly gash of a scar running down his sternum and into his stomach, and the slashes, lower down, where the connections for the artificial heart had entered his abdomen. But the redness was already fading, and soon he would have just cold, white lines as reminders of his surgeries.

When he put on one of his business suits, he was dismayed—pleased, certainly, but also distressed, because he liked to look neat and sharp—to find that the waistband of the trousers had four inches of slack flapping over his belly. He had to fold and tuck in the excess at the back and hold it with his belt—unless he wanted to postpone his return and wait for a tailor. His dress shirts also bagged around his midsection. And his single-breasted jacket now had enough material to wear double-breasted—if he'd had the buttonholes and buttons for it.

Once dressed with the help of a few discreet safety pins, he went downstairs to kiss his wife good-bye, rolled his Obsidian Black E-class Mercedes out of the garage, and headed downtown. He arrived at the headquarters garage at a quarter past ten. He didn't think anything of the time, because he knew his parking space was reserved. But when he pulled around on the first level, the chairman and chief executive's space held Leonard's blue F-type Jaguar. All the other reserved spaces were filled—even Callie's, with a car he didn't recognize. So Praxis had to swing around, out and in again, and draw a visitor's ticket, which cost ten dollars for twenty minutes. He fought down a surge of annoyance. *Oh well, someone upstairs can stamp it for me.*

He took the executive elevator to the thirty-eighth floor with his personal key and walked past the receptionist's stealthily armored desk. Behind it was a young woman he didn't recognize, but he didn't give her more than a passing glance.

"Sir! *Sir!*" she called behind him. "You have to sign in!"

As he turned, she came running after him. Blonde, with hair bobbed and lacquered. Pretty—under the Urban Assault makeup that was all bruised blues and grays. Dressed in a tailored suit with miniskirt and stiletto heels. Slender enough to be a fashion model herself, but making suspiciously good time on those heels. The only thing out of place was the bulky lump under the jacket below her left breast.

"You don't have to worry about me, darling," he said. "I own this place."

She frowned and her eyebrows came together, clearly recalling a mug book she had memorized. Then her face smoothed. "Oh, Mr. Praxis—*the elder,*" she added by way of mnemonic. "I'm sorry. I didn't recognize you."

"No reason you should," he said. "I imagine I'm from before your time."

He continued up to the electrically locked doors that provided entry to the inner offices, and the woman got back to her desk just in time to buzz him through.

No one on that floor paid attention as he walked down to the chairman's corner. The desk outside for his executive assistant, Ivy Blake, was empty, so he unlocked the double doors to his office and went in.

Nothing was the same. His pair of Modigliani ladies no longer graced the inner walls, having been replaced by a triptych of hideous modern art in glaring yellows and reds that would not look out of place at the local Holiday Inn. His engineering degrees and honorary doctorate were gone. There was a three-foot-high Chinese vase in the corner holding a spray of purple-dyed pampas grass. The telephone had been moved from the right-hand side of the desk to the left.

Well, Callie did try to warn me. Leonard had certainly settled in—like a tick on a dog.

"Oh, Mr. Praxis!" Ivy said behind him. "No one told me you were coming."

He turned to face her, and she rushed up to give him a quick hug. Twenty years of fielding his calls, managing his correspondence, and keeping his schedule—not to mention his secrets—gave her privileges.

"I probably should have called ahead," he said. "Where's Leonard?"

"He's out," she paused. "Entertaining the Millbank delegation."

"I'll just get to work then. Please load the current backlog onto my tablet, along with the most recent emails, and then—" He paused when he saw her bite her lip. "What is it?"

"Mr. Leonard is keeping the job reports now, sir."

"Well, of course. But now that I'm back—"

"I report to Mr. Leonard now," she said, clearly torn between loyalties. "They've set up a new office for you, down on Thirty-Seven—the 'Emeritus Suite,' they call it. And you'll be working with a new admin, Kay Sheffield—from the pool."

"When did all this start?" he asked icily.

"About a week after your heart attack."

"I see. Maybe you'd better show me."

Ivy led him back along the row of senior executive offices, through the security doors, past the reception desk—where the young woman nodded gravely at him—and down one elevator button to the floor with the international vice presidents. Ivy took him over to a barren, three-quarter glass cubicle fronting a narrow office in the middle of the back row.

That office had a single outside window which gave a limited view of gray high-rises on the building's landward side, rather than his familiar panorama of the Bay Bridge, the Embarcadero, and Treasure Island. It had a desk but no phone, no chair, and no decoration, except for his two Modiglianis hanging side by side on the wall—with no lock on the door to protect them. Maybe the ladies were too obscure, too modern and crude-looking, for anyone to think about stealing them.

The desk out in front had Kay Sheffield's name plaque, but there wasn't any identification on his own door. "Emeritus" was clearly a temporary position—one way or another.

"What am I supposed to do down here while Leonard plays chairman?"

"I don't know, sir. Really. You'll have to discuss it with him."

"When's he due back in the office? I'll see him then."

"He won't be back until tomorrow morning."

"Then I've wasted a day, haven't I?"

"It seems so, sir. I am sorry."

———

At her first art therapy class, as recommended by her speech therapist and held at the local community center, the instructor gave Antigone Wells a box of colored pencils and chalks, three sheets of heavy vellum paper, and the suggestion that she "express your feelings, perceptions, and imagination … whatever comes to mind, from wherever inside you."

Wells looked around at the other students as they seemed to meditate for a moment, carefully selected from among the rich palette of colors, and began tracing lines and curves across their own pieces of paper.

She refused to close her eyes, but she did try to look inside herself. All she could feel was the descending darkness of the stroke, the floor becoming the ceiling, and her sense of falling into deep, soft snow. Not a good memory. Not a place she wanted to commemorate. If she tried to draw that, she would have to sketch the acoustic tiles and recessed lamps in the conference room at Bryant Bridger & Wells in shades of gray and silver, then slowly cover them over with black chalk until the whole paper was solid charcoal.

She took another peek at the developing images the others were making. Bird wings—no, from the angle, those were stylized angel wings. Hands clasped in prayer. A vase of flowers. All in pastel blues and rosy blushes. However, one woman with unkempt hair was drawing a snarling black dog with vampire fangs. Wells didn't know if the woman was being more honest or simply displaying a different kind of predictability.

She looked across the room to the wall behind the instructor. To the left of the bulletin board hung a fire extinguisher: bright red enamel bottle, yellow classification label, silver anodized bracket, black hand grips and hose with a flaring black nozzle. Since her mind was so empty, she might as well draw that. At least it had all the colors in her pencil box.

She picked up the red pencil and began drawing the extinguisher's bottle. She made two straight, vertical lines for its sides, a rounded curve for the hemispherical top, a shallower curve for the flat bottom. Suddenly she remembered what she had hated about art class in grade school. Artists—and the people around her doing praying hands and angel wings—knew some special technique for making an image leap off the paper in three dimensions. But when Wells tried, she could only draw the outline and edges of things, flat images in two dimensions. She had no feeling for depth, perspective, or surface contours. Her drawings had all the depth and subtlety of an eight-year-old child's. *I'm caught in some kind of Byzantine icon*, she thought. *Trapped in Flatland.*

This wasn't a new fault she could attribute to the stroke. Wells had always been a terrible artist. She could *see* depth in the works of others, of course, and appreciate the reciprocal play of light and shadow, highlighting, and texture. She could understand the principle of perspective intellectually. But she just couldn't make her hand, the tip of her pencil, reproduce the sense of depth on paper.

She owned artworks, of course. Her apartment was full of them, mostly floral still lifes, many incorporating the orchids she loved, some realistically drawn, some more impressionist, but all alive with color and leaping off the page. Antigone Wells fancied herself a connoisseur of botanical art. But she couldn't draw worth a damn. Her medium was words, the structure of a good logical argument, the advantage gained over an opponent by the presentation of compelling facts. That was what made her study law and become an attorney—not this mucking about with pencils and chalk.

Wells put down her red pencil and stood up.

The instructor came over to inspect her work.

"Done so soon?" the woman asked.

"No. I can't do this. It's not me."

"Everyone feels that way at first."

"For me, it's a good place to stop."

She picked up her jacket and purse, thanked the woman, and went out into the hallway. This late in the afternoon, the center was busy with children doing after-school activities. As Wells walked down toward the entrance she passed a room with a hardwood floor, mirrors, and ballet bar, designed for aerobic exercises and dance. She glanced through the open doorway and saw young boys and girls in white pajamas, standing in rows, moving in cadence. Their movements lacked the flow and rhythm of dance. Instead, they looked more like jerky robots. She focused on the action and guessed they were practicing some kind of martial art: step forward, punch, step forward kick, step back, block then punch—all at the direction of a young man, also wearing pajamas, who faced them and performed the same movements while barking short words in what she guessed was Japanese.

After two more sets of advance and retreat, the instructor gave a quiet command, and the ranks of students broke up into pairs. Then he came toward the doorway where Wells was standing.

"Can I help you?" he asked politely.

"No, sorry. I was just watching."

"Is one of these students yours?"

"No. I was taking an art class."

He nodded and moved away.

"Is that karate?" she asked suddenly.

He came back. "Yes, a style called Isshinryu."

Without thinking, she said, "I suppose I'm too old …?"

He paused. "There's also a *tai chi* class. It's perfect for people of all ages."

Wells had seen them: old people, frail people, moving in slow motion, pushing on invisible stones, being pushed back by invisible waves, silent as mimes. *Tai chi* was too static and lifeless for her taste, but at least it was more rhythmic than yoga, less chaotic than modern dance.

"Couldn't I try your thing?" she asked. "This Iss-shin-something?"

"It's a mind-body discipline that takes a long time to master." He hesitated. "Okay, sure. Our adult class is Monday and Thursday nights. Beginners welcome."

Then he turned away to guide the sparring pairs.

Wells went back to her apartment and her orchids.

2. Slow-Motion Train Wreck

"We've got to convince Dad to retire," Leonard Praxis told his brother at a private meeting in the chairman's office. Their sister was calling in from Denver on speaker phone—kept at a low volume so the conversation wouldn't be heard beyond those walls.

"Doesn't Human Resources have a policy on that?" Richard asked. "About everyone retiring at sixty-five? We could simply wait a few months and let that kick in."

"That's just for employees," Leonard said. "And even there, we've granted exceptions in the past. The policy has never been tested against senior executives—or family members."

He paused for Callie to chime in, but the connection remained eerily silent.

"Dad's the biggest shareholder," Richard said slowly, "with thirty-five percent of the company."

That gave Leonard an idea. "I hold fifteen percent and, among the senior executives on the board, I know I can swing another ten percent. You each hold ten. So together we can force him out."

Richard was nodding thoughtfully but didn't commit himself.

The speaker box made a small noise, perhaps a muffled cough.

"I'd need both of you with me on this," Leonard stated flatly.

"Dad's done a pretty good job over the years," Callie said. "He's kept the company on an even keel—despite current difficulties. I trust his judgment."

"Except that he's had a near-death experience," Richard said. "Who knows how much brain damage he suffered? He's now an untested quantity."

"He seemed pretty sharp to me," their sister replied.

"The point is," Leonard said, "he had a massive heart attack. And what's running inside his chest now is, at best, a science experiment. There's no telling how long it will last."

"He's held the reins for almost twenty years," Richard put in. "We knew this day would come sometime, when the next generation has to step in. Dad is not going to live forever. This is an opportunity for him to bow out gracefully."

"And I'm already—" Leonard started, then stopped himself. How was he going to end that sentence? In place? In charge? *In control?* It sounded bad. "I'm not doing such a bad job here, am I?" he ended lamely.

"You're not doing badly," his sister admitted. "But you don't have his experience or his connections. And the position you took on that St. Brigid's fiasco—"

"The Legal Department backed me on that!" Leonard shot back.

"So? They were wrong, too, not to settle. I'm just saying another year or two of grooming under him—and paying attention this time—couldn't hurt."

"So we don't have your shares?" Leonard said.

"No, not at this time," she said. "Not like this."

"Then I hope we all get the luxury of waiting."

The Great Crash came three weeks after John Praxis returned home from the hospital.

He was out jogging that morning, following the challenging road that curved up through the fog from Sea Cliff to the Legion of Honor museum, listening to KCBS in his ear buds. The first news story simply said that the People's Republic of China had sold a block of U.S. Treasury bills.

Praxis noted the fact, buried among the weather and traffic reports. *People and countries must be rolling over their investments all the time,* he figured. He continued his morning run.

The second version of the story mentioned a *large* block of bills, ten-point-two trillion dollars worth, which—the announcer read in the same monotone—accounting for inflation, represented ninety-five percent of the Chinese government's holding of the U.S. national debt.

Praxis stumbled, caught himself, and then took two more steps. He really didn't want to break his stride, not when he was all hooked up with his heart rate monitor and pacing himself, especially when he was almost at the top of his run, with the square façades and colonnade of the museum just appearing out of the mist ahead. But he did stop. *That's not a sale, that's a dump!* he realized. And in a flash it occurred to him: *Who's around to buy up that much paper?*

He turned and loped back downhill, taking long strides in triplets to the rhythm in his brain: *This is bad … this is bad … this is bad!*

Within forty-five minutes he was downtown in the thirty-eighth–floor conference room watching the story unfold on the widescreen with his two sons. They switched back and forth between the world news on CNN and the financial news on CNBC. In either case it was bad.

The Dow Industrials were down about a thousand points, heading toward a loss of fifteen hundred for the session, or a drop of about seven percent—and that was only the beginning, all the commentators warned. The Chinese had announced their intention to "get out and stay out" of the U.S. debt market until the government stopped "intentionally inflating" the supply of dollars in order to "erode the value of its obligations." Praxis's original suspicion had proved accurate: No buyers existed for that much suddenly available paper debt. In fact, Japan, the Caribbean banking centers, Brazil, and the major oil exporters—the next largest holders of U.S. debt—were all following China's lead. The credit rating agencies had announced that at two o'clock Pacific time—after the markets had closed on the East Coast and before they were due to open again in Asia—they would officially adjust the rating of federal debt instruments.

"This is bad," Richard said, echoing his father's earlier sentiments.

"Thank God we don't hold any T-bills," Leonard said with a chuckle.

"You don't understand," Richard said. "There goes half our backlog in government projects."

"Or worse," Praxis added.

"We surely don't have that much going with the Feds," Leonard objected. "The wharf at the Norfolk navy yard and the ring road at Sheppard air base, sure, but we've been light on federal projects since—"

"You still don't understand," Richard insisted. "Every project backed by government bonds is now in question. That's all our transportation work, all the water projects, half the power plants. Even if that backing is no more than five or ten percent, losing it puts the whole financing package in question. And don't think this won't spread to the states, too. This is just terrible."

John Praxis made a decision. "Start an analysis, Richard. See where we stand. See if we can come up with some kind of strategic plan."

"What plan?" Leonard demanded. "What can we do?"

"We can start by suing for breach of contract," Richard said.

Praxis sucked his teeth in disgust. "That only works if the client has *money*. Look, I don't know what we can do yet. But if we start by demanding strict terms and payment assurances, we'll lose these customers for a generation. Maybe we can somehow signal our willingness to go long on the payment schedule."

"Then we go bankrupt," Richard said. "We have suppliers and subcontractors to pay, too, you know."

"Yes," Praxis agreed. "But it's better to stretch than to break—which is what will happen if we get pushy with our clients. We need to show a willingness to work with them rather than fight them. Maybe even trade payment up front for some kind of equity position, where feasible."

Richard was aghast. "And become—what? A banker?"

"Be reasonable, Dad!" Leonard said. "We don't have enough credit to cover—"

Praxis interrupted them both. "We have a damn sight bigger credit line than our government clients right now. Let's be prepared to use it. We're in a whole new world, boys. And if ever there was a time to go all hands on deck, this is it."

The day Antigone Wells returned to the offices of Bryant Bridger & Wells, the legal secretaries chipped in to buy a box of Krispy Kreme donuts and left them on the desk of her administrative assistant, Madeline Bauer. Although the pastries had no aroma to speak of, their scent—or simply the rumor that free food was available—wafted through the four floors of the law office like invisible pheromones. No one told Wells, of course.

That morning she was sitting at her desk, wondering what came next and afraid to discover she no longer fit into anyone's plans. For an hour she played with the computer, refamiliarizing herself with the software for managing emails, caseload assignments, and accounting of billable hours. It was all vaguely familiar, but she still had nothing to enter, no messages to send. Wells ended up reading months-old emails that Carolyn Boggs had already answered, trying to remember the details of cases where she was referenced and the circumstances of those where she was not. She felt like a fraud.

A young woman—early thirties, daringly dressed, face hidden behind a donut—popped her head into the open doorway. "Hi, Auntie!"

Wells groped for a name. Giselle-something. "Can I help you?"

"Oh, um, yeah." The woman swallowed hard. "I'm, um, trying to find Thorvaldsen Electronics in the files. Which side did we represent?"

Wells stared at her. Then, like the answer floating up at the bottom of that old toy, the Magic 8 Ball, the word appeared in her mind. "Defendant."

"Oh, right! Thanks, Auntie!"

"You're welcome!"

Two minutes later, Sully Mkubwa stuck his head in. He wasn't eating a donut but held one wrapped in a paper napkin. "Welcome back, ma'am," he said, then paused. "I forget, who is the psychologist at the American Forensics Institute that we go to for expert testimony?"

Wells stared at him for a moment, then the information tumbled out. "There are two, actually. Amy Lewis does our civil cases. Peter Behrend handles the criminal work."

"Thank you, ma'am!"

"Oh, Sully?" she called after him.

"Yes, ma'am?" His head came back into the doorway.

"Didn't you and Amy date a couple of summers ago?"

"Why, now you mention it, I believe we did."

"Then you're a heartless cad, Sully."

"Thank you, ma'am!"

After three more of these pop-up exchanges, including one where Carolyn Boggs—also bearing a donut—asked about one of the emails Wells had just read, she became suspicious. She stalked out of her office and found Madeline applying bright-red varnish to her nails.

"I'm glad to see you're keeping busy," Wells said.

"Hey! I've been working my ass off in the pool for three months. I'm just happy to get back up here and relax. Is there something you need me to do?"

"Tell my why everyone has a sudden case of amnesia this morning."

Madeline glanced at the big white box with the green polka dots. By then the donuts were half gone. Wells walked around her desk and found a note in front of the box: "Help yourself, but be sure to say 'Hi' to Auntie and ask her a question."

"Are they testing me?" Wells asked suspiciously.

"I think they're trying to make you feel needed."

"Well, isn't that just humiliating!" Wells fumed.

"In a nice, pathetic, disparaging sort of way, yes."

"I don't suppose *you* had any hand in this?"

"No, ma'am. I *hate* Krispy Kremes."

Before Wells could comment, one of the legal secretaries came up to Bauer's desk, reached for a donut, then froze, withdrew her hand, and ran back down the corridor. Wells turned to follow the direction of the woman's glance and saw Ted Bridger coming from the other direction.

Bridger was carrying a gray-cardboard file folder, not very thick, a case in the early stages of documentation. He reached for a donut with his free hand, paused to read the note. "Are you ready to get back to work?" he asked. "Oh, 'Hi, Auntie,' by the way."

"Hello, Ted. Of course, I want to work, but—" She lowered her voice. "I'm just not sure how much law my battered old brain retains right now."

"Shh! They'll start saying that about all the partners," he said, smiling.

"I'm serious, Ted. Two weeks ago I could barely read a newspaper."

"So … do you need to take some tests, or pass the bar again?"

"Nothing that formal. I'm just not sure how sharp I am."

"And will that fix itself by wondering about it?"

"Well, no …"

"Then here!" He shoved the folder into her hands. "Simple case. Two parties. Dispute over contract terms." He paused. "If you want, take Carolyn and Sully along as training wheels—in case you get stuck."

"Thanks, Ted. I appreciate your confidence in me."

He reached into the box again. "For that, I get a donut."

―――

"And hell followed after," John Praxis murmured to himself, echoing *The Book of Revelation*, as he followed the financial news.

After more than a decade of benchmark interest rates in the sub-single digits, the straps had come off when the U.S. government essentially defaulted on its obligations. Everyone understood that the Federal Reserve had tried to stimulate a flagging economy by holding down the cost of money—and thereby hold down the interest the government would have to pay on the national debt—while at the same time trying to prime the economic pump by printing trillions of dollars in "quantitative easing." With the failure of this monetary policy, the laws of economics took over. Within two weeks, the federal funds rate shot up to twenty percent, and the interest that banks charged their best customers went to twenty-five. The interest rates that the average person paid in mortgages and car loans went above thirty percent. Revolving debt like credit and charge cards went to fifty percent. The national economy, which had been promising recovery for almost all of that same decade, rolled over and died.

He didn't really blame the Chinese for starting the landslide. The real culprit was a generation or more of powerful men who sat around long tables of polished hardwood, dribbling cigar ashes and imagining they were smarter than everyone else on the planet. The seeds of collapse probably dated back to 1971, when the Nixon Administration took the country off the gold standard, ended the Bretton Woods system of exchange rates, and turned the U.S. dollar into a fiat currency.

Ever since then, these masterminds had played chicken with the U.S. economy, theorizing about how much stress the monetary system could stand and then pushing against that limit, then out beyond it, into the void. What had started as calculated risks eventually required bold moves to recoup the losses, and after the bold moves came the desperate gambles. These were not wise or good men, but they dabbled like sorcerers with complex equations that pretended to control forces no one could fully understood, let alone foresee the consequences three steps down the road. When you played with other people's money, you took risks you would never attempt with cash from your own pocket. Economic charlatans! Witch doctors! Fools!

But then, having mentally vented his spleen on the folly of the age, John Praxis refocused his mind on the meeting at hand and matters within his own company. *What to do? What to do? What to do?*

"Three more customers have put their projects on indefinite hold, pending a filing for bankruptcy," Richard was saying. He started counting off on his fingertips. "The Coshocton Towers development, the Stirling Chemical headquarters, and the Georgia Gophers stadium renovation. All told, about nine percent of our backlog."

"Is that adjusted for being down seven percent last week?" Leonard asked.

"Ah, yeah," Richard replied. "Nine percent currently."

With every week's erosion, Praxis realized, it was taking less and less of a bite to weaken them more and more. Where did it end? … Short of losing their last customer and declaring bankruptcy themselves?

"Are we cutting staff as projects wind down?" he asked his sons.

"Well, yes," Richard said. "With the usual benefits."

"What benefits are those?" Leonard asked.

"Severance, COBRA, ERISA …"

"But keeping core staff?"

"Well, of course."

"Okay, then."

"What's that?" Praxis asked. "Who are you defining as 'core staff'?"

"Oh, um," Richard began, looking at the ceiling. "Accounting, Legal, Human Resources, Information Technology—all the backroom functions that keep us going." These were also the parts of Richard's personal empire.

"But you're cutting those groups proportionally, too?" Praxis suggested.

"Well, that gets tricky. You see, there are minimum levels below which—"

"I don't think you understand," Praxis said. "We are not operating in normal times anymore. We've just run out of road, and like that coyote who chases the big blue bird, we've gone airborne. Revenue is going to be down a third to a half this year, and next year looks to be worse. We have to consolidate. And where you can't consolidate, liquidate and outsource. All hands on deck!"

He could see Leonard and Richard taking covert, eyes-only glances at one another.

"Does that include family, too?" Leonard asked. "Or the senior executives holding personal shares—shares granted to them in *your* day and in Grandpa Sebastian's?"

Praxis could see where he was going with that. Callie was in the middle of construction on the Mile High Performing Arts Center outside of Denver. It was a major complex with a concert hall, opera house, and three museums—celebrating modern art, history, and science—plus an aquarium, all with the latest technological enhancements. If that project went belly up, was John Praxis going to call for sending baby sister out into the cold? When all of Richard's departments were outsourced, would *he* be expected to go as well? And a number of those shareholding executives were Praxis's personal friends and supporters on the Board of Directors. If all the projects in their various divisions were eventually to disappear, was he in favor of divesting them as well?

"We'll burn that bridge when we come to it," he replied, knowing it was a dodge.

"You going on record with that?" Leonard asked with a cruel grin.

"Don't mock me, son," he said. "This isn't the time."

―――――

Antigone Wells spent all day Thursday working on bankruptcy filings. Because she was a partner in the firm, it was considered beneath her position to actually fill out the forms for petition, application, lists of creditors, schedules of assets. So instead, Wells pretended to review the work that the paralegals were doing and that Carolyn and Sully had already checked. "Quality control," she called it. But as she waded through the folders on her desk—Chapter 7's, Chapter 11's, the rare Chapter 12 for a farmer or fisherman, Chapter 13's for people with assets—it occurred to her that clients in bankruptcy were unlikely to be *paying* clients, and a good many of the individuals and smaller businesses wouldn't remain any kind of client in the future. As the day rolled grimly forward, the magnitude of the disaster impressed itself upon her.

She and her associates would be in and out of court for months, maybe years, as they followed each petition through to discharge. That might look like steady work, but the process would slowly, inexorably, break them. It was almost like an algebra problem—or more likely the finely chopped incremental summations of calculus. Given their annual budget for salaries, office rent, phone service, utilities, and other expenses, how fast can you take clients out of the billing cycle before assets of the firm are returned to zero? And then, who does the bankruptcy filing for Bryant Bridger & Wells, LLC when they no longer have any lawyers on staff?

All in all, it was six o'clock by the time she left the office, with gym bag in hand, a black cloud of doom over her head, and an hour to get across town to the community center for her first karate class. There she found that the only place to change was in the ladies room with four other women, where she stripped out of her business suit, nylons, and heels and put on sweat shirt, sweat pants, and tennis shoes. Then she went down the hall to the exercise room with the mirrors and the ballet bar, where she was invited to dump her bag with her street clothes and purse in a corner and remove her tennis shoes and bobby socks.

"I'm more comfortable in shoes," she told the young man who seemed to be in charge. He wore a brown belt made of folded and stitched canvas that tied in a complicated knot to hold his immaculate white uniform jacket closed.

"We all practice barefoot," he said. "It's customary."

"See here, young man. I would really prefer to wear my shoes."

"You should call me '*sensei*,' ma'am. And as to shoes, see the class rules."

When she registered and paid her class fees to the community center's representative, Wells discovered that she was also required to sign a waiver indemnifying the center, the class teachers and organizers, the International Okinawan Karate Organization, and all the other students against any injury she might suffer as a result of class participation. She also was explicitly promising to obey all rules, conform to the dress code—which included barefoot practice—and do whatever the *sensei*s required of her. As a lawyer she knew the waiver was not binding and she could break it in court in about thirty seconds. But as this was her first day in a new environment, she decided to go easy on them and not press the issue. She signed and handed back the pen.

"*Ha-ji-may!*" shouted another *sensei* on the other side of the room, and everyone hurried to get into formation—five ranks wide and ten rows deep. Before Wells could decide where to stand, the first *sensei* pulled her and a half-dozen other students, obvious beginners, out of line and assigned them to a young woman wearing a green belt.

"Hi, I'm Judy," the girl said. "I'll get you started on the basics." She took them over to a corner away from the others, lined them up, and showed them the "ready stance."

Wells thought she already knew how to stand, but she was wrong. As Judy worked with each student individually, using curt comments, gentle molding pressure with her hands, and little slaps and pushes up and down their bodies, Wells discovered just how much she had to learn: feet parallel according to imaginary lines running between the second and third toes back through the heel, weight evenly distributed, knees straight but not locked, pelvis forward, back straight, shoulders back, head up, elbows back, and hands curled into fists on top of her hipbones. She supposed that Marines going through boot camp had to know all this, but even they wouldn't spend fifteen minutes just learning how to brace in the "ready stance."

When they all were standing like toy soldiers to Judy's satisfaction, the girl showed them how to make a real fist: first joint of each finger folded flat against the third joint, then folded again until the nails bit into their palms, and thumb folded over index finger. The girl molded their wrists flat against an imaginary line running from between the index and middle fingers back through the elbow. The result was a fist rigid with tension and yet self-supporting, like a box.

"Practice making that fist and holding it straight," she said.

"So do we ever get to *move?*" Wells asked.

"Right now. We call this first stance '*seisan*.'"

The girl took the ready stance and moved her right leg and foot forward in a sweeping arc, lightly skimming the floor, still parallel with those invisible lines. She planted it at the outer corner of an imaginary box, with her feet shoulder width apart. Her center of gravity had only moved about six inches. She showed them how by glancing down she had sight lines past her bent forward knee to her toes on the right and inside her straight back leg to her toes on the left. Through the whole movement, Wells noted, the girl's head stayed in the same plane, without bobbing up and down. She moved smoothly, mechanically, like a robot.

Then Judy had them all practice that swinging step, forward and back, right foot, left foot. The wonder of it was, for all of Wells's clumsiness since the stroke, she never once lost her balance or started to fall during the exercise. Keeping her feet panted in stance or skimming the ground, and minding the even distribution of her weight, she felt more in control, more confident. She found a new center of balance just below and behind her navel.

"That should do it," Judy said.

"Do what?" Wells wondered aloud.

"Get you through the first stance," the girl said.

Wells was startled to find the ninety-minute class was over.

"Go home and practice what you've learned tonight," Judy said. "A little bit every day. Stand straight, make a fist, step in, step back. Next week we'll work on punches and kicks."

Later, as Wells bent to put on her socks and tennies, she was surprised to find how stiff she was. Just by standing and stepping, curling her fingers, and pulling back on her elbows, she had used muscles that hadn't moved in years. She wasn't sure she wanted to continue with this. It all seemed so finicky and precise. But a tiny voice inside her suggested this was the way of true knowledge. Law school had been made up of such little pieces and parts, too, all finicky and pedantic. Maybe that was the only way to learn anything that stuck in your brain and lasted.

She decided to give karate another week.

When he got home that night, Praxis decided it was time to discuss the realities with Adele. He had already missed dinner, so after he made himself a bowl of soup in the microwave and spooned it down, he went to find his wife. As usual, she was in the "family room" watching television. She slumped in her favorite chair and stared with heavy-lidded eyes at the screen—some show that paired contestants in flashy, beaded outfits doing the tango. He wasn't even sure Adele was awake, until she reached for the glass of neat bourbon on the end table by her elbow.

"Dear, we have to talk …"

Adele slowly shifted her gaze to his face. At the same time her hand lifted the remote and muted the television. "So talk," she said.

He sat down next to her. "The boys and I have been going over the books at the company, and it looks pretty bad. Since interest rates have shot up—"

"You know I don't understand that stuff," she interrupted.

"Well, the economy's in bad shape. Projects are closing down. We're losing customers. Revenues are going to be way off this year."

"You'll figure something out." She didn't say this as a form of encouragement. It was her way of dismissing the problem.

"My take-home will be way down as a result."

"Huh!" It was more a grunt than a comment.

"We're going to have to start economizing."

That caught her attention. "How? Where do we ever *go*? What do we ever *do*? You spend all the money around here."

"I'm going to be looking at my expenses, too," he said quickly. "But they're mostly on company accounts, and those will be cut back automatically. I was thinking of the Jag. You hardly ever take it out. You don't drive anymore. So—"

"You leave my XK alone! I bought it with my allowance."

"And I pay insurance and upkeep. That's a hell of a bite—"

"Not open for discussion," she said. So the ruby red coupe, which last time he looked sat under a thick layer of dust, would continue to molder in the garage.

"I was thinking we might move to a smaller house. Even get an apartment. Property values here in Sea Cliff are holding, so far, and I think we could get out from under the mortgage and taxes—"

"You're not taking my house," she said distinctly. "You want my car. Now you want my house. I *earned* this house. All those years in the jungles and deserts, practically dying of dysentery, bored out of my skull. This is my life now. You're not going to take it away because *you've* got money trouble."

"All right, we keep the house," he agreed, then paused.

It was hopeless, he knew, trying to change her ways after all these years. But the Thunderbolt and its aftermath had given him a new perspective. Rather than swimming aimlessly, like a fish in the open ocean, he now sensed the flow of time. He knew he was swimming upstream, against strong currents, toward the inevitable end of life. Time—and his ability to meet it head on, overcome it, *survive* it—had become important to him. He wanted her to share this sense of renewal, of fighting the inevitable, too. She had been strong once. She could be strong again.

"You know," he said finally, even though he understood it was a mistake, "you might feel better if you started taking better care of yourself. Maybe get some exercise. Maybe you could, sometime, come out for a run with me. ..."

Adele just stared at him. Then she raised her drink in mock salute. "I'm glad you're enjoying your exercises, John. They'll probably save your life. Good luck with that." Then she poured rest of the bourbon down her throat, looked back at the television, and turned up the sound.

3. The Twenty-Nine Points

Ted Bridger stopped by Antigone Wells's office with another gray folder, another case for her and her team. She tried to smile as she reached for it.

"You'll enjoy this one," he said. "We're going after your old friends at Praxis Engineering. Seems they've been stiffing their suppliers on accounts payable, and one of them finally decided to sue."

Wells paused with her hand out, fingers touching but not yet clutching the cardboard cover. "I don't know if I can take this," she said.

"What? The St. Brigid's suit against them was your great triumph. Don't you want to go back for another bite of the apple?"

"I—uh—I'm not sure, but I think Praxis has us on retainer."

"You *think*? Not *sure*? Who am I talking to here? My trusted senior partner who eats defendants for breakfast? Or those regenerated cells which are now giving you brain farts?"

"I'm all right, Ted. It's just that I met the chairman, John Praxis, and he was so impressed with our handling of the case against them he wanted to put me on retainer."

"When was this?"

"In the hospital."

"I thought so. You refused, of course."

"Well, he asked so nicely. And he's not a bad man. I gather it was just his legal team pressing that silly *force majeure* defense. John himself seems pretty responsible."

"I think you've gone soft in the head—no offense, Antigone."

"Well ..." She grinned. "It's a bit of a blur, but he did mention putting us on retainer, although I don't actually remember accepting."

"You didn't file an agreement."

"No, it was all fairly … casual."

"Then you'd better straighten it out before we take this case against them. I don't care which side we represent, and at this point I wouldn't mind taking their retainer fee as well as racking up some court time. You'd better go over there and get a signed agreement."

"Yes, sir. Right on it."

Every morning John Praxis read the *Wall Street Journal,* which he paid extra to have delivered in paper form rather than reading it online. He trusted the order and emphasis given to the stories and summaries when the editors laid them out in page format. He had trouble focusing when all the stories blinked and rotated in the same screen space and all seemed equally important. He felt he might miss something more demanding of attention than all the rest. But not this morning. This morning the news and its import were inescapable.

A week ago the United States had applied to the International Monetary Fund for debt support. All of the economic pundits noted the irony in this, as the nation was the fund's single largest contributor, with nearly 18 percent of its "special drawing rights"—which was a euphemism for a potential claim on the country's non-gold foreign exchange reserves. But nearly all of the pundits also noted that the U.S. had gone broke partly through its foreign aid and international police activities "in service to humankind." And others had sermonized about turnabout being fair play.

This morning the International Monetary Fund had responded with a preliminary agreement, but one based on the U.S. accepting certain underlying principles of the United Nations program for sustainable development. The media quickly dubbed these the "Twenty-Nine Points." They included, as a series of bullet points, raising fuel taxes to curtail energy use and cancelling extraction leases on public lands; imposing new air and water controls and "improving" land-use permitting to limit growth and development; establishing new land-use policies designed to "bank" large areas of the countryside as wilderness or "future wilderness" areas; creating agriculture and food distribution policies designed to curtail meat production, limit dietary intake, and provide food stores for famine areas; setting educational and cultural standards designed to encourage "appropriate" understanding of the world situation and compliant behavior; setting media standards to ensure "correct" reporting of news; imposing weapons controls on all citizens; establishing defense guidelines, including de-emphasis on military and nuclear technology; setting transportation and housing standards to de-emphasize private travel and "isolationist" living conditions; and controlling medical spending to avoid "unnecessary procedures"—"Like my new heart," Praxis guessed—with immediate means testing for Social Security, Medicare, and health insurance benefits provided through the Patient Protection and Affordable Care Act.

The stated goal—stated plainly, in the preamble, for everyone to see—was to control the size and activity of the U.S. population through energy use, environmental, and economic controls and to bring U.S. lifestyles into line with the rest of the world population. Compared to the Twenty-Nine Points, the earlier requirements of the European Central Bank for bailing out the overspent countries of the southern euro zone were the equivalent of a harsh lecture and being sent to bed without supper.

It'll never happen, Praxis thought to himself. *The government will never accept these terms. ... Well, maybe not the U.S. government in abstract, as representative of the American people in all their wealth and power. But how about* this *government, the current White House and the ideologues staffing it? Would they be willing to fall into line?*

Suddenly, anything was possible.

Praxis called his assistant, Ivy, and told her to dig Leonard and Richard out of whatever meetings they were in and send them to his office.

Half an hour later his sons were sitting in the guest chairs on the other side of his desk. He had found the article in the *Journal*'s online version and put it up on the screen. "Read that," he told them. "Starting with the bullet points."

"I saw it already," Richard said.

"Then let Leonard read it," Praxis said.

After two minutes, Leonard lifted his head. "So?"

"It's not going to happen," Richard said, echoing Praxis's first thought.

"Yes, true, that's probably the way to bet," Praxis said. "But with this administration? Which is halfway there already on sustainable energy, environmental, and defense issues, and just bursting to pile on more regulations?"

"Even if they accept the terms," Leonard said. "What's that to us?"

"Oh, come on! Think strategically!" Praxis said, nearly shouting. "Look at our current backlog. Automobile use goes down—but then we hardly support it anyway, except for highway and bridge construction. Mass transit is even more favored, and that's a plus for us. Water projects go away—but we might see an upswing in dam removals and environmental amelioration. Nuclear power stays dead—but then the government puts even more into solar and wind farms. Maybe we need to team up with or buy into a company making solar panels and wind turbines. Meat processing drops—but we see a rise in high-energy foods. So that's more factories, with more processing lines. These Twenty-Nine Points are a roadmap to the new winners and losers in our business. We have to take them seriously."

"What do you want us to do?" Richard asked.

"Study the backlog of projects, to see where we're vulnerable. Study our current capabilities and marketing goals, to see where we can shift into the new paradigm."

"This is all premature," Leonard said. "We don't even know if any of these programs will pass. Legislation could be years away."

"You don't get on top of a market swing by waiting 'til it's already under way," Praxis said. "When any fool can see what's going on, it's too late to start moving your feet."

"Well, I guess it couldn't hurt to take a look," Richard said.

"But—" Leonard began, and his brother elbowed him.

"Thanks for the, um, heads up, Dad," Richard said.

Outside, in the broad hallway of the thirty-eighth floor, safely beyond the closed doors to the chairman's office, Leonard turned on his younger brother in anger. "What was that all about?"

"Isn't it obvious?" Richard said. "He's clutching at straws."

"Getting senile, if you ask me. Making us sit down to read the newspapers, like we were kids back at the breakfast table."

"He doesn't have a plan. He's gone totally reactive. He thinks the government can bail us out with a slew of new programs, when it was government spending—on the infrastructure programs that are now drying up for lack of funding—that got us into this jam in the first place."

"What are we going to do?"

"Oh, I'll look at the projects in hand, make a few calculations, write a report. By the time it lands on his desk, Dad will have forgotten all about this."

"Until he gets some new bee in his bonnet."

"Then we'll write a report on that one, too."

Antigone Wells was certain, intellectually, that she had once before visited the thirty-eighth floor of the building on Steuart Street. She must have come here during the St. Brigid's pre-trial negotiations, when they were seeking a settlement with Praxis Engineering & Construction. But she could call up no actual memories of the place. The walnut-veneer paneling with their framed views of famous bridges and dams, the beige-colored carpeting—so hard to keep clean—and the glimpse of sunshine on San Francisco Bay and Treasure Island beyond the broad window at the end of the hallway, these should have been memorable. But the memories must have died when her brain exploded and was overwritten by new cells ready to make fresh memories.

The rather severe young woman from the reception desk—all angular shoulders and legs and rhythmically swinging butt—led Wells down the hall to the last secretarial station, which was situated in front of wide double doors. The elderly woman sitting there looked up with a smile. "Nice to see you again, Ms. Wells."

"Ah, yes, um—" Wells couldn't hide her confusion.

"I'm Ivy Blake, Mr. Praxis's personal assistant."

"Of course you are, Miss Blake."

"He'll see you now."

The woman took her into the chairman's office. The first thing Wells saw was the paired portraits of two young women, both with ruddy features, skeptical eyes, and notably unsmiling mouths. Both existed against quickly brush-stroked backgrounds. Seeing them, she felt time slow, and she was more certain of her questions than her answers. Then something undefined in her brain whispered, *Modigliani,* and the world started moving again. Did she know that from before? Or was she guessing?

She focused on the man behind the desk. She recognized John Praxis immediately this time, from their encounters on the rooftop. He seemed younger somehow, more alive, more alert. She guessed this was because he was also thinner than before, taking better care of himself now. She also guessed that he was farther from death's door than before. They both were.

"I'm glad you could take time to see me, Mr. Praxis," she said.

By now he was standing, coming around the desk, taking her hand. "We used to call each other by our first names—Antigone."

"Yes, we did. But that was friendship, and this is business."

"Uh-oh! Are we in trouble again? Do we face each other at sword's point?" He offered her a guest chair and resumed his seat.

"Well, you'll have to tell me," she said. "One of your subcontractors—Subatai Electric—wants to bring suit against you for nonpayment of their bills. They approached us to take the case, but I believe we have a conflict of interest here."

"I'm not familiar with them," he said mildly. "Accounting practices happen in the bowels of administration. Should I call our chief financial officer? He would be the one—"

"The conflict isn't between you and Subatai," she said quickly. "Rather, with our firm. I believe you once intended to put Bryant Bridger & Wells on retainer. You spoke of it the last time we met. *That* would create a conflict."

"Oh, yes. I did intend. I mean, I still do. You're a good attorney, Antigone. With the mayhem that's coming, we're going to need all the talent we can afford." He paused. "Oh, not against this Subatai thing. I'm sure our Legal Department can settle their hash with one hand tied. But with the federal government in default, rough times are ahead."

"Do you foresee a lot of lawsuits?" she asked.

"I foresee a lot of *new law* being made. And then challenges and suits coming out of that. Our corporate staff know how to navigate in calm waters—routine, rule-based stuff like contract and tax work. But this is a new situation, and we're all in a barrel going over the falls."

"I hear you," she said quietly. "Although … I don't know whether to be excited or afraid."

"Fear is a good choice. But I find excitement the more attractive response. Since I've already been dead, more or less, it's hard to work up a feeling of decent terror over a little thing like a national bankruptcy."

Wells smiled at that. "Death does give one perspective."

"Shall we start at a hundred thousand a month? Subject to the usual constant-dollar multiplier? It's been a while since I've retained a personal attorney, but I think that covers the math—if inflation still applies when the money's all gone south."

"Is this a personal arrangement?" she asked. "I thought you meant corporate."

"I can't guarantee this firm will exist beyond the next couple of months, Antigone. But I know I'll be here. Either way, I'll need access to a good legal mind."

"All right, done. We'll tell Subatai to take a walk."

"And get ready for the high jump ourselves."

———

When John Praxis went home that evening, he found the house dark and empty. From the garage he entered by the back door, through the laundry room, and into the kitchen. For all its being in shadow, the interior's hard surfaces, the counters, cabinets, and appliances, were immaculate and gleamed with moonlight reflected from outside. This was not Adele's doing, except in a loose, supervisory capacity. Their cook, Miranda, took pride in leaving the kitchen—and as much of the rest of the house as she considered her province—spotless.

He went from room to room, lighting lamps and calling Adele's name. It was just conceivable she had gone out—but where? Her Jaguar was still parked in the garage. He didn't expect her to leave him a note. That kind of thoughtfulness was no longer Adele's style.

Praxis found her in the upstairs bathroom, across from her own bedroom and down the hall from the master suite. She was lying facedown on the marble floor, one arm angled up and the other down, like a broken semaphore. Her hips were cocked and legs spread out, with her toes pointing in. She was dressed, as he had often seen her in the morning, in a blue chambray blouse, khaki slacks, and red-velvet bedroom slippers. Her face was turned toward—or rather pulled away from, leaving a filmy smear—a puddle of clear bile edged with greenish froth. It smelled sourly of stomach acid and Jim Beam. She most have gone into the bathroom for something, stumbled or simply passed out, fallen, and then vomited.

"Adele!" he called, suddenly afraid of her terrible inertness.

"Adele!" He knelt beside her, wedging between the tub and toilet bowl.

"*Adele!*" He touched her shoulder, shook it, and her upper body rolled loosely.

If she had breathed in any of that vomit, she might have drowned. He shook her again and lifted her face away from the puddle. That action stirred something, because Adele coughed once, back in her throat, and started snoring.

"Come on, dear," he said softly. "You can't lie here."

Praxis managed to stand over his wife, work his hands in under her armpits, and lift with his thumbs pressing at the soft flesh over her shoulderblades. He walked backward, pulling her up from the floor, onto her knees, and then upright and sagging against him. He half-walked, half-carried Adele into her bedroom, sat her down on the bed, and laid her across the quilted coverlet. He got dampened towels from the bathroom and wiped her mouth and face. He removed her slippers and clothing, then rolled her to one side, pulled at the bedclothes, and rolled her back, until she was lying under the sheets.

He went to the medicine cabinet and got her bottles of aspirin and vitamin C and a big glass of cold water. He removed the child-guard caps, which Adele always found so difficult, and set everything up on her night table. He went back into the bathroom and used more towels to clean up the puddle. Then he sat down on the chair at her dressing table to watch and make sure she was breathing easily and not going to vomit again.

It had been two or three months since he had last found her like this. Usually, she was asleep in her chair in front of the television, or on the couch with a magazine in her lap, and would rouse easily enough with a bit of coaxing. Most nights she was already in bed and snoring.

He couldn't help comparing Adele, who was willfully extinguishing her mind with alcohol, to Antigone Wells, who had suffered a massive vascular accident that took away her mind and then had fought bravely to regain her memory, her skills, and her mental acuity. The two women were enough alike in age—allowing Adele a few extra years—but they seemed a generation apart. Antigone's face was clear and her eyes bright, her manner alive, her movements quick, and her outlook positive. Adele's face was puffy and her eyes clouded, her manner dead, her movements slowed, and her outlook negative.

Praxis knew he was being disloyal, but there it was. His wife was killing herself slowly. His new attorney—his former nemesis and then his friend from the hospital rooftop—had dragged herself back from extinction.

He looked at Adele's sagging face, tipped back and snoring, and wondered what it would feel like to see Antigone sitting there in bed. She would be smiling, sharp witted, erect, ready for anything. ...

It didn't pay to have such thoughts. He was too old to learn how to betray his wife, take on a mistress, and keep half of his life hidden in secrets.

And Antigone Wells, he suspected, was not the sort of woman to accept a life in obscurity living with just half a man.

―――

"Quick, turn on CNN!" Antigone Wells heard Ted Bridger say as he charged into her office.

"What's up?" she asked, fumbling for the online feed.

"Just look!" he pointed to the crawler.

"... Federal government to adopt U.N. criteria in exchange for monetary support ... OPEC votes to discontinue pricing oil in dollars, all transactions in euros ... Dollar loses status as reserve currency amid flight to euros and yuan ..."

"Interesting times, indeed," she observed.

"You know, this could be a bonanza for us," he said.

"It would—if any of our clients had money. But give me your thinking."

"If those 'Twenty-Nine Points' get adopted as law, and land-use policies are officially redirected toward wilderness and sustainability, that will all but shut down commercial and agricultural development. We'll see a lot more work under the takings clause of the Fifth Amendment. Then those new media and 'cultural' standards—whatever that's supposed to mean—will bring us more First Amendment challenges."

"Unless they just do away with the Constitution and Bill of Rights altogether."

"The government can't do that without, first, a supermajority of two-thirds in both houses of Congress, then ratification by three-quarters of the states."

"Unless they just do away with Congress and the states."

"Don't be silly." He grinned. "No one would do that!"

"Ted, I don't know what anyone would do anymore."

"Well, you may be right. But if this goes through, people won't like it."

"Yes, but will their indignation rise to the level of a lawsuit?"

"It will if new statutes hit them where they live."

That night when Wells got home after her karate class, Jeanne Hale was watching the *10 O'Clock News,* which was serving up refinement and commentary on the day's headlines about the U.N. demands and the crippling of the dollar.

"Did you *see* this?" the nurse asked.

"Yah. I've been hearing it all day."

"What do you think it means?"

"Lot of high-level wrangling."

"That's all?" Hale asked.

"No effect on you or me."

"How can you *say* that?"

"Well … how did you get here? Drive? No, and neither did I. We take the Muni bus or streetcar, sometimes a taxi, because it's silly to own and park an automobile in this city. Do I live in a mansion? No, in an apartment carved out of the top floors of an old house that was built right after the '06 fire.

Do either of us eat that much meat? No, just a little chicken in the salad on Tuesday. We live about as sustainably as possible. What more could anyone ask?"

"Okay, I get it. But what about your contractor?"

"My *who?*" Wells asked, thoroughly mystified.

"Your fella who's in the building trades, John Praxis."

"He's not a contractor. He runs a major engineering firm."

"Okay, so he builds really big things. How's that going?"

"And he's not my 'fella.' Actually, he's now my client."

"Interesting development! So what does this U.N. stuff mean for him?"

"Even he doesn't know. He says his firm might go under next week, but I seriously doubt that. They've got clients all over the world. Still, his workload's fallen off. Not much call for new infrastructure. And all his clients have gone slow-pay, like the rest of us, so he's in a bind. It seems dollars are scarce." Wells thought for a moment about what she'd just said. "Dollars are supposed to be plentiful—not worth a whole lot though, but supposedly coming out of our ears—and yet they're scarce. How's that for trouble?"

"But still 'no effect on thee or me'?"

"Well, not so much on us as the big folks."

"You'll be sorry to see your man lose his business."

"He's not 'my man.' In fact, he's married."

"What does that matter?" Hale asked.

"Not at all. I'm going to bed now."

"Sweet dreams to you."

"Shut up!"

Leonard Praxis was on the phone, planning his weekend getaway, when his brother came into the president's office unannounced, closed the door behind him, and took a chair in front of the desk. Richard's expression was, as usual, baleful.

"Call you back," Leonard said into the mouthpiece and hung up.

"Do you know what Dad has done?" Richard said.

Leonard closed his eyes. "What is it this time?"

"He's hired a lawyer on his personal account. And not just any lawyer, but the same woman who took us apart over that St. Brigid's thing."

"That's damned insulting. Did you ask him? Did he say why?"

"He won't tell," Richard fumed. "Oh, he claims he has a reason. He says he met her in the hospital while he was recuperating. He says she was there recovering from a stroke—"

"I heard about that. Cheered me up for the whole day."

"—and says she's really a much nicer person when you get to know her."

"Well, that's certainly baloney. He's up to something."

"Yes, but what?" Richard said. "He's top of the food chain in this company, both chairman and chief executive. He owns a third of the shares outright. And he has enough cronies on the board to swing any vote against us. So what does he need outside legal muscle for?"

"Maybe he's just crazy," Leonard said. "Some residual brain damage from the blackout during his heart attack. So now brain-damaged Dad meets brain-damaged lady lawyer, and they're off to smash windmills and slay giants together. It could be harmless, like he said."

"I don't know. He doesn't seem mentally incompetent to me. He may be acting a little hyper about the money crisis, but it's a *good* hyper, a creative reaction, even if I think he's clutching at straws."

"And he's getting stronger, too. With all this jogging and exercise, he even *looks* younger. If this health kick holds, we may have to put up with him for years to come."

"We can still gather votes against him. Force him to retire."

"How? Callie is still throwing her shares behind him."

"I think I may have an idea," Richard said slowly.

"What is it? If there's anything we can do—"

"Not now! You must not ask me about it."

"Well, why ever not?" Leonard asked.
"Because you want deniability."

While his son Richard, as chief financial officer, and Alison Crowder, PE&C's head of Human Resources, discussed the company's current situation and the savings to be realized by laying people off versus the expenses to be incurred in severance packages and government-mandated benefits support—with Richard shouting at this point, "*What* government? *What* mandate?"—John Praxis thought through everything he had recently been reading about corporations and their place in society.

They were meant to serve the economy, surely, by providing a product or service. They were also meant to serve shareholders—in this case, the Praxis family and those top-level executives they had rewarded over the years—by earning profits and investing in the business. But they also had a duty to their employees, those willing heads and hands who made the business into a "company," what the dictionary called "an association of persons engaged in an enterprise, voyage, or military expedition." As the credit crisis evolved, as their projects in hand either folded or went into suspension and the backlog collapsed, PE&C was being forced to jettison the very people who made it capable of providing a service and earning a profit.

The first to go had been the temporary workers brought on to fill gaps during the last expansion. Then, as each contract closed down, they had to send away the backbone of engineers, technical staff, and support services—long-time employees and familiar faces—who had fed directly off that project's accounts. And now, in the discussion this morning, they were planning the decimation of division and department heads and the pool of senior engineers currently engaged in marketing. This was the nucleus of experts who, in the better times to come, might be expected to seed re-entry and growth in the various industries and sectors PE&C served. The national crisis had already eaten alive most of what he and his family had built over the generations. Now it was stealing their future.

The adage says a rising tide lifts all boats. Praxis now realized that the reverse was not true. *An ebbing tide leaves some boats stranded higher up the beach than others, or stuck on shoals and sandbars, while the strongest, the best-managed, or the most maneuverable boats are able to navigate to safer waters.*

Corporations which were still viable and could afford it—damn few, but not unheard of: Archer Daniels Midland, ExxonMobil, Safeway, and others necessary to prevent food riots—were actually stepping in and offering additional benefits for their key workers. They were providing premium-grade medical insurance to cover defaults in the various government insurance programs, mortgage and consumer loans where banks had refused to lend, and accelerated retirement funding to replace benefits lost from the now-insolvent Social Security system. This benevolence had the effect of increasing the tension between the haves and have-nots in society. If you had a job and long-term prospects that your employer could bank on, you might sail through the crisis with minimal discomfort. If not, you were suddenly back in the Stone Age with neither corporate paycheck nor government safety net. Of course, those who remained employed were also entering the Dark Ages of feudal serfdom, because who would dare quit a job that had become a lifeline?

Corporations which had their roots, their headquarters perspective, or a largish fraction of their business overseas—construction firms like Hochtief and Taisei, auto companies like Toyota and Honda, and pharmaceutical makers like Bayer and Roche—were circling the wagons against the U.S. government's encroachments and pulling key functions and services out of the country. U.S.-headquartered corporations with large overseas holdings and markets were also preparing to move assets and expectations offshore.

Even states whose governments had good budget balances and relatively low tax profiles—those in the middle of the country, especially the plains and mountain states with heavy investments in the energy and extractive industries, and those in the economically rejuvenated south—offered better prospects for PE&C's line of work. The company backlog was drying up fastest on the Coasts, in the Midwest, and the Northwest, where insolvency was growing, taxes were rising even faster, and public attitudes were closely aligned with the Twenty-Nine Points. These high-tax, high-spend states—California among them—had already begun the process of surrendering their sovereignty to the federal government and its U.N. backers, while at the same time they were demanding life-support from a partially refinanced Treasury Department.

At one point Praxis had discussed with the boys whether they should liquidate PE&C's business in California and reincorporate in the more viable middle of the country. He was a builder, Praxis said, but with less and less around here to build. The need for new construction still existed in California, perhaps more than ever before, but people lacked the money and the will to make it happen. He wanted to get out and work on real projects backed with real financing—not struggle through this confusing shadow play of debt and default.

But when he put the question of relocating to Leonard, his son—rather than raise his eyes to the far horizon—had stubbornly focused on the near term. "We've already lost the Sheppard air base project in Texas. They cancelled two weeks ago. So the south is no garden spot, either." Praxis had refrained from pointing out that the air base was a federal defense project and so subject to the default and collapse.

Richard had simply exploded. "Liquidate! *Why*, for Christ's sake? Our debt is way down. We've managed the company very conservatively. Why throw in the towel now?" Praxis had refrained from trying to argue tax structures with the financial expert.

Instead, all he said was, "Our debt position doesn't much matter if we don't have customers. Without cash flow, you don't have a business."

But the truth was, Praxis himself wasn't all that keen on a move just yet. Tensions in the country were rising. Lines were being drawn for a conflict that would soon erupt. And that would be a time to hunker down and survive, rather than get creative with your assets and your loyalties.

John Praxis was beginning to understand how his namesake, great-great—great?—grandfather Ioannis, must have felt during the Greek War of Independence. He'd had to decide whether to stay and fight the long hand of the Turk or flee to safer ground. It was an art, knowing when and where to jump. And sometimes you fell and died.

Now, sitting in on this pointless discussion about cheese paring and staff reductions, he wondered if he was going to be in the same position as Ioannis. Then he wondered if Alison Crowder, who talked so dispassionately about shedding employees, understood how close she was—in months rather than years—to losing her own job. Or, eventually, Richard, his.

Antigone Wells wondered why, with everything else in the city around them collapsing into fits and starts over disputes about pay and pensions—regular police patrols, Muni bus service, streetlight repairs on major thoroughfares—the local community center had managed to remain open and her karate classes continued meeting. She supposed it had something to do with student fees being paid up for the quarter.

She found comfort and stability in the new movements that the green and brown belts were teaching her with every class. The straight punch pistoned forward in time with that swinging step into *seisan* stance, her fist making a half turn from palm up to palm down, planting those tightly folded knuckles in an imaginary opponent's solar plexus. The blocks whipped across from the hip, again in time with a half-circle step, pivoted on the hinge of her elbow in an arc either upward or downward to sweep the vulnerable areas of groin, solar plexus, or face. The straight kick brought the knee of the rear leg up and the foot forward in an arc, with toes pulled stiffly upward to tighten the foot and ankle bones, struck at an imaginary groin, then snapped back twice as fast, planting the foot again in the square *seisan*.

The movements were as mechanical as clockwork, yet strangely fluid. She was constantly reminded to hold her trunk still, her head level, and her center of gravity evenly balanced between her two feet—even when one of them was off the floor and flying. She was told that her energy must be controlled and contained, with blocks stopping precisely at the edge of the body, deflecting an incoming blow to just past her side but no further than necessary. The punches and kicks were held to mere touches and taps, which supposedly would transmit their kinetic energy into the opponent's vulnerable nerve centers. It was all precise, concise, specific.

When Wells asked about this kinetic energy, this *chi*, the instructors told her it would come in time, as she learned to control her muscles. "First you learn the movements," Judy the green belt said. "Then you learn to make your muscles soft and smooth in motion, but rigid and hard on impact. It's called 'focus.'"

"How long did that take you to learn?" Wells asked.

"Well, I *understand* it, but I can't *do* it yet."

"How long have you been studying?"

"About a year and a half now."

"That's a long time."

"Not really."

Wells thought about all this as she walked home. As a method of self-defense, the classes were going to be a bust. It seemed karate had no trick, no special technique, that would give her superhuman powers. In fact, one of the black belts, Daniel, had told them: "If you want to protect yourself against a mugger or a rapist, buy a gun." But she was learning the purpose of the class, which was mental and physical discipline through mastering a complicated and difficult set of movements.

She had never been much for physical exercise. The treadmill and the stationary bicycle bored her. Yoga poses made her feel silly and vulnerable. But the clockwork movements of karate—the tiny perfections of motion linking shoulder, elbow, wrist, and fingers into a solid punch, or linking hip, knee, ankle, and toes into a perfect kick—that fascinated her. It was like ballet, except that instead of representing fanciful literary objects like waving willows and fluttering swans, the movements had a precise, technical, even lethal purpose. And it appealed to the fighter in her. What she had long ago learned to do with words in the courtroom, she was learning to do with elbows, fists, fingers, and toes on the *dojo*'s polished wood floor.

Not to mention that she had lost five pounds and could touch her toes again. Her balance was better. Her breathing was easier. And after a workout she felt like Wonder Woman.

―――

Richard Praxis stayed late at the office one night, waiting until he was sure that most of PE&C's employees—and everyone on the thirty-sixth floor, where the Accounting Department was located—had gone home. For what he was about to do, it probably wouldn't matter if anyone was around, physically, but he just simply better knowing he was alone.

He logged out of his computer, cancelling his personal identity, then started it up again, this time as a "guest." It was as if someone else had taken control of his machine. Normally, a computer running in this state would not have full administrative access to all of its software and settings, but Richard didn't need that, just an internet connection and a little piece of code stored in an innocuous folder on his hard drive. The code was named PRETZEL.EXE.

Richard was not supposed to have that program. No one was supposed to have it. But one of the system integrators working for Intelligeneering Systems Inc., the firm that had installed and customized the accounting package on PE&C's computers, a man named Louis Petzel but whom everyone called "Pretzel Man," had given it to him on a thumb drive, "in case you have to make any interim reconciliations."

"Isn't that illegal?" Richard had asked, accepting the memory chip.

"Well, technically." The man grinned. "But sometimes you have to run system checks with test data that you don't want to leave hanging around. Besides, occasionally you might need to push a penny into this column or that. This will keep you from later having to fill out the *long form* with the Financial Accounting Standards Board or whoever."

As Richard understood these things—and he admitted his understanding of modern security systems was that of a complete idiot—the piece of code went onto the internet and poked at a specific port from among the 65,000 attached to the computer that ran the accounting software. This had the effect of setting up a virtual server which bypassed all of the company's internal security—the firewall, the logon process, and intrusion detection. For that little trick to work, the accounting package itself had to have secret instructions, known as a "back door," written into its source code so that it listened to that one port and responded appropriately. Pretzel Man had made it sound like this was a service they provided for all their clients.

Sometimes Richard lay awake at night, wondering how many of the grinning computer geeks of this world had the key to the back door of his company's accounting systems—to his company's *money*—but then he always got to sleep by assigning that worry to the category of "things I cannot change." This night, he was glad to have that key himself.

Well, one advantage that Richard had—and any random hacker wouldn't, unless it was Pretzel Man himself—was he knew his way around the PE&C accounting structure. All of the active data and running totals were organized by account number, rather than the account name. Names as pieces of text were kept in a separate file and only linked to the numbers as needed—say, for a billing statement or a financial report. Unless you knew and entered the account numbers, you were lost in the system.

What Richard was about to do was a simple matter. He even thought of it as "reconciliation." He made complementary changes in two accounts that no one would ever think were related. Then he deleted one record entirely to hide the change. That done, he exited by the back door, no logoff required, and shut down his computer.

Tomorrow morning, when he came into the office and started it up, it would show no trace of what he had done.

4. Breaking Up Is Hard to Do

CABLE NEWS WAS reporting on a convention held in Kansas City over the weekend by the "middle states," which included roughly the same areas John Praxis has been watching: the Plains, the Mountains, the Old South, plus Texas and Arizona. Polls during the past week had shown that, while the national attitudes in general ranged from unenthusiastic to complaisant about accepting the Twenty-Nine Points of the U.N. guidelines, for the middle states their imposition was a cultural and economic death sentence.

That's not hard to understand, Praxis thought.

In places where the majority of the population lived in urban areas, as on the East and West Coasts, and people rode bicycles for health and pleasure, only taking the family car out for trips to the beach or the mountains, then they could remain calm about pending legislation to boost the price of gasoline to European levels and eventually outlaw internal combustion. Where the most property people owned was 1,500 square feet of condo in Berkeley or Menlo Park, they didn't mind EPA restrictions on wet lands, dry lands, runoff, and dust pollution. Where they had already bought into Green Planet thinking on nutrition and diet, they didn't mind outlawing beef and pork.

But in places like "flyover country," where most of the population lived forty-odd miles outside of any large town and ten or fifteen miles from the nearest high school, they depended on their cars—more likely a pickup. Where the local economy was farming or ranching a couple of hundred or a thousand acres, and everyone hoped for a windfall from drilling for gas or oil on their property, they wanted the federal government to stay farther out of their lives rather than moving closer in. And where people worked hard and played hard outdoors seven days a week, they didn't want to try subsisting on 1,500 calories of brown rice and kale—that was stuff they fed to the cows and pigs.

As legislation and regulations enacting the Twenty-Nine Points poured out of Washington, D.C., the middle states had at first discovered they had an identity, then that they had common ground, and finally, over the past weekend, that they had a cause. Twenty-six states, from North Carolina to Idaho, had come together to form a Committee of Secession. As with everything else in politics, the voting was neither unanimous nor uncontested. Florida and Nevada were tepid about the move, as were Minnesota and Wisconsin. New Mexico never even showed up. But so long as secession was still in the talking stages and, to quote the governor of Idaho, which was halfway to the Left Coast itself, "Nobody's going to *do* anything," the committee was formed and began drawing up plans.

This is getting serious, Praxis realized. So that morning he decided to call his daughter Callie in Denver and find out what effect any of those plans might have on her project, the Mile High Performing Arts Center.

"Hard to say, Dad," was her response. "Denver might be San Francisco, as far as the political climate goes. Everyone this morning is pooh-poohing the goings-on in Kansas City."

"What happens if your project ends up on the other side of a national border?"

"I don't know. What happens when we work in Shanghai or Dubai?"

"Same thing, I guess. Except we're not at war in those places."

"Do you really think it will come to that? To civil war?"

"It did the last time," he said. "But shooting aside, we could see all kinds of interruption. Tariff restrictions. Rules against employing foreigners. Currency exchange—as if that would make much difference, now that the dollar has cratered. I think this imbroglio puts your whole project in jeopardy."

"So what do you want me to do, Dad?"

"I don't know—well, keep your ears open. Keep a bag packed. And memorize the flight schedules out to either coast."

"Do you think things are going to happen that fast?"

"Do you have any reason to suppose they won't?"

"Fair point," she conceded. "I'll keep in touch."

"You do that, Daughter," he said and hung up.

When Antigone Wells got home at the end of a long day, she went up the terrazzo steps lightly, quickly, hardly bothering to breathe. As she got out her keys at the front door, she stopped to think how different that was from a few months earlier, when she was released from the hospital. Then she had gone slowly and clung to the railing. It was proof that with diet and exercise you really could recover from a near-death experience.

In the hallway at the top of the inside stairs, she found a pair of suitcases. Almost immediately Jeanne Hale came out of the kitchen. She was dressed in her winter coat—although the day did not require it—and a hat.

"I left a note in the kitchen," Hale said. "In case I didn't see you."

"What's this?" Wells asked. "Are you going somewhere?"

"You obviously don't need me anymore. I should go."

"Oh? Do you have another assignment lined up?"

"Well, no, but MaxStaff will find something."

"Funny," Wells said. "When I got their bill last month, they announced they'd be closing their doors. Gone bankrupt. Surely you heard about that?"

"I'm a trained nurse. I can always find work."

"Not if the agencies themselves are going toes up. Look, we can eliminate the middleman. What say I write you a check for the full amount each month?"

"But you don't *need* me. I think you're stronger than I am now."

"Ah, you never know. I'm due for a relapse. One day I might slip and fall in the shower."

"Then you can get yourself a beeper. Or call nine-one-one."

"Can't wear a beeper in the shower. And I could drown before I got to a phone."

"I don't like to take charity," Hale said.

"This is not charity. It's life insurance."

"Well ... so long as you understand, I still don't do cooking or cleaning."

"I know. I have a woman who comes in for that," Wells said. "But you can carry those cases back up to your room, can't you?"

Hale picked up the suitcases. "So ... dinner in half an hour? Chinese takeout?"

"Sure. Let's have that water chestnut thing again."

―――

Adele never joined him for breakfast anymore, or not on workdays when he had to leave the house early. Occasionally on weekends, as this Saturday, she would come down and have coffee with him. And then he could smell the bourbon in it from across the table. Praxis had discreetly asked their cook, Miranda, whether Adele ever ate anything before lunch. The woman grimaced. "Better to ask if she eats anything before dinner. A few crackers, maybe. I make her a sandwich and she eats maybe half the bread."

This morning Adele sat across from him, staring out the window at the lawn of the house next door, where nothing was happening, while he read the paper. Praxis had long ago given up trying to start a conversation at times like this, because she would only answer in grunts and negatives, shutting him down. So it was unusual that she would try to start one herself.

"John ...?" she said clearly, distinctly, as if calling his attention to something.

"What, dear?" he said, not bothering to look up from his newspaper.

"John!" she said louder, as if alarmed at whatever she'd seen.

He glanced out the window—nothing—then back at her.

Adele was sitting bolt upright, eyes wide. The hand holding the cup halfway to her lips was shaking. She tried to put it down, missed the saucer, and dropped it on the tile floor, where it smashed. Her whole body was rigid and shaking now, with some kind of fit.

"Adele!" he called but knew at once that she wouldn't hear him. He moved around the table, grabbing her silver teaspoon and wrapping the handle with his napkin. He got two fingers into her mouth, pried her jaw open, and inserted the padded restraint. By this time she had lost all control and flopped sideways, off the chair and into his arms. He lowered her gently to the floor and cupped his hand under the back of her head to keep it from banging on the tile.

"Miranda!" he shouted. "Call 9-1-1. Get an ambulance. Adele's having a stroke."

The seizure lasted only a minute or two but seemed longer. By the time Miranda came into the breakfast room to tell him the emergency team was on its way, Adele had already stopped convulsing and was lying quietly with her eyes closed. He took the spoon out of her mouth and let her head rest on the floor. After another minute, she opened her eyes.

"How did I get down here?"

"You had some kind of fit."

"Really? I don't remember."

When she tried to get up, he urged her to stay down, and that was how the EMTs found her when they came into the house with their satchels of medicines and bandages and cases of equipment. They hooked her up to one machine to take her heart rate, blood pressure, blood oxygen, temperature, and other vitals. They gave her Tylenol when she complained of a headache, and put an oxygen mask on her. Then they lifted her onto a gurney and took her out to the ambulance.

Praxis asked if he could ride along, but they discouraged that, saying he could meet them at the California Pacific Medical Center in Pacific Heights. When he arrived there, Adele had already been admitted to intensive care and was scheduled for a brain scan. Two hours later, he met with one of the staff physicians, Dr. Meyer.

"The good news is we didn't find any lesions, no clots, no ruptures, no tumors. Does your wife have a history of epilepsy?"

"No, I've never seen anything like this."

"No prior seizures, convulsions?"

"No, nothing of the kind."

"Does she have any medical conditions of which you're aware. Diabetes? Heart disease? Liver or kidney troubles?"

"Well, she does drink pretty heavily."

"So describe 'heavily,' " Meyer said.

Praxis pursed his lips. "Pint of bourbon a day. Maybe more."

"For how long has she had this drinking problem?"

"Ten years. Maybe fifteen. All her life."

"Okay, we'll run a panel for liver toxins. We'll also schedule a biopsy."

"But she's going to be all right, isn't she?"

"I'd like to be reassuring," Meyer said. "But your wife may be a very sick woman. We'll keep her here for a few days of observation, see how she responds to enforced abstinence. We'll know more then."

―――

Antigone Wells was going over the practice's accounts with Ted Bridger, in his office with the door closed. It had become a first-Monday ritual that neither of them relished.

"This is worse than last month," he said as they compared the reports for accounts receivable against revenues.

"Too many clients going bankrupt," she replied. "Or going slow-pay, no-pay."

"Are we still making our nut?" By which he meant BB&W's monthly cost for maintaining the office and utilities, paying staff salaries, and subscribing to information feeds like LexisNexis, Bloomberg Law, and ProQuest. After flipping through pages of the accounting software printouts and fumbling with them twice, he found the answer. "No, I guess not. But the shortfall is—"

"—fifty thousand eensy-beensy American dollars," Wells supplied from her own reading of the bottom line. "That's not so much, in the scheme of things."

"Yeah, but suck it out of your veins every thirty days, and sooner or later you're losing real money."

"What do you want to do, Ted?"

"Can't cut back on the lease or the utility bills. Without the databases and news feeds we might as well be reading palms. I'd sell the furniture, except we're sitting on it. That just leaves—"

"—people," she said bleakly. "Layoffs."

"Not much of dent letting the admins go."

"No, it'll have to be one of the associates."

"At least one for now. Maybe more later."

"You don't have any staff, do you, Ted?"

"Who, me? Halfway out the door myself."

"So really it's down to Carolyn or Sully."

"Do you want me to pick for you?" he said.

"No, I can do it," she said. "I'm a big girl."

"And before the end of the month, please."

She nodded. It was going to be hard, firing one, maybe both, of the people who had carried on so valiantly while she was in the hospital. And it wasn't as if associate positions at prestigious, boutique law firms were going begging during the currency crash.

Well, on the bright side, with a start like this, the week couldn't get much worse.

―――

Callista Praxis was sitting in the construction trailer at the Mile High project site on a Monday morning when the call came from Harold Cromwell, her liaison with the Denver Arts Commission.

"We got a problem here, Callie."

"Oh? I'm sorry to hear that. What's up?"

"Our accounting firm just called. They say you issued a duplicate invoice on the last progress payment."

"Well, if it's a duplicate, you can probably ignore it," she said.

"Yes, except it came with a notice saying the original invoice was never paid, the sum is now overdue, and we have to pay a penalty. I'm sweating blood here, because we're talking a bit more than forty million."

"Let me check something." She cradled the handset against her shoulder, turned to the computer on the trailer's desk, logged in with her headquarters identity, and brought up the project accounts. She ran down the columns of numbers and did a quick mental calculation based on amounts of previous payments. "Yeah, Hal. I could be mistaken, but it seems we really *are* short on that last invoice."

"No way! I remember signing the check myself. That was over a month ago. I know how snail mail's been all bollixed up—which is why we send everything certified, registered, insured, and the rest."

"Okay, fax me what you've got and I'll look into it."

An hour later she was looking at three sets of documents. From the Denver Art Commission's third-party accountants, she had the original invoice with initials authorizing payment, as well as the duplicate PE&C invoice with formal notice that the original amount—$43.6 million and change—was now overdue and carried a ten-percent penalty. From Harold Cromwell himself, she had his photocopy of the original check with his signature and a postal return receipt signed by "B. Glaser" at PE&C's San Francisco headquarters. And finally, from the Denver Art Commission's bank, she now had a fuzzy electronic image of the cleared check, front and back, with a stamp that sure as hell *looked* like PE&C's endorsement. All the dates matched Cromwell's story, and Callie had no reason to doubt his good faith. The art commission had been an excellent client to work with all down the line.

She called her rep in PE&C Accounting, Julia Schottlander, and explained the mystery as much as she understood it.

"Yep," Julia said, "and nope. Money's not here, and no record of our receiving the check."

"But they have a postal receipt from someone named B. Glaser," Callie insisted.

"Let me pull up the company directory. Yep, first name Bernie. In the mailroom. He probably signs a thousand of those things a week. It must be a mistake."

"What should I do?"

"Tell your client to void the first check and send us another—on the second invoice, please," Julia replied. "And if it helps keep you on the client's good side, tell him we can waive the surcharge—but just this once!"

"That's not going to work," Callie said. "Their bank shows the check's been cleared. So the money is already gone from their account."

"Whoops!" Schottlander said. "Well then, it's got to be somewhere. Likely somebody intercepted the check in the mail, faked our endorsement, and cashed it."

"Who would have the balls to cash a certified check for forty-three mill made out to a publicly registered corporation?"

"The thieves these days are pretty sophisticated."

"You'd better find this Glaser fellah and grill him."

"We'll surely do that," Schottlander promised.

"And then run an audit to find the money."

"We'll do whatever we can on our end."

Then Callie called Hal Cromwell back to break the bad news. When she stopped speaking, the line was quiet for a moment. Then he said quietly, "Son of a bitch."

"Look, Hal … this is nothing you and I can unsnarfle here in Denver. I've already referred the matter to our accountants for a full audit. And either way, I'm pretty sure we have insurance that covers against this kind of loss."

"You might carry such insurance," he said. "I know the art commission doesn't. And I just checked the U.S. Postal Service website. They don't insure anything for more than twenty-five thousand—which is about the cost of the envelope."

"Don't worry. We'll figure it out."

"Somebody better," he said and hung up.

It was a mystery, pure and simple, and Callie Praxis hated mysteries. But then, she was an engineer and architect, not an accounting or finance expert. Someone in the firm would find out what happened. Callie packaged the whole mess of documents with a note to Julia Schottlander, reminding her to start a formal audit, and fed it all through the trailer's fax machine. By the time she was finished, the morning was shot and she had accomplished almost nothing.

John Praxis ran in the Presidio 10K, his first organized run, on his sixty-sixth birthday. He thought it would be a good choice, because the course wound across the flats of Crissy Field, the former army airfield right inside the entrance to the Golden Gate, and then up through the hills on the old army base, the Presidio—familiar territory since he'd started his daily exercise program. Of course, ten kilometers was longer than his usual morning run, longer than any three of his runs put together, so he gave himself the option of stopping at the five-kilometer mark and not feeling bad about it.

Standing with a thousand other runners on the roadway before the start, he shivered and could feel his skin contracting into goose bumps. A stiff westerly breeze was coming through the Gate. The feeble morning sunshine of late April hardly warmed him. Coupled with the cold, he was feeling self-conscious. He knew people had seen him out on the public streets, or at least running along these wooded roads, wearing just a tee shirt and running shorts. But this was the first time he had put on a numbered bib and pretended to be a competitor.

When the race started, he let the crowd sort itself out and adopted his own pace. After an initial lap around the field, the pack headed onto the service road that climbed through the trees below Doyle Drive. The crowd thinned even more as the grade took its toll. For Praxis, who ran from Sea Cliff uphill to the Légion d'Honneur and around the Presidio Golf Course every morning, the ascent was a simple matter of adjusting his pace and breathing.

In a few minutes they passed through the parking lot of the Golden Gate Bridge visitors center and out onto the roadway of the bridge itself. Praxis had assumed the race course would follow the pedestrian walkway, but with automobile traffic generally thinned out by the price of gasoline in a euro-dominated market, the race organizers were able to get three of the bridge lanes cleared and coned off. Surprisingly, after the thinning out on the grade, Praxis found himself running in a tight cluster near the front. He realized he was committed to reaching at least the end of the bridge, because if he slowed down here in midspan, stumbled to a stop, and bent over clutching his knees, he would block runners behind him—perhaps even cause a number of them to go down.

The wind on the bridge deck, two hundred feet above the water, was even colder. Streamers of fog blew in from the ocean and threaded between the orange-painted suspension cables a hundred feet above his head. But Praxis found he was warmer, now that he was moving. He thought about what it would mean if he quit at the north end of the bridge. He would have to wait at the exposed overlook for someone to come pick him up. And who would that be? Even though he had a cell phone tucked into his shorts, he couldn't call Adele. She hardly drove anywhere anymore. The only other person at the house, Miranda, didn't drive. He couldn't call either of the boys, because they would be off somewhere with their families. And Callie was in Denver on her project. He would have to call for a taxi, and they would take forever on a Sunday morning with a big race going on nearby.

Praxis realized that he really had no choice but to turn around at the north end, come back with the pack, and finish the race. If he took his time and paced himself, he just might do it. He glanced at the heart monitor built into his fancy GPS watch, which read signals off a belt strapped around his chest. The display showed a steady 130 beats per minute. He kept his eyes on the number over the course of half a mile and it didn't change. More than two beats per second, and his new heart was working like a well-oiled machine.

He probably should have discussed entering this event with his cardiologist. But what was the doctor going to say? No? And would John Praxis have listened to him even then? At this point, it wasn't his heart that was going to give out. Not unless it went spectacularly, *blooey,* like an overheated tire exploding. But so far he sensed no distress, nothing impending. If anything was going to fail, it would be his sixty-six-year-old ankles or knees. But in his chest he had the full-grown heart of a baby less than a year old, and he had toughened and trained it over the months since its creation with his morning runs.

Praxis made the decision to take more time each morning, start earlier, and double or triple the length of his daily run. And then, if his legs could stand it, he might even try a marathon next.

―――

Brandon Praxis was pulled out of his civil engineering class, CE436 Structural Steel Design, at Stanford University by a U.S. Army recruiting sergeant from Menlo Park. The sergeant wore his battle dress uniform, or BDUs, in urban-camouflage gray and didn't bother to mention his own name, although the tag on his chest said "Roxbrough." As they stood in the corridor outside the classroom, the man held up and read aloud Brandon's commission as a second lieutenant, swore him in with the officer's oath, and handed him a sealed envelope containing his orders. He then saluted Lieutenant Praxis and informed him he had two hours to pack his gear and get down to Moffett Field in Sunnyvale.

"Excuse me, but what gear is that?" Brandon asked.
"Your ROTC stuff. Better wear battle fatigues."
"But—but what's all this about, Sergeant?"
"The Army needs you, sir. Right now."
"But you don't understand. I'm not a soldier. I'm a student. My dad runs one of the world's foremost engineering

companies, and he expects me to graduate in June and join him in the business."

"That's nice, sir. But no, sir. You've had three years of military training. You're a gear head. And your country assumes that, being a bright California boy of good family, you have the right attitude. This is a national emergency, and you've been called up to serve."

The sergeant saluted again, turned on his heel, and hurried off. He was already consulting a printed list and pulling another set of commission papers from his gray-camo messenger bag.

Brandon stood with his mouth hanging open. He had started with the Reserve Officers' Training Corps during his sophomore year, primarily as a backup plan. He knew all along that his family—his father Leonard most of all—expected him to step right out of college and into a responsible position somewhere on the upper rungs at Praxis Engineering & Construction. Brandon felt he didn't have the courage to refuse this future outright, and he'd majored in civil engineering as his father recommended. But still, he wasn't altogether comfortable with the prospect. Joining the family company, becoming the "golden grandson" of the fifth generation, meant he would never have the opportunity to prove himself. It also meant everyone around him might be whispering secret doubts about his actual abilities. So he had hedged his bets by joining the Army ROTC.

It wasn't exactly a blind choice. He remembered his grandfather John once mentioning the good work the Corps of Engineers did in maintaining the country's waterways and environmental resources, and how much he admired their public service when they could easily take home two or three times their military pay by joining the private sector. Brandon also liked the idea of playing around with the hydrology of big systems like the San Francisco Bay Delta or the Mississippi River. But he never took the program's scholarship money, and it was always going to be his choice whether to finally accept the commission. He never expected the U.S. Army to just come and take him.

Two and a half hours after being sworn in, Praxis and a dozen other military personnel were marched aboard a C-130J transport at Moffett. As the plane taxied for takeoff, he opened and read his orders. They told him he was being attached to the U.S. Army Ordnance Corps under the command of a Major Anthony Ruysdael. Their mission was to fly to Flagstaff, Arizona, relocate immediately to Camp Navajo, which was ten miles to the west, and secure any and all strategic materiel there. His orders noted that, although the camp was officially maintained by the Arizona Army National Guard, its munitions storage facility remained an inspectable site under the Strategic Arms Reduction Treaty, or START.

He held up the paper for the soldier, an older man, who was strapped into the webbing seat next to him. Praxis pointed out the reference to munitions storage. "What's that supposed to mean?"

"It means support for nukes, son."

"And we're going to get them?"

"Does seem to be the drill."

"With our bare hands?"

"If necessary, yes."

But then the man waved at the cargo strapped to the deck just beyond their knees: two Humvees, each mounting a .50 caliber machine gun in its roof, and an eight-wheeled armored car with a blunt, boat-shaped nose, the Stryker Transport/Combat Vehicle.

"Are we expecting hostilities?" Brandon asked.

"We are expecting anything at this stage."

"I not going to be any good at this. I mean, they taught me to march and shoot a rifle. And I might be able to drive that jeep-thing, given some time to practice. But you understand I'm really just a student, civil engineering."

"That's sweet, son, but no," the soldier said, echoing the anonymous sergeant who'd sworn him in, what, three hours ago now? "We are anywhere from two months to two days away from a shooting war on this continent. We will need every able and committed soldier to make sure this thing goes down the right way. So … what's you're role? I guess you'd better stick close to me. You can take notes when we start inventorying the ordnance. And if we need to blow up a bridge or knock down a door or something, then your education might come in handy."

"Thank you, I guess. Um, what's *your* name, soldier?"

The man turned in his seat and pushed out his collar tab with a thumb. It had a splotch of brown thread sewn on in the shape of a leaf. "Ruysdael, son. You can stand up and salute me later."

———

Late in the workday, the internet news services flashed a report that the federal government had ordered units of the U.S. Army and U.S. Air Force to move into any of the states that had signed on to that "Committee of Secession." Their orders were, first, to disarm the local National Guard units and, second, to "establish a presence" in the state capitals. Some of the correspondents, and various members of Congress they were interviewing, were already calling the action a "coup." But the official language described it as a "preventive measure" necessary to "maintain the peace."

Antigone Wells was with Ted Bridger when the news came up. He stared at the screen thoughtfully. "What are the legal ramifications of open warfare, I wonder?"

"A lot of wrongful death suits," Wells said. "Maybe."

"A whole lot of property damage, too, I would guess."

"Too bad we aren't practicing in Texas or Oklahoma."

———

Richard Praxis hardly blinked when Julia Schottlander, an analyst from the Accounting Department, brought him the report on a misplaced check for the Mile High project in Denver.

"Why bring me this?" he asked. "You should take it up with my sister. She's managing that project."

"I know, sir," Schottlander said. "She tossed the problem over to my department in the first place." The woman closed the door to his outer office, walked over to the chair in front of his desk, sat down, and slid a manila folder across his blotter. "Before going back to Ms. Praxis," she went on, "I thought I should talk to someone higher-up first. I showed this to my manager, and he said I should come to you."

Richard opened the folder and saw on top several pages of data extracted from the company's accounting software. In a couple of places, lines and entries were highlighted in yellow marker, including some conspicuous blanks. Further down in the folder were half a dozen pages of fax, including two of the company's invoice forms and various images of checks, front and back, from the Denver Arts Commission. "So what's going on?" he said. "Walk me through this."

"We believed—or rather, our accounting system believed—we were missing a progress payment on the project and issued a second invoice. The client called Callista, saying he was sure it had been paid the first time. He even had an image of their cancelled check—" Schottlander turned over the pages in front of him. "—there. But when Callista looked in the system, there was no record of it."

"Somebody stole the check and cashed it?" he suggested.

"Well, sir, there's the problem. We've got no record the check was ever received—and that triggered the second invoice. But two days later we do have a log entry that shows the accounts receivable clerk stamped our endorsement on the check, and another entry a day afterward shows it was sent in a batch for bank clearing."

"How can you have log entries for a check that doesn't exist?"

She shook her head. "Different parts of the database, apparently. They just enter the project account number, invoice number, check number, and date. The system doesn't bother to verify original receipt of the check because … well, they've already got it, haven't they?"

"So, what are you telling me?" Richard pressed. "What's the mystery?"

"If we had never received the art commission's check in the first place," Schottlander said, "and it was someone else who cashed it, we'd have no record of it in the system at all. But this looks like someone tried to *hide* the check and didn't think the whole thing through."

"That was clumsy of them," he said dispassionately.

"Yes. And it suggests this was the work of a person, a human being, not a simple software glitch."

"A glitch?" He tried to sound alarmed. "In my system? Is that possible?"

"Well, we've never seen one before. So we did an audit of the entire system. And guess what we found?"

"I hate guessing games. Just tell me."

"A duplicate amount, forty-three point six million, showed up in another account entirely—in Callista Praxis's personal retirement account. It was not a valid entry, of course, because there's no corresponding line item or entry code, no paycheck against which it might have been drawn. The money just appears there."

"Wouldn't a transaction like that leave a trace—the perpetrator's logon, or something?"

"Yes, it would. And no, it didn't." Schottlander shook her head. "It's almost as if a ghost—or the software itself—made the transfer from project account to retirement account."

"Well, now you can transfer the money right back out again," Richard said. "We can't ask the Denver people for another check, can we? Not when we know where their money went."

"No, sir. But that's a problem for us. You see, the system is not designed just to shovel money around. It needs the paper trail, the proper entries in the proper sequence. We'll need authorization to make the restoration without explaining how the money was moved in the first place."

"You've got it. I'll sign whatever you need to square things."

"And then ... there's the matter of Ms. Praxis's account."

"Oh? What does she say about it?" he asked casually.

"As I said, we haven't told anyone. Not even her."

"Well ..." he waited three beats, as if considering. "If it really was a human being who made the transfer, and not a computer problem, then it's a clear-cut case of attempted embezzlement. You should refer this to the Legal Department for their assessment before anyone talks to Callie." He paused. "But I sure hope it's just a system error. I'd hate to think that my sister ..."

"I know, sir," Schottlander said. "Everyone in the company likes her, too."

———

"Hello, Auntie," Suleiman Mkubwa said as he appeared at her office door. "You wanted to see me?"

"Oh, yes, Sully." Wells put down her pen and put aside her notebook. "Yes, um ... You may have noticed that things have slowed down around here lately."

"Oh, indeed!" the young attorney said brightly.

"Our practice has reached a decision point."

"And are you about to let me go, Auntie?"

"Yes, I'm afraid so," she said gravely.

"Oh, thank God! I am so relieved!"

"No, Sully. We're *laying* you *off.*"

"I understand," he said. "Fully. I am released. But I am also *relieved*. I had feared you would let Carolyn go instead of me."

"Oh, and why were you afraid for her?"

"Because this is her home, and she has no place else to go. I should not divulge a confidence, but she was afraid of losing her job. Whereas I have been thinking of going home to my family for a long time."

"Your family is in ... Baltimore, isn't it?"

"Oh, no. That's just my mother. I mean my whole family. I have an uncle in Nairobi who for years has been asking me to join his firm of barristers. I'll have to practice a different kind of law, of course. And also wear a horsehair wig. But it will be better for me."

"I'm sorry you want to leave America."

"Oh, America is fine. I am proud to be a citizen. But right now …"

"This is just an economic downturn," she said. "A rough patch. We've been through them before."

"Oh, yes? Well, frankly, I can buy more with a Kenyan shilling than I can with an American dollar. But that's not why I want to go. We Kenyans have our revolution and civil war behind us. The country is good now. But you Americans have war ahead of you. It will not be so good."

"I'm sure that's all just newspaper talk," Wells said. "Just politics."

"Yes, ma'am. Von Clausewitz said war is politics by other means."

"It won't come to an actual war. Not here. I'd bet my life on it."

"Not your life, Auntie. But bet your dollar against my shilling."

Brandon Praxis figured he had heard wrong when Major Ruysdael said they were securing 'nukes,' because it turned out that all Camp Navajo had were the first-stage rocket engines for Minuteman III and Trident C4 and D5 missiles. And while those launch vehicles were designed to carry nuclear warheads, it would take a whole lot of tinkering, plus a truckload of parts, plus a factory—plus the warheads themselves—to turn the camp's inventory into strategic weapons.

What Ruysdael had neglected to tell him at first was that Camp Navajo was also a training facility for all the service branches. At any one time it could accommodate a battalion of troops and train them in mountain and airmobile operations, land navigation, and proficiency with squad-level infantry weapons like M4 carbines, M249 light machine guns, and hand grenades. Where people trained, there the government tended also to stockpile large amounts of resupply. So Camp Navajo was a major arsenal for any military operations in the Southwest.

What Ruysdael—or the people who had sent him into Arizona with two Humvees, a Stryker armored car, and a dozen men—did *not* know, however, was that the camp, which was supposed to have finished its scheduled training with the North Dakota National Guard's 2/285th Helicopter Assault Battalion, had extended their exercises by two days. The U.S. Army's little task force had rolled up to the gate expecting to encounter a skeleton crew of clerks, contractors, and cooks but instead found the base swarming with more than 500 troops, technical support personnel, and helicopters.

The sentry on duty had passed Ruysdael and his men through and directed them down the road to the Administration Building. Because the major had told Praxis to stick close, Brandon followed his superior officer right into the commandant's office, where together they saluted Lieutenant Colonel Darrell Young of the Arizona Army National Guard, removed their BDU caps, and stood at ease.

"I'm surprised to see you boys," Colonel Young said. "You're not on my list."

"Yes, that's because we're in advance of an activation order," Ruysdael said smoothly. "We're here to secure this facility." Then he added, "Sir," just in time to keep it from being an insult.

"Really?" Young pulled his glasses forward on his nose and looked over them at Ruysdael and Praxis. "You're acting under orders of the President? Is there a national emergency?"

"Near enough. My orders are to inform you and then put your facility under my command as part of the U.S. Army Ordnance Corps."

"I see," the colonel said. "Is that just our industrial operations, which includes your strategic munitions, or the whole camp?"

"My orders aren't that specific. I must assume the whole camp."

"Of course. Well, Major … your men must be tired after a long flight. I'll have my clerk see to a billet and get you tickets to the chow hall. You don't mind eating on the State of Arizona's dime, do you?" Colonel Young grinned.

"Not at all." Major Ruysdael barely smiled.

It had all been very polite and almost friendly. Brandon Praxis was surprised how easily it had gone done.

The next day they toured warehouses and machine shops and even the strategic bunkers with their solid-fuel rocket motors, which were potentially dangerous enough to require a separate facility. Everywhere they went, various of the camp's personnel went before and followed after them. Brandon didn't have to take any notes, as Ruysdael had once suggested, because the staff handed him printouts of everything. It all seemed pretty complete and … secure.

On the second day, however, at ten o'clock in the morning, the atmosphere changed. Their unit was requested to return to the Administration Building for an urgent briefing. In the lobby, an armed detachment of North Dakota guardsmen met them with rifles leveled, relieved them of their personal weapons, and escorted them to a conference room. The television there was playing a national news channel, which they watched for half an hour. Ruysdael protested, but no one would answer him.

At eleven o'clock, a breaking bulletin announced that twenty-six of the former United States had just seceded to form the "Federated Republic of America." By voice vote of their legislatures, they adopted verbatim the U.S. Constitution and all 27 of its amendments, forming a new government in parallel with the old one. Sitting congressmen from those states were invited to form the new Senate and House of Representatives in Kansas City. Election of a president and vice president would follow within sixty days.

When the announcement was finished, Colonel Young came into the room flanked by armed camp personnel.

"I just got off the phone with the governor, Major. He rejects your presidential order and suggests I escort you off base. We've called a couple of taxis to take you and your men back to Flagstaff. The governor's aides will arrange tickets with the Southwest check-in at Pulliam Airport to fly you wherever you want to go. I suggest you head back to California, as Southwest doesn't have as much as coverage east of the Mississippi."

"It doesn't end here, you know," Ruysdael warned.

"Oh, I hope it does, Major. For both our sakes."

5. Total Loss of Control

JOHN PRAXIS WATCHED with a kind of clinical fascination—by turns mixed with frustration, anger, and horror—as the country came apart. He was eerily reminded of those film clips in biology class, where the cell divides, the nuclear spindles form, and invisible threads draw the chromosome pairs apart, like pulling down on a zipper. From everything he read in the papers, saw online, or heard on television, it seemed that the various states had simply lined up on different sides of the room, dividing over the question of the country's political and economic future: Continued reliance on free markets and unfettered growth, or adoption of U.N.-imposed restrictions and sustainable limits? Cultivation of American exceptionalism, or adherence to a One World sameness? Sovereignty or submission?

He found hope in the fact that the newly announced republic created in the middle of the country had adopted the same form of representative democracy with the same founding documents as the old United States. It suggested that, once they could resolve these political and economic differences, the states could just pull up the zipper and knit the country back together.

So far, how any of this would affect PE&C's day-to-day operations remained unclear.

Leonard thought the Federated Republic of America would adopt an entirely new regime of licensing, review, and legislation. "We'll have to start all over again on every project," he complained. "That will force wholesale rewrites of our energy and transportation contracts throughout the area. It will just destroy our accounts receivable."

"At least we can hope that the new government will rethink a lot of the old regulations," Praxis said. "The federal bureaucracies we've had to work under—EPA, Energy Department, Transportation Department, HUD, and HHS—will probably come in for critical review and resizing over there. In the meantime, pent-up demand for new infrastructure will begin calling for our engineering services."

"If there's any money to pay for them," Richard warned.

"Well, with half the country repudiating the federal deficit," Praxis replied, "I'd say they just bought themselves a brand-new credit card."

"Maybe we should move to Texas?" Richard suggested.

"I thought you were against that," Praxis said. "Probably too late now anyway."

But in the midst of these external concerns, Praxis discovered he had bigger problems closer to home.

Adele had been showing a progressive deterioration that he could track practically from one day to the next. At their age, it was one thing to occasionally forget a word, lose the thread of a conversation, or misplace your glasses—which was why he kept pairs of drugstore reading glasses for himself all over the house. But Adele was becoming increasingly vague, muddled, hesitant, and fretful. It was as if the seizure she had experienced a couple of weeks earlier had set off an inexorable process. In the beginning, Praxis thought this confusion was the first sign of a more gradual and much longer slide into garden-variety dementia or Alzheimer's. But when it became apparent she was rapidly falling apart, he discussed her symptoms with their family physician, Dr. Valone.

"Sure, I could run tests," the doctor said. "But you saw the tox panel they did at Cal-Pacific. It suggests she's suffering from brain poisoning because her liver is breaking down and pumping toxins into her blood."

"Is the brain damage reversible?"

"Is she still drinking? The liver won't heal so long as she keeps assaulting it with alcohol. We have to control that first."

"I've tried to talk with her." But any suggestion that Adele should stop or cut down she met with instant hostility. She dragged out every stupid, wrong, or hurtful thing Praxis had said or done in their long life together and used it to prove her sins paled in comparison. "Is there some program we can get her into?" he asked now.

"Sure. Alcoholics Anonymous."

"I mean, one where she doesn't have to … cooperate."

"You mean, like a rehab or recovery center? She'd just call a cab and leave."

"What about one under lock and key?"

"Involuntary commitment is a legal issue. If she's a danger to herself or others, then you can get the police to 5150 her. But that's just a hold for observation, seventy-two hours. Hardly long enough for the detox to take effect."

"But can't *you* just—?"

"Not without a court order."

The legal ramifications of a commitment were nothing he wanted to discuss with the family attorney, because the man was socially close with both of them—and maybe closer to Adele than to Praxis himself. And the matter really fell outside the competence of PE&C's corporate lawyers. So he decided to give Antigone Wells a call.

After the polite exchanges—"How are you doing?" "Stronger every day!" "That's good to hear!"—he broached the matter of Adele, her drinking, and the fearful cost of it that was now catching up with her.

"No, you can't just get her committed," Antigone said, confirming the doctor's verdict. "If she tried to kill herself, or pulled a gun on you … Is she able to take care of herself?"

"What do you mean?" he asked. "She dresses every morning—most days."

"The law about involuntary commitment includes a person's being gravely disabled. But she'd have to be living on the streets, eating out of dumpsters, unable to provide for basic needs like food, clothing, or shelter."

"That's never going to happen," he said stoutly.

"Of course not. So are *you* taking care of her?"

"I try to help, but mostly I'm down at the office."

"Is there anyone else in the house?"

"Well, there's our cook, Miranda."

"But no nurse or anything like it?"

"I hadn't thought … Yes, I suppose it's either that or put her in a nursing facility—which she'd never agree to in the first place. She'll need someone on hand who can deal with her spells and help her stay—I don't know—*focused*. But getting Adele to trust someone coming into her home is another matter."

Antigone paused, then said slowly, "The woman who helped me when I first got out of the hospital is pretty good."

"Is she available?" he asked.

"I know for a fact, she is."

One day later, a woman in her forties showed up on his doorstep in the evening after dinner. She presented her own card—"Jeanne Hale" it read, from the MaxStaff Agency, but the agency name was crossed out—and one of Antigone Wells's business cards as proof of the referral. "Miss Wells said you would be needing some help."

Praxis noted the woman had two suitcases at her feet and a taxi waiting at the curb. Well, the house certainly had enough bedrooms—unless Adele screamed and threw her out, and in that case keeping the taxi waiting was a good idea. "Come on in, Ms. Hale."

They found Adele in front of the television with the picture turned on but the sound muted. She wasn't actually watching, and her hands lay in her lap like a pair of wounded crabs. Sensing a stranger coming into the room with her husband, Adele struggled upright, pulled her hands up on the arms of the chair, tried to stand, missed her balance, and plunked back down. Defeated by the effort, she quavered, "Who—who're you?" She had tears in her eyes.

"My name is Jeanne, dear. I'm here to help you sort things out."

"But I don't need—" his wife began uncertainly.

"Sure you do! We'll have a *good* time together."

Adele looked confused at this, but then her manners took over and she gave a shy smile. "Jeanne," she said by way of greeting. Then she looked at Praxis. "Is it all right?"

"Very all right," he said jovially—and tried to mean it.

Hale turned to him and said quietly, "Why don't you go pay off my taxi?"

As soon as Antigone Wells got home from karate class, she wanted to try out what she'd learned. That would help fix the precise muscle movements in what the instructors called "somatic memory," which was another way of saying somewhere down there in her cerebellum.

After weeks of practicing the thirty basic exercises of Isshinryu—the isolated punches, kicks, and block-punch combinations, plus a half-dozen stretching exercises and hold breaks—Wells was feeling pretty confident about her moves. The black belts had been watching her, too, as they watched everyone. Tonight one of them, a young man named Eric, had taken her aside to begin teaching her the first of the *kata*s, or forms. These were mock fights with imaginary opponents and constituted the body of the Isshinryu style itself. This first one was called Seisan, named after the basic fighting stance, which featured in most of its movements.

Studying her living room, Wells thought she could make enough space available if she pushed the couch this way, the chairs and end tables that way, and backed the television into the corner. She took her place in the middle of the open area and performed first the formal bow—but with eyes directed upward, in case the opponent launched a sneak attack—then the traditional warning sign—"I don't want to fight, but I can if I have to"—with a flat hand over a fist at groin level, and finally a ready stance with arms straight and fists aligned with her thighs.

She stepped off into a *seisan* with left foot forward while doing a brief crossover with her arms that brought her left fist up in guard position and right fist back to her hip. She retracted her left fist to her hip as she punched an imaginary opponent with her right, then pulled it back into guard. That was one. She stepped into right *seisan,* retracted her right fist and punched with her left, pulled it into guard. That was two. Then left step, right punch, and guard. Three. She brought both fists together down at navel level, made a step-slide, and brought them up in a double head block against two imaginary chops to her collarbones. Then she spun on her left foot and came down facing in the other direction with both hands chopping downward and backward against imaginary attackers who were coming up behind her on either side. That ended the first series of movements. She stepped forward into the next series, consisting of blocks, chops, and grapples with a pair of imaginary attackers … and so on, through twenty or thirty more movement combinations to the final ready stance and bow.

Wells never did get a count of the total number of moves in Seisan *kata,* because some of combinations blurred one into another. And the instructor, Eric, told her not to think of *kata* as separate bits, like the basic exercises strung together, but as a flow, a rhythm, supporting a melody of blocks and punches. Like music.

"What if one of the attackers doesn't come in on time?" she had asked. "Or nobody comes in from behind? How do you know the fight is going to follow this exact pattern?"

"*Kata* teaches you combinations and sequences," Eric had said. "Block-and-strike, block-and-kick. It's the most compact way to learn, practice, and perfect your technique. When an actual fight comes to you, your brain will be programmed with these sequences and will know instinctively what to do."

Wells thought about it a moment. "So … is that a 'yes'?"

For giving him sass, Eric made her drop and do ten push-ups on her knuckles. Black belts were as touchy as hawks and did not take smart-mouth from white belts. But for all of her skepticism, Wells could sense the beauty of the *kata,* the precision, the complexity within simplicity.

In past weeks, she had also begun working on close order drill with various partners in class, a kind of proto-sparring. Two long lines of students faced each other across a three-foot gap. On command, one would step forward and throw a punch, lightly brushing the opposing student's solar plexus without actually landing the blow. The other would step back, try to block it accurately, deflect it, and throw a countering punch. In these exercises, Wells was always slow, awkward, fumbling. Her brain had not yet assimilated the sequence, its range and timing, and her execution. She could not turn the series of individual movements into a single response. But if Eric was right, if she could believe in this mystical reliance on "somatic memory," then *kata* would be the way to acquire speed and grace.

And even if she never got into a real fight, it was pretty good exercise.

The charge was serious enough that John Praxis called his daughter back to San Francisco: drop whatever she was doing on the Mile High project, turn over all her notes and instructions to an assistant, and catch the next flight out.

Praxis could not actually believe that Callie would be stupid enough to steal forty million out of a project account and then try to hide it within the system in her own retirement account. The point of embezzlement was to get the money safely out of the company, divert it to invoices from bogus suppliers or consultants, and then invest it in diamonds or Swiss francs, far away and preferably offshore. But an exhaustive diagnostic of the company's accounting system had shown that the transfer was neither a software glitch nor a random event. Someone had moved the money deliberately, and the only person who could possibly benefit, or would have enough detail about the Denver Arts Commission's progress payment to begin with, was Callie. The PE&C Legal Department was already drawing up a case against her.

"What's all this about, Dad?" she said when Ivy ushered her into his office.

"Sit down, please," he said, waving to the chairs in front of his desk. "The Accounting Department has uncovered an anomaly—at least, I hope it's just that—which they think you can explain."

He passed her the folder containing copies of her faxes from Harold Cromwell at the Denver Art Commission, her note to Julia Schottlander, and highlighted extracts from the accounting system. Also included were printouts of software diagnostics, the paper trail of scheduled project milestones and Callie's authorization to issue the missing invoice, and the company's telephone logs showing the date and time of all calls among Cromwell, Schottlander, and Callie. "These are certified copies of everything," he explained. "The Legal Department is keeping the originals for now."

She studied the material, flipping methodically through the pages, and once backtracking to check something. He studied her face as she did so and saw her beetled eyebrows and compressed frown relax into a smile as she looked up.

"Oh, good!" she said. "This explains where the money went. For a while I thought someone had snagged the art commission's check and cashed it. They couldn't possibly afford to pay that whopper twice."

"The money has now been properly distributed," he said quietly.

"Then why bring me back in such a rush? I've got a job—"

"Because everyone thinks you took it in the first place."

"What! That's nonsense! Why would I do that? *How* would I do that?"

"Temptation? Insecurity? Greed? The money ended up in your account."

"You mean, I just put it in there and hoped no one would notice? Like 'finders, keepers'?" She riffled the pages. "Look, even with the recent inflation, that amount is a hundred times my usual quarterly statement. And without a line of code to explain it, that entry sticks out by a mile. Does everyone think I'm stupid?"

"No, not stupid. But we've got Schottlander's analysis and the software diagnostic saying *somebody* moved the money. If not you, then who else?"

"But … I don't even receive the checks. I didn't know anything was wrong until Harold Cromwell called me. I'm on the construction end the business—pushing dirt, concrete, and steel—not in accounting. I *never* handle the money."

"You initiated that invoice."

"Because it's part of my job."

"Look, dear, I believe you. I wish that settled it," he said with a sigh. "I wish I could just wave a hand and make this go away. But we're an international company with financial regulators tracking our every move in sixteen different languages. I have to tell you formally, the Legal Department will be coming after you."

"So I'm going to need an attorney?"

"I think so. But I know a good one."

"Better than our handpicked crew?"

"Someone who's beaten them before."

Before she would put her fate in the hands of her father's lawyer, Callista Praxis decided to do some research on her own. Before trusting what everyone else was saying about the company's accounting software, she wanted to hear the expert view. But she had not been present—or even in the country—when the system was installed five years ago, so she knew none of the people who had done the work. She only knew the name of the installation contractor, Intelligeneering Systems Inc. So she started there.

As with all corporate contacts, it took five layers of phone tree, buffered by four bad choices which dumped her back to a dial tone, before she could speak with a representative from Technical Support. It was a young man named "Andy," who spoke with a lilt that reminded her of Ballywood movies.

"How may I help you today?"

"I'm calling from Praxis Engineering and Construction. I'm a vice president with the company. And I want your advice about a clerical error that the accounting package your people installed seems to have produced."

"Oh? Would you give me the error code, please?"

"Um, I don't have that information."

"Did you run a diagnostic?"

"I believe they did."

"And what were the results?"

"I don't have them in front of me."

"Are you not the system administrator?"

"No, I'm—well, I'm kind of on the wrong end of this," Callie said. "You see, the program has made a huge error. The software itself—or someone using it—secretly moved a large amount of money, forty million dollars, out of one account and into another. I want you to tell me if that's possible."

"The system does not make decisions or transactions on its own, ma'am, unless they are written into the logic of the code," the rep replied with perfect, almost inhuman courtesy. "No one can make such a transaction without having the right kind of access and without leaving a time stamp linked to their authorization."

"I understand all that. But aren't there secret ways—back doors and Easter eggs—that would let someone do this without—"

"No, ma'am. Such things are fairy tales. They would undoubtedly call into question the integrity of your system and permit doubts about the accuracy of its results. Trapdoors are highly illegal and would create for you many problems with your Internal Revenue Service, Securities and Exchange Commission, and other fiduciary regulators."

"So there's no way anyone could move the money secretly?"

"No, ma'am. And if there were, it would be highly improper for me to tell you. You must not think of doing such things."

"No, I'm not trying to—"

"Thank you for calling Intelligeneering Systems. Remember, my name is Andy. If you need to reference this call in the future, please use transaction number four-two-two …" And he recited a string of ten meaningless digits that she didn't have time to write down. "Have a nice day," he concluded, and the line went dead.

The young woman sitting in Antigone Wells's office bore a strong resemblance to the father. She had the same shape of face with high forehead, straight nose, wide jaw, and full mouth. But where John Praxis's hair was cut short and silvery white, giving no clue to its original color, Callista's was dark brown, almost black, flowed in waves around her face, and touched her perfect cheekbones. Also, where his eyes were brown, kindly, and wise, hers were green, sharp, and watchful. But that sense of lizard-like watchfulness might well be due to her present circumstances.

Wells had met the sons, Leonard and Richard, when she was taking depositions and conducting negotiations during the St. Brigid's case. Neither had impressed her as being very intelligent nor half as quick-witted as the elder Praxis. If asked, Wells would have guessed that the family had finally passed over from its days of growth and glory as entrepreneurs, empire builders, and risk takers into the long days of decline and dwindling fortune as administrators, conservators, and trust-fund beneficiaries. But now, seeing the daughter, she wasn't so sure of that assessment.

John Praxis had already briefed Wells on the situation and confirmed his belief in his daughter's innocence, although he remained frankly perplexed by the whole affair. Now Wells made Callista describe her predicament as she understood it. The young woman did so, retelling her interview with Praxis and her own call to the system integrator, and concluded by saying, "I didn't do any of this. I wouldn't even know how to begin faking a thing like this. But, of course, I can't prove that."

Wells finished taking notes before she would speak. "In a court of law, you wouldn't have to," she said. "The evidence against you is purely circumstantial—if we can really believe they don't have a link between your logon access records and the transfer event itself."

"There's no time stamp on the transaction at all, they say. And none on deletion of the invoice."

"So, not your fingerprints. Not *anyone's* fingerprints. And the software people say a system error is simply not possible."

"So *God* did it?" Callista asked angrily.

"I don't think you want to take that line of defense," Wells replied. "It didn't work so well last time. If I could break it in court, so can others." She thought for a moment. "No, it seems like the entire case against you is *cui bono*—who benefits?

"In dealing with a case of employee theft like this," Wells went on, "we operate with something called the 'fraud triangle,' or three elements necessary to explain the act. First is *motive*—the pressure that might have driven you to commit fraud in the first place. It had to be strong enough to overcome your sense of responsibility to your employer. For example, did you need the money to support a drug habit? Do you have an extravagant lifestyle? Are you in debt?" She paused.

"None of the above," Callista said. "I'm doing fine. I have a stake in the company—ten percent of shares. And if I wanted money now, why would I put it into a retirement account?"

"Of course," Wells said. "The second element is *means* or *opportunity*—your ability to commit the fraud. But that remains gravely in doubt, doesn't it? Third is your *rationalization*—what you would tell yourself to justify stealing from your clients or your employer. Have you been passed over, say, by your brothers? Has someone wronged you? Do they not appreciate you?"

"No, I'm good. I'm doing what I want, which is building big projects. I don't want power over people—which I guess is Leonard's thing—and I'm not an administrator like Richard."

"So it's a mystery all around. Tell me, has your legal staff preferred charges or brought a suit against you?" Then she answered herself immediately. "Oh, of course not. If they had, you'd have the documents in hand, wouldn't you?"

"All I know is what my father tells me," Callista said. "I haven't even talked to the company's lawyers yet. They have me in some kind of quarantine."

"Now isn't that odd?"

"You tell me."

"If I were to guess, I'd say they won't go to court, won't inform the authorities, won't move on this at all. They've put the money back where it belongs, so your client is not damaged. And now they have you dangling over a pit. Tell me, do you have any enemies in the company? Any reason for them to hurt you?"

"No, I'm just … Of course, being a member of the family, holding shares and all, makes me different from the regular employees around me. My career path is assured, where other people have to scramble."

"Any particular hard feelings? Dirty looks? Threats?"

"No. I go out of my way to be nice to people, try to treat them fairly."

Wells thought for a moment, tapping her pen on her notepad. She didn't believe for an instant that someone could not have secret access to the accounting files. Human beings were always smarter than any machine or system. So … Wasn't it Conan Doyle who said that once you eliminated the impossible, whatever remained, no matter how improbable, had to be the truth? As soon as they took the one technical impossibility out of Callista's story, the inviolability of the system, the answer became obvious. Someone was seeking advantage, creating a pressure point. But to achieve what? And how could she and Callista use that knowledge?

"If they never formally charge you," she asked, "what happens?"

"I suppose they could still terminate me, for cause."

"We could challenge that with a lawsuit."

Callista shook her head. "A lot of bad publicity there."

"Exactly what you don't want, for professional reasons, and neither do they. They want you to plead *nolo contendere* and go quietly."

"Who is 'they'?"

"Whoever set this up."

"And why would anyone do that?"

"I don't know. But my guess is someone—someone with a lot of access—wants you out of the company. They'll offer you the chance to quit quietly in exchange for their not lodging a complaint with the Board of Professional Engineers and getting your license revoked."

The young woman thought with her eyes closed. Then she opened them. "I could fight that—"

"—but it will be messy. If they won't throw the stink bomb of a lawsuit, you'd have to. So tell me, what are your goals here?"

"To clean up this mess and put it behind me."

"And if that's not possible, will you do what's best for yourself, or for your company?" Wells asked. "Which comes first?"

More thinking. This time her eyes were squeezed shut. When she opened them, they were filmed with tears. "The company, I guess. … I can always find other work."

"Then I'll help you negotiate a deal."

―――

The meeting took place in a conference room on the thirty-eighth floor. As a precaution, John Praxis had ordered the building's security team to sweep it that morning for listening devices. Half an hour beforehand, he met with Leonard and Richard, as well as Vice President and Chief Counsel Winston Burke, to finalize their negotiating position.

"I want it understood," Praxis told them, "that my daughter is to be treated with respect. She is still a member of this family and this company. I believe the principle of 'innocent until proven guilty' still exists in this country."

"This is not a court of law," Burks pointed out.

"We will still hold to that standard," Praxis insisted.

"Very well, but it makes our position somewhat weaker."

Richard twisted in his chair. "I'm afraid we have more proof at this point, rather than less," he said. He dug another folder full of printouts with yellow highlighting out of his briefcase and laid it on the table. "I asked Julia Schottlander in Accounting to check on Callie's other projects. And this morning she brought me evidence of more irregularities, although in smaller amounts and older accounts. These establish a clear pattern of theft and deceit—almost as if Callie was practicing for stealing the Denver Art Commission's check."

Praxis was dumbstruck. "But … I thought you said you ran a system audit."

"Only of the Mile High project," Richard said. "But then I thought we should dig deeper, to make sure that was not just a fluke."

Praxis's heart sank, but he tried to rally. "And is her time stamp on any of them?"

"No, not a one," Richard said. "It looks as if she's found some way around the firewall and password system. I didn't think that was possible, but there it is. I really should take responsibility for letting this happen—"

"It's not your fault," Leonard said quickly.

"Of course not," Burke said.

Praxis kept quiet.

"So …" Leonard said. "Do we all agree she must leave the company, one way or another?"

"I think it's for the best," Richard said. "We can then plug the cash flow and keep publicity to a minimum."

"I still believe we have enough evidence to prosecute," Burke objected.

"That would not be a *minimum* of publicity," Richard said.

"What do you think, Dad?" Leonard asked quietly.

"I want to hear what Callie has to say."

"You know she'll just protest her innocence," Richard said.

"And that just might be the truth," he replied.

"She always was your favorite."

A soft knock on the door interrupted their discussion. Ivy Blake opened the door and escorted Callie and Antigone Wells into the room. As his executive assistant withdrew, Praxis said, "Please wait outside and see that we're not disturbed."

Ivy nodded somberly and closed the door behind her.

Antigone and Callie moved to the empty side of the table, across from his sons and Burke, leaving Praxis at the head in the dubious and undeclared position of arbitrator or moderator. That suited him fine, as he wanted to be fair to his daughter but also to the facts. He nodded at Antigone to speak first.

"Let me begin by saying that my client and I want what is best for this company," Wells said quietly. "While we dispute the evidence that has been made available to us and the interpretation you gentlemen are placing on it, we have no intention of dragging the Praxis name, either as family or corporation, into a public scandal."

When it was clear she had finished, he nodded for his sons to make their case.

"About that evidence," Richard began. "We have conducted a more thorough audit of all Miss Praxis's earlier work and uncovered even more irregularities." He lifted his folder and shoved it halfway across the table to a point equidistant between Callie and her lawyer.

Callie grabbed it, spun it around, opened it, and began poring over the details. By the third page her face was bright red. "Oh, come on!" she exclaimed. "Where did all this come from? What's happening here?"

Antigone laid a hand upon his daughter's arm. It looked like gentle restraint, but her fingers were arched and her grip taut to prevent another outburst. Callie subsided. Antigone casually drew the folder in front of her, glanced at the first page, and flipped it closed. She looked across the table with a serene expression.

"We're prepared for you to stipulate," she said, "that one or more unexplained computer errors have embarrassed my client and even cast doubt upon her professional reputation. We don't require an apology at this point, but we would have the company's commitment, in writing, to root out and fix the source of these errors."

Burke laughed out loud, but he was alone in doing so.

Antigone's expression did not change. Her eyes were as opaque as stones.

"We have enough to show fraud and grand larceny," Burke said. "Not to mention a pattern of previous criminal behavior."

"And it benefits you to disclose this—how?" Antigone asked.

"We don't want a scandal, either," Leonard said quietly, more to Burke than to her. "In fact, we'll withdraw all charges if Callie will simply admit her guilt and leave the company."

Richard and Burke frowned at this but nodded their agreement.

"We will admit nothing," Antigone said. "However, my client feels that her services may no longer be appropriately valued at Praxis Engineering. She is eager to be released from her contract and try her hand at new endeavors."

"Fine by us," Leonard said. Richard, and then Burke, nodded.

"Of course," Antigone went on, "she would expect to receive the basic severance package and a glowing reference from her immediate supervisor and his management team."

"She'll certainly have my support in that," Praxis said.

The boys and Burke just looked sour.

"You will also," Antigone continued, "distribute her vested amounts in the company retirement plan—minus whatever unearned benefits your faulty software may have awarded her—into a tax-protected individual retirement account."

"We can do that," Leonard said slowly.

"Wait a minute!" Richard began.

Antigone rolled right over him. "And, lastly, she will keep her privately held shares in Praxis Engineering and Construction as a family member in good standing."

Leonard looked around uncertainly. "Are we allowed to do that?"

"No, we can't," Richard said. "It's in the bylaws. Shares can only be held by active employees. There's no provision for releasing them outside the company."

"Fine," Antigone said. "Then we'll take cash."

Richard paled. "But—but—that's easily—" He looked at the ceiling while evidently doing sums in his head. "Twenty times the amount she stole."

"You mean," Antigone said crisply, "the amount you and your computer misplaced."

Richard gaped at her, his mouth working like a salmon thrown up on the dock.

"We realize," Antigone went on, "that you can't liquidate a tenth of the corporation's asset value on short notice. So we're prepared to give you—" She glanced at Callie. "—a month from date of separation?"

"Three months would be fair," his daughter said.

"Three months then."

"No!" Richard said. "It would hollow out the company. It would break us."

"Those are our terms," Antigone said with a shrug. "Otherwise, you can take us to court. Then we will bring in our expert witnesses to dismember your accounting software line by line. I believe you remember how thorough my witnesses can be? All sorts of little secrets might come out then."

Praxis studied Antigone, who sat utterly still, with not a tremor or a blink, a sphinx carved in stone, one eyebrow lifted and every strand of her glorious golden hair held in place with a wide tortoise-shell comb. Beside her, Callie was trembling but sitting stiffly erect. Both of them had their gazes fixed on Richard, who looked as if he'd been stabbed in the heart. What piece of the puzzle involving his daughter, Praxis wondered, was he missing? What did Antigone already know? What did she suspect?

"All right," Richard whispered. "We'll get the money somehow."

"Excellent!" Antigone said, smiling now. She rose and lifted Callie out of her chair with the same hand clutching her arm. "Do let us know when we can come back and sign the paperwork."

At the door, which opened to her knock, she stepped aside for Callie to go through and said to Ivy in passing, "Don't worry about us. We'll find our own way out."

When the Southwest flight carrying Major Ruysdael and his team out of Flagstaff had landed at LAX, Brandon Praxis expected to be demobilized and allowed to return to Stanford for final exams and graduation. Instead, two master sergeants were standing at the gate with a sheaf of envelopes they distributed to each member of the team by barking out their names, just like mail call. The others broke the seals and read their new orders on the spot, then took off in different directions. His own package included orders for him to report immediately to Fort Hunter Liggett, a couple of hundred miles up the coast, to begin again with a new battalion being formed under the 91st Training Division of the Army Reserve. Brandon was confused, because in Arizona the reservists and national guardsmen were the enemy, while here in California they were friendlies. He still didn't understand the politics. The envelope also contained a one-way ticket on SkyWest Airlines to the Monterey Peninsula Airport, departing four hours from now, onward transportation to be arranged.

Brandon had wrinkled his nose, but he knew better than to protest. He looked around for Major Ruysdael, who was holding his own orders and looking grim as usual.

"Well, Major, sir," Brandon said, saluting. "I guess it's been … educational."

"Yee-ah." He snapped off a return salute. "Keep your tail clean, Lieutenant."

In keeping with Army practice, Brandon had turned then and run off down the concourse toward the SkyWest terminal. But once he was out of sight, he paused to think. The first thing was to let his family know where he was, because Ruysdael had put them all on "radio silence"—by which he meant no personal cell phone calls—as soon as they spotted the unexpected helicopter traffic above Camp Navajo. Nothing in Brandon's new orders said his destination or assignment was secret, although he sensed he wasn't supposed to explain too much to civilians. His father would understand that. So he called Leonard Praxis at the company number and was passed through by his administrative assistant.

"Oh, God, Bran! Are you all right? Was there trouble in Arizona?"

"No, Dad. It seems it was all some kind of weird mix-up."

"The news makes it sound like we're at war."

"No, the thing was almost … cordial."

"When are you coming home?"

"I don't know yet."

"What can you tell me?"

"I'm assigned to an army base up near Monterey for training. I'll try to get in touch with the university and see what they're doing about my exams. I hope I can join you at the firm by the end of the summer session, maybe."

"As to that," his father said, "well, you go ahead and fix up your degree. But, about your position with the company, I wouldn't hurry too much."

"Did you say, 'Don't worry'?" Brandon was confused.

"No, I mean, there's no rush for you to join us."

"Is there a problem? Now I *am* worried."

"No, just some business wrinkles to iron out."

"Can you at least tell me what's going—?"

"Son, I have to take the other line."

And the call had ended abruptly.

So Brandon Praxis flew up to Fort Hunter Liggett, nestled into the Santa Lucia Mountains. For the next month he led a platoon of forty-five infantrymen, fresh out of basic, on field exercises through the chaparral. His team was broken into three rifle squads and a weapons squad, each led by newly promoted sergeants and corporals, whom Brandon was required to train, inspire, and evaluate. They navigated by map and compass, by the stars, and by dead reckoning when the fog rolled over the mountains from the coast. They set ambushes against other platoons and learned to avoid ambushes in return. They ate Meals Ready to Eat, griped about them at first, and soon wolfed them down. They fired their weapons on the range—Brandon's first practice with an M4 carbine since his initial year of ROTC, and his first ever experience with his officer's M9 Beretta service pistol—and earned their marksmanship ratings, or not.

He was learning to be a soldier himself, and not merely an onlooker. He was learning to lead men and earn their respect, and that would be a useful skill to have in whatever career finally claimed him.

―――

The separation papers came in the mail two days after the negotiation. Callista Praxis received them at the house in Sea Cliff, where she was staying with her father, as she usually did during her brief visits to San Francisco. She took the documents downtown to the offices of Bryant Bridger & Wells and reviewed them page by page with Antigone.

"It all seems to be in order," the attorney said when they finished. "This gives you everything we asked for."

"Except the apology," Callie said—not that she much cared.

"Funny how they'd rather shed ten percent of the firm than admit an error."

"Men! More ego than brains sometimes."

"No, seriously," Antigone said. "It makes you wonder."

"Do you think they're going to find a way to wiggle out of this?"

"No, the terms are ironclad. If your brothers balk, we'll eat them alive in court. I'm just curious what else is going on that we don't understand yet." The woman stared at the documents with pursed lips. "Whatever it is, you're free and clear, with a tidy fortune to boot."

"I'd rather have my old job back," Callie said.

Antigone shrugged. "Go buy yourself a company."

"It still wouldn't have the Praxis name on it."

"Then start your own," Antigone said.

The attorney called in her administrative assistant, Madeline, who was also a notary public. She witnessed Callie's signature in five different places, affixed her seal, and handed the papers back.

"Do you want us to mail those for you?" Antigone asked.

"No, I want to throw them in Leonard's face myself."

"Do you think that's wise?"

"Of course not."

But she went down to Steuart Street anyway, because she still had to return her electronic building card and the keys to the trailer in Denver and to her company car, a leased vehicle she'd left at the airport. When she arrived at PE&C headquarters, neither of her brothers was available, but the security staff in the lobby directed her to the Legal Department on the thirty-fifth floor.

Winston Burke met her at the elevator, escorted her into his office, and received the documents. He inspected her signatures and the notary's seal, countersigned in the appropriate places, and didn't offer to have it witnessed or notarized. He handed Callie her copies in exchange for her pass and keys. Then nodded curtly.

"This releases my shares," she said. "What happens to them while I'm waiting for the money?"

"They'll go into escrow," Burke said. "And when you sign for the receipt, they'll either be redistributed to eligible members or sold to new board candidates."

"Who decides that?" she wondered.

"The Board of Directors." He shrugged.

She remembered that Burke was the company secretary. He served the board but was not a shareholder himself.

"Then I will expect your check," she said and turned to leave.

"Um, let me call security to escort you to the lobby."

"But I'm not going down to the lobby."

"I'm afraid you must, Ms. Praxis," he said.

"Then they can escort me to my father's office.

John Praxis had made no arrangements with Callie that morning, but since it was her last day he expected she would come up to say a formal good-bye. It was odd, however, when the female Myrmidon from the front desk escorted his daughter, practically holding her by the elbow, through the door of the chairman's office. He rose from his desk, came around it, and gave Callie a hug.

"You can go now, Pamela," he said. "She's not going to steal the furniture."

The severe young woman nodded curtly and withdrew.

"You know she's going to wait outside and take me to the elevator," Callie said.

"Not my orders."

"Burke's, I think."

"Undoubtedly."

"Him I can understand," she said. "But what happened to Leonard and Richard? What did I ever do to them?"

"It's a mystery to me, too."

"At least this nightmare is finally over."

"You're well out of it. Free to do what you want."

"I *want* to complete the Mile High project."

"You'll find other work, of course."

"In Europe, maybe. Or China. The situation in this country is too unsettled right now. Nobody's starting anything bigger than a freeway interchange."

"At this point," he said slowly, "you may survive Praxis Engineering."

"Seriously, Dad? I know it was a blow, taking out my shares. But you've got some reserves, don't you?"

"A lot of projects got cancelled when the dollar went south. And our prospects overseas are hardly better. You may end up the heiress of this family. You can retire to the Riviera and buy yourself a pretty husband."

She wrinkled her nose. "I'd still rather have a job."

"I'll see you tonight? We'll go out to celebrate."

"Sure, the first day of the rest of my forever."

6. The End of an Era

"The Coup"—as John Praxis would later describe it—came at the third item on the agenda of the monthly Board of Directors meeting. Herb Longacre, the executive vice president for international marketing, introduced a measure requiring mandatory retirement at age sixty-five for all employees—not exempting senior executives, as in the current rules.

Praxis looked at his two sons, sitting on either side of the table next to him. Both had their heads down, studying the papers in front of them, while Longacre detailed his reasons for the measure, which had something to do with accelerated shedding of aging staff. Leonard's own eyes shifted sideways and upward, to catch Praxis looking at him. Then Leonard lifted his head fractionally and glanced across at Richard.

Ah so, Jessica! Praxis thought, *as the Japanese would say*. Longacre was a longtime friend and ally of Leonard's. And this move was directed upward, at Praxis himself, as the "aging staff" in question. Well, he still had the votes to counter the measure. With his own thirty-five percent of shares, plus Callie's ten percent held until her payout, and the ten percent held by other board members who were loyal to him, the motion was doomed.

When it came time to vote, however, the ayes and nays went as he expected—with both of his sons and their allies voting in favor—until the very end, when the issue of Callie's shares arose.

"According to the corporation's bylaws," Richard said, "shares held in escrow are voted at the discretion of the chief financial officer."

"Is that a fact?" Praxis asked.

"I didn't know that," Leonard said in mild wonder.

"Article One, Section Seven, Subsection Three," said Burke as secretary.

"And I am voting those ten percent of shares in favor," Richard concluded.

"The vote is fifty-five percent to forty-five," Burke said. "The motion passes."

The rest of the meeting proceeded, as far as Praxis was concerned, in a haze of meaningless activity. When it was over and everyone was standing, he gathered his sons by eye and said, "Would you gentlemen please come to my office?" If indeed it was still his office.

As soon as the doors were closed, he turned to his eldest son. "What did you two just do in there?"

Leonard was aghast. "Us? Do? Nothing! It was Herb's motion, to handle some personnel problems he's having in the international division."

Praxis did not miss the fact that, of all the business transacted that afternoon, Leonard knew exactly which piece of it his father meant.

"But it never occurred to you that I'm now over sixty-five?" Praxis said. "This forces me out of the company. The two of you have been asking me to step down since the heart attack."

"Only for your own good, Dad." Richard said.

"It's the direction you've been taking for a long time," Leonard said.

"Well … hell!" Praxis said. "Things are different now. I'm *better* since the heart attack. My weight's way down. My stamina's up. I'm stronger than before. I run *foot races* for ten and fifteen miles at a time. And now the company's in a rocky place. It needs me."

"We can handle the company," said Leonard. "Just like you taught us."

"And, besides," said Richard, "you'll want to stay on in a non-voting role as 'chairman emeritus,' just like Grandfather Sebastian did."

Praxis stared at him. That would keep his shares in the company, too. But because his employment status would officially become "inactive," the shares would be held in trust—"in escrow," in fact—which would give Richard a forty-five percent vote between his own and his father's shares. Actually, fifty-five percent until Callie's payout was finalized. That was too much control. On the other hand, if Praxis opted to leave and cash out his shares immediately—forcing the liquidation of more than a third of the company's assets—that would spell the end of Praxis Engineering & Construction.

But wasn't the company headed down that road anyway? With the falloff in contracts, the shrinkage of federal and state budgets, and looming economic uncertainties for a country that was cut in half by economics and politics and on the brink of war—what were the company's prospects? Whatever was to come for the nation, the bloodier it was, the greater would be the need to rebuild one day. And that was some kind of future, if a distant one, for PE&C. But in the meantime the country had to negotiate the passage of a great, gray unknown, a nexus where all plans and expectations broke down. And the company would also have to pass through a fiscal sinkhole, wide as a lake, deep as the ocean, with bankruptcy lurking at the bottom.

For the past year Praxis had felt like the pilot of an airplane running out of gas and losing altitude. He had tried, or proposed for his sons to try, everything he could think of to keep the business going: new ways of financing projects, new customers and industries in more prosperous sectors, new work methods and practices. But since Leonard and Richard had taken control after his Thunderbolt, everything they touched had turned to ice cream. True, the troubles were not always of their own making. But they seemed blind to the tasks at hand. They lacked the capacity to adapt and learn.

And now the question came down to his own immediate course of action. On which side of the equation governing the future was he going to stand? Stay and take the emeritus position in order to preserve the family business and its slender, doubt-filled future? Or leave to preserve as much of his own fortune and financial future as possible? Take the money, and devil take the rest? *Wasn't it a French king who said, "Après moi, le déluge"? Ah, but was that a cry of selfishness, or despair?*

"I think not," he quietly told his youngest son.

"Dad!" Richard said. "You can't seriously mean to take—"

"If you want to precipitate a landslide in the middle of a hurricane," Praxis told him, "then be prepared for the consequences."

"Now, now, now," Leonard quavered. "There's no need for hasty action. There's plenty of time for us to sit down and work through—"

"Work through *what?*" Praxis asked angrily. "How will these circumstances change if we delay until tomorrow? Or next week? Next month? You've forced me to a decision, and I've made it. What can change now, except your arguments and my mind?"

"Then we'll survive without you." Leonard said, suddenly cold.

"We've survived a lot worse than this," Richard said.

"I hope you're right," Praxis replied.

"We've reached the tipping point," Ted Bridger said quietly as they went over the practice's books for another month. Antigone Wells could see what he meant.

Having let Carolyn Boggs go as well as Sully Mkubwa, and put her assistant Madeline on part time, they had nowhere else to cut in terms of staff—unless Wells wanted to open her own mail and type her own letters, as well as Ted's, like a rookie just starting out from law school. Their income for the month barely covered office rent and utilities.

"Where did the huge fees of the last couple of years go?" she wondered, thinking of BB&W's share of the recovery in the St. Brigid's case—the last of her glory days.

"To keep us afloat through the thin times of the past year," he said.

"I guess I haven't been as productive as … before."

"Neither have I, come to mention it."

"Are we getting too old?"

"I am. You're not," he said. "I swear, Antigone, you look younger and more alive than you ever did ... before."

"Before my brain exploded, you mean."

"Well, whatever it was."

"I'm getting better. Soon I'll be back up to my usual pace, you know."

"You might, but I won't. I've grown senile, my dear. Time for me to go."

"What's the—" She hesitated. "—the protocol for a situation like this?"

"You should offer to buy me out. But ..." Now *he* hesitated. "Don't."

"I have resources of my own," she said. "I can manage the cost."

"I know. And the value of the practice has declined to the point where you could probably afford to buy it outright. But honestly, in these times? With this future?"

"Lots of work. Nobody able to pay."

"If you bought my share, you'd still be bankrupt next month—and personally broke to boot."

"Then ..." she said, "I'll draw up the liquidation papers and alert the landlord." She ran her hand over the burled maple of her desktop. "The furniture ought to fetch a good price. And we can sell the computers on eBay."

"Not much value in liquidations," he said. "Anymore."

"What will you do?" she asked.

"Tend to my garden. And you?"

"Oh ..." She realized hadn't ever considered a life beyond the law. *Best Damn Attorney in San Francisco, now bankrupt, seeks suitable employment* ... "Live off my hump for a while," she said. What could she get for a top-floor condominium apartment on Divisadero Street? "Maybe travel for a bit. I've got a sister Oklahoma I haven't seen in a couple of years."

"Isn't that on the other side of the border?" he asked.

"What border? They're not another country yet, are they?"

"Well, go then. But just take care of yourself."

———

Callie Praxis was performing a bit of rudimentary bonsai on her mother's purple African violet, trimming away dead leaves with a pair of kitchen shears. Yesterday Adele had looked at the plant, walked away, turned back, and touched the pale brown leaves with a frown. Working on the theory that, if her mother could still love anything in her confused state, it might be a living thing, Callie had taken the plant in hand and tried to coax it back to life. She had found some liquid fertilizer in the garage, and as soon as she'd cleared enough of the leaves to give the plant breathing space, she planned to apply it.

Her cell phone caught her in mid-snip. When she picked it up, she didn't recognize the number. It was from somewhere in Texas. She answered it anyway, because her days were just not that busy anymore. "Hello?"

"Hello, Miz Praxis? My name is Kevin Lowe, and I'm a marketing vice president with Intelligeneering Systems Inc. I got your private number from the operators at Praxis Engineering—"

"Uh-huh? Right, Mr. Lowe. You need to know that I'm no longer with that company and not in a position to recommend your services." She had her fingertip poised to press "end."

"I understand that, ma'am," he said quickly. "They told me you'd left. But I'm following up on a call you made two weeks ago to our technical support line. The subject matter was unusual enough that they referred it to my attention."

"Oh? Yes … 'Mr. Andy.' "

"Yes. I've listened to the recording. This is not something we reveal in a routine service call, you understand. But as you are—or were—an officer of the company, our legal staff has asked me to contact you and tell you the information he gave out was not entirely accurate. It's in the fine print on your contract that, during installation and testing of any software package, we may from time to time interrupt the various databases for the purposes of seeding sample data. And then, of course, we delete it. Such additions and deletions are not recorded in the system access files, for obvious reasons."

"Name one."

"Excuse me?"

"Tell me an obvious reason for not recording a transaction," she said.

"Well, during testing, we're not making actual accounting entries, nothing that would show up on your company's books. So we don't want to clutter your system with meaningless data."

"And when you're finished with the installation, you—how do you say—remove that access? Close those back doors?"

"Yes, that would be customary."

" 'Customary'?" she said. "Don't you have a *rule* about it?"

"You must understand, Miz Praxis. Every installation is a major undertaking and a lot more complicated than you can imagine—"

"I can imagine quite a bit."

"Sometimes, when our engineers know they may have to return for additional troubleshooting, they leave these access points in place. It's a precaution we take for your benefit, actually."

"Does anyone in Praxis Engineering know about this unsanctioned access?" she asked. A picture was beginning to form in her mind.

"We don't make it widely known, for obvious reasons. But as I said, it's noted in the contract. And we make a practice of informing the most senior executives in the financial end of the business."

"But would anyone inside Praxis Engineering have that access?" she pressed. "Would they know how to *use* the back door?"

"Oh, I doubt it!" Lowe said, almost but not quite laughing. "The coding is very subtle and requires a piece of software with the right keys. Your average senior executive would be lost, really. And your information technology staff should know better than to try poking around."

"I see," Callie replied. She remembered that Richard had been a math wizard as a child. He had cried for his first computer, an old S-100 hobby system running CP/M, at age eleven, and a year later he was making it do tricks that weren't even in the manuals by coding at what he called "binary level." The rest of the family thought it was adorable that he thought he could actually make sense of all those paired zeroes and ones glowing in green on the monitor screen.

Of course, there was nothing she could do about his implied treachery now. The paperwork for her removal was all signed. The Coup—as her father called it—had already taken place. The company was effectively broken and launched on a glide path to destruction. And no amount of angry accusations, techno-babble, and hate-filled he-said-she-saids could ever put it back together.

"Thank you for your call, sir," she told the man on the phone. "You've answered my original question."

"I'm glad we could oblige, ma'am."

And then she did press "end."

―――

Antigone Wells understood that John Praxis owned a house in Sea Cliff, but she had never seen it. When he asked her to come out one evening and gave her the address, she didn't know what to expect.

He met her himself at the front door, took her through into the study, and sat her down at his eighteenth-century desk, taking one of the chairs in front for himself. On the green leather blotter was an envelope in heavy, cream-colored vellum.

"What is this, John?" she asked.

"My revocable living trust and a durable power of attorney."

"I see." Wells had kept in touch with Jeanne Hale, who was now the full-time caregiver for Praxis's wife. Without violating a confidence, Jeanne had let her know that the woman was failing fast. "You want to change the terms, I guess, in case your wife … does not survive you?"

His gaze held steady. "No, the succession is fairly clear and covers a number of contingencies. I want it changed now so that my daughter Callie becomes trustee, chief inheritor, and agent on my behalf."

"Oh!" Jeanne had also mentioned some kind of upheaval at the engineering company, after Callista's forced withdrawal. The daughter had moved into the family home full time, John himself was spending most days at home, and the entire household had suddenly gone tense and quiet, except for the fitfully dreaming Adele. Using admirable discretion, Jeanne had only discussed her sense of foreboding, not any juicy tidbits she might have picked up from overheard conversations.

"You can pretty much make that change with a word processor and a notary public," Wells said now. "You don't need an attorney for that."

"Let's just say I'm cautious. I want this ironclad and unbreakable."

"I understand." She opened the envelope, unfolded the documents and began scanning them.

"My sons can be very persuasive," he went on. "And they will have a lot of power at their backs. I want to be sure any attempt they make to overturn this gets stopped dead in its tracks." His voice was calm enough, but under the surface she could sense a suppressed rage.

"I understand." A thought occurred to her. "What about Adele's will? If it follows the pattern here—with your eldest son as trustee, followed by your other son, and only after him your daughter—and Adele should outlive you …"

"It don't think that's a reasonable possibility."

Wells nodded. She turned a page and was studying the list of assets. Praxis was a wealthy man, she found, even by the standards of Sea Cliff.

"One other thing is that list," he said. "Right now, it's all tied up with shares in Praxis Engineering. I will soon be surrendering those outright. So we'll need to show cash or some other liquid asset. I'm not sure what I'll convert the shares to right now. Times are so unsettled. This has to be a work in progress."

"Don't worry. I'll help you get started, John," she said. "But I may not see it through. We're dissolving the practice, Ted and I, and I may not be in town much longer. I'll handle the trusteeship and inheritance issues right away, of course. But you may need to find someone else to work on the assets. I know two good attorneys, former associates of mine, who can do that for you. And you will want to stop my retainer as of the end of the month."

"Oh?" It was his turn to look puzzled. "I didn't realize you had … troubles."

"Not trouble. But it feels like all the air's gone out of the room."

"I know what you mean. Like we're all on short time."

She gathered the documents. "We'll survive."

He took her hand. "I sure hope we do."

―――

Praxis entered in and ran the San Francisco Marathon that June. Although the organizers offered a pair of back-to-back half-marathon courses, he decided to try for the full twenty-six miles, which meant climbing and descending elevation changes of two to three hundred feet at least five times. He sternly told himself to have no expectations. He would run until he was tired, then he would drop out, cool down, and go home.

He gave himself the longest possible estimated finish time, six hours, and received a bib with the number 80,679. He would be starting a full hour after the fastest runners, but still early—six-thirty on a Sunday morning. Toward the end of the race, around noon, he thought he might be stumbling over a course littered with dispensed water bottles and fallen bodies.

The starting point was the Ferry Building at the foot of Market Street. The course went around the waterfront on the Embarcadero, through Fisherman's Wharf, Marina Green, and Crissy Field. Then he was on familiar territory, up over the Golden Gate Bridge and back. From there he went down the western slope of the city, passing within three blocks of home, and across the Avenues. The course looped forward and back through Golden Gate Park, then proceeded east on Haight Street, crossed to 16th Street, down to the foot of Potrero Hill, and finally back along the Embarcadero to within a block of his office—his former office—on Steuart Street. It only felt like he was running half of the famous Forty-Nine Mile Drive around the city.

He did not push himself too hard, but he never let himself give up, either. He passed many younger, stronger people who sagged by the side of the road in defeat. For the last six miles his knees and ankles, shins and thigh muscles were throbbing, and he knew he would be hobbling around the house for a week. He wondered what it would cost, and how painful it would be, to have to have the doctors replace the joints where cartilage now rubbed against bone with implements of steel and ceramic, or maybe new bearing points grown from his stem cells. He was staggering and gasping and hating himself for the last mile.

But his heart felt fine, clocking a steady one hundred forty beats per minute.

He was a mess. He was a wreck. He was invincible.

———

Callie tried to spend at least an hour a day with her mother, to be there even if Adele wasn't always aware. On the good days, when her mother decided to dress, they would sit downstairs and watch daytime television or maybe go out into the garden when the sky was clear and the sun warmed the wrought-iron bench. On the bad days, Callie would sit by her bedside while Adele nodded and dozed.

Once, when Callie had first come home, her mother asked her for a drink. Callie had consulted with the caregiver, Jeanne, who pursed her lips and frowned. "She's not supposed to have it," the woman said. "But I can't see it makes a bit of difference now."

So Callie had mixed a tablespoon of bourbon in three fingers of soda and given it to her mother. Adele took it, gulped it down, grimaced, and burped from the bubbles. The "daily soother" became a morning ritual, until Adele forgot to ask, then forgot who Callie was, and finally forgot who she was herself. But still Callie sat beside her and held her thin, pale hand.

When her mother seemed capable of hearing, Callie helped Adele remember her life through the stories from Callie's childhood. She recalled the time Leonard tried to make a pet of a stray mongoose, when they were all living at the dam site in Ghana, and the animal bit him. She told about the time the family traveled to see the tidal bore, the "Silver Dragon," on the Quiantang River in China. She remembered the mountain lion that chased Callie and Richard up a tree when their father was renovating the missile site in Idaho, and how Adele shot the beast in the shoulder—her father always claimed it was through the heart—with a Winchester rifle. She remembered the time she and her brothers, who had been raised on four different contents and in six different cultures, finally went to Disneyland and simply goggled at Main Street, the Mississippi riverboat, and the Fantasyland castle—although Richard said he'd seen bigger ones in Germany.

Sometimes Adele smiled. More often she simply nodded or shrugged. Once she asked, "Was I there?" And Callie said, "You were the glue that held us together, Mom."

Lately, Adele simply slept. Fifteen hours a day. Then twenty.

Jeanne Hale took Callie and her father into the study one evening and said quietly, "There's only so much I can do. Soon she's going to need real medical support—the sort she can only get in a hospital or skilled nursing facility."

Her father nodded. "Can you help with arrangements?"

"Of course. I'll start making calls tomorrow."

"She won't like leaving the house."

"I doubt she'll know about it."

"A blessing, I guess."

———

Because the community center had no locker room for her to change in, Antigone Wells had vastly simplified her preparations and dress for going to and from class.

Instead of more complicated layers of underwear, she wore a simple pink nylon leotard under sweat pants and a fleece jacket, and slip-on sneakers without socks on her feet. Then, when she got to the ladies room—or even out in the corridor or in a corner of the exercise room—she could simply strip off the pants and jacket, shed the sneakers, and pull on her white cotton uniform *gi* trousers with their draw-string tie and the loose-fitting jacket that was closed only by the heavily stitched white *obi* belt around her hips. The leotard took care of any modesty issues as she bent and twisted during the workout. She had long ago stopped carrying a purse but instead put her house keys in one pants pocket, her money and cards in a billfold in the other. All she had to carry then was the *gi*, which she rolled into a compact bundle and tied with the belt.

That lack of encumbrance probably saved her life.

Wells was walking home after dark on Divisadero Street, and once again the streetlights were out. She could navigate only by the indirect light coming from the few open store fronts, lit porch lamps, upper-story windows, and the occasional sweep of headlights from passing cars. Otherwise she moved from shadow to shadow, and she could feel the tension rising in her neck and shoulder muscles.

She kept to the middle of the sidewalk and alternately scanned the dark spaces between buildings and the gaps between parked cars. Several times she paused on approaching the most densely shadowed areas. But each time she made it through alone and without incident.

Then her luck ran out. A figure in black detached itself from the side of a building and moved on a line to intercept her. "Hello, little lady!" said a cooing voice.

She didn't know whether to speed up or slow down, engage or turn and run away. They hadn't cover this kind of encounter in karate class, only the moves to make after a fight had actually started.

She was holding her *gi* folded and tied together by a loop of her *obi* belt. It formed a mass that hung about eight inches below her hand and glowed whitely in the darkness.

As the man came toward her, she swung it up hard, aiming for his face, the side of his head. He batted it away with a chuckle and kept on coming, his hands reaching out for her throat.

Her fists dropped below navel level.

She took a short step-slide toward him.

Fists jammed upward in a double head block.

When he stepped back, her rear leg came forward.

Toes arched, struck his groin, and whipped back faster.

As he doubled over, her hands came down in one-two chops.

She pushed him away, and he collapsed against the building wall.

She scooped up her *gi* and ran off down the street ... all the way home.

Wells didn't know if she had hurt the man, or whether the chops—which landed somewhere around his neck and upper back—had broken anything. If he was injured, or even dead, then she supposed she bore some legal responsibility. But she didn't care. She couldn't identify him, and it was a safe bet he couldn't identify her.

But at the back of her mind was the glowing thought: *How about that, Wonder Woman? This stuff really works!*

Leonard was in the chairman's suite on the thirty-eighth floor—finally, at last, his office by rights—when Richard called for an emergency meeting. Leonard agreed that his brother could come up, and when he did, Richard was carrying a sheaf of printouts full of numbers.

"What's all this?" Leonard asked.

"We're going to lose the bid on Hetch-Hetchy restoration."

"That's not been decided yet, so it's too early to say."

"We were third in line, and that's announced."

"So what's your point?" Leonard said.

"We've lost out on the Seattle flood control, the Beijing airport expansion, and the Stanford accelerator double loop. With Hetch-Hetchy gone, I started running our numbers in earnest." He spread his papers across Leonard's nice clean desktop. "Our backlog of projects is down to fifteen percent of where it stood a year ago. Not down *by* fifteen percent. Down *to* fifteen percent." He pointed at another sheet. "Top-line revenues are down to twenty-five percent of year-ago. That's old jobs being cancelled, including, most recently, the Mile High arts center, which they just took back and sent to our competition." He pushed the two pieces of paper together. "Old jobs going away. New jobs not coming in."

"I know things are tight," Leonard said.

"No!" His brother shook his head. "They were tight a year ago." He picked up a third sheet. "Now—we are not even covering expenses. Forget profits and dividends. Think core staff, office rentals, computer and telecommunications, taxes on this building, heavy equipment in the field, *people* in the field, even the cash in hand to buy the next brick and pour the next batch of concrete on projects where we're already committed. It all adds up to more than we can possibly collect. Ten percent, maybe twelve percent more."

"What do you want me to do?"

"Nothing—not unless you can pull a big fat lollipop out of your ass. Find us a sure-fire gigabuck contract, up-front loaded with one hundred percent profit."

"There's no need to be insulting."

"I'm trying to make a point, Len."

"All right, we're in trouble."

"No, we're already dead."

Leonard stared at him.

"Start proceedings with Burke today," his brother told him. "I'll try to get us twenty or thirty cents on the dollar for any assets that aren't already in hock. Then we'll have to cancel our current contracts and pay a slew of penalties. Hopefully, the one will just about balance out the other. We can close the doors next quarter, if not next month."

"But … this is a hundred-and-twenty-year-old company!"

"No, Leonard. It's a walking shell just bleeding money."

"You to have do something. You have to save it!"

"No, you shoot it and put it out of its misery."

―――

The final ceremony of the funeral was held at the Praxiteles family plot in Colma, with an open grave prepared and blanketed with bright green turf, right next to John Praxis's mother, Phoebe. The rosewood coffin sat suspended in a framework of gold-colored posts and rails.

On its left side stood Praxis and his daughter, along with various friends of the family, including Jeanne Hale, and senior staff from the company, including Ivy Blake. On the right side stood Leonard and Richard with their wives and the five children between them, including the eldest, Brandon. The boy, who had been released on compassionate leave to bury his grandmother, looked good in his dark-blue service uniform.

They stood in silence while the priest, Father Demetrios from Holy Trinity on Brotherhood Way—his father's church, not his own, not anymore—chanted the final Trisagion at the graveside: "Holy God, Holy Mighty, Holy Immortal, have mercy on us," and repeated it twice more.

In addition to the traditional service with its hymns and psalms back at the church, Callie had asked to give a eulogy. She recalled events from her mother's life, seen through the eyes of an adoring daughter, and told stories that even Praxis had forgotten. When he glanced sideways to where his sons were standing, he saw Leonard blotting his eyes with a handkerchief and Richard nodding his head in remembrance, while their children stood transfixed, solemn as owls, at the thought of their grandmother shooting a lion.

Now, facing his boys across his wife's casket as it sank into the ground, he saw only stern frowns and, when they would meet his gaze, hard eyes. He knew they blamed him and Callie for the failure of the company. But the collapse of the dollar and the economy it sustained had already done that. By cashing out his shares, and his daughter taking hers, they might have hastened that end by one or two quarters, but no more. And in doing so they had preserved at least part of a great family fortune that would ultimately have evaporated in claims, lawsuits, and debt service. At least some in the family were now whole.

When the ceremony was complete, Praxis nodded to his sons, their wives, and his grandchildren, not knowing when he would see any of them again. Callie took his arm, holding it between both hands. Whether his daughter was intending to support him, or his arm was giving her strength, he could not say. Together they walked back to the limousine, sealed themselves inside, and told the hired driver to take them home by way of Highway 280 and 19th Avenue. They sat side by side and did not speak another word.

———

Because he stood six-foot-four, the problem Brandon Praxis always had with airline seats was the short knee room. Now, however, he also found that his side arm and holster didn't fit between his hip and the armrest, and he had to tug the weapon around on his web belt until it was covering his stomach and groin before he could even find, let alone fasten, his seat belt.

The other thing was that his Kevlar PASGT helmet clunked on the low ceiling every time he stood up, and it caught on the seat back when he was sitting down, but Captain Ramsay had ordered all helmets secured on heads for the entire flight. They couldn't stow them in the overhead bins, because those were jammed with each soldier's field pack, M4 carbine, and other equipment that had to be ready to hand and couldn't ride in the baggage hold. Nobody wanted those rifles loaded and rattling around in the pressurized cabin during the flight, so they went up into the bins with their magazines detached and safeties engaged. "Each man check your teammates on this," Ramsay had warned.

Two days earlier, his Bravo Company of the newly formed 1/22nd Combat Infantry Group, California Army National Guard, had been mustered out of Fort Hunter Liggett, boarded a fleet of gray-painted school buses, and transferred to Travis Air Force Base, just outside of Fairfield, California. They bivouacked in temporary lodgings—essentially a two-star hotel on base called the Westwind Inn—but were told not to get too comfortable. This morning before dawn they were bussed out to the flight line and boarded an American Airlines 787—one of seven that were sitting on the pavement nose to tail. Unlike a civilian airport, they boarded by climbing a mobile ramp rather than walking down a jetway.

As an officer and platoon leader, Brandon had attended a briefing the evening before with about fifty other young men. The officer giving it was a two-star general of the regular army named Beemis. So now Brandon was in a position to know what was going on—even if he didn't quite believe it.

Supposedly, all flights throughout the country, in the Federated Republic as well as the old United States, were still coordinated by air traffic controllers who reported up to the Federal Aviation Administration—an arm of the old government. Apparently, the newly seceded country had not had time to appoint all of its own centralized services and their supporting bureaucracy. Working with the Pentagon, on the following morning the FAA was going to quietly divert traffic and clear the air space over Kansas City. Just about the time Bravo Company and other units of the California Army National Guard were going wheels up, teams of rangers with the elite U.S. Army Special Operations Command would be parachuting into the city from high altitude.

One detachment would land at Kansas City International Airport and secure the tower and field. Others would take over police, fire, and other municipal services. A large detachment, made up of men with former transit experience, would take over the Metro bus yards and commandeer their rolling stock. The SOC headquarters unit would land and secure the city's Municipal Auditorium, which was the temporary meeting place of the F.R. Congress. Then the California Army National Guard would land without incident, offload onto the Metro buses, and deploy into the city. By noon, the capital of the Federated Republic would be in the hands of the legitimate federal government.

Similar strikes were being coordinated at key cities throughout the region. At the same time, convoys of light armor and mechanized infantry were starting on the ground from bases on the East and West Coasts to penetrate the heartland and secure military facilities. U.S. Air Force fighter and attack squadrons were going to overfly the air bases in the secessionists' hands and make sure retaliation strikes never left the ground.

After the briefing, Brandon had given his platoon leaders details of their assignments.

"We're not going to dock at the jetways or anything like that," he said. "When the plane stops rolling, we open the doors and drop the slides. Everyone goes down feet first, on your butt, with your weapon at port arms. Pick yourself up and get out of the way for the next guy. Right?"

"Yes, sir!" the men chorused.

"Then look for white buses with blue and teal stripes."

A hand went up. "Teal, sir?"

"It's a kind of blue-green."

"What if I'm color-blind?"

"Then follow someone who isn't," Brandon snapped. "The buses will cluster at the planes, and Captain Ramsay will give the drivers our assignment. So you just get on the nearest bus and find a seat. Got that?"

"Yes, sir."

So on that next morning he was sitting hunched over in this too-narrow seat as the Boeing 787 trundled down to the end of the runway, made its final turn, briefly locked its brakes, ran up its engines, and rolled smoothly forward for takeoff. As the acceleration increased and the expansion joints in the concrete thumped faster and faster under the wheels, the grip of his pistol pressed against the armrest, causing the muzzle to dig into his thighs. The rear lip of his helmet snagged on the top of his seat back and pushed the visor down over his eyes.

What a ridiculous way to fly into the history books, he thought. But how historic this moment actually was, he did not know. If everything worked out the way General Beemis had described at the briefing last night, they would execute a flawless first strike, paralyze the enemy, and finish up this silly civil war by Friday. Then it would just be a minor incident pursuant to a political misunderstanding—not much different from the National Guard getting called in to stop an urban riot.

A flight halfway across the country would take two or three hours at least. If this had been a commercial trip, Brandon would have powered up his smartphone, logged onto the plane's complimentary WIFI service, and done some surfing, or traded texts with friends, or read one of his ebooks. But once again, the operation was under radio silence and all cell phones were ordered turned off under penalty of six months in the stockade and a bad conduct discharge. He checked the pocket of the seat in front of him, but someone had thoughtfully removed the in-flight magazines. With nothing else to do, he pulled the helmet further forward over his eyes and tried to sleep.

He woke up as soon as the engines changed to a lower pitch and a definite lightness under his butt told him they were descending. Brandon prepared himself to execute his own special set of orders. Throughout the plane, he knew, other second lieutenants were getting ready for similar tasks.

As soon as the plane's tires touched the runway and the jets went to reverse thrust, he unbuckled and stood up—letting the hard deceleration pull him forward out of the seat—and clunked his helmet once again on the underside of the overhead. He stepped sideways into the aisle, ran through first class, and prepared to unlatch the forward starboard-side door. Through the oblong view port next to the opening mechanism, he watched patches of grass punctuated by numbered taxiways flow by the fuselage and disappear under the wing. He saw the terminal complex and its central control tower go by, and still the plane continued at brisk taxiing speed. They passed the last of the great circular concourses lined with jetways and kept on going. The plane made a hard right-hand turn at speed and proceeded down another set of runways. The seconds ticked by as if they were minutes. Something about this long parade around the airport didn't feel right.

Finally the plane began braking—a weird, hollow wailing that came up from beneath his feet—and slowed almost to a stop. Brandon looked out the port again, trying to identify where in hell they were. Nothing but open field and green grass. Not a bus in sight. Not white with blue and teal or any other color.

He swung the door's locking bar over and threw his weight against it. The plane was still rolling, but suddenly its smooth forward motion changed to a sideways lurch and wiggle. The wailing of brakes became the harsh grinding of bare wheel rims on concrete. Somehow the plane had blown all ten of its tires at once. Brandon hung onto the locking bar and managed to stay upright as the fuselage jerked to a stop.

He pushed hard on the door, and the articulated arm carried it out and away.

A bullet spanged off the doorframe, missing his head by inches.

"Son of a bitch!" he shouted, dropping to the carpeted deck. He'd caught the muzzle flash out of the corner of his eye. Over in the tall grass, thirty yards northeast of the plane. He drew his M9 and returned three spaced shots. A pair of combat boots stopped on the carpet beside his head.

"What is it, son?" Ramsay asked.

"We're under fire, sir!"

"Son of a bitch!"

"Yes, sir!"

Ramsay turned and called for the men with light machine guns to set up firing positions on either side of all the cabin exits. Then he told Brandon to pop the inflatable slide. The captain handed him an M4. "Go fast, son!"

"You're kidding me, sir!"

"Make a streak, Lieutenant! You're holding up the line!"

Brandon tapped the carbine's magazine as he'd been trained, pulled the charging handle to chamber a round, held the weapon across his body, and launched himself, feet first and butt down, onto the yellow rubberized cloth. Above his head, the machine guns roared. He could only hope that the people in the weeds now had their heads down or, if they didn't, then at least that they might not know how to lead a moving target. When he hit the end of the ramp he had to jump to his feet, and his momentum carried him forward into a hard roll across the concrete. There he flattened himself out and started firing short, controlled bursts, just like on the range.

At the same time, the odd thought floated up into his mind: *Whatever this is, it isn't going to be over by Friday.*

Part 3 – 2028: Plumbing Work

1. In the Ninth Year of War

JOHN PRAXIS WAS building a brick wall. He was doing a favor for a neighbor, Nora Graham, who lived three doors down from the small house he had bought for himself on Balboa Street in the Richmond District. It was the closest he could get to his old home in Sea Cliff, which he had been forced to sell years ago.

Nora wanted to build a series of low walls at the back of her lot to divide the vegetable patch and the flower garden and both of them from the compost heap. But the cost of a city-licensed contractor was beyond her means. So she had talked it over with Praxis, who had become the neighborhood handyman, and he drew some plans, roughed out the job, and told her how many used bricks to buy and at what price from the local scavenger, or more politely, "unlicensed urban recycler." That had been a month ago, and since then Nora had set her two boys to sorting the bricks and chipping off old mortar after school. The weekend before, Praxis had dug trenches according to his plan and poured the concrete footings.

This morning he had mixed the grout—a trough of fine portland cement, this one prepared without aggregate—and now he was troweling it carefully onto each layer of bricks, working along two or three bricks at time, putting just the right amount of cement on the butted ends and using a string stretched between two stakes to keep them in a straight line. When each couple of bricks were set and tapped down with the heel of his trowel, he used the edge like a knife to cut away the excess grout that oozed out and slung it back into the trough. Then he used his bare finger to smooth the gap into a nicely finished curve. It was patient, methodical work of the kind he had come to enjoy.

The two boys, Tommy and Joey, ages eleven and nine, watched with fascination. They helped by bringing him bricks from the pile and adding measured amounts of water, sand, and cement powder to the trough whenever it went low.

"This one's broken," Joey said, holding up half a brick.

"Nuts," Praxis said. He took the brick and studied its broken end, which was nearly perpendicular and could easily enough be made to fit. It would stagger the line, of course. He looked at the diminished pile, spotted more broken bricks, and knew it would be a near thing to finish all the wall with what he had there.

"We'll use it anyway," he said.

"It'll mess up the pattern," Tommy objected, pointing to the neatly spaced bricks in the existing layers.

"Naw, it will give your wall character," he said. "Besides, you don't want to trap a devil inside the wall, do you?"

"What?" the older boy said.

"Sure," Praxis said, "all great artists leave a little flaw, a break in any regular pattern, so the devil can find his way out of it. The ancient Navajos did it all the time with their sand paintings, leave a little nick in one line, so as not to trap spirits in a perfect design. I think the word 'glitch' even comes from the Navajo language."

"You're just making that up!"

Praxis turned to the younger boy, whose face was clouding up with this talk of devils and spirits. "I'm sure glad you found that brick, Joe. It kept us from making a terrible mistake."

The little boy tried to smile.

"Now be sure to find me another one like it real soon," Praxis said, "so we can come out even at the end of the line."

"Would've been better if my mom had bought new bricks," Tommy said.

"Well, you know," Praxis replied, "we can't have everything we want."

He finished the long wall between the vegetable and flower gardens and started the shorter one around the compost pit. He laid three bricks on the first course, straightened up to reach for the next one from Tommy's hands, and felt the world go gray.

Praxis stood there, feet rocking gently in the loose soil, holding himself upright by muscle tension alone and not by any act of his own will. The trowel slipped from his fingers and fell a long way to earth, a distant thump. He stared into the golden sparkles that lit up just behind his eyes and knew that if God was going to take him, now was the time. And that was all right, too …

After a moment the dizziness passed. He walked over to the wall he had just finished and sat down, and be damned to what his weight might do to the still-wet grout.

"You okay, sir?" The two boys were staring at him with fear in their eyes.

"Sure," he said. "I just get a bit dizzy sometimes. It passes."

The little fits, due to low blood pressure, were coming more regularly now. And some days he felt just … tired. No energy. No pep. He wasn't eating as much as he once did, either, and these days he was not much interested in food. He had been thin since he took up running after his heart implant, but now he was getting downright scrawny. He still tried to run at least a couple of times a week, but his distances were getting shorter and his breath giving out faster. It had been months since he had gone as far as five kilometers at one time, and that on level ground. A marathon was out of the question—not that any city in his part of the country had the money to stage those anymore, not even a Fun Run 10K for a good cause.

Hell, he was just getting old. He would turn seventy-five this year. His heart was still going strong, but the connective tissue seemed to be giving way. It was called life. Old age happened to everybody.

He stood up, looking back to make sure the wall hadn't gone swaybacked under him. He looked over at the pile of remaining bricks, the trough full of grout.

"That's enough for today, boys. We'll finish up next weekend."

"Aww!" Joey said and made a face. His brother punched him.

"You know where to dump that?" He pointed at the trough. "And how to clean it out without killing the grass?"

"Yes, sir," Tommy said.

"Good then. Next week."

"I told the damn thing both mares was due for foaling, and it would take about six months," Edward Hopper said. "Still the dummy went ahead and ordered oats and hay like usual, vet service like usual, shoeing like usual, stabling and grooming—"

" 'Like usual'?" Antigone Wells supplied, with a smile.

"Yes, ma'am. You'd think a computer could add and subtract. Two horses minus two horses means how many horses do I got to feed? Quick now!"

"You told your system the horses would be foaled?"

"Yes, ma'am." Hopper had now quieted down some.

"Did you say *where?* I mean, they'd be moved out of your stables?"

"Well, it *had* the waybills, transport fees, and insurance."

"And is that on the same account?" Wells asked.

"As which?" Hopper's eyebrows knitted.

"As the one that maintains your mares."

"Well, no, transportation's different."

"What app are you using?" she asked.

"Farmer John two-point-something."

"Yeah." Wells didn't even have to check with her tech specialist. "That's an older model. They don't cross-link."

"I thought these robots were supposed to be smart."

"Well, some are true intelligences, and some just clever programming."

"Anyhow, it finally cancelled all the orders," Hopper said, "but the feed store won't take back and restock without a charge, the vet and stable will only add months to my account, and the blacksmith had already spent my payment."

"So what do you want me to do?" she asked.

"Cancel 'em properly. Get my money back."

Hopper was an old man—older than Wells herself. Over the years she had learned the peculiarities of computers in order to stay current in the legal business. It had taken time and patience, but the brainwork seemed to keep her young. Hopper was just that much older and probably thought he could simply install a piece of software on his smartphone and let it run a part-time stock-raising and stud business spread over four farms and six private stables in three different counties.

"You know," she said, "that software comes with disclaimers."

"Lawyer stuff." He shrugged. "Didn't read 'em."

"Of course. Still, this matter has been tried in court—all the way to the High Court here in the Republic and the Supreme Court back in the States, parallel rulings. A properly installed intelligence system has *de jure* as well as *de facto* power of attorney. It's like you bought those things yourself. That's the only way the Integrated Commerce System can work."

"But I didn't *want* 'em."

"That's as may be. You got 'em."

"Well, this has been a complete waste of my time." He paused. "You ain't gonna bill me, are you, seeing as you can't help me?"

She squinted at him. "Just because your horse is feeling horny, do you give your stud away for free?"

"What's that got to do with—?"

"My 'bot will talk to your 'bot."

Hopper jammed his hat on his head.

"Good day to you … young lady."

"Nice try—but you still owe me."

In the last nine years, Antigone Wells had also had to learn the ways of country people, which was "a fur piece" from her former law practice in San Francisco. She had gone to Oklahoma to visit her sister Helen, got caught on the wrong side of a shooting war, and been interned as an enemy alien. She spent six weeks on a cot in detention at the National Guard

Armory in Shawnee until the paperwork could be cleared to release her into Helen's custody.

"I'll bet you're loving this," she told her younger sister.

"Shut up and get in the car ... *war criminal*."

As an essentially stateless person, because the borders were closed to both the East and West Coasts, Wells lived for six more months under house arrest, then applied for citizenship in the new Federated Republic. Two years after that, including a year at the Oklahoma University College of Law, catching up on the New Constitution and all the reformulated precedents, she passed the bar and set up Wells & Wells, LLC in Oklahoma City. She didn't actually have another "Wells" in the firm, because Helen's married name had been Carter and she just helped out in the office, but it looked more stable and professional. If asked, Antigone Wells said it was a "me, myself, and I" kind of partnership.

Over the years she had come to specialize in what she called "human-cyber relations." Amazingly, the course of the war—complete with military raids, economic sanctions, occasional civilian rationing (worse in the States than in the Republic), and crushing public and personal debt (again, worse over there than here, but not so good here nowadays)—had not at all affected the march of twenty-first-century technology. Next generations of smartphones and watches, neurostims and biolinks, across the spectrum of hardware, software, and squishware, still appeared at the end of every summer and at the midwinter geek shows. All of it had vastly improved human communications and data management. And every year the devices grew smaller, faster, smarter, more intuitive, and more seamlessly connected to the human body and fringes of the nervous system, not to mention integrating people's social relationships, commerce, banking, medicine, and government services.

Perhaps all that technological growth was actually a function of the war. An assassination drone could now be made the size of a sparrow, find your street address in GPS coordinates from two hundred miles away, and pack the explosive power of ten pounds of Semtex. A spy drone could be made the size of a bumblebee, travel a ten-mile radius through wind and rain, transmit over more than twenty miles, and still hear in broadwave, see in plex-pix, and fake a retina scan. So why shouldn't the labs sell their goodies from three generations back onto the commercial market?

Wells might not be able to get a cup of real Sumatra coffee through the U.S. blockade on the Gulf Coast. Yet she could wear an agent on her wrist which scheduled her days, ordered her lunch, did the grocery shopping, and contracted to get her car fixed. She could wear eyeglasses—well, *faux* lenses in her case—that with a blink recorded everything she saw and read, received her emails, and communicated with her wrist to help it plan her social life. She could wear earrings that let her pick up conversations across a crowded room just by turning her head and triangulating. And all this stuff was voice activated, touch sensitive, and had the good sense to go dead the minute the physical device determined itself to be lost or stolen. Her wrist companion also kept track of her vital signs and, should they ever stop or change beyond certain limits, it would signal her current location and medical history to the nearest medical facility. If she felt threatened, she could whisper a code word to summon the police—her current panic word was "Shazam!"—not that she ever felt *that* threatened.

Antigone Wells—and every other adult she knew—walked through a virtual world that was webbed in various dimensions and at various wavelengths with personal contacts, social obligations, commercial and medical support, and information and entertainment resources. To be a citizen in the Federated Republic was to be a *wired* citizen. It meant she was never alone, unless she chose to be. And whatever she might consciously have surrendered of her privacy, she had won back many times over in terms of convenience, speed, and connection.

———

Business used to be personal, John Praxis kept telling himself, like some kind of old man's mantra. Time was, running a business either as a buyer or seller was all about relationships, about finding people he could trust, people who offered good service at fair prices, who could expedite and solve problems, who could make things happen and tell a joke along the way. Over the years Praxis had become accustomed to the business phone tree having replaced a live human person at a switchboard. He had even come to accept that most branches of that tree would take him to automated responses, where he had to speak slowly, annunciate clearly, and repeat himself until the machine stopped saying, "I'm sorry, I didn't get that …" Sooner or later he would press zero and be talking to a person again.

But five times in the past two weeks, when he dialed one of his suppliers he got neither a person nor a tree but a disembodied female voice: "Your call is being transferred to our automated ordering system." And after that, rather than more robots painfully working on their language recognition skills, he got the high-frequency buzz of machine talk, an earful of static, one machine trying to communicate bits and bytes to what it supposed was another but was actually a live human person, Praxis himself.

This time he was trying to order flapper valves from *etoilets.com*. He just hung up. And that wasn't getting the work done.

Praxis was a corporate buyer for PlumbKit, the West Coast branch of a plumbing services center representing "23,000 independent contractors nationwide"—or at least that part of the nation represented by two separated coasts. His job was to maintain a virtual warehouse that provided just-in-time delivery of everything from copper pipe to septic tanks and whatever came in between: faucets, valves, sinks, toilet bowls, urinals, shower stalls, and sidelines in the new electrostatic precipitation systems and composting closets that used no water at all.

Once he had been personally responsible for building huge dams and power plants, freeway and transit systems, commercial and residential skyscrapers, and mechanized facilities covering acres of land that designed and built automobiles, airplanes, and all the other necessities of modern life. Those were the new turnkey factories, which took raw materials and commoditized components like screws and ball bearings in at one loading dock and spit out finished goods in your choice of model, features, and colors at the other. But in the ninth long year of war between the United States of America and the upstart Federated Republic of America, nobody wanted that kind of infrastructure anymore. Correction: everybody wanted and needed it badly, but nobody had the money to pay for it.

But, so far, and as bad as things got, everybody still needed a toilet that flushed or did whatever the local ordinances allowed. So John Praxis had gone where he could be useful … at least until this morning.

Bernie Gutierrez, head of Praxis's department, stopped by his desk. "How's it going?"

"I just got another carrier signal. Sounded like an old modem."

"Like a what?" The younger man looked blank.

"Or dialing into a fax machine."

"That's okay, John."

Gutierrez was somewhere in his thirties. Praxis suddenly realized he was talking about technology that had been dead before this man's childhood. He could read *silly old geezer* in Bernie's facial expression.

"Anyway …" Gutierrez lifted his head above the angular partition that separated Praxis's section of desktop from the buyer next to him in line. "People?" he said, raising his voice. "Meet in the conference room in five minutes? Let's go team!" And he actually clapped like a cheerleader.

On all sides people broke off conversations, shed headsets, and stood up. Praxis followed them down the hall. When they were all seated around the table, Gutierrez stood up and applauded them.

"I want to tell you personally what a fine team you have been. We could not have achieved our success without each and every one of you."

Around Praxis people exchanged nervous glances. *Business used to be honest, too,* he thought.

"However," Gutierrez went on, "word has come down from Corporate in Philadelphia. In two weeks we will be rolling out OSMA—the Order and Stock Management Analyst." Praxis could hear his voice emphasizing the capitals. The man sounded positively giddy. As if he didn't know that without a team of buyers, Gutierrez himself would have nothing to supervise. The supervision of his own department would become an Information Technology function.

"We will be keeping a number of you on board for the transition period. Your job will be to teach OSMA everything you know. For the rest, you'll be getting severance packages with extended benefits commensurate with your years of service." Which would average about six weeks, Praxis knew, because PlumbKit believed in new blood and promoted rapid staff turnover.

"So everyone keep up the good work during these exciting times."

It was a dismissal, and the team took it as such. They filed out of the room to go back to their desk sections and headsets. All but Praxis, whom Gutierrez took aside.

"You know, John, there's a company policy on overage employees."

"I didn't know that," Praxis said. "What's the policy?"

"Since you're already hooked into Social Security and Medicare, the company automatically waives your severance and extended benefits."

"Oh," he said. "I see."

In fact, although he had paid the maximum amount into the federal Social Security system all of his life, Praxis never actually applied for benefits when he became eligible at sixty-two, or any year after that. He had never told Gutierrez nor anyone else at PlumbKit how, once upon a time, he had been an extremely wealthy man. Once, he could have bought their little plumbing supply business—all the franchises, on both coasts—with just pocket money from a month of his average income.

Praxis had salvaged as much as possible from the wreckage of a family business that had taken four generations to build and a single year of economic chaos to destroy. He had tried to manage wisely the wealth that remained to him, investing it in the stocks and bonds of companies which made necessary goods and offered necessary services like food, housing, clothing, and military supplies. He invested in productive land that bore good harvests and supported people. And when the government had appropriated those enterprises for technical violations of its ever more complex regulations—basically, for the good of society—Praxis had shown better sense than to try and fight those actions. And he still had resources, held in bank accounts and other assets, that amounted to many millions, for the family fortune had been huge before it went mostly away. Those resources were meant to provide for his old age and for the future of his children and grandchildren.

Still, the government in his half of the country yearned to redistribute such wealth. It had long ago found a way to tax literally everything that moved, throve, and made a profit. But the federal government had no history, no legislative provision, allowing it to simply expropriate private property without a public reason and suitable compensation under eminent domain. Bank accounts, assets held in trust, and private capital were still protected by the "takings clause" of the Fifth Amendment. So, much as the government needed Praxis's money and that of other wealthy men to survive, it could not just appropriate it. Besides, that looked bad. It left a sour taste in the mouths of citizens who still placed sentimental value on notions of "freedom" and "independence."

But the U.S. could offer Praxis and others like him the deal of a lifetime. In the fourth year of the war, under the pretext of a public emergency, the federal government held a sale of national assets. Monuments, national parks, reclamation areas, disused military reservations, and other public property held in trust for the people were all put on the block. The deal was that men like Praxis would donate their unattached wealth to support these public treasures, thereby freeing the government to win the war. In return, the man who accepted the deal was granted a one-time, nontransferable right to acquire the asset at the end of a specified time—usually thirty-five years—unless the government had repaid its obligation in full before then. In the meantime, the asset would continue as public property, and the grantee agreed to support it as a public service.

The deal that was offered to John Praxis involved the Stanislaus National Forest. It comprised almost 900,000 acres centered on the Stanislaus River in the Sierra Nevada, just north of Yosemite National Park. Out of curiosity, Praxis had asked about acquiring Yosemite itself, but it had already gone to a branch of the Buffett family. Still, the Stanislaus was a prize worth far more than the amount Praxis would pay for it. The value of the timber rights was a prime consideration, even after a third of the acreage had been burned over and virtually destroyed in the Rim Fire a decade earlier. That land would not be worthwhile as forest for another generation or more. But the mining prospects—for gold had once been found there, and much was still believed to be locked in the granite bedrock—would compensate him richly, not to mention the land's worth when developed for housing and resorts. All of this value was prospective, of course, as he could not touch it for another thirty years yet.

It was a cunning wager to dangle before a man who had just turned seventy. He would, in all probability—given the advances of modern medicine and the care he was taking with his body since the heart replacement—live to somewhat beyond one hundred and five. And then title to the land would be his, unless the government chose to pay him off and reclaim it first. He could hope to live long enough after that to secure possession and develop its riches for his family and heirs.

It was an attractive deal, despite the numerous downsides. First, and most obviously, he might succumb to accident or illness in the intervening years. Second, because his pre-contract income and assets had by now indexed him out of the Social Security system, he would remain ineligible for the term of the Stanislaus National Forest contract. Third, and finally, the bulk of his remaining assets was pledged to the annual expenses of maintaining the land, which included advancing the reforestation effort, repairing fire roads and trails, clearing brush season by season, dredging silt-clogged lakes, and paying the salaries and administrative costs of on-site foresters, park rangers, and firefighters.

The remainder left him just enough to live on, if he watched his pennies, same as everyone else. But because he liked to keep busy, he had taken the job at PlumbKit as a "supernumerary worker."

"Sure, Bernie," Praxis said with a shrug. "The government's taking good care of me."

———

On Monday and Thursday nights, Antigone Wells drove to the First Presbyterian Church in the central part of Oklahoma City. It offered a big fellowship hall in the basement, and at six o'clock the brown and black belts went in to move chairs and tables up against the wall and mop the grime of foot traffic off the linoleum floor. They also brought out and hung an oil painting that one of the students had made of the *Megami*, the Goddess of Isshinryu: a beautiful Asian woman in a black leotard rising from the sea, her right hand raised in a fist to strike and her left held low to offer peace and protection; a dragon flew in the sky above her head and another swam in the sea around her waist. It was all based on a dream that had come to Master Tatsuo Shimabuku, the style's founder. The Presbyterian church fathers agreed to regard this painting as a cultural icon, and the Oklahoma Okinawan Martial Arts Association agreed to call her the "spirit of karate."

Once the chores were done, Wells changed in the ladies room. She still wore what had become her trademark pink leotard under the white *gi*. But now, in addition to the uniform, she carried to and from class a collapsible *bo* staff made of black fiberglass, which screwed together in the middle like a pool cue, and a pair of stainless steel short swords called *sai*, whose handles were wrapped in purple cord. After almost ten years of training she had learned all the forms associated with the style, including the weapons *kata*s, and had achieved the rank of third degree black belt through testing with *Sensei* Peter Greenwood up in Kansas City.

At seven o'clock sharp, Wells stepped barefoot onto the *dojo* floor, performed the traditional bow to honor the teaching space, looked around to make sure she was still the ranking belt for the evening, and shouted *"Hajime!"* to call the students to order.

The ninety-minute class took the usual form: half an hour of basic exercises as a group, half an hour of individual technique with the students lined up facing each other, and half an hour devoted to various forms of advanced instruction.

During the basics, led by a budding green belt, Wells walked around and corrected the students one by one: angle of a foot here, alignment of an elbow there. During the technique session, she usually worked with one student each night trading punches and blocks, holds and breaks. And during the advanced session she divided her time between teaching a *kata* to one or more students and a small group doing *kumite,* or sparring.

This evening she was sparring with a white belt, a young man named Brian, a college student not yet twenty who stood a head and a half taller than Wells. He was all elbows and knees, with puppy-dog hands and feet. He was nervous, and it obviously bothered him to trade blows with a woman—especially one old enough to be his grandmother. Also, he couldn't keep his eyes where they belonged, which was over her shoulder, gazing passively past her body, using only his peripheral vision to detect and track her slightest movement. Mammals had developed that kind of seeing-but-not-looking to protect themselves out in the open. But this boy's eyes kept moving to the fold of her *gi* jacket, seeking a glimpse of the pink nylon across her chest.

The distraction made him slow and stupid. It was time to teach him a lesson. And a number of other students were standing in a polite circle, watching. All to the good.

She and Brian took their ready stances. She was in a sideways *seisan* with her right fist on guard at shoulder level, left fist held low in front of her groin. He was in a *seiunchin,* the straddle stance, with his hands hanging loosely somewhere near his chest. Again, he was looking down at her cleavage.

In one fluid motion, she opened her right fist, curled her fingers back, plucked at the lapel of her *gi,* and pulled it open, exposing a firm breast held taut by the nylon. His eyes went wide. At the same time she made a small step-slide, lifted her forward foot, cocked her hips, and kicked him lightly in the ribs. His mouth was still hanging open as she completed the move.

"Eyes above my clavicles, Brian," Wells said.

"Your *what,* ma'am?" he asked blankly.

For answer, she hop-stepped and planted the toes of her rear foot in his unprotected solar plexus, hitting him just hard enough to trigger a muscle spasm in his diaphragm. He gasped and sank to his knees.

The women in the circle shrieked with laughter.

"Ladies, help him to the sidelines, please." Wells straightened her jacket, then called out, "Next!"

After class, as she was changing into her street clothes back in the bathroom, Wells paused to use the toilet. When she stood up, she was horrified to see a dark red stain filling the bowl. She had only seen it once before, after she had been kicked in the kidneys during a sparring session some years ago. She had spent two days in the hospital then. But no one else had been quick enough to tag her kidneys—or get anywhere near them—in a long time.

She whispered her finding to her wrist agent. It consulted the bioproctor implanted in the wall of her abdomen, which reported a rise in C-reactive proteins, indicating an inflammation somewhere in her body. However, it reported negative for the kind of protein loss attributed to kidney disease.

"Shall I make an appointment with your doctor?" Wells's agent whispered into her ear.

"I guess you'd better," she said and finished dressing.

Three days after Francesco di Rienzi was killed in an automobile accident, the newspapers still hadn't reported it. That was odd, because he was reputedly a member of the Italian minor nobility and styled himself a *conte,* or count. And after four days the *Polizia di Stato* had yet to release either his body for burial or his mangled Ferrari for the insurance claims and ultimate disposal.

"The investigation is continuing," was all anyone would tell Callista di Rienzi when she called the police headquarters in Torino to inquire about her husband.

So the dry-eyed widow decided she had to appear at the station in person. She dressed appropriately in black, although perhaps with more style than the occasion required. Her suit was tailored in black satin with a fitted jacket and short, tight skirt. She also wore sheer black stockings and black leather pumps with three-inch stiletto heels. After nine years in the country, Callista di Rienzi knew how to be taken seriously by Italian men.

"Cesco was an excellent driver," she told the uniformed sergeant at the desk. "I can't believe he would be killed in an *incidente stradale,* a mere accident."

"That may well be," the man said. "Still …"

"Do you suspect something more? Perhaps foul play?"

"*Scusi, signora?*" he asked with a confused squint.

Callie was standing in an open hallway busy with people both uniformed and civilian. She could not know what ears might be listening. She raised her hands just above the edge of the rail that fronted his bench, left hand cradling an imaginary gun barrel, right hand around an imaginary stock, with forefinger pulling an imaginary trigger. "Eh-eh-eh?" she said softly at the back of her throat.

The sergeant's eyes widened. His lips compressed. And he shrugged.

That told her as much as she needed to know.

―――

The first email waiting in John Praxis's queue that evening was from the Janet Bormann, Secretary of the U.S. Department of Health and Human Services. It carried the notation "Personal and Confidential." It had the subject line "Happy Birthday, John Praxis."

When he opened the file, it blossomed into a computer-generated animation of friendly adult faces, appropriately weighted for gender and ethnicity but not for age. All of them were elderly. Although uniformly fit, lively, and smiling, all bore the marks of age in graying hair, double chins, and wrinkled skin. Behind them floated balloons and colored streamers. They were gathered around a cake decorated with a candles—not a bunch of separately burning sticks, as on most birthday cakes, but big, molded wax numerals with candy-red edging that spelled out "75." The flames had a weird sparkle, almost like the burning of Roman candles—or lit fuses.

After flickering just long enough for Praxis to take in the happy message, the animation dissolved into a formal document, using a calligraphic typeface, like a diploma or an official declaration. In so many words the document invited him to prepare for his upcoming "Environmental Sacrifice," reminded him of the benefits that would be made available to his children and grandchildren (if any), and directed him to a website with a helpful planning book and the addresses of convenient, local, and painless service providers. It was not an order. More like a suggestion.

In the creeping, soft-spell socialism that had settled over his half of the country, the government wanted no whiff of coercion. Unlike the books and movies that had informed his childhood notions of tyranny, from Koestler's *Darkness at Noon* and Orwell's *1984* to Bradbury's *Fahrenheit 451* and Burgess's *A Clockwork Orange*, the voice of authority came not with jackboots, peaked caps, and truncheons. Instead it presented its demands with smiles, party balloons, and gentle reminders. The architects of his society had studied and learned from Huxley's story of planetwide control through community, identity, stability ("I'm really awfully glad I'm a Beta …") in *Brave New World*.

Praxis had the right to refuse his Sacrifice, of course. But then, unfortunately, there would be penalties. For one thing, his medical status would automatically change to PTO—Pain Treatment Only—which meant that the cure for whatever ailed him would be a morphine drip. He would also forfeit those promised favors for his children and grandchildren. And he would embarrass himself with his friends and neighbors: he would show the world he did not know how to behave, how to be a good little *Romper Room* "Do Bee."

Eleven years ago the doctors had given him a new heart and the promise of a long and fruitful life. Now the health service that controlled many of those same doctors was inviting him to commit "ethical suicide"—the other, less grand word for it—so as not to become a burden on society.

"Ain't life precious?" he muttered and dragged the email notice into his trash folder.

Four days after Francesco di Rienzi was killed, his widow decided to do the unexpected and visit his uncle Matteo at the villa east of the river. She wore black, although not in any fashion to influence a man, because Matteo was family—however distantly and by reputation only. She took along her eight-year-old daughter Rafaella, because the girl liked to chase the cats in Matteo's garden. She was still dry-eyed.

The guard at the gate passed her through with a wave. Matteo himself was waiting for her on the front steps, with his son Carlo by his side. As she parked her Alfa Romeo and opened the door to release Rafaella into the garden, the old man came down to open Callie's own door for her and hand her out onto the gravel driveway.

"Contessa!" he said with a face full of sadness, holding onto her hand as if to support her in her sorrow. "*Mio cordoglio!* My condolences."

"Cut the crap," she said in a low voice. "Just this once, please."

"Of course, Callista." The man's face did not change. "Come inside."

As they crossed the entry hall's mosaic floor—the god Neptune in green and blue, complete with trident, scales, and fishtail, in keeping with the originally maritime nature of his business—and passed into the sitting room, he offered her coffee, tea, or "something stronger."

She waved him off. "This is not exactly a social call."

"I understand. You are upset. That is natural."

She remained standing while the two men arranged themselves on the embroidered satin settee facing her. "All this time I've kept my peace," she began, using the speech she had been rehearsing in her mind for four days now. "I've been a good wife to Cesco. I tried to be an *Italian* wife. I never asked what his business was. I turned a blind eye—"

"And this has been noted," Matteo said quietly.

"—to his gambling, and his drinking, and even to his whoring—"

Carlo, who was straitlaced, flinched. The old man bore up better.

"—and when he asked me for money, I gave it to him. The more he asked, the more I gave, because I loved him and he was the father of my child."

"You also knew the marriage laws here," Carlo said. "What each brings to the marriage belongs to the marriage."

"We had a prenuptial agreement. You know what that is?"

"Yes, of course," Matteo said.

"I never called him on it. And when he made 'investments' with you, I never questioned him. I gave him my support, as a wife, even if I did not agree."

"As was proper," Carlo said.

"Now Cesco is gone. I do not ask under what circumstances. I do not seek to place blame …"

The old man pursed his lips and nodded at this.

"But I must think of my future and that of my daughter. I plan to take Rafaella back to the States. So I need to redeem whatever shares Cesco had in your business."

Matteo looked pained. "This is not a convenient time, Contessa."

"I understand. I am prepared to be patient. Work out a repayment—"

"You do *not* understand," Carlo said. "There will *never* be a good time."

"I still have the prenup he signed. It is binding on his family as well."

"Ah, but you see," Matteo said, " 'family' is a term with many meanings."

"This is a legal document," she said quietly.

"And you would enforce it—*how?*" Carlo asked with a grin. "In an Italian court? As a woman? And a foreigner? Against *us?*"

"If necessary." Callie was determined to stand her ground.

"Americans are no longer much loved—or feared—here."

Matteo placed a hand on his son's arm. "Please, *mio figlio*. She has some justice on her side, I think. And Francesco was not always wise. Loyal, yes, but foolish. His wife, on the other hand, is not such a fool."

Callie looked at him with narrowed eyes. She knew instinctively to keep her mouth shut while he worked out a compromise in his head.

"Contessa," the old man went on, "truly, I cannot pay you back what your husband took from you—and lost with us. But I do acknowledge your situation. We owe you a debt of honor."

"Father, please!" Carlo protested.

"What we cannot repay in money," the old man said, "we can pledge to you in service. I will, of course, put you and your daughter under my protection. And you may call on me at any time—"

"But, Matteo … I will not remain in Torino for long."

"I understand. I will see that you are equally well known to our American affiliates—on both sides of the border. We are an 'old, established firm,' as the English like to say. And we understand the nature of blood obligations."

Callie considered. She had lost to her husband, to his schemes and his whims, a good deal of the fortune she had rescued from the collapse of the Praxis family business. But she still had enough to get herself and her daughter home to America and to live on—frugally, for a couple of months, until she figured things out. But the Italian dream was over. And if she could not be made whole financially, it was not a small thing to have a man like Matteo di Rienzi acknowledge a debt to her.

"I see," she said. "I think I see …"

The old man smiled warmly. Carlo stiffly nodded his acknowledgement.

She was smart enough to know she would never have anything in writing. She could claim no assurances. Nothing would stand up in a court of law. But for as long as these two men lived, she would hold a Get Out of Jail Free card. Not because she had anything on them. Not because she could threaten them in any meaningful way. But because they believed in a concept that was fast disappearing in the world. Matteo had used the magic words: "honor" and "blood." She knew the code. And she had no alternative but to accept.

"I understand," she said at last. "Thank you."

"Come now," Matteo said more easily. "Let us see if your daughter has caught any of my cats."

2. Sixth or Seventh Armistice

Lieutenant Colonel Brandon Praxis checked the morning roster on his Tactical Tracker. The 2nd Battalion, 3rd Combined Arms Division, temporarily stationed at Fort Dix in New Jersey, was at half strength: 575 combat effectives, plus staff, support, and mechanics. His company of Tortoise Fighting Vehicles had gotten badly shot up in the attack on Atlanta last month, and repair and resupply were slower than in the early days of the war. The Air Force still had plenty of C-17 Globemasters for putting his battalion in the field, but he didn't have enough troops and vehicles to make it worthwhile. Praxis made requests. Command made promises. Everyone bided their time.

He studied the device on his wrist: a little slab of silicon glued on one side to a piece of armored glass and on the other to a ceramic antenna and button-sized battery. The loops for the wrist strap were cut directly into the glass, the strongest part of the Tactical Tracker-109. Total cost to replace this tech sandwich was about three dollars, and his people went through a lot of them, even though Praxis had taught his men to wear them on the inside of their wrists instead of outside and cover them with their cuffs—less banging into things that way. The technology of the device itself was insignificant, having been around for a decade or more. But the web of data that it tied a man into—his chain of command on secure links upward and downward, his own medical stats through the biobead punched into his belly, his senses through more biobeads in his eye sockets and ear canals, and the status and location of every piece of equipment and supply he needed to support himself in the field through RFID tags and barcodes—that was priceless. With it, Praxis could contact anyone under his command, look through his eyes, hear through his ears, and place him—or her, because this man's army boasted lots of good women—at any point of an operation.

It was a far cry from his first big assault nine years ago, the supposedly surprise attack on the capital of the breakaway republic in Kansas City, as well as other key points in the seceding territory. Yes, every soldier had something like the TT-109, but it wasn't army issue and it wasn't secure.

What neither the commanding general—what was his name? Beemis? Gone now—nor his own Captain Ramsay could know, and Brandon himself would only piece it together in the weeks that followed, was how difficult it actually was to coordinate a massed invasion with thousands of soldiers. Many of them, like his own Bravo Company of the 1/22nd Combat Infantry, had been fresh out of training and experiencing a strange new adventure. The officers had instructed the platoon and squad leaders about the need for secrecy. But, unlike previous wars, this one was being fought in a society that was saturated with smartphones, social media, photo sharing, web logging, and the pervasive and childish mindset that "Information wants to be free." Before Bravo Company even boarded their commandeered airliner, details of the strike were slipping out in personal updates and posted images on Facebook, Twitter, and MySpace. Not to mention heartfelt good-byes to wives, sweethearts, brothers, fathers, the banks that held their auto loans, and their bail bondsmen. So long, Mom! Look for me on TV! They were all such a bunch of babies back then: college boys with some physical training and a new rifle, but not really military-minded.

Pundits and bloggers had immediately begun translating hints from these various social feeds into a historical perspective. Radio talk-show hosts were actually taking bets on the outcome of the raid. And of course the strike teams themselves, who were maintaining "radio silence" that morning, knew none of this. The initial wave of rangers from Special Operations Command had landed in a cross fire of combined forces from the Missouri National Guard, local sheriff's deputies, and municipal police SWAT teams. By the time Bravo Company was crossing the Utah-Colorado border, the strike had effectively failed. But for good measure, the Missouri National Guard commander at the airport ordered the air traffic controllers, at gunpoint, to bring the fleet of 787s from Travis AFB on in. Then he had the tower instruct them to taxi to the end of Runway Two-Zero West. There a team of police snipers in the deep grass shot out the tires. Praxis and his squad had fought their way off the plane, but for all their firing they never hit any of the snipers.

How had he gotten out of that one? Oh yeah, returned a month later in a prisoner exchange. Those were the good old days, when the war was fought by gentlemen and everyone thought it would be over by Christmas.

It had been a long and bitter war. They came within an inch of being invaded by the Chinese, out to make hay while the Americans devoured themselves in civil war. But social disruption in the Middle Kingdom prevented any real occupation. First came popular revolt against the crippled hand of the ruling Communist Party, then the revolt of the *Fennu Xiong*, the "Angry Bears"—the legion of young men deprived of female companionship, family life, and progeny by the gender imbalance resulting from the One Child Policy. No, China had been in no position to follow up on the first air strike in Seattle. Neither was anyone else ready to invade. Russia still feared the U.S. government's nukes. And no one in Europe, the Middle East, or the Subcontinent had the wherewithal to go adventuring.

Brandon Praxis had lost his father and mother. After the family company fell apart—and wasn't it a good thing he had not graduated a year earlier to join in that debacle?—Leonard had tried to recoup his fortune with real estate deals in a declining market. Then, as the war grew worse, he made the fatal mistake of confusing remoteness with safety. Leonard and his wife retired to a vacation lodge north of Lake Tahoe and disappeared in the predawn strikes of the Federated Republic's narrowly successful Donner Incursion.

Who was left now? His grandfather John was still in California, doing something with plumbing services. His uncle Richard and his wife had moved to Texas, where he joined a firm involved in computer design—computers had been his uncle's first love anyway. And his aunt Callista had taken herself to Italy and become a countess. His own brother Paul had joined the U.S. Army, been wounded in North Dakota, and was now in physical therapy with a bionic leg. His sister Bernice was married to a soldier named Littlefield, out on the West Coast. His cousins had gone along with their father and mother to Texas: Jeffrey was fighting for the other side now, and Jacqueline had trained as a mechanical engineer and immediately gone into defense work in a cyber-munitions plant. So the Praxis family was represented on both sides of the war, as well as outside of it.

War had torn his family apart. But then, hadn't the family been in full disintegration mode the summer before, for reasons Brandon Praxis had never really understood? These days, he actually felt closer to the men and women in his unit than to the people who shared his genes. War had taught him about the different kinds of blood, and that blood spilled was stronger than blood shared.

But how much longer could this war go on?

He sent another repair requisition up the chain.

It couldn't hurt. They were only electrons, after all.

After a combined three hours of waiting for security clearance, first in Milan's Malpensa Airport and then at London Heathrow, followed by a twelve-hour flight over the pole, and four hours clearing U.S. Customs in San Francisco, Callista di Rienzi was exhausted and her daughter Rafaella had passed from unusually irritable to unconscious.

It took another hour to find transportation into the city because of restrictions on vehicular traffic and Transportation Commission permits. Her Electrocab pulled up in front of her father's house sometime after one o'clock in the morning. But the lights were still on in the living room, and the window curtain twitched as she was getting out of the passenger pod and hoisting her sleeping child up on one hip with arms draped around her neck. The front door opened before she had figured out which buttons to push and where to insert her card to pay the fare. Because she was still thinking in euros, the amount seemed exorbitant, but Callie was too tired to argue with a machine.

"Do you want me to take her?" John Praxis asked.

"No, she's okay. Can you get the bags?"

He opened the bin lid and took out their suitcases and travel packs, setting them on the sidewalk. The machine wouldn't leave until all the luggage was cleared, but her father still hurried, as if he was inconveniencing it. He carried the first two pieces up the front steps behind her.

"I hope you've got a spare room," Callie said. "She's down for the count."

"Sure, top of the stairs, first door." He motioned with a suitcase.

"*Chi è che, mama?*" the little girl asked sleepily.

"Your grandfather, Raffi. Say hello."

"*Buona sera, Nonno.*"

"In English, honey."

"Good night, sir." And the little head went back down on her shoulder.

When they got to the room, Callie left it darkened, laid her daughter on the freshly made bed, and slipped off her shoes. Washing up and undressing could come later. John put the bags down in the hall and went down for the rest of their luggage. As he returned with the last of the pieces, he was breathing heavily. In the overhead light in the hall, his face was gray and slack, with shadows under his eyes and in the hollows of his cheeks.

"My God, Dad! You look terrible."

"It's just age catching up with me."

"A year ago you were running marathons."

"More like ten-kays, and a couple of years ago."

"Sure you're all right? What do the doctors say?"

"Well … you know doctors these days."

"But what did they *say?*"

"Some kind of hormone imbalance. They prescribed some pills for me, but the California Medical Service ruled they were 'age inappropriate' and won't issue them."

"What hormones? You mean like testosterone?"

He shook his head. "Cortisol and aldosterone. My adrenal glands don't seem to make them anymore. I need corticosteroids."

"That doesn't sound like too much trouble."

"They're not approved for a man my age."

"Well, that's just nonsense, if your body needs them."

"It's the law now, Daughter. Welcome to California."

"And finally," Philip Sawyer, chairman and chief executive of Tallyman Systems, Inc., announced to the firm's assembled directors at the monthly board meeting, "the 'grand enterprise' proceeds according to plan, with indices showing we're thirty-five days ahead of schedule."

Richard Praxis stared out over the spaghetti tangle of freeway interchanges that lay to the west of downtown Houston. His eyes tracked the pulsed arterial flow of monomeric units—colloquially, "cars and trucks"—through its concrete channels, and he nodded soberly. So did everyone else around the table, although with greater and lesser degrees of understanding. They all appreciated, in general, what the "grand enterprise" represented. However, the board minutes would show no more detail than that single reference. Praxis, as vice president of Government Affairs and one of the original architects of the project, knew that not much more documentation existed anywhere else within the company. He could only hope that the project's clients and ultimate benefactors were being just as discreet.

Inside Tallyman Systems, the people most responsible for the enterprise believed they were testing a proposition in game theory, a mammoth "what if" that had no practical purpose in itself but that might, with a major amount of tweaking, one day be sold into the internet gaming market. For now, it was an intellectual exercise under the project name "Realpolitik."

Richard had come into the company not long after the mammoth failure of the family business that had borne his name. Tallyman was a startup working on artificial intelligence, originally with neural networking. This was on the premise that complicated problems in distribution, routing, and leveling, as well as problems that had to draw on diffuse and poorly integrated data sets, could best be solved by networks of independent but massively interconnected computing nodes, like neurons in the human nervous system. Rather than a single processor working to a strictly linear algorithm, the network nodes all worked in parallel. Each node would already have been taught a single pattern which activated it, or not, based on inputs received from neighboring nodes. Each node then applied its own pattern to the problem's outputs. Neural networks could learn. They could weigh choices. And that meant they could solve problems where the programmer himself had limited knowledge. The programmer might have understood the nature of the choices involved and the tests to be applied but have no idea how to approach a solution.

The company had hired Richard Praxis because of his expertise in construction of major projects. They wanted to apply neural networking to problems in public policy, population density, city planning, rights of way, transit system and highway grade design, and water and power grids. The fact that he had dexterity with computer systems was a plus. So Richard had moved to Texas just before the war's outbreak and settled his family in the Houston area.

More recently, Tallyman had been pursuing analysis of the same kinds of complex, diffuse problems through evolutionary theory. In nature, evolution applied random genetic mutations to living organisms that were experiencing environmental change. The changing environment imposed a new set of criteria—a new set of survivability tests—without specifying what bodily forms or traits would best be able to meet them. Living animals and plants suffered mutations all the time, tiny modifications in DNA coding that might or might not affect the structure of their proteins. And those modified proteins might or might not affect the organism's metabolism, tolerance for bodily insults like heat or cold, physical structure, or some other functional characteristic. In a stable environment, where the old biological pattern had been proven to work, most mutations were either unimportant or minorly helpful or hurtful, while some were downright lethal. In a changing environment, with new criteria for survival, a small number of tiny, marginally beneficial modifications suddenly mattered.

Evolutionary design solved problems in form and function where the designer himself had limited knowledge, understood the nature of the choices involved and the test to be applied, but had no idea how the system under stress actually worked or what success might look like.

Microbiologists had been using "directed evolution" for more than a decade to improve the function of proteins such as antibodies, enzymes, and other biological agents. Without any knowledge of a protein's folding pattern, molecular bonding sites, or its mechanism of operation, the researcher could set up a hundred or a thousand samples of the original DNA that had produced the protein, modify each DNA strand in some random way, code newly modified protein from those induced mutations, and test each new protein to see if it worked better or worse in the specified application. If better, the researcher kept the new protein and modified its DNA again. If worse, the researcher discarded it and started over with a fresh sample. By repeatedly applying random changes, testing the results, and discarding the failures, biologists could eventually cook up a protein that worked better at what they wanted—moderating a chemical reaction; breaking, joining, or copying DNA strands; fixing a blood clot; inactivating a virus; whatever the function was—without ever having to know what the internal structure of "better" might look like.

The same principle worked in the physical world, too. For example, an aircraft designer might create a new airfoil by knowing everything about curves and airflows, lift and drag, and other abstract principles. Or he could just take a flat piece of sheet metal, give it a whack to bend it, mount it in a wind tunnel, and see if it generated lift. Do this a thousand times with a thousand pieces of metal, keep any bent metal that moved the gauge, discard any metal that didn't budge and replace it with new flat metal, and start randomly whacking everything again. Sooner or later, the designer would get a better airfoil in a shape no one had ever—or could ever have—imagined.

Of course, the evolutionary approach yielded its failures. A lot of failures. Mostly failures, in fact. Proteins that had been getting slightly better at their job through the baby steps of random mutation might take one more mutation to their coding and suddenly become totally useless. Nearly perfect airfoils might take one more whack and become junk. But with persistence, through sheer, dogged, blind keeping on with the task at hand, a researcher using directed evolution eventually produced a success. Evolution was cruel, too: a lot of individuals in any species—most of them, in fact—died along the way to producing something new that could hope to survive in a changed environment.

Tallyman Systems, Inc. was advancing the technique by applying vast, neurally networked computing power to directed evolution. They went beyond taking a physical sample, modifying it, and testing it in a petri dish or wind tunnel. A computer could model the intricate folds and bonding domains in a new protein, or the lift properties of battered metal in the laminar flow of a virtual airstream. A computer could mutate, test, and mutate again on a thousand or a million samples in the time it would take a human with restriction enzymes to modify just one strand of DNA, or bend with a hammer and test in a wind tunnel just one piece of metal.

The process wouldn't work if the computer programmer didn't understand at least some of the principles involved—like how a protein's sequence of amino acids might actually fold and how that arrangement of positively and negatively charged atoms might interact, or how lift and drag might balance each other across a curved surface. But for well understood principles like chemical reactions, aerodynamics, fluid mechanics, structural stresses, heat transfer, and many other applications, the developing science of Iterative Stochastic Evolutionary Design, or ISED—where "stochastic" stood for the randomness of the changes to be made, and "iterative" for their many repetitions—was bearing results in all sorts of ways.

The process worked especially well in reverse, too. When you had a system in equilibrium with its environment, or under a certain amount of identified stress, and you wanted to see what changes were necessary to throw it completely out of whack, iterative stochastics were the ideal computer exercise. And that, of course, was the basis of the "grand enterprise."

At the request—made privately, without competitive bidding or any such business niceties—of the Federated Republic's Department of Cyber Warfare, Tallyman had been testing various models of the U.S. government's operational systems. Under simultaneous analysis were its tax laws, revenue distribution patterns, monetary policy and financial regulation, Social Security and Medicare programs with their supporting algorithms, and the U.S. Pentagon's systems for supplying, allocating, and distributing personnel and equipment. "Realpolitik" was an exercise in multi-front economic warfare. Its product was not a game program for bored teenagers with genius-level IQs, but a stream of small attacks, regulatory deflections, program interruptions, and seemingly unrelated service demands that the Federated Republic's allies, cyber spies, and paid turncoats could inflict on the enemy's economy.

And, according to the chairman's report this morning, after three years of subtle and continuous pressure, they were now thirty-five days ahead of schedule.

―――

Antigone Wells's internist referred her to a urologist, Elise Paterson, MD, who had an office in the same building and an opening in her schedule. The woman was polite but brisk. At the second visit, following up on a battery of tests, including a cheek swab for genetic analysis, she said, "You have kidney disease—specifically, autosomal dominant polycystic kidney disease—although the conditions are a bit unusual."

"What do you mean, 'unusual'?" Wells asked.

"For one thing, the onset is late. Normally, you should have gotten this in your thirties or forties, and you're what?" Paterson consulted her computer screen. "Sixty-seven. And no history of urinary tract infections?"

"One or two." She shrugged. "Years ago."

"No history of back pain? Headaches?"

"I just thought everyone got those."

"But not enough to see a doctor?"

"Not really. But … you said I 'should have gotten' this thing years ago. Is that because this is a disease for younger people?"

"No, because it's genetic. And you have the pattern."

"So … what's happening to me?"

"The CT scans show your kidneys, both of them, are already starting to grow clusters of large, fluid-filled cysts—bubbles about the size of double-ought buckshot. They break down the organ's structure and impede its function. Sooner or later—possibly sooner—your kidneys will quit entirely and you'll go into end-stage renal failure."

"Dialysis?" Wells made a face.

"It'll save your life," Paterson said.

"And leave me sick for half of the time."

"Things are much better now. And we can look into organ replacement."

"There's only my sister. I don't know that she'd give up a kidney for me."

"They're doing wonderful things with stem cells, these days."

"I know. About ten years ago I got brain support after a major stroke. But … if this is a genetic disease, won't the regrown kidneys have the same kind of cysts?"

"Eventually, maybe. Are you planning to live another thirty years?"

Wells squinted at the doctor. "For as long as I can."

"You know, those parts boys are pretty smart. By now they should know how to patch up the genes before inducing pluripotency. With this disease, you might go on to get cysts in your liver and pancreas one day, eventually even your heart valves and brain. But the new kidneys will be pristine."

"And when those new cysts start to form?" Wells asked.

"Then some other doctor will chase them down and make you a new liver and whatnot."

"When do we get started? I mean, assuming we want to avoid that end-stage stuff and go straight to the fix."

"I'll book you an appointment at the Mayo Clinic."

"Thank you, Doctor. I'll clear my schedule."

―――

The electric shock of the TT-109 stung the inside of Lieutenant Colonel Brandon Praxis's wrist like a wasp. He actually jumped in his seat. So did his staff officers—G1 Manpower and Personnel, Major Frieda Hammond, and G3 Operations, Major Stephen Swarovski—who both rubbed surreptitiously at the bands on their wrists.

Brandon had gathered the two into his office that morning to discuss the latest FUBAR. An outbreak of salmonella poisoning in the chow hall had taken another forty-three combat effectives off the line. And then the hospital had run out of packaged rehydration supplements, with no resupply in sight, and was now dosing its growing number of dehydration patients with plain tap water, which lacked the necessary electrolytes. Estimated time of his people's return to duty was the full seven days. But the simultaneous shock from all three of their wrist units signified a message that was both urgent and operational. His subordinates were eyeing him expectantly.

"Okay, take a look," he said, and turned his own wrist over to read the screen.

The time stamp was 1459 UTC, which translated to 1059 local. The originator was simply CIC, which translated to the Office of the President—a step above even the Joint Chiefs. The message content was simply: "All units stand down."

"What the hell?" Swarovski muttered.

"We *are* down," said Hammond.

Brandon turned to the computer screen on his desk and keyed up the newsfeeds. The rolling ribbon at the screen bottom was headlining another ceasefire which, in the blink of an eye as the clock moved to the hour, became an armistice. The United States of America and the Federated Republic of America had just signed an electronic treaty pledging them to end the fighting. He held his breath.

"That's what? The seventh one so far?" asked Swarovski, who was reading over his shoulder.

"Thirteenth ceasefire, but the sixth armistice," said Hammond.

"Do you think this one will hold?" the major asked.

"Do we have a choice?" Brandon said.

The two subordinates stared at him. "Sir?" they echoed each other.

"Well, look around you," he said. "Are we combat effective? We barely got out of Atlanta with our lives. This army hasn't had a win in the field in the last eighteen months. Our navy and air force can't blockade their ports and ground terminals. Their GDP is up; ours is way down. Their currency is strong; ours is still weak. We're not just losing this war, we've already lost it."

"We still have our nuclear arsenal," Swarovski observed.

"And you're going to use that on *Americans?*" Hammond scoffed.

"This is defeatist talk," Swarovski warned.

"No, the colonel's being a realist."

"Still, we should report—"

"Oh, shut up, Steve!"

"Pipe down," Brandon said. "The both of you."

After a pause, Hammond raised her head. "So, what comes next, sir? I mean, assuming this armistice holds."

"If we're smart, we apply to join the Federation. Then we ask for assistance."

"That didn't work too well the last time, did it? I mean …" She shrugged. "Reunification. Reconstruction. Carpetbaggers and scalawags. Destitution and humiliation."

"That was a victorious republic reclaiming the secessionist states and punishing them for breaking away—as well as for the institution of race slavery," he said. "I have to believe this time will be different. We're both working from the same set of governing documents, after all. We just had a differing interpretation about the uses of power. Besides, this time the secessionists will have proved their point."

"And what point was that?" Swarovski asked.

"I'm a military man, not a political theorist."

"Go ahead, sir," Hammond said. "If the walls are listening, we're all cooked anyway."

"Well, just that you can't control everything. Hayek and Freidman were more or less right about the nature of human activity and the generative power of markets. Keynes and Greenspan were more or less wrong in thinking they could fine-tune an economy with decisions made at monthly meetings in Washington, D.C. … Or that's my worm's-eye view."

"Get ready for the scamsters and con artists," Swarovski said.

"Well, maybe there will be some of that. But I remember the unification of East and West Germany a couple of decades ago. That went off pretty well, and they started from a lot farther apart."

"I hope you're right, sir," Hammond said.

"Not like we have a lot of choice, Major."

When his daughter had first broached the subject of finding a second opinion about his adrenal glands, John Praxis said he didn't think that was allowed under the California Medical Service.

"Nonsense," she replied. "Even doctors agree they're not infallible."

"Sometimes." He smiled. "But it's useless to contradict them."

He had already explored his options under the law and found that, for a person of his age and income level, one diagnosis was deemed sufficient. And if the State of California wouldn't pay for another, it wasn't going to happen.

"Then we'll find an out-of-state doctor," she said next.

"It's a federally mandated system," he said. "No doctor outside of California will touch my voucher. Nothing in it for them."

"Well—Jesus, Dad! Then we go over the border to Phoenix. They still practice medicine over there."

"You might get a visa, I guess, with your Italian citizenship. I would be an enemy alien. It wouldn't solve my problem to be interned or shot."

So the matter stood between them until the day of the armistice, or at least the day after. And then Praxis advised his daughter to give it another week, to see if the treaty would hold this time, to see if it might result in peace. And all the while he became weaker, now with joint and muscle pains. He fatigued more easily, had more fits of low blood pressure, and lately unexplained bouts of nausea and diarrhea. He spent more time in his favorite chair, trying to read and dozing off.

Finally, Callista packed him a bag, as well as ones for herself and Rafaella, rented a car she could drive herself—having gotten used to driving in Italy—locked up the house, and headed out of the Bay Area and across the Central Valley.

"Where are we going?" he asked from the back seat.

"Reno," she said. "I spent last night on the phone with Saint Mary's Regional Medical Center. Their kidney unit has agreed to see you."

"Nothing wrong with my kidneys."

"Your adrenal glands sit on them."

"How will we pay for all this?"

"How's this for a concept?" she asked in full sarcasm mode. "They take cash. They'll even take euros. And I've got a bunch of them."

"You shouldn't be doing this."

"I'm saving your life, Dad."

Interstate 80 through Donner Pass was open—or, at least, damage to the road surface from the last battle in the area had been repaired. Praxis listened closely as Callie quietly told her daughter this was where her Uncle Leonard, whom the girl had never met, once lived. She didn't go into how he died. She also explained that a huge freshwater lake of incredible blueness lived just over the horizon to their right.

Fifteen miles east of Truckee, they came to the Nevada border and a huge, new glass and stainless steel checkpoint under a neon sign with the blue-and-white Department of Homeland Security eagle. The uniformed guard examined Callie's and Rafaella's passports and Praxis's driver's license—his passport had been automatically revoked at the start of the war, along with those of most other private citizens who did not hold essential military, government, or commercial positions.

"Reason for leaving the country, ma'am?"

"Meh—" Callie started to say and paused.

Praxis held his breath. He knew she was going to say "medical," and he wondered if she understood that evading the federal health care system was a class-three felony with a mandatory three-year prison sentence.

Callie faked a sneeze and excused herself. "My daughter and I are visiting from Italy. She just loves the old cars, and begged to see the National Automobile Museum in Reno." Here Rafaella looked up at the man and smiled. "My father—" Callie jerked her thumb toward the back seat. "—wanted to come along, explain all the technical stuff, and share his memories. That's all right, isn't it?"

The guard paused for two seconds, then smiled. "Sure, ma'am. I'm told it's a great museum." He went back inside his booth and dropped the crash barrier.

A mile down the road, they stopped at the crossing into the Federated Republic, a one-story cinder-block building with the gate permanently raised. The guard just waved them through.

Two hours later, Praxis was admitted to Saint Mary's, and Callie and her daughter checked into a nearby hotel. That afternoon he was assigned a batch of blood tests, followed by a CT scan of his abdomen and MRI of his skull to check his pituitary function.

"You have Addison's disease," the assigned physician, Dr. Kendal, told them the next morning. "It's an immune system malfunction that causes the body to attack the adrenal glands—either that, or you've had an infection centered on them sometime in the past. The treatment is relatively simple, a course of hormone replacement therapy."

"Do hormones fix the problem?" Praxis asked, knowing the answer already.

"Well, they will *address* it. You'll take them for the rest of your life."

"I understand, Doctor. But, you see, since I live in California—"

"—they've put you on the index," Kendal finished. "Jesus!"

"Are the drugs so very expensive?" Callie asked.

"My dear, I think the bureaucrats are making a separate point," Praxis told her. "So, Doctor, what are my other options?"

"They're doing wonderful things with stem cells," Kendal said. "If they can grow whole organs in a bottle, they can certainly grow an itty-bitty set of glands."

"What about the immune system attacking them?" Callie asked.

"They can boost the histocompatibility signature to warn it off."

"Can you do the culturing and implant here in the hospital?" Praxis asked.

"That's still somewhat advanced for us. One day …" Kendal said wistfully. "Until then, we refer our regeneration patients to the Mayo Clinic in Minnesota."

"Can we get an appointment there?" Callie asked.

"I don't see why not? Shall I send your records?"

3. Getting Into Bed

WHILE CALLIE AND Rafaella were off parking the car, John Praxis registered at the admitting desk of the Mayo Clinic in downtown Rochester, Minnesota. He was having trouble convincing the clerk and her cyber that as a United States citizen he was in the country legally; that he wasn't a member of La Raza Centra, Kaiser, or any other medical association with networking privileges; that he wasn't planning to use his California Medical Service voucher for payment; that he did not qualify for charity support; and he was prepared to cover the full cost of his procedures and hospital stay with euros drawn on a bank in Turin, Italy, from an account registered to his daughter, who was styled "Contessa di Rienzi." The latter would not pass cybernetic muster, of course, until his daughter could show up with her bank cards and passport.

Looking around in frustration, Praxis caught sight of an almost-familiar figure across the room. She was facing away from him, but the upward sweep of ash-blonde hair and the square shoulders on a trim body—or what he could see of it—brought back memories. For a moment he thought he could smell her perfume, but in his weakened state, his mind sometimes played tricks.

Praxis turned away from the reception desk and started across the lobby, slowly at first but gaining speed the closer he came. "Tippi!" he called under his breath. Then louder, "Antigone?"

The woman turned. She had the same beautiful face with the strong jaw and high cheekbones, the same gray eyes that went wide in surprise, and wider in recognition. "John!" she called. Then something in the set of his face, in the slight stagger as he walked, must have alarmed her. Her smile of recognition changed to a frown of concern.

They met in the middle of the lobby with people moving all around them. The quick hug of old friends, the touching of cheek to cheek.

"What happened to you, John?" she asked, holding him at arm's length.

"What else? I got old." He drank her in. "You haven't changed at all."

She tipped her head. "Same old outsides, but going rotten inside."

"Oh, no! What's wrong?" He could not believe she was sick.

"Kidney disease. Incurable. I'm here for a new pair. You?"

"Endocrine trouble. Adrenal glands. Need a pair, too."

"I lost track of you," she said quietly. "I went to Oklahoma, the war started, and …" She shrugged. "Two different worlds ever since."

"I know. I guess you picked the right side."

"Luck picked for me." She paused again. "I heard your business failed."

"Can't do civil engineering with the economy crashing around your ears."

"And your wife died. I was so sorry to hear about that."

"There was nothing we could do. At least she went quietly."

"Dad?" Callie asked, coming through the crowd with Rafaella.

"Oh! Yes! You remember Antigone Wells."

"Of course. You got me out of a terrible jam."

"Easy trick," Antigone said. "And who's this?"

"My daughter. Rafaella di Rienzi. Say hello, dear."

"*Buona sera, signora,*" the little girl said shyly.

Antigone looked straight at Callie. "I'll bet there's a story here."

"You have no idea," his daughter said. "Are you checked in, Dad?"

"I was just negotiating the process. I need your help." He turned to Antigone. "Can we see you at dinner, or something? Chance to catch up?"

"Sure, I'm just doing tests and samples this afternoon. Say, six o'clock?"

"Gosh, you people eat early!" Callie remarked.

"This is the Midwest," Antigone said. "We go to sleep with the sun, too."

———

As she recovered from kidney surgery, Antigone Wells renewed the acquaintance—no, to be honest, the flirtation, or the budding romance—with John Praxis that had begun on a rooftop in San Francisco almost a dozen years ago. This time the affair was carried out in the Mayo Clinic's cafeterias, libraries, and physical therapy rooms amid the serious work they both needed to get healthy again.

John seemed to be gaining strength and vitality day by day. When she asked how the surgery to replace his adrenal glands had gone, he told her he never went under the knife. Apparently, the doctors had a new technique that turned mature cells into totipotent stem cells right inside the body. Then they could manipulate the genes in those baby cells to grow up into fresh, healthy tissues. It was all done with needles.

She gathered from things John said in passing that he was no longer a rich man. She wasn't really surprised, since he had lived in a country with a stated policy of redistributing private wealth, and that country had just endured nine years of war—and lost. True, the conflict had been more on the level of economic and psychological attrition than territorial invasion and aerial bombing. But both sides had conducted targeted raids intended to reduce public infrastructure—things like transit, water, sewage, and power systems—and so disrupt public comfort and safety. The Federated Republic had made much of news stories about the suffering on both East and West Coasts.

John's daughter apparently had financial resources, either left over from the cash which Wells had helped her take out of the engineering business or from some new venture. Callista Praxis made no secret of her connection with minor Italian aristocracy—a connection now rumored to be deceased—but Wells understood that Italy had just as much of a redistributive bent as California, and Callie's title by marriage, "la Contessa," was purely decorative.

As the end of her rehabilitation period neared, Antigone Wells found herself suddenly becoming hesitant. The future was a question mark, and she hesitated to ask John outright, "What are your plans now?" That would force her to confront her own situation, her feelings for him, and their future together—or, once again, apart. But finally, on the day before her discharge, with John still having some days to go because of his previously weakened condition, she could put it off no longer.

"Oh, I'll go back to California," he said.

"It's not a question of citizenship, is it?" she asked. After the armistice, the exact nature of the national borders and limits of the U.S. government's authority were still in transition. But she was sure she could get Praxis and his family permanent residence in the Federated Republic and eventually citizenship—unless amnesty and repatriation resolved the issue first.

"No, that will take care of itself, I think." He paused. "I was thinking of the opportunities."

"There's lots more opportunity here in the Republic," she said. *With me,* she added mentally.

"Really? I would have thought it was the other way around."

"What? Oh—you just haven't seen this country, not really. We have a vibrant economy, good manufacturing base, academic centers featuring advanced technology and biomedicine, plenty of energy resources, rivers that drain a continent, farms that run to the horizon, mines and forests under able management, free markets, solid currency, and stable finances. What do you have in the former United States to compare with that?"

He grinned wickedly. "Collapse. Ruin. Decay and deferred maintenance. Not to mention paths of destruction five miles wide. The place is just a mess."

"And that's an opportunity because—?"

"Somebody's got to rebuild it. This time better than before."

"But you don't have a company anymore."

"I have a Rolodex. I know top-notch engineers hungry for work."

"But where will you get the money to pay them?"

"Money?" he asked. "Money's like air. When you need it, it's just there."

"I don't—I mean—you're seventy-five years old. Isn't it too late to start over?"

"And miss out on the biggest engineering boom in a century? Not on your life!"

"I admire your spirit, John," Wells said at last.

"And I do have an ulterior motive," Praxis said. "I have some unfinished business." He told her about the deal he had made to acquire future title to nearly a million acres of prime timber and recreational land held in the old National Forest System. If he could survive another thirty years or so, and still manage to pay upkeep on the preserve, he would become one of the biggest landholders in California.

"I never heard of that program," she admitted.

"They kept it pretty quiet. Still, the deal is entirely legal."

"But ... it's a contract with a government that may no longer exist."

"I understand. There is risk," he said. "Everything depends on whether the Federated Republic will recognize obligations of the old United States. That would be a gesture of good will, I think. History has too many examples of bad things happening to victors who extracted punitive measures. Reconstruction after the first Civil War and rise of the Ku Klux Klan in the Old South, for one. Versailles at the end of the First World War and the rise of Nazi Germany, for another."

"You're going to need a lawyer to pull all this off."
"Probably. Do you know a good one?"
"I'd better come with you."

With the armistice apparently holding and turning into a peace process, Richard Praxis had reason to preen at his next one-on-one meeting with Philip Sawyer. The chief executive was among the few people at Tallyman Systems who knew the true success of Project RealPolitik, which for everyone else in the company was still in early-stage development. And Sawyer was the only one in a position to congratulate Richard, however privately.

"Yes, our clients are very pleased," Richard said. "They're even talking about some kind of covert honor, to be awarded anonymously and kept at Cyber Warfare headquarters—until everything is declassified in a hundred years or so."

"Well, you and your team will certainly be getting a bonus."

"Ah, as to that. I'll take the money, of course, as part of the regular executive package. But the team doesn't know the project is actually over. Special recognition rewards at this point would be out of place."

"You could still sell the software as a game, couldn't you?"

"That would be considered insecure. Somebody might twig."

"Well, then, what's the next move for you? Destabilizing Japan?"

"Oh, yeah!" Richard laughed. "Like they'd need any kind of push."

"Seriously, Richard. What has your group in Government Affairs got lined up for next quarter?"

"Oh, um … Well, there are still the projects I came in on: infrastructure leveling and alignment for water and power, transit, demographics. They're going to need a lot of intelligent rebuilding out on the coasts."

"Are the algorithms for stochastic evolution ready to roll on real-life projects?"

"Well, no. Maybe in a year or two. First, we need to get some small-scale demonstrations going. We're still at the dream-time stage."

"Why is that?" Sawyer asked.

"My group was pretty busy with that other thing."

"You have to multitask around here, Richard. Everyone else does."

"Of course, sir." Richard thought fast. "We could put together some proposal packages, aimed at whole city rebuilds: optimal population density, work-life balance, logistics and traffic control, water and sewage scaling, substation gridding. The sort of municipal master planning my old firm did for the Saudis back in the seventies, or the Chinese in the oughts—but done using Tallyman techniques."

Sawyer frowned. "That sounds like Twenty-Nine Points stuff. Didn't we go to war about the government imposing that kind of control?"

"Well, yes. But it's still applicable to places like Atlanta and Sacramento, where the fighting was hardest. And, of course, being both *evolutionary* and *stochastic,* the algorithms will ape—um, *approximate*—results from market forces."

Sawyer nodded. "Put together a package and we'll take a look at it."

The four of them took a flight together from Minneapolis-Saint Paul into San Francisco. They made the trip with half the restrictions and a third the documentation required during the war—or at least during its active phase. Upon landing, John Praxis went off to arrange ground transportation while Callie and Antigone collected their luggage and kept Rafaella amused. He managed to book an Electrocab big enough for all of them and loaded their bags at the curb.

He punched the address on Balboa Street into the GPS screen, then paused. "Can we drop you at a hotel?" he asked Antigone.

She looked at her wrist. "It's after nine, and I don't have a reservation."

"Well, then …"

"Let me go home with you, and I can call around from there. Okay?"

"Sure thing."

When they got to the house, he unloaded the family's bags but left Antigone's in the bin. He glanced over his shoulder. "You want to pay for the cab to wait?"

"I can always get another, can't I?"

"We're pretty far out in the Avenues."

"I'll chance it. I'm feeling lucky."

He took his and Callie's bags, with Callie carrying Rafaella's, up to the front door, and then on up the second, interior flight to their bedrooms. Antigone stood by her suitcase just inside the front door. When he returned, she was using her phone and frowning, shaking her head.

"Must be a convention in town," she said. "All the places I know are full."

"Ah, well …" Praxis didn't know what else to suggest.

"Put me up for the night?" Antigone asked.

"Well, um …" He caught his daughter looking at him with slitted eyes.

"There are only two bedrooms," Callie said with a shrug. "Small house."

"The couch down here—" Praxis began.

"—is hard and lumpy," Callie said. "And we don't have sheets for it."

"Oh … dear." Antigone finished with a sigh.

"Why don't the two of you work it out?" Callie suggested with what Praxis took to be an evil grin. She corralled her daughter and took her up the stairs to bed.

"I guess …" He hesitated, then picked up her suitcase. "This way, please." He took her up to the landing and down the hall to his bedroom. Fortunately, he'd left it neat, with the bed freshly made up, and all of his clothes either hung up or in the hamper. "You can sleep here and I'll take the couch downstairs. Just let me get a few things."

"That's a queen-size bed," Antigone said, running her hand over the polished walnut footboard. She was unbuttoning her jacket and slipping off her shoes. "Plenty big for two people."

"Well, if you don't mind. I mean, if you really want to—"

"Please don't make me beg, John."

———

John Praxis was shy, which Antigone Wells had suspected all along. She had to take matters into her own hands, unbuckling his belt and unbuttoning his shirt. To do so, she stood close to him with her face upturned, looking directly into his eyes. When she got to the fourth button, he bent and kissed her full on the lips.

She put her arms around his neck and held on. They were gentle kisses, almost chaste, with no presumption. His day's growth of beard tickled, and she smiled.

"I'm afraid I'm out of practice," he said.

"We both are. Unbutton me, please."

His fingers shook as he worked the little pearl buttons of her silk blouse, keeping straight down the middle. He was plucking at the material, clearly trying not to brush up against her breasts with his fingertips or knuckles.

"It doesn't mean anything unless you touch me," she whispered.

He stopped, looked at her in surprise, and gently cupped her breast with his palm. He slowly rubbed the silk against the lace and glazed satin of her bra.

She felt her flesh tighten in response. She closed her eyes. After a moment, she finished the unbuttoning herself, slipped out of her blouse, pulling the silk out of his hands. She turned slightly away, self-conscious about the reddened scars low on her back over her new kidneys. "Unhook me, please."

Neither of them had any words after that. He finished undressing her, kissing her in new and exciting places. She ran her hands over his upper arms and then his shoulders as he worked his way down her body. When he moved away to undress himself, she turned down the bed and climbed onto the crisp, white sheets. She arranged the pillows behind her shoulders and the small of her back and then arranged herself among them.

He climbed onto the bed and knelt between her legs. His member was stiff and questing. He started to sink down into her, then froze.

"What?" she asked, alarmed.

"I don't have a condom!"

She laughed aloud.

"I mean, seriously," he insisted.

"What could it possibly matter?"

He nodded, but he still hung over her. She chafed his back and sides, as if to warm him up, and then pulled him down. He moved slowly into her. She adjusted her hips and moved with him.

"I'm not hurting you, am I?" he asked.

"I'm a lot tougher than I look," she said.

After a time without counting, he climaxed. She followed immediately.

He lay with her for a moment, cheek against cheek, then withdrew and rolled onto his back. She sighed and put an arm across him, dropping the back of her hand onto his chest. After a pause, she slowly rubbed her knuckles in the wiry hairs there.

"Thank you," he whispered.

She flopped her hand over and ran her fingers and palm down his stomach, across his damp groin, to the top of his thigh. There she rubbed gently. "Don't make me beg."

After midnight, when they were finished and both of them were almost unconscious, Antigone Wells raised herself on one elbow and looked around the darkened room.

"This house needs growing things," she said. "Orchids, I think."

The rebirth of Praxis Engineering & Construction Company took place, not in a glass-and-steel tower overlooking San Francisco Bay, but on the third floor of a four-story building on Sansome Street in North Beach. The elevator up from the lobby was a brass-bound cage run by hydraulics with electromechanical switching, technology that had been developed in the age before electronics, and spent more time in breakdown mode than in operation. At least the stairs were cast-iron and nonmechanical. Everyone involved with the startup was healthy enough to climb them two or three times a day—more if they happened to go out for lunch. The lease was just for six months, by which time John Praxis figured they were either in business and could move uptown, or out of business and would no longer need the space.

According to the articles of incorporation, which Antigone Wells had drawn up as the new chief counsel, Praxis was chairman and chief executive, Callie was president and chief operating officer, and Rafaella was their biggest shareholder, because her college fund had supplied the first infusion of working capital.

So far, they had five desks, a single divisible landline, their personal smartphones, a webwall for virtual meetings, and three console computers with the firepower to run 3D architectural CAD, a project management-purchasing-logistics package, and basic accounting. It was a start.

Praxis clicked off on his thirteenth call of the morning. He announced to the room at large: "Axel Brod's with us. He can start Monday."

"Can he make coffee?" Callie asked. "Because yours is terrible."

"We need one of those machines—the ones with the little caps."

"We need a lot of machines, Dad. Coffee's the least of them."

"So, how many people does that make?" Antigone asked.

"Counting us?" Callie said. "Six. With five engineers."

"Then we'd better hire a marketing department."

"Nah! Everybody sells until a job comes in."

"And when is that?" Antigone asked.

Callie looked across at her father.

Praxis stared back, shrugged.

"I thought you *said*," Antigone began, turning her attention back to him, "there was all this vast opportunity. Well, I can see the *need*. Two bridges out there hanging by a thread. Electricity that goes on standby two days a week. Tap water full of brown rust. And potholes that could hide a hippopotamus. The people in charge of this city should be beating our door down to fix these things. What's the holdup?"

"Money," Praxis said. "California's broke. The U.S. is broke. And the Federated Republic hasn't geared up to bail us out yet."

"You said money was like air—there when you need it."

"That was just to get our business started," he said. "Now we've got some run time, thanks to Rafaella's certificates of deposit. But state money's different. Everything has to go through a process—committees, public comment, appropriations, bond underwriting, environmental impacts. You're a lawyer. I thought you understood this."

"It's just that—" Antigone shook her head. "From the perspective of far-off Oklahoma, I would have thought people out here on the coasts might be further along."

Callie shifted in her chair. It squeaked. "Why don't I …?" she began.

"Yes?" Both Praxis and Antigone now turned toward her eagerly.

"Random thought," she said. "Not worth thinking, really."

Late in the evening, Callie told her father she needed to go out for a walk and asked him to keep an eye on Rafaella until bedtime.

John was sitting on the sofa with Antigone Wells. They sat shoulder to shoulder, hip to hip, with their stocking-clad feet nested together on the single ottoman, playing slow-motion footsie. They were studying something on Antigone's tablet, something colorful but with static imagery, judging from the reflections Callie could see on their faces. Maybe it was some kind of catalog. Maybe they were picking out linens and place settings—as if the things John already had in the house weren't up to Antigone's standards.

Her father looked up and frowned. "But it's dark out," he said.

"Don't worry," Callie replied. "I'm not going far."

His frown deepened. "That's not the point. This isn't the city you grew up in, sweetheart. Even around here, after dark is—"

"I'm not a child, Dad. I have protection."

"What do you think constitutes pro—?"

She opened her purse and showed him, in its shadowed interior, the butt end of a Glock 17. It fired nine-millimeter rounds, and she had a spare magazine in a side pocket. "Satisfied?"

His jaw dropped. "Where the hell did you get that?"

"Italy. I brought it home in my luggage."

Antigone looked up and caught sight of the gun as it disappeared. "Do you know how many laws that breaks in California?"

"Only if I get caught."

"Only if you use it," Wells said.

"Then I'll stick to well lit places, I promise."

John and Antigone turned to stare at each other with raised eyebrows.

"Make sure you have your cell phone with you," John said.

"Of course," Callie replied. "I always do, don't I?"

Indeed, she wasn't going far, just the two long blocks north to Geary Boulevard, and the streetlights were working and lit her path all the way. Half a block down on Geary, she found a Starbucks that was still open. She ordered a double cappuccino and settled with it at a vacant table buffered by empty chairs on either side. And indeed, she was carrying her phone—which was the whole point of the excursion. Now she took it out and dialed an international number.

"*Pronto*," said a young voice she recognized after a second.

"Carlo? It's Callie di Rienzi. I need to speak to Uncle Matteo."

"Who again?" he asked in English.

"Your first cousin. Callie? Calling from America?"

"Eh … Matteo is not at home."

"It's seven in the morning there. Where else would he be?"

"Then he's sleeping."

"Wake him, please. This is important."

After a long pause that stretched to a minute or more, a familiar voice came on. "What is it, Contessa?"

"How are you fixed for investments, Matteo?"

"Eh, 'fixed'? Is, ah … what are you saying?"

"Do you have spare cash to loan at a good return?"

"If this is about the money you think we owe you, I tell you it is not available."

"I'm not asking for that—not yet anyway. This is about investment opportunity." She went on to explain the situation in California and the rest of the old United States. Work needed to be done. Talent and material were available to do it. But the government had no money. The situation called for bridging loans, pump priming, greasing the wheels. Investments that would be paid back tenfold—twentyfold, or likely more.

He listened without comment. When she stopped, she could hear his breathing. Finally, "California is a long way off. Its affairs do not concern me."

"Oh? So you've got more going on in Europe, do you?" Callie could read the business newsfeeds. The continent under the failing European Union had not prospered while the two halves of America battered each other. Europe was succumbing to the Japanese devaluation sickness.

"My associates and I," he said with dignity, "we are getting by."

"Is that all you aspire to? 'Getting by'? Your grandfather, and his father, grew rich by rebuilding *Repubblica italiana* after the Second World War. This is your chance to duplicate that achievement."

"And how would I know where to invest, what are the good prospects?"

"Because I will point them out to you. I know this business, Matteo."

"You would do this out of your good heart? For family loyalty?"

"I would do this for a finder's fee, of course. Fifteen percent."

"Seven," he replied crisply.

"Ten."

"Of the profits."

"Of the project."

"Then eight," he said.

"Make it nine and it's a deal."

"Now don't be greedy, Contessa."

"And don't you be short-sighted, Uncle."

He sighed. "Do we need a piece of paper between us? Lawyers?"

"I have a good one. But we can do this on trust. For the family."

"I will send out someone to mind my affairs, learn the ground."

"That's not necessary, Matteo. I can—"

"I insist. It will be discreet."

Callie realized that her share in arranging any deals would diminish in proportion as this intermediary person gained knowledge and confidence. But the finder's fee was not her immediate objective, and she only pressed Matteo about it to ensure his sincerity. Her real goal was to get projects off the ground and paying into Praxis Engineering's backlog. "Very well then," she said.

He mewed to signify his acceptance. "*Ciao,* Contessa."

"*Grazie,* Uncle." And she clicked off.

4. Family Ties

WITHIN THREE DAYS of completion of the peace process and signing of the Treaty of Louisville, which ended the war, Brandon Praxis was standing on State Street in Trenton, New Jersey, having just stepped out of the Clarkson Fisher Federal Building and U.S. Courthouse—soon to be renamed for a senator from Missouri—where he and his senior officers from 2nd Battalion, 3rd Combined Arms Division, had renounced their commissions and signed oaths of allegiance to the Federated Republic. He was wearing civilian clothes for the first time in nine years, still rubbing at sore spots on his face, neck, and belly where his biobeads had been surgically removed, and absent-mindedly trying to consult with a chipset on his wrist that would only give him the time, weather, and basic newsfeed.

"What do we do now—uh, boss?" Frieda Hammond asked, stumbling over his new rank.

A decommissioned officer with good service behind him routinely got a bump in rank, if not in pay, as he was removed from command. Under normal circumstances, with forty-one sorties and three Purple Hearts to his credit, Brandon would have mustered out as a full colonel. But according to the new peace treaty, former officers in the U.S. Department of Defense were to be brevetted two ranks lower, once for no longer serving in wartime conditions, and once more for having lost the war. He could assume the courtesy title of captain—if he wanted it.

"I don't know, Frieda," he said with a smile. For the first time in six years he was using her given name, rather than call her by her new rank of lieutenant. Relationships were changing all around him. "The only career I've ever known has been the war."

"What did you study in college?"

"Civil engineering. At Stanford. But the country went south before I could take my bachelor's degree. So I know how to fire a rifle, organize a regiment, coordinate a ground strike, and lead men and women into battle. It'll probably be a while before anyone needs those skills again. … You?"

"Sociology. Actually, I have my masters."

"What does that qualify you for?"

"Human resources someplace—like my specialty in the army."

"Well, congratulations, ma'am."

"It's just not going to mean as much, doing it for a corporation."

Behind them, Stephen Swarovski came skipping down the steps. "Free at last! Free at last!" he chanted. "Thank God almighty I'm—oh! Hello, Colonel! Major."

"You look happy, Steve," Brandon said. "Where are you off to?"

"My family, of course." Swarovski had a wife and two girls in Newport Beach, Virginia. "I'll spend a week or two weeding the garden and painting the kids' rooms. Then I take up my old job." He had been an architect with the nation's—the old U.S.A.'s—largest builder of new, made-to-order homes. There he had done most of his work inside a shared-universe computer program called Second Life®. There his clients could adopt temporary avatars and walk around a virtual mockup of their dream house, look out the windows, check out the closet space, and arrange the furniture—all before the sheetrock was even ordered. He had once promised to build Praxis a home as soon as they won the war. Now, with so many service people demobilizing, demand for new housing was going to be huge.

"Well, good luck with that," Brandon said.

"Thanks, sir. It's good to be a civilian again."

Richard Praxis was growing desperate. His position at Tallyman Systems depended on his finding a project or a program that would prove the value of a modified and somewhat truncated Stochastic Design & Development® package. He had canvassed his government contacts inside the Federated Republic, and each of them had pulled at their lips and made long faces—much as Philip Sawyer had predicted.

"We don't actually operate that way, you know," one Iowa state commissioner had told Richard. "When we need a water or a sewer system, it's because someone is putting up a housing development and has already filed the permits. The utilities do their substation planning the same way. If we put a bridge over a river, it's because people have written letters complaining about how far out of their way they have to drive to get where they're going. And we know we need to widen a freeway, route a bus line, or put in a light rail feeder because we can see where traffic is already bogging down.

"Your piece of software there might be clairvoyant," the man went on. "It might actually have the second sight, like my great aunt Sybil. But if it's wrong—well, then we've got hell to pay, don't we? And otherwise, we're spending how many millions just to find out what people are already telling us?

"No, my uncle Walter ran Parks and Recreation in Des Moines for years. He used to say if you want to know where to pave a walkway, just look for where people's feet have burned holes in the grass."

And that story more or less condensed every other interview he had in the Federated Republic. The lack of vision among public officials was just astounding.

Of course, the need was greatest in the old U.S., as he had told Sawyer in the first place. Stochastic Design was the perfect fit for burned out cities that needed to recalibrate their infrastructure—power, water, sewage, transit—all at once for a newly reduced population level. But where the trouble in the Heartland of the Republic was lack of imagination, what the once technically advanced East and West Coasts lacked was funding.

"Gosh, could I use that!" the mayor of Portland had said. His city once had eight major bridges over the Willamette River—three of them now falling to age, four already down because of war damage. "We could rationalize our entire traffic system and rebuild the downtown on a scientific basis.

"And you know," the man added with a nervous grin, "if I had two nickels to rub together, you'd get one of them. But until this reunification thing gets some dollars behind it, we're just patching and piecing, trying to find the greatest need. I'll be lucky to get the Steel Bridge rebuilt next year. I can't even think about doing them all at once."

Richard's eye, which his father had trained long ago to see the big picture where construction was concerned, could see no movement yet, and maybe not for another year or two—which was too late for his purposes. The one city that seemed to be digging out and rebuilding on its own was his old home town, San Francisco. Those projects, his sources told him, were being funded largely with foreign money. And when he followed the money trail to its logical conclusion, he was both shocked and surprised. In every case, the projects with such funding were those being built or managed by Praxis Engineering & Construction.

Somehow, the old firm had survived the crash and the war! But then, survival was simply not possible, as he knew too well from having personally presided over the cratering of the old PE&C's finances. So a new firm bearing the family name had risen from the dead.

Maybe Stochastic Design & Development® was just the thing to help coordinate all the business this new firm was handling. But, to his ultimate frustration, Richard knew he was the wrong person to sell it to them. The family history was just too strong—and not in a good way.

———

Callista di Rienzi and her father arrived at the jobsite on Franklin Street at seven-thirty in the morning, forty minutes after the call from the project manager had awakened them at the house out in the Avenues. The site's chain link fence was intact, and the gate was open. The broad white sign off to the left announced the rebuilding of the War Memorial Opera House—to replace the Beaux-Arts structure built of granite, steel, and terra-cotta in the 1930s that had collapsed in the one aerial bombing the city had endured during the war. The sign said it was a project by Praxis Engineering & Construction, listing the architect and various subcontractors, under authority of the City of San Francisco, with exclusive funding by Torino Investment Partners, SpA. It also announced a completion date two years into the future.

"More like three now," her father said as they walked onto the site. They were both wearing their office shoes, but that didn't matter now. Another sign informed them that hard hats were required beyond that point. Also irrelevant, considering the state of the work.

Two men were standing on the muddy ground inside the gate: Will Chapple, the project manager, and Sonny Deeths, construction superintendent.

"I sent the crew home for the day," Chapple said. "Nothing for them to do."

"Are we still paying—?" Callie started, but her father laid a hand on her arm.

"You've got a chain on the gate and a padlock on the chain," he said, pointing behind them. "Were they broken or cut?"

"No, sir," Chapple said. "All locked up."

The elder Praxis turned to look out over the site, and Callie turned with him. It was a hole, a big one. The ochre mud of the surrounding ground quickly gave way to layers of darker, compacted alluvial soil, then bedrock. Because the opera house was a new project and not simply renovation or reconstruction of the damaged building, they had been obliged to dig below and remove the old foundation. The only thing left was a hole, two hundred and forty feet wide by three hundred feet long, with more mud and water at the bottom.

"What equipment did we have on site?" Praxis asked.

"You noticed, huh?" Chapple said. "Three Caterpillar D9s, subassemblies for the concrete batch plant, and rigging for a tower crane."

"And they are now …?"

"Gone, sir."

"Somebody had to load all that out with flatbeds."

"Yes, sir."

Callie looked around. "Where's the office trailer?"

"Gone, too," Deeths said. "Anything with wheels."

"Did you have anything else on site?" Praxis asked.

"Well, three loads of that special rose-colored marble."

"That's not on the Gantt chart for months!" Callie said.

"Didn't you have anywhere else to put it?" Praxis offered.

"Well, um, we figured it was heavy, so why move it twice?"

"Of course. All the eggs in one basket. Makes perfect sense."

"We've also lost two generators, floodlights, and a mile of cabling," Deeths said. "The thieves probably took them for the copper."

"But you weren't working night shifts," Callie observed.

"Well, the schedule called for that to start next month."

"So someone knew just when to hit us," Praxis said.

"That's about the size of it," Chapple agreed.

"It's all insured, isn't it?" Deeths said.

"Of course," John replied. "We'll get the equipment replaced, but that's not the point. Our premiums will go through the roof—not to mention rental rates and liability on anything we lease from now on."

"And whoever did this will be watching for another chance," Callie said.

Her father was looking at the ground, thinking. He suddenly pointed about forty feet away. "What's that?"

Callie saw a glint of something gold. As she walked toward it, the glint resolved into a bright oval. It was a shield engraved with "Nocturna Security" and a badge number. She took it back to the men.

"Torn off in a fight?" Chapple suggested.

She turned the badge over. The pin was intact with no torn cloth under it.

"It was left as a message," Praxis told them.

"You just can't trust anybody these days."

Mariene Kunstler pressed the elevator button a second time, then a third, thinking the signal must not have gone through, although the white plastic disk with its upward-pointing arrow was still glowing. Nothing happened—no rattle of doors on the floors above, no hum of motors in the shaft. She shook her head and walked across the marble floor of the lobby to the flight of stairs decorated with metal vines in badly flaking gold leaf.

This was what Matteo di Rienzi was investing in? This was the powerhouse construction firm that was going to rebuild California? And they couldn't even maintain an elevator?

"Don't be fooled by the people you will meet," he had told her over the phone before she flew out of Zurich. "The family was great once, and they survived the war." He paused. "The Contessa survived my nephew Cesco. That should tell you something."

Arriving at the third floor, Mariene found a long corridor stretching away, paved with tiny white hexagonal tiles, paneled in darkly varnished wood, and offering three widely spaced doors, each with a pebbled glass window and brass knob. But only one of them had a brass name plate beside it, "Praxis Engineering & Construction LLC," and lettering on the glass said, "Enter Here."

She didn't bother knocking—that wasn't her style. She turned the knob and walked in. The wider hallway beyond the door was carpeted with blocks of indoor-outdoor fiber in a color the old Bundeswehr had called *Feldgrau*. The reception desk positioned sideways in the entry was unattended, with not even a telecomm bot.

"*Hallo?*" she called.

A dark-haired woman—tall, good figure, well-tailored business suit—put her head out from one of the doorways leading off to the side. She had a headphone boom slung from her ear. She tucked it down, away from her mouth. "Are you from Hotto-Potto?" she asked.

"Excuse me?" Mariene was confused.

"The sukiyaki place on the corner?"

Ah, now she understood. It was a reaction Mariene Kunstler had met many times, especially when she wore her loose-fitting travel clothes. In the land of American giants, she stood just five feet tall, had a silhouette easily mistaken for a boy's, and wore her white-blonde hair cropped short all around. Her features were small and her face pale—except for black-black eyes and a slight fold to her eyelids that her father had attributed to a great-grandmother who might have been Chinese. In certain lights—and until she put on her stiletto heels, miniskirt, and a scarf or makeup to conceal the Black Widow tattooed on the side of her neck—she would pass for the punked-out delivery boy from an Asian fast-food restaurant. It was a useful trick, sometimes.

"No," she replied. "Are you the one they call the Contessa?"

The woman blinked, then nodded. "I am Callista di Rienzi."

"We need to talk. Your uncle Matteo sent me."

The news did not surprise this woman. "I see. Come in, please." She took Mariene into her office and closed the door behind them. "When did you arrive?"

"Two hours ago—from Switzerland."

"Do you want coffee, or anything?"

"Let us assume my social needs are taken care of." Mariene took a chair and waved for di Rienzi to sit behind her desk. "We should get right to the point. I want a position in this firm that will give me a high degree of authority but also latitude as to hours and movements. Matteo wishes me to keep an eye on his investments here and increase them wherever possible. He specified the opportunity to travel and meet important people. So that would exclude some make-work job like personnel or accounting."

"I see." Di Rienzi frowned. "Do you have a degree in engineering or anything technical?"

"Of course not. I studied German medieval and renaissance poetry at the University of Hannover in Lower Saxony, then transferred to the faculty for political science and economics. I took training with and served three years in the Bavarian State *Polizei*, four years in the Italian *Carabinieri*, and two months at the European Union's Department of Justice and Equality."

"I take it you didn't like Brussels?"

"No, Brussels didn't like me."

"So you're a police officer."

"Not exactly. I … blend."

"Come again, please?"

"I can make my way into and out of strange and difficult situations. I can gather information, retain and process it up here." She tapped her forehead. "I can read people and know what they're thinking. I can disappear into the background when necessary. I blend."

"That's, um, a useful set of skills. Anything more … concrete?"

"For reasons that won't concern you, I am loyal to Matteo."

"We're really too small right now for anyone logging non-billable hours."

"That's your problem. You can assume my salary and expenses will be paid out of Matteo's interest. What I need is a base of operations, high-level connections, and a set of business cards."

Di Rienzi squinted at her. "This part of the country is still somewhat in transition. We've had a rash of industrial thefts recently, really quite damaging to our job progress. Someone with police investigative—"

"I don't think you understand. When Matteo speaks of protecting his investments, he's not talking about chasing thieves and vandals. Your insurance people can do that. He is concerned with the other end of the business, the money end—where the clients are."

Di Rienzi thought for a moment. "We don't have anyone in charge of marketing yet. How does executive vice president sound?"

"That would be perfect. Does it come with a car?"

"Don't you wish! Right after I get one."

In the weeks since Antigone Wells moved into the house on Balboa Street, the family had established a comfortable morning routine. Callie was usually the first one awake, rousted out Rafaella, and started getting her ready for school. Then John Praxis got up, left Antigone asleep in their bed, and went down to make coffee. And finally Antigone came slowly awake, sleepwalked into the bathroom, and locked the door for half an hour.

But this morning the routine seemed to have changed. Praxis roused early, aware that he was lying in a cold and empty bed. He listened for sounds from the hallway and heard only light snores coming from Callie's and Rafaella's bedroom. But he detected muted sounds of bustle and clatter from the kitchen. He stumbled down the stairs and found Antigone there in her bathrobe.

The refrigerator door was wide open. A carton of milk and six brown eggs were warming out on the counter. A number of steel and ceramic bowls of different sizes stood next to them, and three of his graduated, cast-iron frying pans sat on top of the stove. Antigone herself was standing at the open flatware drawer, holding up and considering a spatula in her left hand, a whisk in her right. The coffee maker was still cold and empty.

"Good morning, m'dear," he said, walking over and kissing her cheek.

"Oh, hello, John," she replied absently, still studying her implements.

"What are you doing, Tig?" he finally asked.

"I got tired of eating breakfast burritos at the office. I'm making pancakes."

"Oh … good." Praxis looked around the room. Pancakes appeared to be some hours in the future. "I didn't know you could cook."

"I know how," she replied. "Well … I've seen it done."

"Pancakes sound wonderful. Rafaella loves them."

"Where do you keep the flour?" she asked.

"Cabinet by the stove. But I think we ran out."

Baking was not his strong suit—or Callie's.

"And the yeast?" Antigone prompted.

"Do you put yeast in pancakes?" he asked.

"I'm sure there must be some."

"Aren't you following a recipe?"

"I couldn't find your cookbook."

"Well, try baking powder instead," he suggested.

"That would probably work. … Do you have any?"

"I don't think so." He paused. "Do you mind if I make the coffee?"

"No, go ahead." She put down the utensils, turned, and looked around the kitchen: empty bowls, cold skillets, and eggs and milk as the only available ingredients. Praxis could see the light of reason slowly dawn in her lovely gray eyes. She sighed. "I guess I could scramble some eggs."

"That would be a lot of work," he said.

"Um … I don't suppose there's cereal?"

"Try the cabinet above the refrigerator."

"I'm sorry, John. Better luck next time."

"It's all right. We just need to stock up."

"Brandon Praxis," Callie said, trying to keep her voice level.

"Yes, ma'am," replied the mature man seated before her.

She tried to focus on his resume, which was skimpy enough, but her eyes kept drifting upward to his erect posture and lean, tanned face. In her mind's eye, she saw the young nephew of eighteen or twenty years old, with his father's softly rounded features and incipient paunch. That boy had habitually worn—and that included a few Christmas dinners and family birthday parties—a cardinal-red sweatshirt blazoned with the word "Stanford" and khaki cargo pants draped two inches below his hips. The boy of twenty had never called her "ma'am" in his life.

This man of thirty-one or so was no fashion plate now. His suit was clearly bought off the rack, with sleeves that ended an inch above his bony wrists and the trouser cuffs up around his ankle bones. His shirt was oxford cloth, and its collar points and tabs were three years out of style. His tie blended colors that belonged on a candy wrapper. From the resume in front of her, Callie guessed he was used to having the military pick out his uniforms—and that most of them had been battle fatigues in a cement-and-brick-dust camouflage pattern.

"Why do you come to us, Brandon?"

"Well, ma'am, you can see I just—"

"You used to call me 'Aunt Callie.'"

"Okay, Aunt Callie." He smiled. "I just got demobed from the army. I'm looking for an opportunity to use my talents and experience productively, and … well … here …" He broke off and hesitated.

That sentence was going to end badly, she knew, whatever he said next. Brandon Praxis might have many talents and much experience, but the only reason he would bring them to PE&C was the family connection. Clearly, he had heard that the engineering business was starting up again. Obviously, he hoped the place that once would have been made for him as eldest son of the president and chief operating officer was still available—ten years and a lifetime later. Maybe in another dozen years, when the family business was back on top of the heap. But right now they had no room for useless mouths—or *more* useless mouths, after the woman Uncle Matteo had recently forced on them.

She flexed the single-page resume. "I see a lot of military courses and training exercises listed under 'education,' but no academic degree. You were studying for a BS in—what? Civil engineering, wasn't it? But you enlisted first."

"Actually, inducted at start of the war. Nothing voluntary about it."

"You were in your senior year. How many credits shy of a degree?"

"Fifteen. And I'd done the course work. It was a week until exams."

"We could use an engineer—although at this point we need experienced people," she said. "Could you go back to campus, take a makeup or something, and get—"

"After this long …" He sighed. "Most of my credits have lapsed, and with all the technical developments since then, I'd be looking at about two years worth of work. I've already checked."

"And I suppose you'd have to eat in the meantime."

He smiled again. "That would be the preferred option."

Callie chewed her lower lip. Much as it pained her, she didn't have anything for Leonard's boy. Unless … "I suppose you know all about running a military operation," she said. "Motivating people, making them work as a team, moving toward a goal."

"Sure, it's what an officer does. I could see myself in project management—"

She dismissed the idea. "That would need still more course work. Plus logistics and cost accounting. But you *do* know about weapons, tactics, use of force?"

"That's all I've done for the past nine years."

"And have you ever mounted guard duty?"

"Do you mean 'walked the perimeter'?"

"Well, have you set up under hostile conditions?"

"Inside enemy territory, ma'am. Every night."

"Brandon," she said, "you might think the war is over. But unsettled as things are, given the collapse and confusion, and general lawlessness, plus human nature, our construction sites sometimes resemble a war zone. And it goes on every night."

His eyes brightened. "And you need someone to set up a countering force?"

"Someone I can trust implicitly," she agreed. "Family would count."

"I'd have to see what weapons are allowed, then get licensing."

"Given our losses to date, you'd have a sizeable budget."

"So when do you want me to start, Aunt Callie?"

"There's a desk down the hall. Take off that tie."

As Richard Praxis entered the lobby off Sansome Street, with its musty smells of faded varnish, old plaster, and lemon-scented cleaning products, he realized he was entering a San Francisco preserved from the middle of the last century. It was a place of modest elegance with even more modest expectations. It reflected a San Francisco far from the power centers of New York and Chicago, when California was still provincial, at the long end of rail lines and steamship connections, but trying to project a solid appearance of business on the small scale. As he rode up in the elevator's brass cage with its discreet spots of tarnish, a sense of claustrophobia oppressed him. Once the city had risen by its own will power from the devastation of earthquake and fire. Now it was trying to rise from the devastation of war and economic collapse.

As he stepped out on the third floor, with its dark paneling and shadows, he remembered the steel and glass tower down on the Embarcadero with its views of the Bay and Treasure Island. *Father, how you've come down in the world!*

Richard had no sense that he was entering enemy territory until he opened the quaint, half-glassed door to the Praxis Engineering office suite and found his sister Callie inside, as if she had been waiting for him all along. And then, after nine years of isolation due to rebellion and war, she gave him a look that resembled the way Texans dealt with lizards, scorpions, damn Yankees, and folks who turned up their noses at barbecue.

"Hello, Callie."

"Richard."

She led him down a long hallway and into a conference room. There the brass-and-varnish quaintness of last-century California disappeared into a modern workspace with diffuse lighting, a dark-glass reactive tabletop, sprung chairs, and inset video panels on three of the four walls. It was a data-rich environment familiar to anyone who worked in Houston's Carbon Fiber Crescent, such as a vice president from Tallyman Systems, Inc.

Callie settled into one of the chairs, touched a spot on the table, and spoke to the wall. "John? He's here. We're ready."

"On my way," the wall told her.

"Um," Richard said. "Could I have a cup of coffee?"

His sister looked as if he'd spoken in Urdu. Then she pointed to a tiny countertop in the corner behind the door. It had a steam press and a basket of colorful flavor capsules. "Leave a dollar in the dish, please."

While Richard was brewing his coffee and digging in his pocket for change, his father came into the room. The man looked around and found him behind the door.

"Dad!" Richard exclaimed and then, God help him, he rushed forward and embraced his father. The body was thinner than he remembered but not yet frail, the hair no longer silver but the white of sun-bleached stone, the face just starting to go slack with the soft wrinkles of well-tanned deer hide.

John pushed him away gently. He looked deep into Richard's eyes, but he was smiling. "It's been too long."

"You know it," Richard replied.

"You're not here for a job, are you?" his father asked.

"No. I'm—well, as I explained in my text, I have an opportunity for you."

"Richard's going to make us wealthy using his computer skills," Callie sneered.

"It's not me," Richard said, closing the door and moving back to the table, where they all took seats. "The company I represent, Tallyman Systems, has a unique way of running data evaluations—stochastic evolution—here, let me show you." He took out his two-penny data nail, slotted it into the tabletop, and started into the presentation in which Tallyman's marketing people had coached him.

As the story of Stochastic Design & Development® unfolded, he could sense his father becoming interested, even intrigued, while his sister remained hostile, with arms folded and eyebrows lowered.

"That could be a low-cost solution to complex engineering problems," John said.

"If it's really low-cost," Callie replied, "and doesn't need a ton of hand feeding."

"The program is goal-directed and maintains its own data streams," Richard said.

"How many other engineering firms are using this?" John asked.

"You, or Praxis Engineering, would be the first," he said.

"In other words, we're guinea pigs," Callie said.

"Could we get some kind of exclusivity?"

"I'm sure we can work out something," Richard told his father, "based on your service area, market share, penetration, and timing."

"How do we know," Callie began, "this isn't just another ploy to torpedo the company—like before."

"I had hoped we could put that behind us," Richard replied. "The old company was going down anyway. And, after all, I managed to help you and Father separate some value before the collapse."

"You think you were *helping* me?"

"Isn't that how things turned out?"

"But you were trying to get *control!*"

Before he could reply, the door opened.

———

Mariene Kunstler had heard voices in the conference room and decided to check them out. She found the elder Praxis and the Contessa in conversation—tense conversation, marked by flaring nostrils and hurried breathing—with a handsome older man who bore a faint resemblance in face, build, and body language to the other two. "Oh, hello?" she said. "Am I interrupting?"

"Well, at this stage …" John Praxis hesitated.

"Of course not," Callista assured her and made the introductions—giving Mariene the title "our head of marketing," which was close enough. She learned that the new man was indeed a member of the family, a long-lost brother, although apparently not everyone was happy about his return. "Richard is introducing us to a new piece of engineering software," the Contessa finished.

"I'm not sure this is anything Ms. Kunstler needs to know about right now," the father cautioned.

"Why not let her stay?" his daughter countered. "She might have some valuable insights. That is, if Richard doesn't mind …?"

"I'd be delighted," he said, his eyes shining as he looked at Mariene.

She knew that look—and the kind of man who employed it. She could use such a man, especially if he was connected to the Praxis family but not part of their company and perhaps, from the tensions in the room, would at some point be willing to work against them. He might be the ally she needed in her present circumstances, as an outsider forced on Praxis Engineering by Matteo.

However, as he continued his presentation about this Stochastic Design & Development® software, she sensed—never clearly and always from the distance imposed by her lack of technical knowledge—that it was some kind of organically active computer program, almost alive. It was something self-directed, spiderlike, watchful, and hungry. It scared her a little bit. But she liked that, too. Fear kept you sharp!

When he was done, John Praxis was the first to speak. "This could be a useful addition to our toolbox. Especially—" He turned his attention on Mariene. "—if we're going to bid on that big sewer project in Sacramento."

"Where is Sacramento?" she asked.

Richard bobbled and spilled his coffee.

The Contessa just sighed and shook her head.

"Callie will draw you a map," the elder Praxis said.

5. Mad Scramble

THE PACKAGE CAME to John Praxis at Sansome Street but without the name of Praxis Engineering in the address. It was a heavy envelope, made of synthetic paper visibly reinforced with fiberglass strands. From the feel, it contained some kind of binder or notebook. The return addressee was the F.R. District Court for the Eastern District of California, Fresno Division, at the F.R. Courthouse on Tulare Street in Fresno. He opened it to discover a legal document pinned together with three aluminum rivets under a clear-plastic cover, which showed the cover page of a lawsuit.

Praxis sat down in the office hallway by the mail cabinet and skimmed the first couple of pages.

"*In re State of California, F.R.A.* v. *John Praxis* … Case No. 100026-248, Courtroom No. 9, 6th Floor … The State brings forth the following causes of action and alleges the following …

"1. Plaintiff is the Reunified State of California, bearing geographic congruence, demographic inherence, and civil and jurisdictional authority identical with the former State of California in the former United States of America. …

"2. Defendant is an individual, resident of the City and County of San Francisco, former citizen of the Unites States of America and newly repatriated citizen, *re* National Reunification Act, of the Federated Republic of America. …

"3. Defendant is and was one of fifty-two named subscribers to the National Assets Distribution Act, legislation passed in time of war by the former United States of America. …

"4. Defendant agreed under terms of the Act to certain stipulations and requirements as to maintenance and improvement of property formerly known as the Stanislaus National Forest …

"5. Defendant failed to abide by the terms of those stipulations and requirements … in that fire roads and trails installed under his responsibility fail to extend to all areas identified as vulnerable to wildfire combustion on Exhibit C, F.R. Geographical Survey, "Stanislaus Section," 7.5-minute, 1:24,000 topographic sheet ...

"6. Defendant failed to abide ... in that roads and trails fail to meet specifications as to width, grade, surface preparation, and composition in the F.R. Forest Service's Wildlands Fire Regulations, dated ..."

The allegations went on for another half-dozen numbered paragraphs, all having do with his upkeep of the forest property.

"Plaintiff brings forth the following counts in support of the cause of action. ... Count 1 – Negligence: Defendant failed to perform contractually promised duties in a safe and effective manner. ... Count 2 – Destruction of Public Property: Defendant's actions permitted, over the course of his stewardship, seven separate wildfires to consume a total of 6,230 acres of second-growth forest. ... Count 3 – Public Nuisance: Defendant's actions deprived the public of lawful enjoyment of a scenic wilderness area. ... Damages: WHEREFORE, Plaintiff seeks recovery of title to the property identified as the Stanislaus National Forest and reimbursement for real and compensatory damages."

By the time he reached that final "wherefore," Praxis was breathing hard, as if he had just run a 10K race. He got to his feet, still clutching the document, which contained many more pages of exhibits, affidavits, foldout maps, and drawings, and walked down the hall to Antigone's office. She was smart. She was a lawyer. Antigone would know what to do.

"Don't let it worry you, sweetheart," Wells said as she thumbed through the State of California's civil action. "We can fight this."

"I don't see how," John said. He sat hunched over in her office's guest chair, hands clasped between his knees, looking utterly defeated. "Everything in those allegations is true on the face of it. There have been fires. Erosion has washed out the fire roads in some areas. And I don't know anything about the regulations on things like 'grade' and 'composition.' They can certainly prove all that in court."

Wells held her peace and let him talk the negativity out of his system. He was a dear man, but sometimes he could take things so literally. He had not yet learned that the essence of any battle—or negotiation, for that matter—was not the supporting details that the enemy mustered but their overall intention. That was the nut she and John had to crack.

Finally, when he had reached the point of just staring at her, she dropped her eyes to the written specifications and pretended to read more closely.

"For all their huffing and puffing," she said at last, "they can only find seven fires in what? Five years? And those burned a total of six thousand acres—out of how many hundreds of thousands? We're bumping up against acts of God here."

"But what about the road building?"

She pulled out the Geological Survey map marked with "vulnerable areas," then turned to her computer console and keyed in a search for "Rim Fire." The online map of scorched forest dating from the twenty-teens coincided with the State's representation. "You apparently failed to build fire roads through a burned-out desert," she said. "And you said yourself that erosion took out some of them. Uncontrolled erosion usually follows a massive fire, doesn't it?

"Come to think of it," she went on, "did you build those roads yourself? With your own bare hands?"

"Of course not," he replied. "I used a contractor."

"One you chose after appropriate due diligence?"

"The same people who had been building and maintaining fire support under the U.S. Forest Service for twenty years."

"So you used appropriate experts, and they applied their expertise."

"But what about the specifications in the regulations they quote?"

"Those regulations were adopted—" She checked the list of allegations. "—three years ago, while we were still at war with the adopting government, and all this building of fire roads happened on *our* side of the border. The Federated Republic's new specifications may have been subsumed under the National Reunification Act, but they can't apply retroactively to work you and your contractor performed in prior years. That would constitute rulemaking *ex post facto*, which is not legal under Article One, Section Nine, of both our constitutions."

"So we can win?" he asked with hope shining in his eyes.

"That will depend on who we get for a judge. And how much of this mess he wants to send on to the jury. I'm pretty sure we can kick out 'destruction of public property'—but they only put that in there as icing on the cake, anyway. We'll counter with 'acts of God.' The same with 'public nuisance,' because God—or some careless campers—burned out those acres, not you. The toughest nut will be 'negligence,' which has a long and amorphous history in jurisprudence. But so long as we can show you acted in good faith and trusted your contractors, and they performed to the standards in force at the time, it's up to the State to prove otherwise."

He came around the desk and kissed her. "Thank you, Antigone …"

She smiled under his kiss. "We still have to fight, you know. … It'll be fun."

Although he didn't spend much time in the PE&C corporate offices on Sansome Street, Brandon Praxis couldn't help but notice the vice president of marketing. Mariene Kunstler reminded him of Tinker Bell—but without the top knot, or the leaf-green minidress, and with a three-inch spider tattoo under her ear. Yet the resemblance was noticeable.

Brandon was enough in touch with his feelings to know exactly the origins of his hidden yearnings. When he was in grade school he had begged his mother for a Peter Pan lunch box. The Disney people weren't having one of their marketing revivals at the time, and this item was practically a collectible, but he wanted it anyway. He told everyone he liked the adventure story and the artwork, but it wasn't the images of daring Peter or glaring Captain Hook that drew him. Instead, he could stare for whole minutes at a time at the side panel of darling Tinker Bell swooping around in a shower of gold. She was Brandon's first love at the age of seven.

And here she was in the flesh, still elfin and delicate, but life size and grown up—and with a streak of attitude.

He managed to be at headquarters on a Tuesday morning, eleven-thirty, and with not much going on. His aunt and grandfather were out on a job, and Kunstler was in her office and not, at the moment, on the phone. He appeared in her open doorway and almost knocked on the frame when she suddenly looked up.

"Hi," he said, smiling and nodding inanely.

"Hi," Mariene repeated without a smile. Those great, dark eyes held nothing, not even a question. She appeared to stare through him. "Can I help you?"

"Well, it's almost lunch time. I thought, if you don't have plans—"

"I don't have plans," she replied, sounding like a parrot.

"Great! Then, well, do you want to grab a bite?"

She seemed to be processing this into some other language.

"I mean, go out for lunch," he said. "With me."

"I understand. You are a son of the Praxis, are you not?"

"Yes. John's my grandfather. My dad was president of the old company."

"I see. Yes. The one that went bankrupt," she said, as if reminding herself.

"That was before my time. Before the war. I was a soldier till I came here."

"And you want to eat lunch with me. Do we have business to discuss?"

"Well, no. More as a social thing. Like getting to know each other."

"I see. Like a date, but you don't buy flowers or pick me up."

"Well, if you want to put it that way ..."

"I don't think this is a good idea," she said.

"Would it help if I brought flowers?" He smiled.

"It would help if you put me out of your mind." She held his gaze for one more minute, and the whole room appeared to go dark, as if it spread from her eyes. Then she turned her attention back to her computer tablet.

Brandon nodded and silently withdrew. Out in the corridor, he wondered what had just happened. He knew he wasn't all that charming or smooth with women, but what he lacked in style and clever lines he usually made up with earnestness and honesty. He knew he wasn't certifiably ugly. And he didn't smell.

Another man might think Mariene was herself the cause of rejection. A lesser man might walk away thinking that European women were strangely attracted to weird or ugly men, or to women, or to other forbidden fruits. Given the obvious clues from her meager figure and her style of dress, such a man might even suspect she was some kind of transsexual.

But Brandon was mature enough to intuit that she just wasn't interested in him. It happened. And that question about "business to discuss" ... She was all business. Serious, direct, and dedicated to her job. And to the family enterprise.

He was strangely comforted by that.

Back in Houston once more, Richard Praxis scheduled a meeting with one of the Tallyman Systems software designers who had worked on the "grand enterprise." He did not choose the leader of that project, or even one of the section heads. Instead, he selected Potiphar Jackson, an up-and-coming engineer with a reputation for unorthodox thinking. Before the meeting,

Richard had sent him a file with specifications and software schematics.

"What's this?" Jackson asked, when they sat down in one of the private conference rooms and he pulled the file up on his tablet.

"It's an adaptation to the Stochastic Design package," Richard said.

"I can see that. You've got the hooks into the main logic loop all spec'ed. But why? What does it do?"

"It's a one-off, particular to this client. It's not for general distribution."

"You still haven't answered my—"

"The client has special needs. He believes these modifications will improve the software's integration with his other applications and data packages. I don't know all the details. I got that file from their Information Technology manager. Personally, I'm dubious. But the client insists, so hey! What are you going to do?"

"If you want the package to integrate, I'll have to know what software it's got to talk to—and not just the manufacturer's model, but the version number, latest updates, code references, and port addresses."

"That stuff's all in the specification."

Richard had spent two weeks working out those details. Of course, no one in San Francisco had requested any such modification. Praxis Engineering & Construction didn't even have a full-time IT manager, or not yet. They worked with package reps and tech support on the operating system and applications they were running—which was all to the good for his purposes. And Richard knew that window would be closing quickly as PE&C built up its backlog and grew the company.

He had asked Callie to provide a list of their current applications—manufacturer, version, update history—that were of interest to him. "To make sure there won't be any conflicts," he'd told her. Then he went online, using all the various resources available to him as a senior executive at Tallyman, and teased out logic structures, code sections, and ports for each application. He had worked carefully and methodically, as always. But this was the one software modification that would never get a full burn-in and run-up on the client's systems. If he tried to do that, it would spoil the game.

"This will be a rat's nest to test," Jackson said, as if reading Richard's mind.

"I know," he admitted. "And this client is touchy about getting things done right the first time. So we'll have to set up a hardware simulation, the complete system and apps, all running just like in the client's office, and test it out before installation."

"That'll be expensive …"

"I have the budget for it."

"Bill it back to them?" Jackson grinned.

"You got it. Special service and all that."

"But I still don't see … There's data collected *here*, buffered and stored *there*—" Jackson zoomed into portions of the schematic and pointed. "—but the system doesn't *do* anything with it. There's no provision for reporting or readout."

"That information is just a system check," Richard said. "We'll use it for diagnostics and take it out offline. Oh yes, you need to build a trapdoor into the Stochastic Design code, if there isn't one already."

"The client's tech guys won't have access?"

Richard shook his head. "They shouldn't have to. Diagnostic's our problem."

Jackson studied the schematic. "Hell of a lot of information for a diagnostic."

"We want to be thorough."

The man snorted. "There's thorough, and then there's trying to stuff the Moon in your hip pocket."

"I told you, I'm dubious. But this is what the client wants."

"Yeah. I guess. Do what they want, right?"

"My thinking exactly!"

The level of illumination was the same. The silhouette of shadows and window reflections—from dump trucks, Caterpillar tractors, the office trailer, and the material laydown—was the same, allowing for random movements of the equipment during the day. Brandon Praxis knew this because he had stalked the opera house jobsite from outside the fence line for four nights running.

He flipped down the QuadEye NVS barrels attached to his helmet, and the differences sprang into view. Green beams from his team's IR laser targeting crisscrossed the open spaces. Waves of ghostly fog streamed up into the air from the neural inhibitor pads—probably picking up a bit of dust, too. Ranging sensors glowed at key points on the trailer and the truck cabs.

It crossed his mind that if the people they were going to meet carried similar night vision enhancements, then he and his team were screwed in the nude, as they say. But … no, the people who had been working this and other construction jobs in the city were not that sophisticated. These thieves carried flashlights and bolt cutters—the cutters now that they'd lost their inside man on the Nocturna Security payroll. Praxis Engineering & Construction was securing the site at a higher level of diligence these days.

"Sound off," Brandon said, his voice hardly more than a humming mumble in his throat mike.

"Alpha clear … Beta clear …" and on down through the team of six under his command. They were all inside the fence, waiting. He still patrolled outside, moving from shadow to shadow on the other side of Franklin Street, as he used to do during a raid. His jumpsuit, helmet cover, and gaiters absorbed the light from occasional passing cars and trucks, and no part of his equipment—not even the lenses on his goggles—returned a reflection. No one on the ground had ever caught him or his scouts before a night fight. It was always afterward, when his unit had made their strike, secured the salient, and been denied reinforcements by the chickenshit chain of command that the tactical situation went south. Things were different now.

He was his own authority. And these men and women were handpicked from his old command, hired special, and trained in new and better equipment that was paid for by PE&C. All of them except his brother Paul, whom he'd called out of civilian life, now that he was comfortable with his prosthetic leg. "Comfortable," hell! Paul was faster, stronger, and deadlier for having all that spring steel and carbon fiber attached to his thigh—as he kept reminding his older brother. Brandon had installed him as second in command and was grooming him to eventually take over his own team. PE&C really was a family operation.

A dark-colored—possibly dark blue—panel van pulled out of the traffic lane on Franklin and stopped by the curb just beyond the gate.

"Heads up," Brandon murmured for his team.

The driver got out carrying—yes!—a pair of cutters. And as he approached the chain securing the gate, a semi pulled up behind the van and obscured Brandon's view of the actual incursion. What the thieves thought they could take away in the tractor trailer was a mystery, since the jobsite was still basically a hole in the ground lined with concrete. Maybe they were hoping for bulk materials—steel rebar, copper plumbing and wiring, and maybe other early deliveries like window and door frames, glass and roofing tiles—plus the forklift with which to load them.

"My view is partially blocked," he announced quietly. "I'll tell you when everyone has dismounted. Wait until they all cross the pads before engaging."

A series of contact clicks in his earphones signaled general acknowledgement. Because his last instruction was really unnecessary, having been covered a dozen times in training, one voice whispered, "Sheesh, Captain!"

When the last of the doors had slammed on the two trucks, Brandon counted and described five bogeys for his team. After they disappeared on the far side of the semi, he broke cover and ran—a depthless shadow articulating itself under the streetlights—across Franklin Street and crouched behind the hood of the semi's tractor.

From there he could see the thieves walk, or rather swagger, through the gate and head for the laydown area beyond the office trailer. They walked right across the ghostly streaming pads. These were sending up waves of near-ultraviolet light, 300 to 400 nanometers, just beyond the range of human vision but intense enough to confuse the eye, and emitting warbling sounds between 10 and 20 Hertz but at more than 115 decibels, too low to actually hear but strong enough to be felt in cranial and body cavities.

The men staggered, turned, and one fell down. The others had guns and tried to draw or raise them. That was when Brandon's team opened fire. Their weapons—silenced, which also suppressed the muzzle flash—were undetectable from beyond the fence. Brandon only knew they were working because the line of their infrared lasers bucked slightly with each recoil.

In ten seconds the thieves were all down. Master Sergeant Bill Pitt turned off the pads with his master key. One of the thieves was still rolling around—probably the only one wearing a ballistic vest—and First Lieutenant Sally Hungerford stepped out of her hiding place to put the grace shot through his head.

"Okay," Brandon said. "Police your brass."

His team used cartridges doped with a special dye that positively blazed in their night vision goggles. But they had counted their shots anyway.

They bagged the bodies and loaded them back onto the thieves' trucks. Brandon had arranged a second team with a front address at an industrial park across the Bay in Hayward, where human remains could be made to disappear cleanly.

Two of his main team would then drive the vehicles to a chop shop in Nevada which guaranteed to wipe the lojacks and destroy the VIN numbers and plates.

By an hour before dawn, and after Brandon and the remainder of his team had removed their equipment from the grounds, swept the dirt, and resecured the gate chain, it would be as if nothing had ever happened.

Bernardo Gorgoni was not, in Mariene Kunstler's opinion, a particularly handsome man. Oh, he thought so. He had the curling hair, heavy brows, large liquid eyes, straight fleshy nose, and full pouting lips of an old-time Roman senator. She made the connection because she had once done duty in the Musei Capitolini in Rome and seen pieces of the colossal statue of a stern old Roman, including a huge but roughly detached head. One day, Bernardo's swelled head would end up similarly removed from his shoulders—or so she suspected.

Gorgoni was head of Construction Workers International Local 320, the union that would get most of the labor contract on the Southside Sewer Project in Sacramento. They were meeting over dinner at The Firehouse, an upscale restaurant in the Old Town district, which had been untouched by the fighting. Before the salad course was over, Mariene made her pitch.

"What wages will your people earn for the construction work?" she asked.

"What do you care?" he asked. "It's a city job, paid for out of municipal bonds. For Praxis, the cost is a pass-through."

"We might want you to go a little higher on this one."

"No can do. The contract rates are fixed. And public."

"Then find a way to *unfix* them." She made it an order.

"How? The sewer's not critical infrastructure, doesn't involve any Superfund sites, or cut through areas of archeological importance, so there's nothing to—"

"It's in a war zone, for God's sake! Tell them you're worried about unexploded bombs, or getting poisoned from lead slugs and depleted uranium, or leftover traces of chemical weapons—"

"The Federated Republic never used any—"

"Don't be thick, Bernardo!" She sighed. "There doesn't have to be any *evidence,* just the concern. You want to invoke hazard pay or whatever you call it. Praxis will not challenge you in this."

"Why would Praxis Engineering want to pay above union scale?"

"It's a pass-through, right? And you're not talking to Praxis now."

"Okay, then who are you?" He seemed genuinely mystified.

"You're talking to Kunstler. That is all you need to know."

"And if I do this?" His stare was direct and intense. "What then?"

"Well, what could you get? How much of a percentage increase?"

"Oh, maybe seven percent in all classifications. Maybe a bit more."

"Then take that for yourself," she said. "And you pay me four."

"You're going to put my men at risk for a lousy three percent?"

"There's no risk, remember? Besides, when the job starts, the rate will already be written into the contract and the work will proceed as normal. You'll end up finding nothing dangerous at the site, and no one will remember the issue."

"You do know this is all hugely illegal?"

"That's why we're going to keep it quiet. Three percent is your *quid pro quo.*"

"What's that?" Now he was finally becoming suspicious.

"Latin. It means 'you scratch my back'—"

He brightened, leaned across the table, and leered. "I'd *love* to, honey."

She squinted at him. In some lights, perhaps, he was almost as handsome as he thought he was. It had been a long time for her, and maybe tonight was the night. That, too, would be part of the implied *pro quo*.

———

The Robert E. Coyle F.R. Courthouse in Fresno predated the war by several years and had never been touched in the fighting. It was an architectural blend of medieval and modern: medieval for the great square blocks of hewn stone, edged and beveled like the ramparts of a fortress; modern for the banked windows of blue glass, decorated with faux balconies in dark-bronze latticework. It was squat and ugly, with a simplicity that was almost attractive.

As Antigone Wells approached the entrance in the morning sunshine, arm in arm with John Praxis, she paused, turned to him, and asked, "Did your group build that?"

"God, I hope not," he replied nervously. "It looks like a prison. Does it seem like something we'd build?"

"I don't know … it rather fits the function, doesn't it? Federalist brutalism."

Inside, they were directed to the courtroom on the sixth floor, where the clerk led them back into the chambers of Judge Robert Rudolph. The State's three attorneys were already in attendance. They were gray men: short gray hair, clean-shaven gray faces, sober gray suits, hooded gray eyes, and steel-rimmed glasses. They reminded her of clerks in a men's clothing store, earnest strivers, good Rotarians, in the image of Harry Truman. They made Wells, in her cream-colored suit with her pink-and-orange silk scarf, feel like an exotic flower.

Before she and John could take their seats on the left side of the judge's big oak desk, the clerk of the court waited a beat and said, "Please rise."

Judge Rudolph entered with a brisk step, turned, and looked around. In contrast to the sober Rotarians, he was burly, like a lumberjack, with a permanently sunburned face and close-cropped sandy hair. Instead of black robes, he wore a red-plaid shirt, open at the neck, and khaki cargo pants with bulging pockets. It was plain he felt he had no one to impress here.

Antigone Wells had done her homework on the man. He was a recent transfer from the F.R. District Court in North Dakota, where the fighting had been unusually severe. Judge Rudolph had been an early advocate of secession and had opposed the U.S. government's attempts to expropriate judicially—and later to destroy by force—that state's share of the Bakken oil shale on the grounds of promoting carbon reduction. Once she learned he was going to preside in the case of *State of California, F.R.A.* v. *John Praxis*, Wells had started to breathe easier.

"Okay, let's go," Rudolph said and sat down in his leather-backed chair. Thirty seconds later, the court reporter hurried in with her steno machine and apologized for her tardiness—getting a grunt and a nod from the judge. She was the only other woman in the room, and she was dressed in sober brown. The clerk announced the case and the purpose of this conference, which was to hear pre-trial motions. Only one had been filed, the defendant's, to dismiss.

"You may begin, Counselor," Rudolph said.

Antigone Wells proceeded to paraphrase her brief, first summarizing the known facts: That the Stanislaus National Forest was originally controlled by the former Forest Service of the U.S. Department of Agriculture. That the land and its developed infrastructure had been legally disposed of under the National Assets Distribution Act, which was the law of the land at the time. That John Praxis had a valid future claim to this asset under the terms of the Act, and that he had abided by those terms.

She then addressed the State's allegations of negligence, destruction of public property, and denial of public service. She demolished them with the same arguments she had outlined to John back in San Francisco: That he had followed good management practices as defined by the Forest Service at the time of disposal. That he had employed the same contractors as the State, and they had been operating all along under the same principles to maintain the property. That John Praxis was steadily ameliorating damage that had occurred decades earlier in the Rim Fire.

"This brings us to the central question," she said. "As John Praxis is a valid *tenant in fief* of this property, is the State prepared to repay the loan which he made to the former U.S. federal government in order to secure these rights? To invalidate his rights without compensation would be a violation of the Takings Clause of the Reenacted Fifth Amendment to the Federated Republic Constitution.

"Second," she went on, "is the State prepared to compensate Praxis for the costs of maintenance and upkeep which he has expended on the property over the past five years? Failing to do so would also be a violation of the Takings Clause.

"Third, is the State prepared to compensate Praxis for material improvements and the increase in the land's value due to his efforts? Failure to do so again violates the Takings Clause.

"And finally, is the State now capable of maintaining the property in its current improved condition? Or would State appropriation lead to a deterioration of the asset, which is the condition currently pertaining to other publicly held properties in territory of the old United States?"

When she had finished, Judge Rudolph stared at her. "You're placing a lot of weight on the Fifth Amendment, Counselor."

"I understand, Your Honor. But that clause is the crux of the reasoning behind the NADA legislation to begin with. Without the Takings Clause, the State is free to appropriate whatever it likes of a citizen's property by way of a tax or in the interest of the public good, without compensation or consideration."

"Don't teach me the law, Counselor."

"Sorry, Your Honor."

"I'm merely pointing out the narrowness of your argument." He turned then to the State's attorneys. "Do you have any arguments against the motion?"

They did, profusely, copiously, and repeatedly, taking more than an hour to explain and expand on them, until even the court reporter started to look bored and frustrated. Wells could follow the thread of their logic through their thicket of precedents. But when she summed up the matter in her mind, they were only leading back to the State's original allegations: That John Praxis was negligent, had damaged the property entrusted to him, caused everyone intense pain, and should be booted off the land.

When the plaintiffs were done, Judge Rudolph said, "I will take the defendant's motion under advisement. We will reconvene in one week."

He didn't have to bang a gavel for them to know they were dismissed.

Out of sight, under the front edge of the judge's desk, Wells reached over and gave John's hand a squeeze.

By the special courtesy of his being family, Brandon Praxis had been brought into the informal Friday lunchtime meetings of PE&C's senior executives—which at this point included John and Callie as the two principals, Antigone Wells as the firm's Legal Department and his grandfather's unannounced *consigliere*, and Mariene Kunstler as marketing chief, although she was away on business at this particular meeting. Brandon sat and listened as the elder Praxis moved from one topic to the next, covering growth opportunities and business prospects, current operational problems, project details, and snapshots of the cash flow.

"And finally," his grandfather said, "our theft problem has dropped off by—well, to nothing."

"Not even pilferage, shrinkage, or whatever you call it?" Aunt Callie asked. She turned to Brandon. "How did you do it?"

"I just took some professional steps."

"Care to elaborate?" John Praxis prompted.

"Well … we ghosted the people who were causing the problem." Brandon shrugged. "Given the meltdown between the police department and the district attorney's office—" Aunt Callie chuckled at this, then put on a sober face. "—it seemed the best way to handle the situation."

" 'Ghosted'?" John asked, mystified.

"We made them disappear," Brandon said.

"I assume you're not talking about magic tricks."

"You really don't want to know the details, Grandfather."

"But, if you—ghosted—the ones who were stealing from us," he said, "won't there be others who'll come in their place?"

"No. Now everybody knows it's bad luck to break into a Praxis site."

"I take it death was somehow involved?" his grandfather suggested quietly.

Brandon was starting to feel defensive. He'd seen a need and he'd taken action. Where was the problem? "This was the way we did things in the war," he replied. "Create dead zones, establish bright-line perimeters, set limits that people just don't cross."

"These weren't soldiers," the old man said, slowly understanding his point.

"Are they better for having been civilians? Besides, they all went in armed."

"But we're not at war." He was denying Aunt Callie's original assessment.

"Aren't we?" Brandon countered.

Antigone Wells, the lawyer, suddenly sat up straight. "Are you saying you just killed these people?" she asked him. "I can't believe I'm hearing this!"

She was still damned attractive, Brandon thought, despite being an older woman. He found the look of withering scorn she now turned on him daunting.

"Do you know how many laws you've broken?" Wells continued. "How much you have exposed this company to legal consequences?"

"No one's going to come after us," Brandon insisted. "Everyone who crossed the fence line is gone. And no one is going to come looking for them."

He saw Antigone Wells turn to his grandfather with the same bright-eyed glare that Brandon's mother Elizabeth used to give his father Leonard when she wanted him to speak out. Brandon saw his grandfather lock eyes with her briefly, then glance away, perhaps in shame.

"Oh? So no one's looking?" Wells said. "Here's a thought, as I seem to be the only person in the room who's *thinking*. These people may have had accomplices, middle men … certainly families, all of whom probably knew what they were planning and where they were going. And *those* people will come to us seeking explanations, and then they will bring, at the very least, wrongful-death suits."

"And what will they find?" Brandon shot back. "Nothing. No bodies. No evidence. No mark on the fence. Not a sign of disturbance. If anyone went out to break the law that night, they didn't come to us."

"How can you be so sure?" she demanded.

"Because my team is professional, all soldiers. We've done this before. And we have a lot of experience policing up our battlefields."

"I give up," Antigone Wells said. "This is totally outside the law. As an officer of the court, I can't be party to this." She stood up. "On your head be it." And she left the room.

"It sets an example," Brandon said quietly to his grandfather and aunt. "It makes a point. It sends a message."

"A message that won't be read and can't be proved?" Callie suggested.

"Damn right. Mess with a Praxis site and you disappear."

Finally, John Praxis cut off the discussion. "I'll consider whether or not we're in some kind of war with the people who would steal from us. But these are unsettled times, and we probably should keep our options open." He turned to address Brandon directly. "Still, please, before you do anything like this again, let's discuss it in the family. We're all involved in this enterprise. If it goes wrong, we'll all suffer the consequences."

When the case of *California* v. *Praxis* reconvened in Judge Rudolph's chambers in Fresno, Praxis himself had no idea how the judge would rule on Antigone's motion to dismiss. His ears were still ringing from the hour-long harangue of the State's attorneys at the previous session. Praxis could see that they had brought a mountain of evidence and precedent against a molehill of constitutional amendment from Antigone.

After Rudolph came in, still dressed like a backwoodsman, and the apparatus of court procedure was settled in place, the judge launched right in. "I'm going to grant your motion, Counselor," he said, facing Antigone.

This drew a burst of objections from the plaintiffs, which he dismissed with a wave of his hand.

"For the benefit of all present," he went on, "I will explain my decision. You gentlemen—" He turned to the three plaintiffs. "—have tried to end-run the law by alleging the defendant's negligence and creation of a public nuisance, which you have failed to demonstrate. I spent last weekend hiking in the Stanislaus, and I saw no sign of the degradation you claim exists. John Praxis has held up his end of the bargain and, as far as I can see, been a good steward of the land.

"I probably should let this case go to trial in order to prove that," Rudolph went on, "except I'm not ready to set precedent on the National Assets Distribution Act. Not all of these cases are going to be as clear-cut as this one, and some *tenants in fief* have permitted actual damages to occur that need to be redressed. Yet I'm not ready, either, to put the final nails in the coffin of the Forest Service—to which the Stanislaus would revert, unless I found for the defendant. And then, by extension, I would be ruling against the National Park Service, which relinquished similar assets under this law.

"We had something like the NADA in the Federated Republic in the early days of the war. Vast federal lands were released for civilian use and the results were not so pretty. Land rushes, shantytowns, open-pit mining—the worst of the human spirit applied to the best of our natural resources. I don't want to be the one who unleashes that here.

"I realize that with this decision," Rudolph said, "I'm essentially kicking the can down the road for another thirty years—until the point at which ownership and future development of the Stanislaus forest land will transfer to John Praxis as a private citizen. Until that transfer takes place, however, the State may still at any time return the principal it borrowed from him and reclaim the land for itself. And even after the transfer, the State of California and/or the Federated Republic may still challenge any plans he makes for the property under environmental or other grounds.

"With that said, I'm dismissing case number 100026-248 without prejudice to either party." The judge picked up his smartphone and, in lieu of a gavel, tapped its case lightly on his desktop.

John Praxis turned to Antigone—who was also turning toward him—embraced her, and gave her a full kiss on the mouth. Out of the corner of his eye, he saw the judge raise an eyebrow.

"Thank you, my dear," Praxis whispered. "You've made me very happy."

"My pleasure, sweetheart. We've saved the property for now, at least."

"Counselor?" the judge asked. "Would you mind taking that outside?"

6. The Next Generation

John Praxis lay in bed with Antigone, cuddling after a bout of lovemaking. Her head rested against his shoulder and her hand played across his chest. Slowly he shifted to one side and lowered her into the pillows, lifted himself up and stared down at her with a long, thoughtful look. "I wish there was more than this," he said. It was a lack he had been feeling lately, a sense of purpose left unfulfilled.

"What we have is good," she said. "What more do you want?"

"I want to have a child with you, someone who shares the best of us both."

"Then you should have met me thirty years ago—twenty, even."

"It wouldn't have mattered then," he said. "I was still married. Adele was my partner, my wife, 'to have and to hold.' We took those vows seriously back then."

"Do you want to get married again?" she asked.

"We can do that," he said, almost dismissing it. "But a child would join us—"

She wrinkled her nose at him. "You may still be able to get it up, sir. But I'm afraid my uterus is no longer fit for the task."

"Many people these days use *in vitro* techniques and surrogate carriers. That takes the work out of it—except for the first part."

"Maybe for you. But after sixty-odd years, my eggs are long past their sell-by date."

"That shouldn't be a problem, either," he said. "We still have usable bits of DNA all over our bodies. If they can rebuild my heart and your kidneys with the stuff, they ought to be able to find a few good chromosomes to build a fertilized egg. The rest is just chemistry ... plus paying the bills for someone to bring it—him, her—to term."

"And then the sleepless nights begin," Antigone said.

"We can pay someone for that, too."

Melissa Willbrot was a mouse—a powerful mouse, to be sure, because she was assigned counsel to the City of Los Angeles Board of Public Works—but still a mousy little person. She stood an inch shorter than Mariene Kunstler, but there the resemblance ended. Willbrot was thin and twitchy, nervous, with strangely yellow-brown eyes that darted side to side every couple of seconds as they talked, as if she suspected an attack from either direction. She wore her dark hair in a cloud of ringlets, each one carefully permed, and they jittered around her forehead and ears like tiny, silent bells. It made Mariene tired just to spend five minutes with her.

But all that aside, from Mariene's researches Willbrot was shown to be the woman to know in the bidding process on county work. And the subject today was the project for renovating the Long Beach Freeway, the old Interstate 710, which linked the glamorous downtown area and the distant harbor through fifteen miles of sandy lots, dry riverbed, and industrial wasteland. Although the actual construction work would be funded by the F.R. Department of Transportation and the state's own Caltrans, both of those agencies had been cut back by war and reunification until they could only offer minimal planning and accounting services. The real decisions were made at the local level.

Also from Mariene's researches—although not explicit in any database, more to be read between the lines and inferred from the stub-ends of various special committee reports—Willbrot was bent. The whiff of corruption was strong, like the scent of cheese in a pantry, but nothing had ever been proven. Time and again, the finger of justice had tapped others—planning commissioners, city council members, accountants and budget analysts—but never Willbrot herself.

And now that Mariene was face to face with the woman in her office, she could sense that Willbrot was bent in another way. It was nothing overt and suggestive, nothing communicated through words, glances, or gestures. But the woman was definitely interested in Mariene. Not in any dominating way, like a predator, nothing butch and obvious. Willbrot was more like docile, willing prey. In the past, certain people had attributed to Mariene a catlike grace and quickness, a tendency to slash first and ask questions later, and an ability to make surprising leaps to save her life. But now, like a mouse fearing the danger yet hypnotically drawn to it, Willbrot was playing up to Mariene's inner cat. Timidly at first, surreptitiously, but with growing confidence.

All of this was useful information.

"You understand that we have a statutory preference for local contractors," the woman was saying.

"Praxis Engineering is a California company," Mariene said, giving her best smile with plenty of teeth.

"Yes, but you're relatively new and small, with experience limited to Northern California." Willbrot made a little grimace, as if the cheese wasn't ripe yet.

"Our principals have a great deal of experience, going back to the prewar firm, which was an international giant in the construction field."

"Oh yes—the firm that failed." Willbrot shook her head.

"I think you would be honored to work with them."

The woman shrugged. "How honored would I be?"

Aha! The first little kink in their conversation!

"This is a major project," Mariene said in her silkiest voice. "The costs will be huge, eight figures? Probably nine! We haven't even begun to estimate it yet."

"I know! We're still putting together all the elements of the bid package."

"I'm sure there will be many considerations," Mariene said. "With many peripheral expenses to be calculated."

"Of course, I don't make the final decisions. I just help the process along."

"But I'll bet you can be very helpful—very *persuasive*."

"I just do my job," Willbrot cooed, then glanced down at her watch. "Oh, dear! Is that the time? I'd love to discuss the bid process further with you, but I have another appointment. ..."

"Such a pity!" Mariene said. She knew exactly what was going on. Only a fool would say anything definitive inside an office in a public building. Oblique suggestions and polite overtures, the first steps of the dance, to test the waters, as it were, all couched in language that would fool listeners at keyholes and microphones—that much was permissible. Specifics and the basics of haggling—those were for later, outside, on neutral ground of the haggler's choosing.

"Perhaps we could meet later for drinks?" Mariene suggested.

"That would be lovely!" Willbrot agreed, naming a time and place.

Drinks would become dinner, Mariene knew, and then the evening would progress along now-predictable lines. The things she was expected to do for the family!

―――――

Antigone Wells still wasn't sure she wanted a child. After all, she had lived her whole life without becoming totally responsible for another person—let alone for that hypothetical person's genetic inception, birth, growth, intellectual and emotional development, and ultimate presentation as a human being. She had never kept so much as a cat in her apartment. Orchids were as much personal commitment as she felt she could make.

But John was gently insistent, even though he already had three grown children of his own—well, two now, and one of them estranged. He still felt the hunger of fatherhood. And so, for his sake, as well as for their future together, she was willing to give *in vitro* fertilization and all the rest a try.

The trouble was, she didn't know where to begin looking for such services. In the old days, before the world fell apart, she would have gone to her primary care physician, the internist or general practitioner who was her medical insurance plan's gatekeeper to the universe of specialists. Together they would have discussed the problem, what services were available within her preferred provider network, and how much her insurance would pay. But then, did designing a child out of two adult human genomes come under the heading of "elective surgery" or "reproductive therapy"?

Wells could remember when a huge bureaucracy had tried to run the business of health care across the entire country. It had started with the insurance companies and their health maintenance organizations, or HMOs—or perhaps it began with the federal government itself, back in the nineteen-sixties, when it introduced Medicare and Medicaid. In either case, the bureaucracy established huge buying structures, leveraged volume purchases into advantageous price schedules, and forced the development and consolidation of doctors' associations, hospital corporations, and pharmaceutical manufacturers. People who were signed up with the system could get medical appointments, hospital and laboratory services, and drugs for next to nothing, or for just a few dollars per visit—called "copays"—so long as they stayed within that circle of preferred providers. Those outside the system, individual buyers without such leverage, paid much more than the market rate. In fact, there was no market, no matchup of producer and consumer, since everything passed through an impersonal middle man. Consumers got what the bureaucracy could negotiate or they suffered the consequences.

But the business of medicine in California had changed since the end of the war and reunification, although seeds of the old pricing structure's dissolution had been sown long before. For one thing, what was now on offer was no longer "health care," implying some overall responsibility for the human body, human life, and its well-being, served through the primary care physician and designated specialists. The business was back to passing out "medicine"—not a lifetime commitment to the individual but a marketplace for separate ills, procedures, pills, and surgeries. If you wanted holism or top-to-toe health, you went to a spiritual guru or a yoga teacher.

The biggest change was that the government was no longer in the medical business. The economic collapse that had preceded the civil war had taken care of that. Not that the old United States, as practiced on both coasts, didn't try to continue offering some form of government-funded health care—a wheezing steam calliope with a bunch of broken and missing pipes. The Federated Republic had dumped that monstrous obligation in the first year after secession.

Without a national bureaucracy of accountants, working either for the insurance companies or for the Department of Health and Human Services, to support a multi-tiered pricing system, with good deals for the volume buyers and sticker shock for everyone else, the whole system eventually collapsed. Hospitals, doctors, laboratories, and drug makers had no incentive to maintain such a monster. Even with computerized billing to keep track of what they might charge through different accounts, they simply could not explain the fee structures and choices to their patients, and they got tired of the haggling. Consumers—forced for the first time to think about what they were paying—became conscious of price and quality. Prices flattened and then began to fluctuate according to the local supply and quality of service. Competition between providers held prices and service offerings in line with consumer expectations.

After a hundred years of being the country's wealthiest class of professionals, the *nouveau riche* of every community, with pricing expectations to match, the doctors returned to being just fee-for-service working stiffs—the same as any accountant or attorney. After fifty years of being cash cows, hospitals and drug companies went back to being just service providers. Standards slipped for a while, as charlatans and snake oil salesmen practiced their range of gimmicks, and scandals ensued. Finally, the medical fraternity reimposed serious review and licensing, and let their members compete and advertise on the basis of quality, skills, and experience.

Without government support and volume deals, patients suffered for a while. Then they wised up and began paying for their medical expenses in the same way they paid for educating their children or putting a roof over their heads: they planned and they saved. To guard themselves against the unexpected—the original purpose of "health insurance"—people joined mutual funding associations that grew up among neighborhoods, professional groups, social clubs, churches, and even some extended families. Variations included market rating associations for individuals with particular diseases or conditions, and limited liability pools for patients who were more risk conscious. Each association was structured, funded, and paid out a little differently. Since most of these organizations never grew beyond the local community or county level—although some of the professional associations might attain statewide status—they never established the kind of national buying power wielded by the old federal government, and so prices and expectations remained relatively flat.

When Antigone Wells went to explore her and John's options for *in vitro* fertilization and surrogate hosting, she found a number of providers, some offering package deals with genetic analysts and cloning services thrown in, some offering the best low prices on single procedures. Medicine had rejoined the disorganized world of buying and selling that had all along pertained to car dealerships, oil changers, and auto body shops. Medicine had become a commodity once again, like carpentry or house painting—although perhaps with a higher sense of humanitarian purpose.

Wells did most of her shopping online because, along with the advertising of providers and their services, a secondary market had grown up on the internet, modeled off the original Angie's Doc® listing. It was an automated, area-wide, word-of-mouth service that provided reviews and testimonials on quality of care and pricing. But still Wells had to get out her sharp pencil, take notes, figure costs, decide what she actually wanted in terms of service and how much she could afford, and then make her own decisions. It was both daunting and exhilarating.

At first, she thought she should look into cloning services, because that seemed to be the nature of her quest—to copy one person out of two genomes. Since it had become technically feasible, cloning had enjoyed a varied history, filled with social taboos and local restrictions. The biggest disincentive, however, was a popular perception of buyer's remorse. You might want to recreate a favorite cat or dog, or even a deceased loved one, but you soon discovered that genetic material was just the starting point of any organism, and about as important as the yeast in bread dough. Original genes might exist in an embryo, but their expression in the body's different tissue types was controlled by a variety of chemical factors present in the environment. This was the enigmatic realm of "epigenomics." It was why even identical twins grew apart over the years. And, in the case of human beings, nurture and the accidents of life, experience, education, and acquaintance had more to do with the essence of personality than the original genes.

For a while, Wells lingered over consulting services that offered "genetic analysis, realignment, and reassignment." But these people didn't seem to *do* anything. The gist of their advertisements seemed to involve looking at your genetic chart, like some kind of new age horoscope, and offering suggestions about what your and your spouse's baby would become. Wells needed something a little more basic—from people who would actually knit the chromosomes together and make that baby in the first place.

She finally punched her exact requirements into a search tool, creating a parameter of eleven key words without prepositions or conjunctions. The likeliest hit came back in half a second: "parthenogenic reproductive services." It sounded Greek and vaguely antique. Wells had a notion of Athena erupting from the head of Zeus, and when she checked the operative term, "parthenogenesis," it made reference to "virgin birth." That seemed like what she and John were looking for, but without cutting into either of their foreheads.

The medical buzz-feeds had almost nothing to say on the subject or about any of its practitioners—all of two of them in Northern California. So at that point she decided to take her findings back to John for discussion and to see if he really, really wanted to go ahead with this.

After the Tallyman Systems service technicians had installed the Stochastic Design & Development® software on Praxis Engineering's computers—with the help of outside IT contractors, because the firm didn't have its own in-house technical staff yet—Mariene Kunstler was invited to a demonstration. Richard Praxis was in San Francisco for the entire week, holding one-on-one training sessions with each of the senior executives. The purpose of the training was to show them how the software package worked, its basic inputs and outputs, and what it could offer PE&C's clients—for which he was spending extra time with Mariene Kunstler as head of marketing.

Most of it she could have picked up from a brochure. But what she learned from the hands-on was intriguing.

The two of them were sitting side-by-side at her computer console, which tied into the office server. The man was close, with his knee actually pressing against hers under the desk, and his hands brushed her forearms and wrists—once even the front of her blouse—as he reached across to work her mouse and keyboard. She knew without having to think about it that he was interested in her, and that gave her psychological leverage.

When the show was over and he was sitting back in his swivel chair, she asked, "So, what is your game?"

"Excuse me?" He feigned ignorance. "I'm demonstrating a piece of software."

"Oh, I understand that," she said. "I realize it has to make outside connections for feeds from demographic and census databases, tax rolls, land surveys, opinion polls, and all the rest. But I see the program makes some inside connections, too. Accounting. Project backlog. Scheduling and estimating. Even my client list. I wonder why an application that designs sewers and transit systems needs to know so much about its parent company's business."

"Well, that's an integration feature. Those connections let the SD&D software share its data with the project organization, prepare Gantt charts and bills of materials, issue billing invoices, and so on."

"Bullshit," she said, but keeping her voice and manner pleasant.

"I beg your pardon." His manner went all cold and hostile.

"You are using the software to spy on this company."

"That's an outrageous accusation," he protested.

"I'm an outrageous person." She turned her head to make sure he saw her tattoo. "But I'm not a fool. I do my homework. I know the history of the Praxis family. I know how, long ago, you and your brother took the company away from your sister and then from your father. So pardon me for not believing that all is forgotten, bygones are bygone, and you would come to them, install an invasive software package, and not have a few extra features in mind. I think they call it a 'Trojan horse'?"

"You can't prove any of this."

"I can hire an expert to strip that thing—" She pointed at the last SD&D screen left pulsing on her monitor. "—down to its machine code and wring its brains out."

Richard Praxis collapsed—predictably. "Are you going to expose me to John and Callie?"

"Of course not." She gave a low chuckle. "But I want a look at whatever your software finds. Understood?"

"I would think, with your access, you could just—"

"Simply tell me you understand my request."

"I understand. ... Piece of the action."

"Very good. You may go now."

After he stood up and collected his papers, but before he reached the door, he turned back. "I would have thought you'd be more loyal to your employers. To the family."

"Oh, I'm loyal, all right. To the core. The question is, which family?"

John Praxis sat with Antigone in one of three conference rooms in the office of a reproductive medical supplier, Parthenotics, Inc. That was one of two firms she had found online which, presumably, could create a viable embryo—no, a baby—out of their two genomes. They sat side by side and he held Antigone's hand while they listened to Ashley Benedict, a medical technician with the firm, explain details of the procedure. In truth, the woman seemed more like a sales consultant, although she spoke very knowledgeably. She used graphics and video animation software to make her points.

One of the questions that had been worrying Praxis himself was their legal right to become the putative child's parents. Clearly, they would have to undergo some kind of adoption process once the baby was born, because he and Antigone were not married. In fact, they had not really discussed the issue of marriage. As the session progressed, however, it became clear that Parthenotics was only involved in the technical end of things. And that was the end Antigone appeared to find unsettling.

"I understand about *in vitro* fertilization," she said. "You put donated eggs and sperm together in a petri dish, let nature take its course, then implant a fertilized embryo back inside the mother, or in a paid surrogate."

"Well, we do something very similar," Benedict agreed. "Although first we have to make the 'egg' and 'sperm'—or their genetic equivalents—from scratch using your genes. So the process is kind of *in vitro vitro*. By the way, since the active cell is not actually the product of two gametes, we can't legally call it a 'zygote' or 'embryo,' so we have to use the term 'parthenote.' " Praxis suspected the term was also good as a sales tool.

"Your brochure mentioned using stem cells?" Antigone said. Praxis knew they both had some experience with and understanding of that technology.

"No, actually," Benedict said, "we just employ procedures *similar to* inducing pluripotency in a stem cell. What we're doing is taking somatic cells from anywhere in your body and reprogramming them, like an artificial stem cell—except we're taking them all the way back to the embryonic, pre-development stage.

"Here we're not working so much with genetic changes as with epigenetics," the woman said, "which are the basis for most differentiation processes during normal cell development. We use a fairly small set of transcription factors—Oct4, Klf4, Sox2, and c-Myc, collectively called the OKSM group—to convert differentiated chromosomes back into an unexpressed state representing total potentiality. Then we can transfer the nuclear material into oocytes and continue with ectopic development expression."

"It sounds like you've got this down to a science," Praxis said.

"Well, we've been pretty successful so far," she replied.

"But if you're not using genetics," Antigone said, "will we be able to choose any of the child's characteristics?"

"Certainly—within broad limits. We'll select judiciously among the chromosomes from both parents to get the desirable traits represented in one gene set or the other. And to select for sex, of course. From examination of your genomes, we can even detect some of the undesirable recessives and mutations, and then we remove them using DNA restriction enzymes and ligases—along with extending the telomeres on each of the chromosomes, of course. All of the parthenotes we start will have the best possible combinations."

" 'Parthenotes'—plural?" Antigone asked hesitantly. "We only want one child. At least for now."

"Of course," the technician said. "But while our techniques are good, they're not perfect. Some of the proto-embryos will have mechanical or structural damage. Others will have picked up some form of chemical contamination. We raise a number of them until the fetus has developed enough to make sure the specimen is healthy, with no obvious defects, before implantation."

" 'A number,' " Antigone repeated. "Exactly how many?"

"Our routine starter is a thousand parthenotes, before the first cull."

"A thousand embryos … all to get one baby?" Antigone said.

"Yes, ma'am. But don't worry. You won't have to see any of them."

"No, but I'll *know* about them. I'll *think* about them. John, I don't like this!"

"Hush now, darling," he said. "This is the way it has to be done."

"I understand," she said. "Still … all those tiny lives, just thrown away."

He could see she was visibly troubled. "We don't have to do this, you know."

She tried to smile. "If it brings one new life into the world … I'll focus on that."

"The parthenotes are just tissue," the medical technician said. "Not real people."

"Your saying that only makes it worse," Antigone replied.

Praxis tried smooth over the moment by asking the technician, "But you only implant *one* child with a human mother, right? Only one baby is actually … grown?"

"That's right. For now, we still gestate the parthenote with a human host. But we're working on bringing our fetuses to full term in a bioreactor. That will create a more stable environment, with better control of physical conditions, nutrients, and potential contaminants."

"But it wouldn't have the influence of a mother's love," Antigone observed.

The Benedict woman looked confused. "If you mean talking to the baby in the womb or playing Beethoven for it, no. But none of those effects is scientifically proven, either."

"Since these are just 'tissue samples,' " Antigone went on harshly, "how many of your starters would you carry to full term in this bioreactor?"

"Well, not all of them, of course, for cost reasons. But certainly a number of them, until obvious defects begin to appear. That way you get to the best chance of a healthy baby and you can pick from the best of the lot."

Antigone stood up. "Let's get out of here," she said to Praxis.

He started to rise with her, then turned to Benedict. "But you're only speaking hypothetically, aren't you? With a human host, we're still talking about just one baby, aren't we?"

"Of course, sir."

"And so this question of disposing of multiple babies is not really a problem in our case. And, as to the number of embryos or parthenotes you start, that's not much different from the way *in vitro* fertilization works, right?"

"The numbers are very similar," Benedict said. "It ensures quality."

"Then we're talking about standard medical practices."

"I still find it abhorrent," Antigone said.

"But if you want a child …"

"*You* wanted a child."

"But you agreed."

"I think we need to discuss this some more, John. Away from this place." She pointed a finger at Benedict. "Away from *her*. In an atmosphere where we can focus on our desire for a child and not so much on … tissue."

In the end, Antigone Wells had let John persuade her about the rightness of their conceiving a child together, whatever the grisly details. They returned to Parthenotics, Inc., where a different medical technician—at John's request—had taken cheek swabs from both of them. And that was the extent of their involvement. They would never study the gene charts and review potential characteristics and recessives, never see the petri dishes, and never negotiate with or even meet the host mother. The one decision they could not leave up to the Parthenotics people was the child's sex. In the end, they decided the old-fashioned way, trusting to chance and flipping a coin. It came up heads, a boy.

And then, to take her mind off details of the *in vitro vitro* birthing process, and because everything was going so well with Praxis Engineering's business that they could afford the time off, John took her on their first vacation together. They went on a six-week tour of Europe, starting in London and ending in Italy.

Halfway through, in the middle of France, at the Hôtel Le Choiseul in Tours, a mysterious package from Parthenotics, Inc., caught up with them. It was a small, square cube covered in manila paper. John put it in his pocket and said nothing. He probably thought Wells hadn't seen it, but she had, lying in their mail cubby at the reception desk, where she asked the clerk about it. The man said the package was addressed to John and wouldn't release it to her. She couldn't guess what it contained, but her imagination conjured up bloody images of broken and damaged fetuses.

He waited until they were visiting the castles of the Loire Valley, until they found the one they both agreed was the prettiest and most romantic—Chenonceau, on the River Cher. It was the former seat of the King of France's glamorous and notorious mistress, Diane de Poitiers. It was a place made for love and remembrance.

Standing in the formal gardens on a perfect spring day, with billowy white clouds passing overhead, he finally pulled out the box and presented it to her.

"What is it?" Wells asked. She couldn't resist shaking it and heard a faint rattle.

"It's something I asked the Parthenotics people to prepare. It's a special service of theirs, although the actual silverwork is from Tiffany and Company."

Wells ripped off the postal wrapping and, sure enough, inside was the trademark baby-blue paper and white silk ribbon. She opened that and found a heart-shaped pendant, the size of a half-dollar coin, on a silver neck chain. She checked front and back but saw no engraving.

"It's very pretty," she said. "I love it."

"It might not look like it, but the heart actually opens," he said, "although you need the right tools. Inside, in digital notation, there's a chip holding our two genomes, twenty-three pairs each, all ninety-two chromosomes, fully reprogrammed and cleaned up. Essentially, they're the complete instructions for making any children we might ever want in the future from synthesized strands of our DNA."

"That's um … unusual."

"It's the secret of life."

Appendix 1: Praxis Family Tree, c. 2030

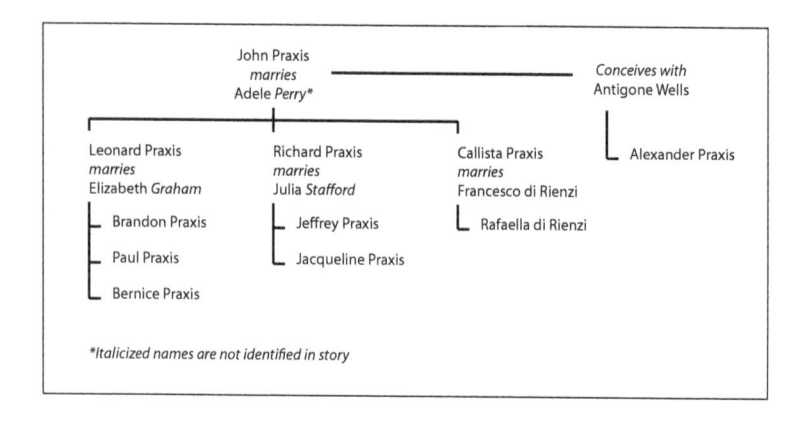

```
                    John Praxis
                     marries                           Conceives with
                   Adele Perry*                        Antigone Wells
    ┌──────────────────┬──────────────────┬──────────────────┐
Leonard Praxis    Richard Praxis    Callista Praxis    Alexander Praxis
  marries            marries            marries
Elizabeth Graham   Julia Stafford    Francesco di Rienzi
  ├ Brandon Praxis   ├ Jeffrey Praxis   └ Rafaella di Rienzi
  ├ Paul Praxis      └ Jacqueline Praxis
  └ Bernice Praxis
```

*Italicized names are not identified in story

Characters Other Than Family

Part 1 – 2018: First You Die ...

Carolyn Boggs, one of Antigone's associates in Bryant Bridger & Wells, LLC

Suleiman "Sully" Mkubwa, the other associate in the BB&W law firm

Ted Bridger, partner in the BB&W law firm

Prabhjot Bajwa, Antigone's doctor at UCSF Medical Center, Mission Bay

Peterson and Jamison, John's doctors at UCSF Medical Center

Anderson and Adamson, stem cell researchers at Stanford Medical Center

Tina Gonzales, clinical technologist at Stanford Medical Center

Gary and Jocelyn, Antigone's therapists at UCSF Medical Center

Elpidia Hartzog, reporter from the *San Francisco Chronicle*

Part 2 – 2019: Run for Your Life
Jeanne Hale, Antigone's in-home nursing attendant
Maritsa, Antigone's housekeeper
Pamela Sheldon, PE&C receptionist on the thirty-eighth floor
Ivy Blake, John's former executive assistant
Kay Sheffield, John's new executive assistant
Madeline Bauer, Antigone's administrative assistant
Judy, green belt instructor in Okinawan karate
Miranda, John's and Adele's cook
Alison Crowder, PE&C head of Human Resources
Daniel and Eric, black belt instructors in Okinawan karate
Meyer, staff physician at California Pacific Medical Center
Harold Cromwell, project liaison at the Denver Arts Commission
Julia Schottlander, PE&C accounting analyst
Roxbrough, U.S. Army recruiting sergeant, Menlo Park
Anthony Ruysdael, major, U.S. Army Ordnance Corps
Darrell Young, lieutenant colonel, Arizona Army National Guard
Valone, John's and Adele's family physician
Winston Burke, PE&C vice president and chief counsel
Herb Longacre, PE&C executive vice president for international marketing
Kevin Lowe, marketing vice president, Intelligeneering Systems Inc.
Father Demetrios, priest at Holy Trinity Greek Orthodox Church in San Francisco
Ramsay, captain, 1/22nd Combat Infantry Group, California Army National Guard
Beemis, general, U.S. Army, coordinator of the attack on Kansas City

Part 3 – 2028: Plumbing Work
Nora, Tommy, and Joey Graham, John's neighbors on Balboa Street
Helen Wells Carter, Antigone's younger sister in Oklahoma

Bernie Gutierrez, head of purchasing at PlumbKit
Peter Greenwood, Antigone's *sensei* in Isshinryu karate
Count Francesco di Rienzi, Callista's late husband
Janet Bormann, Secretary of the U.S. Department of Health and Human Services
Matteo di Rienzi, Francesco's uncle in Torino, Italy
Carlo di Rienzi, Matteo's son in Torino, Italy
Philip Sawyer, chairman and chief executive of Tallyman Systems, Inc.
Elise Paterson, Antigone's urologist in Oklahoma City
Frieda Hammond, major, G1 Manpower and Personnel, in Brandon's unit
Stephen Swarovski, major, G3 Operations, in Brandon's unit
Kendal, John's doctor at Saint Mary's Regional Medical Center in Reno
Axel Brod, engineer with the resurrected Praxis Engineering & Construction
Will Chapple, project manager on rebuilding the War Memorial Opera House
Sonny Deeths, construction superintendent on rebuilding of the opera house
Mariene Kunstler, former policewoman from Germany, among other places
Potiphar Jackson, software designer at Tallyman Systems, Inc.
Bill Pitt, former master sergeant in Brandon's unit
Sally Hungerford, former first lieutenant in Brandon's unit
Bernardo Gorgoni, head of Construction Workers International Local 320
Robert Rudolph, judge, F.R. District Court, Eastern District of California
Melissa Willbrot, attorney, City of Los Angeles Board of Public Works
Ashley Benedict, medical technician with Parthenotics, Inc.

About the Author

THOMAS T. THOMAS is a writer with a career spanning forty years in book editing, technical writing, public relations, and popular fiction writing. Among his various careers, he has worked at a university press, a tradebook publisher, an engineering and construction company, a public utility, an oil refinery, a pharmaceutical company, and a supplier of biotechnology instruments and reagents. He published eight novels and collaborations in science fiction with Baen Books and is now working on more general and speculative fiction. When he's not working and writing, he may be out riding his motorcycle, practicing karate, or wargaming with friends. Catch up with him at www.thomastthomas.com.

Photo by Robert L. Thomas

Books by Thomas T. Thomas
eBooks:
The Professor's Mistress
The Children of Possibility
The Judge's Daughter
Sunflowers
Trojan Horse
Baen Books and eBooks:
The Doomsday Effect (as by "Thomas Wren")
First Citizen
ME: A Novel of Self-Discovery
Crygender
Baen Books in Collaboration:
An Honorable Defense (with David Drake)
The Mask of Loki (with Roger Zelazny)
Flare (with Roger Zelazny)
Mars Plus (with Frederik Pohl)